W9-AAX-855

An Aegean April

Books by Jeffrey Siger

Chief Inspector Andreas Kaldis Mysteries
Murder in Mykonos
Assassins of Athens
Prey on Patmos: An Aegean Prophecy
Target: Tinos
Mykonos After Midnight
Sons of Sparta
Devil of Delphi
Santorini Caesars
An Aegean April

An Aegean April

A Chief Inspector Andreas Kaldis Mystery

Jeffrey Siger

Poisoned Pen Press

First Edition 2018

10 9 8 7 6 5 4 3 2 1

Library of Congress Catalog Card Number: 2017946783

ISBN: 9781464209451   Hardcover
ISBN: 9781464209475   Trade Paperback
ISBN: 9781464209482   Ebook

Poisoned Pen Press
4014 N. Goldwater Blvd., #201
Scottsdale, AZ 85251
www.poisonedpenpress.com
info@poisonedpenpress.com

Printed in the United States of America

*To Sam, Anna, Joe, Minnie, and all those others who fled
one land for another.*

Acknowledgments

Mihalis, Roz, and Spiros Apostolou; Matt Barrett (for his wonderful guide to Lesvos); Michael Barson; Beth Deveny; Diane DiBiase; Andreas, Aleca, Nikos, Mihalis and Anna Fiorentinos; Flora, Yannis, and Alexia Katsaounis; Olga Kefalogianni; Panos Kelaidis; Glenn Kim; Dimitris Kordalis; Nicholas and Sonia Kotopoulos; Ioanna Lalaounis; Lila Lalaounis; Daniela Lorenzottl and friends who wish to remain anonymous; Dimitri Loukas and Niki Kerameus; Linda Marshall; Terrence McLaughlin, Karen Siger McLaughlin, and Rachel Ida McLaughlin; Filippos Menardos; Hdibrahim Mollah; Nikos Nomikos; Elena Panagiotou; Stacey Harris-Pappaioannou; Renee Pappas; Garyfalos Parisis; Barbara G. Peters and Robert Rosenwald; Frederick and Petros Rakas; Dora Rallis; Annette Rogers; Alan and Pat Siger; Jonathan, Jennifer, Azriel, and Gavriella Siger; Ed Stackler; Stelios Tsappas; Miltiadis Varvitsiotis; Christos Vlachos; Stellene Volandes; Barbara Zilly;

And, of course, Aikaterini Lalaouni.

*"You may forget but let me tell you
this: someone in some future time
will think of us."*

—Sappho (630-570 BCE)

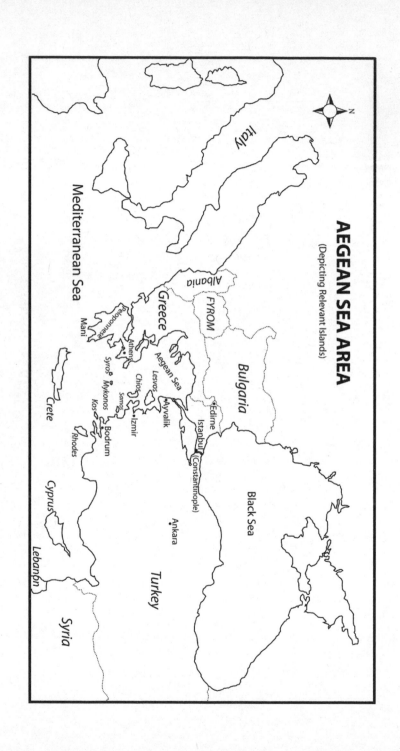

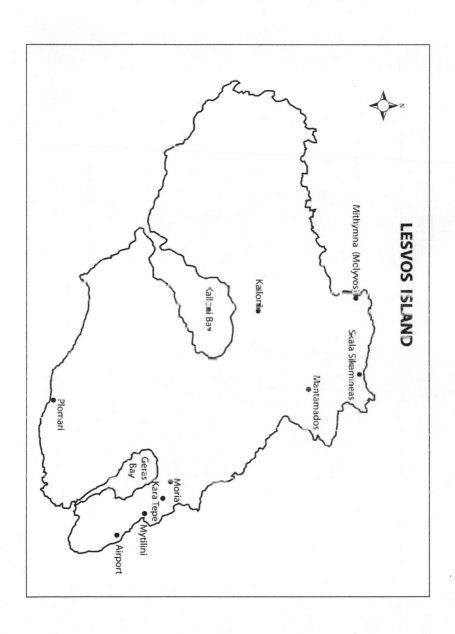

LESVOS ISLAND

Mithymna (Molyvos)

Skala Sikamineas

Kalloni

Kalloni Bay

Mantamados

Plomari

Geras Bay

Moria

Kara Tepe

Myrtilini

Airport

Chapter One

The northeastern Aegean island of Lesvos, a place of quiet beauty, storied history, and sacred shrines, had long drawn the attention of tourists, though never quite the hordes of off-islanders that descended each summer onto some of its much smaller, but far more notorious, Cycladic neighbors to the southwest. Its reputation as the bird-watching capital of Europe, possessing the greatest array of wildflowers in Greece and one of the world's largest petrified forests, drew a different sort of tourist.

Lesvos ranked as the third largest of Greece's islands, behind Crete and Evia, with roughly one-third of its eighty-six thousand inhabitants living in its capital city of Mytilini, an alternative name used by many Greeks for the island. Most Greeks, though, knew very little about modern Lesvos and thought of it, if at all, as little more than the serene agrarian home of Greece's ouzo and sardine industries.

That abruptly changed in 2015.

Virtually overnight, thousands of men, women, and children fleeing the terrors of their homelands flooded daily out of Turkey across the three-and-a-half to ten-mile-wide Mytilini Strait onto Lesvos. Tourists, who'd come to holiday on the island's northern shores, found themselves sitting on the verandas of their beachfront hotels, drinking their morning coffee, watching in horror as an armada of dangerously overloaded boats desperately struggled to reach land.

Inevitably, tourists stopped coming.

But not the refugees, for they saw no choice but to come, no matter the predators waiting for them along the way: profiteers poised to make billions of euros off the fears and aspirations of desperate souls willing to pay, do, or risk whatever they must for the promise of a better, safer existence. In 2015, more than a half million asylum-seeking migrants and refugees passed through Lesvos, looking to make their way to other destinations in the European Union (EU).

The chaos of the modern world had spun out a rushing storm of profit for human traffickers of every stripe, and Lesvos sat dead center in its path.

●●●●●

The sea had always been Mihalis Volandes' friend. He'd been born to it, the same as to his fortune. His father and father before him were islanders who knew the value of owning ships and trading in oil. They stood as part of the Greek elite, protected by the nation's laws and by his countrymen's enduring pride in their tiny country's dominant role on the shipping world stage. The unpleasant fact that little of the shipping industry's revenues ever made its way back to Greece was politely accepted as the nation's cost for maintaining those bragging rights.

Mihalis lived in Kioski, one of Mytilini's old aristocratic neighborhoods, tucked between the new harbor to the south and the 1,500-year-old castle dominating the city's northeast border with the sea. He'd lived through many changes to his island and accepted or ignored most as a part of living in modern times.

One change, though, he could not bring himself to accept or ignore: refugees. Greece had not experienced immigration of the current magnitude since the early 1920s, when 1.2 million Greek Orthodox Christians were expelled from Turkey, an event to which most residents of Lesvos traced their ancestors.

He realized early on what had triggered his nation's modern migration deluge. Under Greece's prior government, the Greek Coast Guard intercepted and turned refugee boats back to Turkey, but in early 2015, Greece's new government ordered its Coast Guard to allow refugee boats to pass into Greece. Germany's later announcement that it would accept one million Syrian refugees that year made what followed inevitable. From that moment on, it would have been irrational for those caught up in war, Syrian or otherwise, to remain in danger rather than risk a journey toward the promised peace and security of a new life in northern Europe.

Mihalis had joined many of his neighbors in doing what they could to help lessen the suffering of the refugees, as did many tourists and off-islanders, but the onslaught soon overwhelmed them. With the arrival of the international media and their cameras, a world outcry arose, bringing non-governmental organizations (NGOs) in to fill the void left by the confluence of EU political paralysis, and Greece's obvious inability to bear the financial burden of caring for hundreds of thousands of new arrivals, while so many of its own eleven million citizens struggled in the depths of a Great Depression-like economic crisis.

Mihalis saw the NGOs' efforts as admirable but severely wanting in both coordination and execution. What troubled him most was the utter absence of an organized plan for addressing the chronic problem of processing and humanely caring for the masses fleeing to safety in Europe by sea.

Threatened bureaucrats entrenched in doing things their own way feared such change. Worried elected officials concerned with playing to their voters wanted no such plan. And, for sure, human traffickers and their allies, who profited from the status quo, didn't want one.

Mihalis saw patience wearing thin on all sides, represented most dramatically in the riots and fires breaking out in the islands' detention centers. Someone had to come up with a broader vision, one that looked beyond short-term expediencies. So Mihalis did just that, with an idea that struck at the heart of the highly lucrative refugee-smuggling business.

He presented his plan to various government authorities, each time receiving a polite thank you from shortsighted apparatchiks who had no intention of considering the proposal but dared not offend someone of Mihalis' stature and influence.

Now, though, with the world even more at war with itself, and no end in sight to the masses fleeing for safer shores, he hoped those capable of instituting change might be more amenable to adopting a sensible, dignified process for integrating refugees into their societies. It struck him as sheer madness to blindly adhere to practices that only engendered anger, resentment, and distrust across generations of souls soon to be part of European society—or returned to their homelands with attitudes forever shaped by their experiences.

But, then again, madness seemed to be in fashion.

Mihalis had spent the day on the neighboring island of Chios, the place of his birth and origin of his family's shipping fortune, trying to stir up support among shipowner friends. He would need their cooperation for his plan to work, and with Chios also a prime target of refugee smugglers, he hoped to get it. For the most part, his friends were receptive to his ideas, and though he would have preferred wild enthusiasm, he sensed they'd ultimately come on board.

It had been a long day, and rough seas made the boat ride back from Chios take longer than expected. His walk from the harbor along the ramble of cobbled and paved streets twisting back toward the old castle also took him longer than usual, but then again, he was tired.

"Whatever," he mumbled as he approached his home. Things finally seemed to be looking up for his project. But if, yet again, no one listened and the situation continued to deteriorate, he could always move to any number of other places in the world. They'd welcome him with open arms, a refugee possessing great wealth. That didn't strike him as fair, but he was a realist—something he wished he could call the EU and his own government.

He fumbled in the dark for his key to the gate in the tall iron fence separating the street from his courtyard and gardens. He wondered why the garden lights weren't on at this hour. Security lights were a relatively new phenomenon here, representing yet another casualty to an island way of life under siege.

He doubted whether, at seventy years old, he'd live to see the world a better place, but with the help of his shipowner friends, he might at least be able to help some of those fleeing its worst places to find a better life, perhaps returning his beloved Lesvos to some sort of normalcy in the process.

But not tonight, he thought as he opened the gate. Tonight, it would be straight to sleep. There was always tomorrow.

He smiled at the thought. "Forever the optimist," his late wife used to call him. She'd have been proud of what he sought to accomplish.

Mihalis sighed as he closed the gate behind him. By memory, he carefully made his way along the marble path to his right. Ahead lay the entryway to his house, off to the right, the tall dark hedges running up against the perimeter fence. He paused for a moment to look up at the sky. Too cloudy for starlight. Just a silent pitch-black night. And the scents of April flowers in the air.

How beautiful.

That's when he heard the *swish.*

• • ● • •

Dana McLaughlin heard the *ping-ping-ping* of a tiny bell long before she saw the battered trash-filled pushcart rambling unsteadily along on two wheels over the flagstones. A blank-eyed, dark-skinned youth edged the pale blue cart through the crowd, tweaking his thumb at the frayed bell cord dangling from its right handle. Mykonos' old-town lanes were far too narrow to safely navigate motorized trash collection vehicles through the tightly packed Easter crowds, and the once-common donkeys only drew gawkers into the jumble. Besides, donkeys were relatively hard to come by these days, and costly compared to Pakistanis, Bangladeshis, Indians, North Africans, and virtually every other dislocated national struggling to find a life in the EU refugee filter trap known as Greece.

She sighed. *So many doing whatever it takes to survive. Even here, on this playground for the rich and sometimes-famous.*

This trip was supposed to be a few days of R & R away from the disheartening campaigns she'd been waging along the front lines of Greece's refugee crisis. If battle ribbons and medals existed for her brand of NGO service in the country's inundated northeastern Aegean islands, besieged urban centers, and mainland relocation camps, she'd have been among the most highly decorated of her under-thirty generation.

In her experience, the effectiveness of NGOs varied broadly. Some, such as her own, performed with dedicated excellence. Others seemed invested in facilitating political positions, rather than in tending to the humanitarian needs of the refugees, while still others seemed more motivated by profiting from their donors' largesse than by doing good works. Then, too, some NGOs, and others who'd come to help, fell victim to unproductive, internecine turf battles that so often plagued competing efforts to do good. It was the infighting that troubled her most, because it so widely missed the mark of the purpose of their work.

Thankfully, in Mihalis Volandes, she'd found a benefactor who shared her vision of what must be done to make relief efforts more effective. There would always be critics and turf-protectors to fight, but together they stood a real chance of bringing much-needed change and sanity to the process.

For this weekend, though, she'd promised herself to put all of that out of her mind and lose herself amid Mykonos' eerily surreal detachment from the ills that haunted the rest of Greece. Here, the nation's chronic financial crisis, and the tourist drought plaguing islands unlucky enough to be headlined in the media's frenzied coverage of refugees in flight, seemed a million miles away.

Mykonos had been a friend's idea, but the friend cancelled at the last minute, leaving her to travel alone. She lay on the beach during the day and wandered through the old town's shop-filled lanes at night. Both left her with too much time to think. She decided she needed to get drunk—but knew that would be unwise for a single woman surrounded by cruising men.

So, instead, she found a gay bar featuring live piano music and sat listening to Broadway show tunes, slowly sipping Kir Royales, not bothered by a soul, and losing herself in childhood memories of growing up in rural northwestern New Jersey.

The gentle buzz of her holiday trance ended abruptly at two, courtesy of the cell phone vibrating in her bag.

• • **●** • •

Andreas Kaldis had just walked into his office when he heard his phone ringing. He picked it up before sitting down.

"Hello, Kaldis here."

"Is this Chief Inspector Kaldis?" The caller struggled to speak Greek.

The question surprised him. "If you have to ask, I guess I should ask how you got my direct number?"

"I'm just…uh…I don't know the word in Greek…*anxious* right now."

Andreas switched to English. "Would you prefer we speak in English, Miss?"

"Yes, thank you. I'm sorry for calling so early."

"It's six-thirty, and you have me now, so why don't we start with who you are, and how you got my number?"

He heard an audible sigh. "Sorry, sir. My name is Dana McLaughlin and I got your number from the Mytilini harbormaster."

"How is Pavlos?" Andreas walked around his desk and sat in his chair.

"He's fine, and said to pass along his regards."

Andreas leaned back. "How can I help you, Ms. McLaughlin?"

"I'm in charge of refugee operations on Lesvos for SafePassage."

He nodded. "I've heard of your organization. My wife tells me it does good work."

"Thank you. That's nice to hear. We try our best."

Andreas heard a deep swallow.

"Last night around two in the morning, I received a call from a coworker that one of our native refugee workers had been arrested."

Andreas picked up a pencil, and began tapping it on his desk. He guessed he was about to be pitched to use his position as head of the Greek Police's Special Crimes Unit to intervene in a local police matter. He wondered why she hadn't asked her harbormaster friend for help. Harbormasters were Coast Guard officers in charge of their jurisdiction's port police. It should be a simple enough favor for him to do for her…unless it wasn't so simple.

"What's a native refugee worker?"

"Some refugees fleeing their homelands find a calling in helping others like themselves. Sometimes they come to work for NGOs like mine. They add a much-needed dimension to our work."

"Sounds admirable. What's your refugee worker accused of?"

She cleared her throat. "Murder."

Andreas stopped tapping. "Oh."

"But he couldn't have done it."

"Why do you say that?"

"Murder is not in his character."

Andreas figured pursuing her basis for that observation would likely take up his entire morning. "Ms. McLaughlin, what is it you'd like for me to do?"

"Investigate. He won't stand a chance if you don't."

"I'm sure the police will be thorough."

"There's too much at stake for the politicians to stay out of it."

He sensed a political diatribe in the offing. "This is not the first time a refugee has been involved in a crime like this in Greece."

He heard her pause and clear her throat.

"It's the first time the victim's been a seventy-year-old Greek shipping tycoon, sliced cleanly in half from neck to crotch with the single stroke of a sword."

Andreas sat up in his chair. "Run that by me again."

"Late last night, Mihalis Volandes, the patriarch of an old-line shipping family, was killed, just as I said, in the garden outside his Mytilini home."

Andreas crossed himself. "My God."

"Precisely."

"Why are they accusing your guy?"

"The police found him at the scene."

"Holding the sword?"

"This isn't funny, Chief." Her voice took on an edge.

"It wasn't meant to be. What's his name?"

"Ali Sera, and, no, he wasn't holding a sword."

"Why was he there?"

"He said he'd received a call telling him to meet Mr. Volandes at his home."

"Who called him?"

"He didn't know the caller."

"Did your guy know Volandes?"

"I can't say for sure that they ever met, but he certainly

knew of him, because our organization publicly supported Mr. Volandes' efforts to develop a new approach for processing refugees."

"Was Ali for or against Volandes' efforts?"

"I'm positive he was for them."

"Why?"

"Because they made sense and would work."

Andreas rubbed at his forehead with his free hand. "Who's in charge of the investigation?"

"I don't know, but I can ask."

"That's okay," said Andreas. "I'll find out."

"So you'll investigate?"

"No promises. For now I just want more details."

"I understand. Thank you so much, and please let me know what more I can do to help." She gave him her cell and office numbers. "I'll be back on Lesvos late Monday, and can get you more information once I'm there, if you need it."

"Where are you now?"

"On Mykonos, for Easter."

"Ah, yes, an island I know well."

"Do you think I should return to Lesvos sooner?"

"Not for my purposes," said Andreas. "I'll give the local police your contact information in case they want to get in touch with you before you're back on the island."

"It's all so unbelievable. I feel so sorry for everyone involved. Mr. Volandes, his family, Ali…."

She seemed to be holding back a sob. "We'd been so close to changing so many lives—an old Greek man and his American granddaughter they used to call us—united in doing good works for the world."

Andreas cleared his throat. "I understand. May I suggest you spend some time in church? After all, it's Easter time and that might help you to process this."

She sighed. "Thanks for the advice, Chief. *Kalo Paska*. Bye."

"And a Good Easter to you, too." Andreas hung up the

phone. He looked out his window at his own building's reflection in the neighboring building's windows.

Sliced in half. He crossed himself again.

● ● ● ● ●

"You're in early, again, I see," said Maggie Sikestes, poking her sturdy, red-haired, five-foot-three-inch frame inside the doorway to her boss' office.

Andreas shrugged. "Lila's feeding schedule for the baby has me up at five anyway. No reason for me to hang around the house."

"Is that your idea or Lila's?"

"Cute. Maybe I should ask my loyal secretary to consider coming in earlier too?"

Maggie feigned a smile, "Feel free to ask."

They'd been bantering back and forth like this since Andreas' return to Greece's Central Police Headquarters in Athens (better known as GADA), following a brief stint on Mykonos as its police chief. He'd returned to assume command of the unit charged with investigating matters of national concern or potential corruption. That's when the luck of the draw landed him with Maggie, GADA's mother superior and source of all knowledge of its many secrets and intricate ways.

Andreas shook his head. "If you'd been here when I got in, you could have screened my calls."

"Ever hear of letting them go through to voicemail?"

"It's the kid in me. I can't resist a ringing phone."

"Why do I sense you're about to tell me something unpleasant?"

"Good guess. A half-hour ago, I received a call from a woman who heads up a refugee operation on Lesvos. Someone who works for her, who happens to be a refugee, is accused of using a sword to murder one of the island's most distinguished citizens."

"Ouch."

"And she wants me to look into it."

"Will you?"

Andreas shrugged. "I've left a message with the Mytilini police commander to call me when he has the chance. Let's hear what he has to say. If it's an open-and-shut case, no reason for us to get involved."

"I sense you don't think it is."

Andreas raised and dropped his hands. "The victim was sliced in half, top to bottom."

"Oh, my God. That sounds like terrorists."

Andreas nodded. "Up to now, we've been blessedly spared that sort of thing in Greece. At least of the foreign-born sort."

"Could it be?"

He shook his head. "I don't know. That's what I want to find out. Tell Yianni to see me the moment he gets in."

"Can I make you some coffee?"

Andreas held up a paper cup. "I got some from the cafeteria."

"My sympathies."

"Also, see what you can find out about the victim, Mihalis Volandes." Maggie's eyebrows rose at the name. Andreas nodded. "There should be a lot. But concentrate on his efforts to help refugees. Also, see what you can find out about the accused, Ali Sera, though I doubt you'll find much, if anything, on him."

"Anything else?"

"Yes, while you're at it, look into the background of Dana McLaughlin." He wrote the name on a sheet of paper and slid it across the desk to Maggie.

"And who would she be?"

"The one who's asked for my help."

"Ah, the ever-trusting soul of my boss."

"Just being careful."

Chapter Two

"You wanted to see me?" said the bull-like man, a shaved head shorter than Andreas, standing in the doorway to Andreas' office.

"Yeah, Yianni. Grab a chair."

Yianni Kouros and Andreas had met when Yianni was a brash young rookie on Mykonos and Andreas his chief. They'd been together protecting each other's back ever since.

"We've got a gruesome murder on Lesvos."

"Maggie told me."

"I'm still waiting to hear back from the cops on the scene." Andreas looked at his watch. "Should be soon."

"If this is terrorists, isn't it something the minister will want to handle directly out of his office?"

"What minister? Our boss, the minister of public order? The politicians are still trying to find someone competent to replace the last one."

Yianni smiled. "That's because you refused to take the job again. I meant our *Prime* Minister."

"I'm sure we'll hear from him, if he's interested in anything more than offering political homilies to the people and routine condolences to the family. My guess is he'll want to play this down, make it seem a local affair, far removed from any sort of international incident. The last word that he or anyone else who cares about our tourism industry will want to hear bandied about is 'terrorism.'"

Yianni nodded. "Look what's happened to Turkey. It's practically deserted. Even the Turks are going elsewhere on holiday."

"Which makes them particularly sensitive to anything that threatens their remaining tourism along the coastline across from our Northern Aegean islands."

"For sure. Remember what happened with Kos? Refugees once poured onto Kos out of Turkey in numbers as large as those hitting our other islands close to Turkey. But Turkish hoteliers in Bodrum complained about how refugees massing at its shores waiting to be smuggled across to Kos negatively affected its tourism industry, and *poof,* refugees miraculously evaporated from Bodrum, and Kos no longer had the refugee problem it once had."

Andreas nodded. "This woman McLaughlin's probably right about politicians getting involved. My guess is they'll want to wrap it up quickly and not let it linger out there as a possible terrorist act."

"Who's McLaughlin? And why did she call you?"

"The guy the Lesvos police have in custody is a recent refugee who works for her. She's the head of the local branch of SafePassage. It's a big NGO based in Brussels that provides hands-on aid to refugees from the time their boats hit Greek waters through relocation into Europe."

"What about the ones that get shipped back to Turkey?"

"They can't help them—which, I assume, is why SafePassage opposes the EU arrangement with Turkey calling for shipping unauthorized refugees from our islands back to Turkey and God-only-knows what conditions over there."

"How do you know all this?"

Andreas smiled and pointed at his computer screen. "Google."

"Chief," Maggie's voice came booming through the open doorway. "It's the Mytilini police commander on the line."

"And the research skills of the possessor of that lovely voice." Andreas pointed Yianni to a chair by his desk, and hit the speaker button on his phone.

"Commander, thanks for calling me back. I'm certain you're very busy with this new case."

"You don't know the half of it, which is probably an insensitive way to put things, considering how the victim died."

Andreas winced. "Yes, I think that's a fair observation."

Yianni rolled his eyes and shook his head.

"Sorry. It's been a long night."

"So, what can you tell us?"

"We received an anonymous call around one in the morning of a suspicious person lurking around the Volandes mansion."

"Any idea who called it in?"

"Like I said, it was anonymous."

"What about caller ID?"

"It came from a throwaway phone with no way to track the owner."

"Did that strike you as unusual?"

"These days a lot of refugees end up using that sort of phone. It's the only kind they can get."

"So, you think a refugee called it in?"

"We recorded the call, and the speaker had a definite accent, making that a distinct possibility."

"Why would a refugee make the call?" said Andreas.

"Any number of reasons, ranging from being a good citizen to a blood feud with the guy the caller implicated. Tribal differences don't disappear when these folks land here. We've got a lot of people who don't get along living in close proximity to one another."

"Hi, it's Detective Yianni Kouros. Sorry to interrupt, but it sounds to me that you think you have your killer."

"I wish I could say that for certain, Detective. Yes, we caught him outside the Volandes mansion with the victim's blood down his face and the front of his clothes. The body was on the other side of the gate, well into the garden."

"That sure sounds incriminating," said Yianni.

"It's why the prosecutor's all hot to go after him." The commander paused. "But something doesn't seem right."

"What's that?" said Andreas.

"The obvious question is why would a killer hang around to be caught? And, yes, I know stranger things happen. But then there's the blood spatter."

"What about it?" asked Yianni.

"It wasn't a lot of blood on him, considering the scene."

"But he was spattered, meaning he must have been there when the blow was struck," said Yianni.

"That's the point. The boy—"

"Boy?" said Andreas.

"The accused is only seventeen. Anyway, the accused, Ali Sera, said when he got there everything was quiet and he saw no one around. He tried peeking inside the gate, but with no moon and no lights, he couldn't see a thing. That's when he said he felt it start to rain."

"Rain?" said Andreas.

"Yes, rain. But we've been bone-dry for days, not a drop."

"So what do you make of that?" said Andreas.

"I don't know. I went back to the crime scene this morning at first light and it's a bloody mess. The boy insists he never went beyond the gate. But I agree it's hard to imagine how the accused could have gotten the victim's blood on his face and down the front of his clothes if he wasn't inside that garden at the time of the murder."

"What about the bottoms of his shoes?" said Andreas.

"Clean. We checked. He must have been careful not to step in the blood, and forensics found no footprints suggesting anyone other than Volandes had been there."

"What about the terrorist angle?" said Andreas.

"That could explain why he didn't run away. He wanted the world to know what he'd done," said Yianni.

"Yeah, but he's not claiming anything like that, nor is any organization. Not yet, anyway," said the commander. "The boy maintains he received a call telling him to meet Volandes at his house right away because Volandes had something important to get to Dana McLaughlin."

"But McLaughlin wasn't on Lesvos," said Andreas.

"Sera knew that. It's why he went."

"So whoever made the call knew that too," said Yianni.

"Assuming there was such a call," said the commander. "Even if the boy's phone shows a call, he could have used a throwaway phone to call himself to create an alibi."

Andreas cleared his throat. "Commander, I hope you don't mind, but could you keep the crime scene protected for the rest of the day? I'm going to have Detective Kouros fly over to take a look at it. I'm sure you caught everything, but this matter could get a bit tricky if someone decides to run with a potential terror angle. I wouldn't want a question hanging out there over why my unit hadn't gotten involved when we had the chance."

"I understand. I also appreciate your effort at not stepping on what you assume are my professional toes."

The cop laughed and Andreas joined in.

"Hold that thought," said Andreas. "Detective Kouros isn't nearly so diplomatic."

"I look forward to meeting him. Is that it?"

"Yep, thanks for your time. Bye."

As soon as Andreas hung up Yianni said, "Thanks. It's just what I wanted two days before Easter. A trip to Lesvos."

"Just catch the next plane out of Venizelos and come back after checking out the crime scene."

"The guy sounds thorough," said Yianni. "Even if his sense of humor could use some work. What am I going to find that forensics didn't?"

"Think of it like diapers. You won't know what you'll find until you look."

"Fine, I'm convinced." Yianni stood up and headed toward the door. "Actually, compared to yours, that guy's sense of humor isn't so bad."

●　●　●　●　●

The 170-mile flight from Athens' Venizelos International Airport to Mytilini International took a little less than an hour, eight hours less than the average travel time if Yianni had taken a ferry. He hadn't been to Lesvos before and, like many Greeks, knew very little of the island's ancient history beyond it being home to the lyric poet Sappho.

He vaguely recalled some mention of Lesvos in the *Iliad* and the *Odyssey* as inhabited as far back as the fourth millennium BCE, and of learning in school that the island had been ruled over time by an assortment of conquerors, from Spartans and Athenians, through Romans, Turks, and other foreign sorts. He also remembered hearing of archaeological discoveries supporting the existence of a Lesvos civilization on a par with that developed in Troy and Mycenae, but that exhausted Yianni's knowledge on the subject of Lesvos' ancient history.

In an airline magazine, he found an article on the island's capital city of Mytilini, which noted that, like Jerusalem, Mecca, Rome, and Athens, Mytilini laid claim to being built on seven hills. Mytilini's seven hills stood on the island's southeastern edge, a little more than ten miles from Turkey. They curved westerly in a north-south arc, embracing to the east the city, two harbors, and a promontory bearing the remains of one of the largest castles in the Mediterranean, rebuilt in the fourteenth century on the sixth-century foundation of another fortress.

When Lesvos came into being as an organized community in the eleventh century BCE, Mytilini stood as a small island separated from the main island by a narrow strait linking harbors at its north and south ends. Time, silt, and defensive considerations ultimately filled in that strait, and Mytilini and Lesvos now stood as one, with the ancient harbor to the north called the upper or old port, and the commercially active passenger harbor to the south, the new port.

Yianni's eyes paused on a line in the article: "Mytilini, like the rest of Lesvos, has for millennia served as a place of exile for those fleeing their homelands."

The more things change, the more they remain the same.

He put down the magazine and stared out the window at a sapphire-blue sea separating mainland Greece from Lesvos. He wondered how many who called themselves Greek today owed the lives they now led to refugee ancestors. Probably a lot more than suspected. Or cared to admit.

Yianni's first glimpse of Lesvos surprised him. He'd expected a large, triangular-shaped island edged in coves and inlets, not the dramatic contrast of land and sea he saw beneath him. Two huge silver-blue bays along Lesvos' southern shoreline drove deeply into a brown and green landmass as heavily ridged as a crocodile's back.

He took the green to be the boundless olive groves and forests of pine, chestnut, plane, and oak trees bragged about by his Athenian friends of Lesvos origins. They spoke of their island's fertile brown soil and warm, sunny year-round climate, countless varieties of vegetation, and abundant water, creating a natural paradise. He'd thought that the kind of clouded nostalgia talk city-dwellers often used when romanticizing the villages they or their ancestors had abandoned in order to earn a living elsewhere. But, from what he saw through his window, perhaps they'd not been exaggerating after all.

The plane banked as it approached the airport's single narrow runway alongside the sea. Time to put away the magazine and focus on the case.

Yianni looked at the tiny gym bag by his feet. He'd only packed what he needed for a quick in-and-out trip to Lesvos. Next time he'd pack more. He had no doubt there'd be a next time.

● ● ● ● ●

Scents of springtime blossoms, carried along a warm summerlike breeze, met Yianni outside the post-World War II-era terminal building. So, too, did a uniformed police officer in a marked car parked at the bottom of the ramp leading out from the main entrance, courtesy of the Mytilini police commander. The cop said it should take about fifteen minutes to cover the seven kilometers to the crime scene.

Yianni asked him about the investigation. The cop said he knew nothing. His orders were to pick up Yianni at the airport and drop him off at the Volandes mansion in town. Yianni knew that by now the Lesvos police grapevine must have spread details of such a horrific murder to every cop on the island, so he took the cop's answer to mean he'd been ordered to keep his mouth shut and not talk to the Athens cop.

No matter, he'd sit back and enjoy the view. They turned north out of the parking lot onto a two-lane road running next to the sea. A single line of trees, perhaps tamarisk, separated the road from the bright blue water to the east. To the west spread open spaces of beige, brown, and green. The closer they drew to town, hotels, residences, and occasional commercial buildings no taller than three stories filled in much of the sea view space with pastel shades of pink, yellow, blue, green, and lavender, all topped with terra-cotta roofs.

They turned away from the sea road onto a two-lane avenue cutting through a more upscale neighborhood of high stone walls, ornamental iron gates, large trees, and green lawns, amid a mix of one- and two-story homes, neoclassical mansions, and uninspired concrete apartment buildings with their ubiquitous slab-sided balconies that plagued all of modern Greece, no matter how well-off the neighborhood.

They met up again with the sea at a broad four-lane boulevard leading toward the new harbor, passing by neatly maintained buildings in colorful pastels taking on a neoclassical air, bedecked in pillars and pediments. Even the usual commercial buildings one expected to find cluttered around any busy harborfront had a softer tone than Yianni expected.

He caught a brief glimpse of the dome of Mytilini's landmark architectural gem, the Church of Saint Therapon, before they turned left away from the harbor, headed the wrong way on a one-way street. Barely wide enough for two cars to pass, the road narrowed still more by light-colored brick sidewalks running flush up against the storefronts of shops that stretched ahead on each side of the road for as far as Yianni could see.

This must be the town's main shopping street. It struck Yianni as more citified than he'd expected for an island town so obviously proud of its architectural past. Then again, from an islander's perspective, Mytilini ranked as more of a city than a town, though not in the sense of metropolitan Athens, with its four million residents. Mytilini's population of thirty thousand far exceeded the total number of residents of most Greek islands. Yes, Mytilini qualified as an island city—complete with urban-style graffiti and an infatuation with modern styling.

The car turned off into a warren of narrow stone-paved streets winding through a decidedly more residential area, one that struck Yianni as a metaphor for the general state of Greek life today: some homes prosperous, some on their last legs, but most looking as if simply trying to get by.

The driver stopped next to a forensic van and a police car parked in front of a fence of black iron spears mounted atop a low concrete wall. Together, the fence and wall separated the street from the courtyard of a meticulously maintained three-story neoclassical mansion. Tightly packed hedges just inside the fence provided the traditional seclusion common to Lesvos' urban residential architecture. An open gate constructed of the same black iron spears offered the only break in the hedges.

A tall, fit-looking man in his forties wearing a blue suit, blue shirt, and no tie stepped out through the gate.

"That's my boss," said the driver.

"He's in charge of police on Lesvos?"

"No, just Mytilini. There are six other commands on the island."

"Thanks for the lift," said Yianni. He shook the driver's hand, got out of the car, and walked toward the police commander, extending his hand as he approached him. "Hi, Commander, I'm Detective Yianni Kouros. We spoke earlier today."

"Pleased to meet you." He offered Yianni a firm handshake.

"Thanks for sending your man to pick me up at the airport, and for arranging to keep the crime scene intact."

"No problem. I'm open to all the help we can get. This is a nasty one."

Yianni stepped up to the gate and looked down at a gray marble path running from the sidewalk into, and apparently around, the courtyard garden. As he stepped inside, straight ahead on the right, five paces away, he saw a massive blood stain on the marble.

"I assume that's where it happened."

The commander nodded. "Yes, blood-spatter analysis confirmed Volandes stood there when the assailant hammered him with the sword from behind."

"Behind?"

"Yes, he likely never saw it coming."

"Where's the sword?"

"Haven't found it."

Yianni knelt and looked at the blood patterns on the marble, stood, and studied the hedges leading back to the gate. At the gate, he looked down at the sidewalk just beyond it.

"Commander, do you mind if I close the gate?"

"Go right ahead, it's been checked for prints."

Yianni pulled the gate closed and, standing inside the garden, ran his eyes up and down the iron spear at the edge of the gate farthest from the scene of the attack. He worked his way back along the gate, studying each spear, until stopping abruptly four spears from the edge of the gate closest to the attack.

"Commander, could you ask whoever belongs to that forensic van out front to step over here for a moment?"

The commander nodded to a young woman dressed all in white.

"Yes, sir, how can I help you?"

Yianni pointed toward the top of the fourth spear from the end. "What's that look like to you?"

She leaned in, squinted, pulled a jeweler's loupe out of her pocket, and examined the spear. "I see what you're getting at… it could be blood."

"But how did it get over here, so far away from the point of attack?" said Yianni.

"It's probably spray," she said.

"That's pretty far from the site of the attack, but even so, from the angle of attack the spray would have been intercepted by the hedges. There's spatter all along them."

The woman swallowed. "Perhaps that's where the perpetrator touched the gate when he left the garden."

"Perhaps, but what about this?" Yianni pointed to more spotting running up and down the fourth spear. "And this." He pointed to similar spots running up and down the next spear over toward the hedges. "You surely don't think he touched both bars in all those places."

She blushed. "No, I don't."

"So what could explain those bloodstains, assuming that's what they are and that they're the victim's blood?"

"I don't know." She looked at the commander and back at Yianni. "I'm new to all this. I'm just an examiner assisting the person who conducted the actual examination."

"And who's that?"

"My boss, the forensic supervisor."

Yianni looked at the commander. "Is her boss one of us?"

The commander nodded. "Technically, he's on the force, but not as a cop, and for all intents and purposes, he's a hand-maiden of the prosecutor's office."

"Is he here?"

The commander gestured no. "He said he didn't have the time to spare for educating visiting Athenians."

Yianni smiled. "I see." He waved for the woman to follow him back to the site of the attack. "So, what do we have here, besides a lot of blood?"

Visibly nervous, the examiner began to stutter. "I, I, I don't know what you're getting at."

Yianni raised his hand. "Relax. Since your supervisor obviously doesn't discriminate as to who he doesn't have time to teach, let's see if I can help out a bit."

The commander smiled.

"Here, in the direction the victim was walking, what do you see?"

She looked like a deer in the headlights.

"Never mind trying to answer that, it's a rhetorical question. What you see is a broad symmetrical pattern of blood spatters. Now look behind the victim and what do you see?" Yianni waited. "That wasn't rhetorical. It's a real question for you to answer."

The woman spoke in a tentative voice, "There's a large gap in the spatter."

"Would you say it seems to just disappear?"

She nodded. "Yes."

"Very good. Now what possible explanation can you come up with for that?"

She paused for a second. Then her eyes opened wide. "The killer's body caught the blood spatter."

"Very good, go to the head of the class."

The woman bristled. "No reason to be patronizing."

"I wasn't trying to be."

She frowned. "But that means there should have been a lot more blood on the perpetrator than we found."

"No, that means there should have been a lot more blood on Ali Sera *if* he was the killer."

"What about the bloodstains on the gate?" asked the commander.

"That's the interesting part, but I think I have an answer. Care to take a guess?"

The woman gestured no. "I know to quit when I'm ahead."

Yianni walked back to the gate followed by the others. "Remember when Ali claimed it had started to rain?"

"Yes, it made no sense," she said.

"But for him it did, because it was raining blood."

"I don't understand," said the commander. "You just said the blood spatter never made it over here."

"It didn't," said Yianni. "At least not from the attack. But think of it this way. The night was pitch-black, and if the assailant wore black, you'd never see him. So let's assume Ali shows up at the gate and peers inside trying to see where's the man he's supposed to meet. That's when he feels raindrops on his face, and blood spattering later turns up running up and down the front of his body." Yianni turned and pointed at the attack site. "If you look closely at where blood pooled up, you might find evidence of what the killer used to pick up some of the victim's blood, like a paintbrush or syringe."

"For what purpose?" said the woman.

"Simple, yet ingenious. The killer carefully gathered some of his victim's blood, patiently waited until Ali peeked through the gate, and then spattered the blood all over him."

"Sounds like you're saying we've got a cold-blooded ninja killer on our hands," said the commander.

Yianni shrugged. "Check the spot on the street where Ali said he was standing when he looked through the gate and felt rain. If you use those two spears in the gate spotted with blood as the point of origin, I think you'll find a blood-spatter pattern on the sidewalk consistent with Ali blocking most of the spatter."

"I get it," said the woman. "It matches the analysis that shows the actual killer catching a lot more blood spatter than we found on Ali. I'll get right on it." She hurried off in the direction of her equipment.

Yianni smiled. "That one has potential."

The commander nodded. "What about the paintbrush or whatever?"

"I doubt you'll ever find it, any more than the sword or garment the killer likely wore to catch the victim's blood spatter."

"I'll get my people checking every trash bin, empty lot, and vacant building in the neighborhood for them all. We might get lucky."

"What's next?" said Yianni.

"Well, neither the prosecutor nor his forensic supervisor friend is going to be happy about what you found. They're both pretty much egotistical pricks, who, incidentally, don't like me any more than I like them. But, in light of what you've come up with, I don't see how they can hold Ali. That's not to say they won't. After all, he's a refugee, not a Greek."

"I get the politics. I guess my real question is whether you'll be searching for the real killer."

The commander shrugged. "If the prosecutor won't drop it, he's not going to take kindly to my trying to prove he's wrong. He might make things difficult for me."

"What about the victim's family?"

"They'll likely want closure, and if the prosecutor can bring them that by sacrificing Ali, that might end it."

"I was afraid you'd say that."

"Afraid?"

"Because once my boss thinks this kid is getting framed, he's going to have me living over here until we get to the truth."

The commander smiled. "Lesvos is lovely this time of the year, and if you're here on Easter, you're welcome to come to my house."

"Thanks, but I've plans with my family down on the Peloponnese. Besides, I don't think much will happen before Tuesday."

The cop nodded. "Well, that'll give me a few days to see what I might be able to come up with before the prosecutor starts thinking about shutting me down. Which reminds me, I better tell the examiner not to mention any of this to her boss quite yet."

"Will she listen?" said Yianni.

"Of course."

"How can you be so sure?"

"She's my daughter."

Chapter Three

"It's Yianni, calling from Lesvos," came the shout through the doorway into Andreas' office.

"Thanks, Maggie." Andreas picked up the phone. "Afternoon. So, what do you have for me?"

"Probably not what you'd like to hear. It looks like the kid in custody isn't the killer."

Andreas exhaled. "I was afraid of that."

"Whoever killed Volandes took great care to make it look like the kid did it." Yianni told him about the blood spatter patterns, what he'd found on the gate, and specks of blood found by the examiner outside the gate.

"The actual killer had to be one strong son of a bitch to slice clean through a man from head to crotch in a single blow."

"Yeah," said Yianni. "And I doubt Ali had the strength to do that."

"Adrenaline."

"Maybe, but nothing else matches up."

Andreas smiled. "Sounds like once again you made me look brilliant for getting you involved in an investigation."

"Flattery works."

"You're welcome."

"A raise would be better."

"Have you spoken to Ali?"

"No, he's been advised by an attorney not to talk to the police."

"Smart."

"Especially since the police commander thinks the prosecutor has a real hard-on for grabbing headlines with a refugee-as-murderer prosecution."

"That's going to be tough to pull off with what you've found."

"The prosecutor has a forensics guy with a reputation for doing whatever it takes to see that the prosecutor gets convictions."

"Isn't that interesting?"

"Yeah, I thought you'd like that."

Andreas picked up a pencil. "I guess that means we'll have to jump in on this one."

"I thought you'd say that, too."

"What's your take on it so far?"

"Looks like an assassination, with two planned victims: the dead guy and the accused."

"The common thread being?"

"Refugees."

Andreas tapped the pencil on his desktop. "Okay, so we had Volandes fired up to change the EU's approach to dealing with refugees, and Ali working for an NGO that supports Volandes' plans. Seems a very neat, quick way to get rid of one half of a problem while undermining the credibility of the other half."

"It also plays into the hands of those who like labeling refugees as terrorists and criminals."

"So, who do you think had the greatest motive and opportunity for pulling this off?"

"There's so much money being made off refugees on all sides, I'm afraid that list is endless."

"We've got to start somewhere."

"Okay, where do you suggest?" said Yianni.

"Talk to the McLaughlin woman."

Yianni voice dropped. "Oh."

"Don't sound so enthusiastic. She won't be back on Lesvos

until Monday. You can talk to her by phone on Tuesday. No need to interfere with your Easter plans."

"Thanks."

"One last thing. What about the murder weapon?"

"It hasn't been found, but it must be an awesome sword to have done what it did."

"I'll take that to mean it wasn't the sort of machete you'd pick up at a local hardware store."

"Not a chance."

"That may be the break we're looking for."

"How's that?"

"Our murderer's likely too fond of his sword to part with it. Assassins generally use generic, untraceable weapons. This guy seems different. Which means, if we find the sword, we might find our killer."

"The police commander has his people searching the neighborhood for it."

"Good," said Andreas, "but ask him if he knows of any locals with access to swords. A collector, perhaps."

"The killer and his sword could have come from anywhere."

"I agree, but anywhere leaves us nowhere. Maybe we'll get lucky."

"The police commander said the same thing. There must be something about getting lucky on Lesvos."

Andreas offered a theatrical sigh. "While you're working on improving your sense of humor, would you also try getting a copy of whatever information that forensics guy has before he realizes we'll be looking over his shoulder?"

"Hmm, I think I know the perfect person to ask."

"There you go again, making me look good."

"It's a tough job, but someone has to do it."

Yianni thought they'd meet at a taverna in the old harbor, for that's where his friends said he'd find the best places to eat. But the commander wanted to be out of town, away from prying eyes, so he picked a tiny taverna nestled close by a small harbor along the road from town to the airport. He assured Yianni the fish was good, with the spartan ambiance of well-worn tables and chairs, and old family photographs adorning the walls, more rustic than they'd find in town. They'd been waiting twenty minutes for his daughter, Aleka, a delay the commander dismissed with a shrug and the taverna owner used to console them with offers of his best local ouzo and a *meze* of the island's famous salted raw *sardeles pastes*, *sougania* stuffed onions, and *giouslemedes*, small fried cheese pies, all compliments of the house. Neither man refused his generosity.

Yianni's mind wandered to what life would be like if he had to make a living as a fisherman on one of those small, brightly colored fishing boats moored just off the beach. He'd been lost in his thoughts when he caught a glimpse of a tall, slender young woman, her deep brown hair cascading halfway down her back, marching toward their table.

He jumped up and extended his hand. "Sorry, for a moment, I didn't recognize you. The last time we met your hair was up." He pulled back a chair with his other hand so she could sit between him and her father. "Thank you very much for coming."

She perfunctorily shook his hand and dropped onto the chair. "I didn't really have much of a choice. Did I, Father?"

"Aleka…."

She raised a hand. "Am I here to receive more lessons on how to behave at a crime scene?"

"No, not at a crime scene," said the commander.

She stared at her father. "Okay, I know, be professional."

Yianni leaned forward. "As a matter of fact, Aleka—may I call you Aleka?"

She nodded.

"Call me Yianni. The reason I wanted to meet with you was precisely because of your professionalism."

She smiled. "Why do I smell a seduction in the offing?"

"Aleka!" said her father.

Yianni raised his hand for calm. "It's okay." He stared straight at her. "View it as you wish, but I'm here to offer you the choice of being inside or outside the tent when it comes crashing down on the careers of some folks you know well."

She blinked. "I don't understand. What am I doing wrong?"

"Nothing, that I know of. And I doubt that even you know. But I'd bet your boss, the forensic supervisor, knows."

She shook her head. "I don't know what you're talking about."

"It has to do with what you did at the Volandes crime scene."

"I only did what my boss told me to do."

Yianni nodded. "I'm sure. Did he tell you to initial evidence bags?"

She nodded.

"And measurements?"

She nodded again.

"What about his notes?"

She hesitated. "He said he needed my signature to confirm he'd made the observations."

"Did you read what you signed?"

She gestured no. "He said I didn't have to."

Her father shook his head.

She bit her lip and glared at her father. "Stop acting as if I did something wrong. I did what my boss told me to do."

Yianni nodded. "I understand that sort of pressure. You didn't want it to seem that you didn't trust your boss and mentor. But now your name's on something you might not agree with. And that could leave you open to taking blame, should something go wrong."

She ran her fingers through her hair. "So, what is it you want from me?"

"Copies and samples of everything having to do with the forensic examination of that crime scene."

"How can I possibly get you that?"

"Do you have access to them?" asked Yianni.

She nodded. "They're kept in the office."

"Then do it this weekend. After all, it's Easter. No one will be working."

She sighed.

"All I'm asking is that you provide that information to a representative of the Greek Police's Special Crimes Unit, for the purpose of ensuring the evidence is preserved. I'm not asking you to alter or destroy a thing."

"But you don't want anyone else to know what you're asking me to do?"

Yianni nodded.

"So, it's not a completely appropriate request." Aleka looked to her father. "What do you think?"

"I think it's the right thing to do if you think the evidence that Detective Kouros wants to preserve supports the innocence of the man in custody."

She rose suddenly. "I've got to run." She nodded at Yianni, exchanged quick kisses with her father, and was off.

Yianni sat quietly staring at the commander as he watched his daughter hurry away.

"What was that exit all about?" asked Yianni.

"In my experience, I think it was a yes."

"I guess it's tough being the father of a strong-willed daughter."

"You can't imagine. Especially when you're in the same line of work. I'm glad you gave her the lecture that you did. She wouldn't have taken it from me."

"When will we know if it actually was a yes?"

"When she shows up with what you asked for."

"Terrific." Yianni smacked his hands lightly on the table. "So, could I trouble you for a lift to the airport?"

"But don't you want to eat first?"

"I'd love to, but I've a got a lot of preparations to do for

Easter and don't want to risk having such a good time here that I miss the next plane to Athens."

"Quite the diplomat, I see. The commander smiled. "No problem, the airport's only a couple of kilometers away. That's another reason I picked this place."

Yianni laughed. "And you're quite the master strategist. When do you think you might hear back from those collectors about the sword?"

"Not before Tuesday, at the earliest."

Yianni nodded. "Easter time in Greece."

"Too bad you can't spend more time here. You should get out of Mytilini and see what our island is really all about. It's like nowhere else in Greece."

"So my friends tell me."

"Forget the places you might have heard of, like Mithymna, Kolloni, and Plomari. Wander around and you'll find all sorts of wonderful towns and villages right out of old Greek post-cards, plus glorious beaches everywhere, museums, festivals, and a million olive trees in between. Trust me, you'll love it."

"I'm sure, and I look forward to doing just that, but this weekend's all about family."

The commander nodded, and raised his glass. "*Kalo Paska.*"

Yianni lifted his. "*Kalo Paska.*"

"Where are you?"

"At the gate, waiting for my flight back to Athens. Thought I'd give you a call."

"Does that mean things went well or not?" asked Andreas.

"That depends on whether the police commander's daughter delivers on the forensics." Yianni described his conversation with the commander and his daughter.

"Seems strange the commander didn't mind you putting his daughter at risk."

"I wondered, too, so I asked him about that."

"Was he offended?"

"No, he laughed."

"Laughed?"

"He said he intends on assigning his most trusted man to keep an eye on his daughter when she's in the office, just in case something goes squirrelly."

"Like her boss showing up unexpectedly?"

"Yep. He said he wants to help me get what I need, but he's a father first."

Andreas smiled. "I like his thinking."

"Me, too."

"I can't help wondering, though, why he's being so cooperative. Local cops don't usually side with us against other locals, especially when the one we're focused on is someone they work with all the time, like a prosecutor."

"I think I have an answer for you on that," said Yianni. "We talked about my plans to spend Easter down in the Mani with my family. He told me the only immediate family he has in Greece are his daughter and a sister with children. His parents and wife died a few years back. His wife's family is scattered across Europe."

"Refugees, eh?"

"His family, too. His grandfather escaped to Greece in 1922 when all Orthodox Christians were forced to leave Turkey. His experiences as an orphan refugee weren't the warm and fuzzy welcoming ones many would like us to believe. But as tough as it was for his grandfather, he still was a Greek, and had it easy compared to non-Greek refugees."

"Sounds like he learned a lesson from his grandfather on how to treat refugees."

"Yeah, the Golden Rule."

"Seems like a good man," said Andreas.

"We could use more like him."

"What about the daughter?"

"Headstrong, but I'm guessing trustworthy."

"A characteristic of your generation." Andreas chuckled.

"In case you haven't noticed, I've grown up. She even called me sir."

Andreas laughed harder. "Well, then, you'll likely feel more comfortable dealing with Dana McLaughlin. She's ancient, like you. Maggie told me she's almost thirty."

"I've got an elephant in the room question for you, Chief."

"Shoot."

"If this really was an assassination, what are the chances of there being other targets out there? If the killer murdered Volandes because of his plans for refugees, doesn't it makes sense that anyone sharing Volandes' cause is a target, too?"

"Good point," said Andreas. "Whoever murdered Volandes took great care to make it look like Ali did it, yet in an attention-grabbing way, guaranteed to send a message about refugees. One dramatic death like his might be all you need to dampen the enthusiasm of anyone considering stepping into Volandes' shoes. It gets you thinking….'This time a sword, maybe next time a car accident, heart attack, slip and fall in a shower, whatever.'"

"Yep, just some uncomplicated cause of death that cops use all the time as a reason for marking a case closed," said Yianni.

"I think we'd better ask Ms. McLaughlin for a list of people who might be considered likely successors to Vola—"

"Sorry, gotta run, Chief. The gate attendant's waving at me like mad. Last call for my flight."

"You better hurry; we don't want you pissing off the Lesvos gate attendants."

"For sure."

"After all," said Andreas to the dead phone, "I have a feeling you'll be seeing quite a lot of them."

● ● ● ● ●

Dana stood at the southern edge of Mykonos' old harbor, close by an assortment of commercial boats with names like *Orca* and *Delos Express*, tied up parallel to the shore. Each morning they ferried tourists the mile or so from Mykonos to the Holy Island of Delos, mythical birthplace of the gods Apollo and Artemis. In the ancient world, Delos stood as the thriving center of Cycladic life until it was wiped off the face of the Earth in the last century BCE for backing the wrong protector.

Maybe tomorrow she'd go there for the day. She wanted a place to reflect and didn't think she'd find it here. Mykonos over Easter was known for offering a preview of its mid-summer, 24/7 high life. Times evoking memories of the nation's EU free money, wild spending days. A welcome distraction for Greeks worn down by a quarter of their population out of work, and an economy that sucked with no end in sight. Those crowds would be far more interested in partying than prayer.

To be fair, she'd come here seeking that sort of diversion, though for a different reason. She sought a few days respite from battling frustrating bureaucrats and their red tape methods of maintaining an unconscionably slow asylum process aimed at keeping thousands penned up in razor wire limbo. Whether one chose to call the victims of the process refugees or migrants— categories she, as many, used interchangeably, despite the legal differences in their status—they deserved better treatment than they received.

For her, Mihalis Volandes' slaughter had destroyed any chance of overcoming that officious muddle, and she could think of no party-time diversion to mask the bitter sense of finality his death had brought to her hopes.

She'd never been a religious person, the result of a Catholic fireman father marrying a Jewish liberal mother, and neither parent wanting to compete for their daughter's religious allegiance. Still, she held a deep belief in the concept of a higher being who guided good works. It's why she did what she did. Though, now she wasn't so sure.

This wasn't the first time she'd wondered if God truly existed. In a world gone crazy, she'd seen far too many righteous slaughtered, guilty praised, and innocents denounced.

Now this.

Volandes' death was almost too much for her to bear. "I don't know if I can do this anymore," she whispered to herself.

She lowered her head, studied the ground for a few seconds, and began to sob. Thirty seconds passed. She tossed her head back with her eyes tightly shut, and drew in and let out a deep breath. "I can't believe he's gone," she said in a firm voice.

She opened her eyes, stared out toward the setting sun, and said aloud for any available god to hear: "I pray for revenge on the bastards who did this."

●● ● ●●

Maggie stuck her head into Andreas' doorway. "If you don't need me, I'm out of here. I've got Easter preparations to finish up."

"I thought you and Tassos were coming to our place," said Andreas.

"That's on Sunday. He's coming in this afternoon from Syros, and I've got a lot of cooking to do to feed him until then."

Andreas tilted his head. "Weren't you putting him on a diet?"

"That's why I'm doing the cooking; otherwise it's takeout *spanakopitia*, *tiropita*, fried potatoes…." She waved a hand off into the air.

"I get the picture."

"These days you'd need a wide-angle lens to take it."

"I'll tell him you said that."

"Not if you value your life," said Maggie.

"He'd never turn on me, I'm the guy who brought you two together."

"He's not the one you have to worry about."

Andreas laughed. "Is he very busy?"

Maggie gestured no. "People don't seem to kill each other as often in the Cyclades outside of tourist season. And thank God for that. If he were busier, he just might consider retiring, and I couldn't handle that. Doubt he could handle me, either. This way we each have our alone time. His with his police buddies on Syros, and mine with you and all the joys of this place." She forced a smile.

"Careful, you're bringing tears to my eyes."

"So, may I leave?"

"Sure, but tell Tassos to give me a call when he has the chance. I want to talk to him about the Volandes case."

"Any leads?"

"No, but I thought with all of Tassos' connections, he might be able to give me some insight into the seamier side of the refugee trade."

"Are you suggesting my cop boyfriend might have friends on the other side of the law?"

"Depending on which side of that line you place our politicians, I'd say he's got a healthy following in both camps."

Maggie smiled and threw Andreas a kiss. "I'll have him call you in the morning. *Yassou.*"

Andreas waved. "Bye."

He picked up a pencil with his left hand and began tapping it on the desktop as he scrolled with his right hand through the document on his computer screen. It was one of many he'd read that afternoon discussing the refugee situation. This one, though, came from FRONTEX, the European Border and Coast Guard arm of the EU responsible for border management. His eyes fixed on the first two sentences under the heading, "Eastern Mediterranean Route:"

In 2015, 885,000 migrants arrived in the EU via the Eastern Mediterranean route—17 times the number in 2014, which was itself a record year. The vast majority of them arrived on several Greek islands, most on Lesvos. Virtually all were seeking asylum as refugees entitled to protection under international law from situations where their life or freedom would be under threat.

The route ran directly through Greece's Northern Aegean islands, and although the EU's March 2016 agreement with Turkey had dramatically reduced the flow along that route, it also emboldened Turkey to threaten to open the refugee floodgates any time its government felt displeased with the EU.

Andreas read on.

People-smuggling has developed into an important industry in Turkey, with networks active not just in Istanbul but also in Izmir, Edirne, and Ankara. The nationalities of people smugglers vary, frequently mirroring the nationality of their customers.

"An important industry in Turkey," struck Andreas as an understatement. Depending on whether a migrant wanted to make the promised two-hour crossing to Greece in a rubber boat built to hold twenty passengers but packed with fifty, or upgrade to a metal boat built for forty passengers filled with ninety, the price varied from a low of 500 euros in winter for the rubber boat, to a high of 2,500 euros in summer for the metal boat. Other traffickers offered a different proposition: 900 euros per person for a landing involving a two-day walk to where processing asylum applications began, or 2,500 euros to arrive closer by.

He already knew that stiff prison sentences for smugglers kept traffickers out of the boats, requiring refugees to pilot their own way across the sea—hopefully, but not always, with enough gas to reach their destination. Some smugglers, though, did risk piloting jet boats across to Greece in a much faster crossing, but the associated risk of capture commanded a price two to three times the normal fee.

Before the Turkey-EU agreement went into effect, the price

for smuggling a family of four from Turkey via Greece's islands into Europe cost on average between eight thousand to twelve thousand euros, or two to three thousand euros per person.

Andreas used his pencil to make some quick calculations. Those nearly nine hundred thousand migrants who made the sea crossing in 2015 generated approximately two billion euros in revenue for the traffickers. Assuming the EU-Turkey agreement reduced crossings by as much as eighty percent in 2016, and without taking into account all that the traffickers managed to steal from the refugees, they still made hundreds of millions of untaxed euros in 2016.

God knows how much they're making now.

Andreas put down his pencil. The most mind-numbing figure of all for him he found in a report from the European Commission's Office of Humanitarian Aid and Civil Protection: 65.2 million people worldwide were in dire need of protection and assistance as a consequence of forced displacement from their homes.

Sixty-five million. That was six times the population of Greece.

Andreas blinked. Lesvos dealt with a half-million refugees in 2015, nearly six times its population, and they're still coming. *Amazing*, he thought, *how things have stayed as calm as they have there.*

He shook his head. The money made by arms-traffickers in fomenting wars that cause millions to flee for their lives leads directly into moneymaking opportunities for refugee-traffickers and their labor- and sex-trafficking colleagues looking to extract the most desirable and vulnerable of the fleeing.

Trafficking enterprises generated tremendous cash volumes, requiring huge money-laundering operations that inevitably brought down legitimate businesses. After all, a bakery, restaurant, or you-name-it sort of retail establishment, set up in a high-volume, upscale location that existed primarily to clean black money, ultimately forced businesses needing to make a profit to survive to choose between closing down or selling their businesses and properties to their money-laundering competitors on desperation terms.

It's not just the smuggled refugees this trafficking scum victimizes. It's all of us.

Andreas leaned back in his chair. A lot of money must be behind whoever killed Volandes. His killer was too smooth and professional to work cheap, and not one likely to leave tracks. Without a break, they'd never find the killer. Make that a damn big break.

Andreas turned off his computer and headed for the door. Now he had something else to pray for in church.

Chapter Four

In his experience, if you tried very hard, you might get Greeks and Turks to agree that they shared a common sea. But good luck at getting one or the other of them to admit they shared much more, such as food, coffee, or some rather distinct cultural practices. Four hundred years of Turkish rule, and decades of bloody wars, slaughter, and unrelenting conflict, had irreparably soured the two nations on each other.

Maybe things between Greeks and Turks weren't that bad these days on a person-to-person basis, but he didn't care if they were. He couldn't have cared less what happened to any of them. Or to Syrians, Afghans, Iraqis, Pakistanis, you name it. They were all the same. Sub-groups of the same lot, trying to pass themselves off as something better than they were.

Greeks could claim they were European all they wanted, but not to him. Line Arabs up on one wall, true Europeans on another, and put Greeks in the middle. No question where they belonged. And toss in the Italians, too. They're just like the Greeks. They even shared the same phrase for describing how much alike they were: "Same face, same race."

He looked at his watch. They were late. They should have been here with his money twenty minutes ago. Naturally, they'd been right on time when they needed him. Now that he'd done the job and it was time to pay up, they were nowhere to be found.

He sat sipping his Turkish coffee. It tasted the same as the Greek coffee he'd had in Mytilini that morning, as he waited for the ferry to bring him back to Turkey on the hour-long crossing to Ayvalik.

Same people, same coffee. They didn't deserve his services. But they paid well. At least promised to.

He watched a dark van drive slowly past the park lined in palm trees on the other side of the street. The second time he'd seen it. If his contacts were inside, they should have stopped. They'd told him to sit and wait on a bench in the park across from the café, but they couldn't be so amateurish as to have expected him to do that. A stranger sitting in an empty, darkened park draws attention. This was Turkey. Police were aggressive here.

Not like in Greece. He hadn't seen a cop the whole time he'd waited outside the harbor for the ferry. And the one who'd checked his papers when he boarded barely looked at him. He probably could have carried the sword on board and no one would have said a word. But it was better to have hidden it. Maybe after things cooled down he'd go back for it. It was his favorite.

He looked at his watch again. If they didn't show soon, he'd go find them. He knew where one of them lived; the stocky one with the limp hadn't been careful after their last meeting. Sloppy.

The van turned around at the end of the park, and headed back in his direction on the café's side of the street. He noticed a sliding door along the rear of the van's passenger side; there'd been none on the driver side. He glanced at the young couple sitting at the table directly in front of him, casually rocking a baby carriage between them. He slowly slid his chair to the right, toward three huge ceramic planters sprouting palm trees.

He'd picked this table because of the planters, leaving the more desirable table in front of the palms to the couple with the carriage. They'd thanked him as if it were their lucky day.

The van slowed as it pulled up parallel to the café, and the side-panel door slid abruptly open.

He dived for the planters as muzzle flashes exploded just ahead of the characteristic spurting clicks of an AK-47 running on full-auto. He hugged the ground while bullets sprayed the café, cracking the planters into bleeding soil, but not collapsing. Ten seconds later he heard the door slam shut and the van speed away. He heard no other sounds. Not from the couple, not from the carriage.

He crawled to the edge of the closest planter and tentatively peered around it to see whether they'd left a man behind to make sure he was dead. That's what he would have done.

No one. Sloppy. Very sloppy.

He stood and glanced at the couple and the carriage. *Bad luck.*

He walked away.

•●●●●•

From the tiny balcony off the third-floor apartment atop the tired, yellow-stuccoed hotel, you could see across the sea to the lights of Lesvos. The promised land for so many seeking a way into the EU from Turkey.

A man in his underwear sat in the dark in front of a sound-less, flickering television, his tightly braced left knee propped up on an ottoman in front of his chair. He flicked his cigarette ash into a saucer on his lap and took another slug of beer from the can in his other hand, his eyes glued to the muted screen.

Even as a low man in the organization he'd made a fair amount of money off the *kebabs*, his favorite nickname for refugees. Others in the smuggling trade called them fish or cement blocks. He'd like to have been one of the middlemen working the streets of Izmir or any of the other places along the coast drawing refugees looking to hook up with smugglers. That was how you made real money, steering them to your boss for commissions, but he didn't speak their languages or have the necessary relationships in the migrant neighborhoods. Those sorts of jobs fell to Syrians, Afghans, Iraqis, and Tunisians. Some of them were so good at what they did that they partnered with Turks who owned the staging points used to launch the boats toward Greece.

But that would never be his life. He'd have to settle for doing the grunt work for his boss' business, like finding places for refugees to stay until the launch, getting them food, life jackets, and other equipment.

He wasn't complaining. He made side deals with the various suppliers, and as long as they kicked back to him, he didn't give a damn if the food sucked or the life jackets sank. That, plus what he managed to steal from the migrants while herding them into the boats, made him a good living. Sometimes near the end, they'd resist and he'd have to stab one or two, or even pull a gun to get the others' attention.

None of that bothered him because they'd all likely end up having to swim for their lives anyway, losing their possessions in the process, or being robbed by someone else along their route north. Why shouldn't he profit, rather than a Greek or some other Balkan-type laying hands on them on their way to Germany, Sweden, or another of those prosperous places in northern Europe?

Northern Europe. That's where that blue-eyed blonde came from. He even went by the name Aryan, according to his boss.

He shook his head at the TV. Still no news.

If Aryan is an important enough assassin for his boss to recruit him from northern Europe just to kill one old Greek shipowner, why did he want him dead too? The assassin's fee was the rough equivalent of what they made off a boatload of refugees on a busy day. It made no sense to kill him. His boss should have paid him and been done with it.

But his boss told him, "No loose ends." Like they were in some American gangster movie.

Aryan hadn't been where they'd told him to meet them, and that turned things messy. They'd had to drive around the neighborhood until they found him. But they had, and they got him. They'd seen him fall.

The man heard the neighbor's dog bark, as it always did when a stranger walked by. That was a good thing, because living directly across from the beach you wanted to know when strangers came around. It barked again. Then stopped.

Whoever had been out there must have moved on. *Good doggie.*

Still no news on the TV. He had to hand it to Aryan, he knew his business. He'd personally delivered his boss' instructions to Aryan that he wanted a meaningful message sent. Slicing the old man in half sure as hell did that. It even made the Turkish news.

He shook his head, took another slug of beer, and dropped the empty can on the floor.

His boss saw the shipowner as intent on destroying the sea-route smuggling business he'd worked so hard to develop into Greece. The damn Greek would have done the same thing to every sea-trafficker's business into Greece, and into Italy, too, if given the chance to show the Italians that his anti-smuggling plan worked.

There wasn't nearly as much sea-trafficking business into Greece these days as in the glory days of past. Smugglers had been forced back to using old land routes across Turkey's narrow Evros River border with Greece, and then north skirting FYROM's notorious fence with Greece, or along new routes through Albania. According to his boss, though, sooner or later the big money would flow again into everyone's pockets. But only if the rich shipowner's plan never came to pass. The shipowner had to be stopped to protect the future of his and every other smuggler's business.

The TV flashed a banner across the screen. *Here it comes.* He grabbed the control and turned up the volume.

"Just in," said a young man wearing a dark mustache in the manner of President Erdogan. "Local police report a drive-by shooting in a seafront town south of Ayvalık. First reports have three killed. It has all the hallmarks of a PKK terrorist attack."

Too bad about that couple in front of Aryan in the café, but at least we got him, and their deaths made it look like a terrorist attack, not a hit. That should make his boss happy.

"The victims have not been identified, but it's been confirmed that the dead are Greek tourists, all from the same family."

"Family?" He turned up the volume.

A photo appeared on the screen behind the anchor's head. "The dead include a husband, wife, and their six-month-old child."

He stared at the screen, swallowed hard, and shut his eyes.

We missed him.

His mobile rang. He knew who that would be. "Yes, boss."

"You killed an entire family."

"Had to."

"And missed the only one I wanted dead?"

"I don't know how that happened."

"I do," screamed the boss. "You're a total fuck-up!"

"The police will never trace this back to us. They think it's PKK."

"I'm not worried about what they think, I'm worried about *him.*"

"Aryan?"

"He's not going to let this go."

"He doesn't know who we are or how to find us."

Pause.

"I want you over here right away."

"It's almost two in the morning."

"I know what time it is. The television has it posted across the screen, along with photos of a dead family. But no dead Aryan. Just get over here, and bring your numb-nuts van driver friend with you. *Now.*"

The phone went dead.

He drew in and let out a deep breath, then pressed a speed-dial number on his mobile and spoke the instant he had a connection. "Haydar, it's Jamal. Pick me up at my place in fifteen minutes. The boss wants to see us."

"Why?"

"Are you watching TV?"

"No, I was sleeping."

"I'll tell you when I see you. Just get over here." He hung up the phone.

This didn't look good. Jamal knew first-hand what his boss did to those who failed him. He took a deep drag on his cigarette and tried to ignore his trembling hand.

Good thing he's married to my sister.

• • ● • •

Jamal stood by a patch of tired oleander in front of the dimly lit hotel entrance, waiting for Haydar to pick him up. He stared up the road running along the beach, searching for headlights. *Nothing.* He looked at his watch. *Ten minutes late.* His brother-in-law must be going nuts.

His sister had married well. They lived in an elaborate villa on a hillside overlooking the sea, surrounded by acres of green and no neighbors. That last part worried him. A lot of deep holes could be dug on that property without anyone being the wiser.

He prayed his sister would be home when he got there.

The neighbor's dog barked loudly. Jamal spun around. He saw no one. He felt edgy; maybe the dog did, too. Could have picked it up from him, dogs are like that. He reached in his pocket for his phone and called Haydar.

"I'm on my way," came blurting out of the phone.

"Where the fuck are you? I told you the boss wants us at his place right away."

"I had to find new wheels. The police are looking for the van."

"You saw the news?"

"What did you expect me to do when you woke me up asking if I'd been watching television?"

"Just get over here."

"I'll be there in three minutes."

Jamal put the phone back in his pocket. He rubbed his hands together and hunched up his shoulders. It was cooler out than he expected.

The boss is going to kill us both. He shook his head. *No, not me. Maybe Haydar.*

A light color, late 1960s 280SE Mercedes convertible, with its top up and windows down, pulled up in front of the hotel, driven by a weaselly, clean-shaven man in sunglasses and a dark watch cap.

"It's about time," yelled Jamal, leaning in through the passenger side window. "Where the hell did you get this car?"

Haydar smiled. "I borrowed it."

"You stole an antique car not to attract attention?"

"I always wanted to drive one of these. The stupid owner left it parked on the street. I couldn't resist. I'll have it back before morning. Don't worry, no one will notice."

If his brother-in-law ever found out that Haydar drove a stolen car to his house, he'd kill him, for sure. Maybe take out Jamal too, simply for being an accomplice to such stupidity.

"You're such a screw-up," said Jamal.

He opened the passenger door, dropped onto the seat with his back to Haydar, and struggled to swing his bad leg into the car. "Let's get out of here." He leaned out to pull his door closed.

The car didn't move.

He turned his head toward Haydar. "I said to—"

Through the open windows on the driver's side a voice said in perfect Turkish, "I'm afraid your friend won't be able to drive you to your appointment this evening."

Haydar's head lay in his own lap, blood gushing from his headless torso as a curved *kilij* saber pointed straight at Jamal.

"I thought it appropriate to use a classic Ottoman sword for the occasion. I know it's not considered as effective these days as an AK-47, but it does have the advantage of being silent, and so many are so readily available over here."

Jamal's first instinct was to scream, his second to run. He suppressed both. "If you're going to kill me, just do it."

Aryan knelt slightly and stared through the open window at Jamal's eyes. "You know, I came to your home tonight planning on doing precisely that, but as I stood in the shadows wondering why you were out on the street at this ungodly hour, I heard you tell your recently departed colleague that you had a boss anxious to see you. I thought, my, isn't that convenient? I'd like to see him too."

"I'll never take you to him."

"Suit yourself. I have the feeling he'll attend your funeral. I should be able to find him that way. On the other hand, if you take me to him we might be able to reach an arrangement that saves both your lives. After all, this is all about money, isn't it?"

Jamal swallowed. "Yeah. It's only about money."

"Good. Get out. We'll take my car. You drive."

Jamal hesitated.

"It would be a bit messy driving in this car, don't you think?"

"But we can't just leave him here."

"Of course, we can. Come along now." The man waggled the sword for Jamal to get out.

Jamal opened the door and swung out his legs. By the time he stood outside, Aryan was next to him, quickly but thoroughly frisking him.

He led Jamal to a dark, beat-up Fiat parked a hundred meters up the beach.

"How did you find me?" asked Jamal.

"I followed you home the one time we met. You weren't very careful." Aryan gestured for Jamal to get in the driver side as he went around to the passenger side. He slid in next to Jamal and handed him the keys. He sat with the sword resting across his lap, the blade pointed directly at Jamal, and his right hand firmly wrapped around the grip.

"We really don't have to do this," said Jamal. "I can get you all the money you want without going to the boss."

"That would strike me as discourteous. After all, it wasn't your idea to kill me, was it?"

Jamal saw only one answer. "No, I thought we should pay you the money."

"Just following orders." Aryan smiled.

Jamal's eye twitched as he nodded yes.

"Just drive, don't talk. I've never had the opportunity to meet your boss, just you and, uh, what's his name—?" he waved back in the general direction of the Mercedes.

"Haydar."

He nodded. "How long's the drive?"

"Twenty minutes."

"Fine, wake me when we're two minutes away."

Jamal thought he'd misheard him. Aryan had to know Jamal would kill him at the first opportunity, and yet he'd just announced he'd be taking a nap. It made no sense. Or maybe it made a lot of sense, because instead of spending the ensuing twenty minutes thinking of ways to outmaneuver him, Jamal spent it wondering how Aryan planned on killing him, should he try to take him out.

"We're almost there," said Jamal.

"Good," said Aryan, his eyes still closed and hand still gripping the sword. "I see you do follow orders."

Jamal said nothing until turning onto a graveled road marked private. "We're here. It's about two kilometers to the house."

Aryan opened his eyes. "Interesting, no security at the gate."

"He doesn't need it. Everyone knows to stay out of here."

"Do they, now? Even curious tourists?"

"Word gets around."

"Why do I feel you're not telling me everything? I'm sure

you understand that I'll be deeply disappointed should I learn you haven't been honest with me…uh…what's your name?"

"Jamal." His voice broke.

"So, Jamal, is there anything you want to tell me before I find out for myself?" He lifted the sword so that the blade rose to Jamal's eye level.

"Nothing. Honest." Jamal swallowed. "Of course, he has men up by his house."

"How many?"

"Three or so."

"Or so?"

"I don't know exactly."

"Anything else?"

Jamal paused.

"Jamal, don't hold back on me." The sword flickered closer to his eye.

"Closed-circuit television starts about a hundred meters before the gate at the main house."

"Good thing I decided to bring these along." Aryan pulled a watch cap and sunglasses out of his shirt.

Jamal looked at him in horror.

"Poor man has no need for them now. Waste not, want not." He pulled the cap snugly down over his ears to cover his blond hair, and masked his eyes with the sunglasses. Next, he pulled up the collar on his dark jacket and hunched down in the seat to shield his cheeks. "Too bad I'm blessed with fair skin, but in this light, they won't be able to tell."

The man opening the gate only gave a cursory glance to Jamal's passenger. He seemed far more interested in delivering a message to Jamal. "The boss wants you to meet him in the garage out back of the house. He said for you to drive straight there."

As soon as Jamal drove through the gate, Aryan said, "Has he ever told you to use the garage before?"

"No."

"Sounds like he's not up for entertaining guests tonight."

"Maybe he doesn't want to wake my sister and the kids."

"What's your sister doing here?"

"She's married to him."

Aryan laughed. "So these *special* arrangements are for your benefit, not mine."

Jamal felt like he might throw up.

"Cheer up. Cooperate with me and this could turn out to be a big surprise for everyone." Aryan paused. "On the other hand, please don't try any last-second heroics. I can assure you the time for that is long past." With a quick thrust of his right hand the tip of the sword pressed at Jamal's right carotid artery.

"Don't worry," said Jamal, his voice breaking again. "I'm not going to do anything except listen."

"Good."

"And pray."

"Even better," Aryan withdrew the sword from Jamal's neck.

No lights shone from the house, but a tiny light off to the right marked a driveway leading around behind the house. Jamal turned at the light and, just past the back of the house, aimed for a concrete structure thirty meters away.

"That's the garage." Jamal stopped the car.

In the dark it was hard to make out more than the shape of three garage doors. Only the center door stood open.

"It looks pretty well lit up inside for three in the morning." Aryan nodded toward three men waiting inside. "Which one's your brother-in-law?"

"Malik's the fat one, standing near the back wall."

Malik waved at the car and pointed to a spot between his two men.

"I guess he wants us to stop there."

Jamal gave him a sidelong glance. "Just tell me what you want me to do."

"Keep driving slowly into the garage. We don't want your brother-in-law getting suspicious." Aryan sat up straight in the seat and gripped the sword tighter. "And turn on your high beams."

Chapter Five

The Fiat crept closer to the open garage door as Aryan fidgeted with something on the dash. The two men closest to the car tried shielding their eyes from the high beams as Malik yelled at Jamal to turn off the lights.

"Just keep driving."

Malik yelled again as the car nosed into the garage.

"Step hard on the gas," said Aryan.

"What?"

Aryan didn't answer, just thrust his sword through Jamal's right shoe, pinning his foot to the gas pedal, and grabbed and spun the steering wheel in the direction of the man on the left, pinning him to the front of the Fiat as it crashed head-on into the solid rear wall.

The man to the right fumbled for his gun, but Aryan was out of the car and slicing him to pieces before he found it.

Malik hadn't moved from his spot by the rear wall.

Aryan turned to face him. "Wise of you not to reach for a weapon."

Malik didn't speak.

"It must have been tempting, though, with me holding only a sword."

Malik's eyes shifted ever so slightly to Aryan's right.

At Malik's movement, Aryan dropped into a crouch and spun counterclockwise, yanking a nine-millimeter pistol from the small of his back with his left hand and putting a bullet in the head of the man who'd moments before waved them through the gate.

"Anybody else out there?" asked Aryan, drawing himself back to his full height. "I mean, anyone you don't want me to kill."

Malik shut his eyes. "Only my family."

"Good." Aryan tucked the pistol back in its place.

Malik opened his eyes. "What do you want?"

"I assume you know who I am?"

Malik nodded.

"Even though we've never met."

He nodded again.

"So I assume you also know my reputation?"

Another nod.

"Then, why do you have to ask what I want?"

Malik swallowed hard. "Money? Revenge?"

Aryan shook his head from side to side. "There's so much revenge out there waiting for me to take, I don't know where to start. And if I did, I'd have no time left for anything else." He sighed. "I guess if the only choice you leave me is revenge, I'd be more than happy to kill you. And your entire family. Family first, of course." He whipped the sword around in the air in flourished strokes.

Malik seemed to hyperventilate.

"Would you like some water?"

"No, no. You want your money."

"Of course."

"How much?"

"Are we bargaining now?" said Aryan.

Malik raised his hands. "No, I just want to know how much, so I can get it for you."

"That's a good attitude. My fee for the task I did for you on Lesvos is now five times what you failed to deliver. Another full fee for each additional kill you've caused me to make. And it shall continue to go up with each person I'm required to eliminate until paid in full."

Malik nodded nervously. "Agreed."

"And now to the part that will greatly benefit us both."

Malik cocked his head. "I don't follow."

Aryan pointed the tip of his sword left and right. "Look around you. What do you see?"

"Dead guys?"

"Incompetence. You surround yourself with incompetents. You were lucky enough to be born into a well-connected local family, and because you knew who to bribe, you've made a fine living picking the low hanging fruit of refugees desperate to pay whatever it takes to cross into Greece."

Aryan patted Malik on the shoulder with the flat of the sword. "Your mistake is in thinking you know how to do anything more than that." He shook his head. "Assassinating one of the most respected advocates of the worldwide refugee movement was not a smart way to better your situation."

Aryan lifted the sword. "If I hadn't taken the time to make his death look like an NGO played a key part, every politician in the EU would be screaming for yours and every other refugee trafficker's head. All you cared about was seeing him dead. My added touch is what gave you political cover."

Aryan rested his sword on his own shoulder. "Now I see it was a wasted gesture. You have no idea how to use it. You're more blunt in your style than terrorists, but a lot easier to track down."

Malik bit at his lip.

"Just look at tonight. Your brother-in-law and his late friend wiped out an entire family in an attempt to get rid of me. And for what? Because of paranoia on your part that I might someday tell someone that you hired me to kill the Greek? Congratulations, genius. Now all of Turkey's looking in your backyard for terrorists who used a van they'll likely be able to tie straight back to you. Good luck."

"Did you kill Jamal?" Malik looked toward the Fiat.

Aryan smiled. "No, that will cost you extra. He's buried in there under an air bag. I only turned off the one on my side. But if I were you, I'd worry more about your own head. You're creating so much heat for your colleagues in the trafficking business, I wouldn't be surprised if they take you out themselves."

Malik looked at the sword on Aryan's shoulder. "How much would they pay you to do that service for them?"

"Haven't asked, but if you and I can't reach terms, they may not have to worry about paying at all."

"I thought we agreed on five times your fee?"

"That's for past services. I'm talking about the future."

Aryan waited for Malik to speak, but Malik said nothing.

"I see you know how to bargain." Aryan smiled. "So here's our arrangement. It's really quite simple. I do your thinking, I take care of all your problems, and you take care of seeing that the refugees pay you to get them across to Greece, or Italy, or whatever new routes I open for you."

"New routes?"

"That's my concern, not yours. You just take care of what you do best, and I'll take care of the rest."

"What's this going to cost me?"

"An equal partnership."

"How can I agree to that?"

"I know, I should offer you less. I guess I'm feeling generous. After all, if I slit your throat, I'm certain any number of locals would be beating a path to my door begging to take me up on that same proposition."

"It's not that simple. There are other people involved."

"I'll deal with them."

"I'll have to think about it."

"I like that, because once you agree, if ever you renege—"

"Malik! What's happening?"

Aryan swung around. A dark-haired woman half Malik's age

stood in the doorway in a cream-colored silk robe staring at the bodies and blood on the floor.

"Go back to the house," Malik shouted.

"That wouldn't show proper hospitality." Aryan waved for the woman to come inside. "Permit me to introduce myself. I'm your husband's business associate." He held out his left hand, his right still gripping the bloody sword.

Her eyes darted between Aryan and her husband. "What should I do?" she asked Malik.

Aryan shook his head. "Don't ask him. I told you what to do."

Malik waved for her to come to him. She made a wide arc around Aryan to reach her husband. He put his arm around her shoulders and yanked her to him.

"Is our business here finished?" asked Malik.

"Almost. First, I need the money."

"I'll get it from the bank tomorrow."

Aryan smiled again. "You're getting a bit cocky, my friend." He stepped forward, swept the sword off his shoulder, and sliced it down through the front of the woman's robe to her beige nightgown beneath.

Malik started to step forward but stopped.

"Another wise decision," said Aryan. "Not a drop of her blood has been spilled." He brought the tip of his sword up against the neck of her nightgown and drew it slowly down along the outline of one breast. "Yet."

"*Stop,*" shouted Malik. "I'll get you the money. It's in the house."

"Good. Now for resolving the matter of our partnership."

"I can't agree to that now. Impossible. There are others to consider."

Aryan used the tip of his sword to lift the wife's nightgown above her panties. With a quick flick of his wrist he sliced them open, and firmly pressed the back of the blade between her legs.

"Malik, do something," she whimpered.

"Fine. *Equal partners.*"

Aryan put the sword back on his shoulder. "Your third wise decision of the evening."

• • ● • •

"I hear you're looking for me," came the voice over the phone.

Andreas looked at the clock on the nightstand next to his bed. "Not at six in the morning."

"Maggie said you'd be up."

"For once in her life she's wrong. Lila's mother took the kids for the night so that we could sleep in."

"Sorry about that. I'll call you later."

"Hold on. Give me a minute to get into another room so Lila can sleep."

"Too late for that," filtered up from beneath a pillow. "Who is it?"

"Tassos. I'll take it outside." Andreas moved quickly out of bed.

"Tell her I'm sorry."

"He says he's sorry."

"I don't believe him."

"She said—"

"I heard."

"He blames Maggie," said Andreas.

"I don't believe that either," mumbled Lila.

Andreas closed the bedroom door behind him and stepped into the adjoining study. As much as he'd grown accustomed to their penthouse view of the Acropolis, the rose-gold glow of morning sunlight moving across the Parthenon always made him pause. He'd come to accept these moments as a welcome consequence of his marrying the heir to one of Greece's greatest fortunes, bringing his wife, in return, such unexpected joys as this early morning telephone call to her second-generation Athens cop husband.

He smiled, *but we do make wonderful children.*

Andreas turned his back to the view, and leaned against an antique French kingwood desk. "So, what's up?"

"I thought you were the one who had the questions," said Tassos.

"I'm looking for specifics on who's making money off the refugee crisis."

"I doubt I know much more than I read in the papers."

"I'm all ears for your 'much more.'"

"That will require me to take a sip of coffee."

Andreas heard his friend swallow.

"Let's start from square one," said Tassos. "It's a mess created by the West that the West wants to go away."

"Nice tag line, but do you have anything more concrete for me?"

"Politicians all over the EU are scared shitless of even the mention of the word refugee. They'll bite at just about anything anyone offers to lower the heat on that subject among their voters."

Andreas stood and turned to stare up at the Acropolis. "Meaning?"

"The UK voted to leave the EU over free migration among EU countries, and every terrorist attack in the West gets the media looking for a refugee connection. Find a way to keep refugees away from northern European borders that doesn't paint its politicians or countrymen as heartless bigots, and the politicians will greet you with open arms. More importantly, they'll pay you."

"Sounds like you're talking about the deal the EU reached with Turkey to take back migrants arriving on our islands by sea."

"Yes," said Tassos. "That and more subtle deals. Look at the former Soviet satellite nations that closed their borders to refugees who never had any intention of staying in those countries. They just wanted to use them as passageways to northern Europe." Tassos took another noisy swallow of coffee. "What sort of sweet deals do you think they received for closing off their borders to the south and east, and taking the worldwide media heat themselves, rather than letting migrants pass through and force their supposedly more civilized northern neighbors to say 'no' directly to those wanting to migrate to their countries? That would have exposed northern EU countries to a blitz of horrible publicity, at least as bad as experienced by the UK and France when refugees massed at the Calais end of the Eurotunnel trying to get through to the UK."

"I get the political analysis, but what I'm looking for are profiles on those who've figured out ways to make money-in-their-pocket profits off the refugees."

"If you're talking about both bad guys and good guys, on a scale from bad to good, we've got refugee traffickers on one end, and NGOs on the other."

"Who's in the middle?" said Andreas, suppressing a yawn.

"It's murky. Traffickers obviously can't function without big-time official protection, and that costs serious money. But because of the subject's acute international political ramifications, other considerations sometimes outweigh the profits to be made from protecting trafficking. That's when the refugee crisis goes into hibernation."

"For instance?"

"Relatively soon after making their deal, the EU cut back on its agreed-upon per diem payments to Turkey, but the Turkish government let it slide for political reasons tied to its wish to get into the EU. Some cynics saw it more as proof of just how little the Turks actually spent on feeding and caring for its refugees, but that's a different story. Later, when the Turkish military's *coup d'état* failed, and Erdogan got pissed at the West, boatloads of refugees began hitting the beaches again in Lesvos and Chios."

"What about the NGOs?" asked Andreas.

"I'm sure most of them are legit, but I'm also sure some

are doing far less than God's work when it comes to how they spend the money they raise. For example, I've heard of some NGO workers getting kickbacks from vendors through inflated invoices to their NGOs, which brings me to the less-than-Christian behavior of some of our countrymen who contract to supply and shelter refugees. With all the money at play, there's a lot of blame to pass around."

Andreas turned away from the window. "I've got a murdered Greek shipowner who planned on breaking the back of Turkey-to-Greece refugee trafficking, and a prosecutor on Lesvos trying to pin it on a refugee who works for the NGO that was the victim's biggest supporter."

"Is that the case with the sword?"

"You heard about it?"

"Who hasn't? Getting sliced in half doesn't happen every day. Especially to rich guys."

"We've no leads, but I'm sure the guy who's in custody didn't do it."

"What do you want from me?"

Andreas sat back against the desk. "As you said, this is the kind of murder that gets everybody's attention. Even hard-assed bad guys."

"For sure."

"There must be chatter out there about this. Maybe you can pick something up on your old-boy network?"

"You mean you want me to go back to hanging out in *Star Wars* sorts of bars, hoping to bump into intergalactic weirdos who might have something to share?"

"You get the picture." Andreas smiled.

"Tomorrow's Easter, and even bad guys take off for that holiday through Monday."

"Tuesday's soon enough."

"How considerate of you."

Andreas laughed. "It's my nature. I'll see you Sunday."

"Assuming Lila doesn't yank my invitation for waking her up."

"I'll see what I can do to soften her heart."

"I guess that means Maggie and I should be prepared to order takeout."

"Not Maggie," said Andreas.

"Bye."

Morning light had broadened out across the city, but the Parthenon still glowed. *As well it should*, thought Andreas. Athenians had much to be proud of in their Acropolis. Some, though, took it a bit too far, claiming that unlike similar wonders of the ancient world, the Parthenon had been built by freedmen, not slaves. That sounded grand, though in truth it only demonstrated how similar were the lives lived by slaves and freedmen—once slaves themselves—working side by side, each class with origins traced to distant lands.

Just like refugees.

●　●　●　●　●

The Saturday morning of Easter Week produced a strange mix of souls on Mykonos' old town streets. During high season, locals knew better than to wander about so soon after the witching hour, but at Easter time they'd not yet ceded their town to the partiers. Old women dressed in black hurried about in determined preparation for a day of church work and services, while stragglers at all levels of intoxication struggled to find their way home from bars, clubs, and other people's beds.

Dana sat in a taverna on the edge of the harbor with coffee and a croissant. She'd spent much of the night in church services, the balance at home trying to sleep, and the morning, since eight, sitting in the port.

Her Friday night had started at the island's lone Catholic church in Little Venice. She overheard parishioners talking about joining a procession beginning at nine at the Metropolis Greek Orthodox Church next door. That seemed a fitting tribute to Mihalis' memory, so she decided to join in.

The procession marched as one of three departing simultaneously from Metropolis and the old town's other two central churches. Each church's clergy and worshipers followed their church's uniquely decorated *epitaphios*, representing the bier of Christ, along a prearranged route winding past the other central churches before ending up back at their own.

It represented the funeral of Christ, and Mykonians and visitors not marching lined the route, some standing on freshly painted balconies sprinkling the participants below with a mixture of rose water and perfumes, the *rodhonoro* used on Christ's body when taken down from the cross.

Dana walked in the middle of the Metropolis procession among young and old, locals and visitors, Orthodox and non-Orthodox, all packed together into the narrow lanes of the old-town route. She sensed that simply by participating in this single night's event, the marchers felt they'd be elevated to a higher spiritual plane than any they could achieve on their own.

If only that were so.

About thirty meters before the turn onto Matogianni Street, Mykonos' compact version of New York City's Madison Avenue high-end shopping locale, the procession passed between a cluster of churches and opened into a much broader bit of lane. But the surge into that wider space ended abruptly as the crowd funneled into another pinch point close by the central gathering place for Mykonos' late-night café society.

Dana stood waiting for the crowd to move on. She looked at the buildings ahead and off to her right. It amazed her how a town as unique and beautiful as this could allow its architecture to be so compromised by transient shop-owners wishing to make it look like someplace else. Madison Avenue-style display windows imposed on classic Cycladic structures—and their rapidly spreading minimalist modern progeny—did not represent thinking outside the box. It struck her as nothing more than an unimaginative denigration of the island's historic natural beauty.

What a shame.

As the crowd began moving, it carried Dana along with it to her left, and she caught a glimpse of a different sort of building. Cycladic white, like all the others, but set back beneath a balcony bearing a discreet sign advertising the island's "accommodations center" on the second floor. A single step, and a knee-high white stucco wall enclosing a small flagstone landing, separated the first story from the road.

Directly up and across from the step, an ornately carved white marble jamb and entablature surrounded a sturdy, six-paneled, blood-red double door, and off to its right, smooth white marble framed a matching six-paned casement window. The only apparent concession to modern times looked to be an open lattice of black iron bars over the window, but the bars matched an ancient, cast-iron cannon set into the road just outside the wall.

This was the sort of classic, nineteenth-century Cycladic design she'd been looking for. She edged through the crowd toward the building. A sign set in marble by the door read, AEGEAN MARITIME MUSEUM.

Dana felt a chill run up her spine.

She stepped up onto the landing and peered through the window. She couldn't see beyond the model sailing ship set on the sill, but that was enough to drive her thoughts to the ships and refugees that occupied her life, and to memories of Mihalis.

"Excuse me, Miss, may I help you?"

The unexpected voice jerked Dana out of her trance.

"Sorry, I didn't mean to startle you. I saw you staring in the window and just wanted to tell you that though the sign says the museum opens at ten-thirty, tomorrow morning it opens at nine, if you're interested." The man extended his hand. "My name is Philipos and I sort of look after the place." Slim, with a scruffy graying beard and long hair reminding Dana of her father's photographs of his hippie days, he looked to be in his mid-fifties.

She shook his hand. "Thank you, I might just do that."

"I think you'll find it unique. It has a garden unlike any other on Mykonos. It is serene and calming." He nodded and left.

How did he know to tell me that? And in English?

Their brief encounter haunted her, and so the next morning, Dana left her table at the harborfront taverna and made her way through the old town to arrive at the museum precisely at nine.

As if to prove he was indeed a mortal Greek, Philipos arrived a half-hour late, but with cakes and coffee for them both, "Just in case you'd be here."

They sat on the edge of the wall drinking their coffees as she listened to Philipos tell her the history of the museum. An individual donor founded it in 1983 for the purpose of preserving and promoting the study of Greek maritime history and tradition, particularly the merchant ship history of the Aegean Sea. Philipos spoke with great pride of the museum's efforts to restore historical exhibits to their original state of design and build.

His words reminded her of Mihalis' tales of his family's generations at sea, which led to thoughts of her murdered friend and his plans, and to tears welling up in her eyes.

"I'm sorry." She took a tissue from her bag and dabbed at her eyes.

"No problem," said Philipos. "Though I must say I'm not used to my little talk on the museum bringing tears to a visitor's eyes." He stood. "Come, let me show you that special place I promised you."

He unlocked the front door and led Dana through a room full of miniature ships arranged in separate glass cases, past walls lined in drawings of seagoing adventurers, their vessels and charts, and across a rough marble floor bordered by artifacts of the maritime life. They stepped into a smaller room of similar appointments, and stopped in front of a pair of red doors in the style of the museum's paneled front door.

"Here you are." He pulled open the doors, and the glass-paneled French doors beyond them.

Dana stood silently in the doorway, staring out at the garden. *I wonder if Alice felt this way at the bottom of that rabbit hole.*

"Our garden is meant to honor those lost at sea. But it also works well for those of us lost on land. Please stay as long as you wish." He turned and left her standing at the door.

She'd not yet asked him why he thought she might need a place like this. *Perhaps it's all too obvious.* Her mother had always said that Dana wore her heart on her sleeve, inevitably eliciting her father's favorite pun: "That's what makes her so disarming."

She should call her parents. Orthodox and Western Easter shared the same Sunday this year. It was also Passover. She'd FaceTime her parents tomorrow and cover all her bases with one call. She knew that family holidays alone were always tough on them.

At the heart of the garden lay a four-hundred-square-meter mat of deep green, flat and smooth as a golf putting surface. A gray flagstone walkway separated the grassy center from a border of olive, orange, hibiscus, bougainvillea, oleander, and other greenery she did not recognize, all running up to a beige stone perimeter wall. The garden was no more than nine hundred square meters, but seemed much larger because, beyond the wall, only treetops and snatches of a few all-white buildings were visible in the distance.

To her left, set off between what looked to be a small storage room and the edge of the grass, stood the top two stories of a lighthouse. A white, twelve-sided metal first story supported a second story of twelve three-paned glass windows enclosing the lamp and lens. An exterior railed metal walkway encircled the base of the second story, and a verdigris dodecagon cupola and weather vane crowned it all.

A plaque to the right of a metal hatchway in the base of the lighthouse commemorated an award at the Paris International Exhibition of 1889 for its lighting, and its subsequent service atop the lighthouse at the northwest edge of Mykonos from 1890 until replaced by a fully automated version in 1983.

An array of relics from centuries at sea stood along the rear wall of the museum: cannon with metal and stone ammunition, a ship's wheel, compass, engine-room telegraph to the bridge, and a collision-avoidance device relied on in a time before radar. She walked past a group of marble columns and slabs set on flagstones by the near edge of the green, and stepped onto the grass heading for three marble markers at the far end of the plot.

She smiled. *It's artificial turf.* A smart decision on an arid, drought-prone island. Three paces later she stopped. She'd realized the markers were marble cenotaphs, each honoring the memory of a sailor who'd not made it back to land. She did not want to tread any further on this spiritual gravesite.

She turned back to sit on a stone bench abutting the rear wall of the museum, and from under the shade of a large olive tree looked out across the garden wall, hearing not a sound, except for the cries of birds.

She shut her eyes.

Why did they kill him?

She already knew the answer. For the same reason they herded families into boats they knew would sink, and offered life jackets—even in children's sizes—they knew would not float.

It's all about the money. Nothing else.

And no one stood up to them. Politicians offered euphemisms and sanctimonious talk, then built concentration camps with fancy deceptive names and considered their work done.

Mihalis had tried to do more. They'd slaughtered him.

She bit at her lower lip, her eyes more tightly shut.

It had to be the traffickers. But which one? Or ones? Mihalis' plan would have affected them all. North of the city of Izmir, traffickers used sea routes from Turkey to Lesvos, west of Izmir routes to Chios, and south of Izmir to Samos.

Refugees arriving on Lesvos always described the same faces organizing their crossings and launching their boats. Chios and Samos refugees had similar experiences. Specific people worked in trafficking to specific islands, with little or no crossover. Those involved in trafficking to one island did not get involved in trafficking to another island. Each had its own territory.

It's a franchise operation. Dana opened her eyes, stared at the lighthouse, and spoke aloud:

"All centered within a hundred miles of Izmir."

Chapter Six

Why did I listen to my father? Aleka kept looking over her shoulder at the door to the lab. She sensed her boss would walk through it any minute.

"What are you doing here on a Saturday morning?" was the question she expected, but she'd yet to come up with an answer. And if he looked at the files she'd been copying, or the bits of physical evidence she'd carefully siphoned off from original samples…she didn't want to think about the trouble she'd be in. Good-bye career, for starters.

But she had to admit, the Athens cop was right. The physical evidence didn't add up to charging Ali Sera with murder. Still, her boss trusted her, and here she was betraying him. Her conscience might drive her to tell him what she was doing— leaving out the part about her father. No reason to draw him into this. Her boss' ally, the prosecutor, would love the opportunity to bring down her father. And using her to do it would only make it all the sweeter for him.

She needed only a little more time to finish copying the reports. Extracting the samples had been the tricky part, taking well over an hour. She looked for her boss' notes, which he'd had her verify at the crime scene, but they weren't where they should be in the file folder. She went through every piece of paper but found no notes.

She looked in unrelated case folders, in front of and behind the Volandes file, on the chance they'd been misfiled. No luck. Then she checked the secretary's desk to see if the notes might be there waiting to be filed. Nope.

She could think of only one other place to look: her boss' office. But that opened her to a charge of breaking-and-entering and bye-bye career, for sure. No way was she going to risk that, even for her father.

She gathered up what she had, stuffed it into her backpack, turned off the copying machine, and took one last look around the lab to make sure everything looked as when she'd entered. Satisfied, she turned off the lights and left.

On her way to the front door, she passed her boss' office.

Something the Athens cop had said made her pause. She'd not read her boss' notes before signing them. And now they weren't where they should be. She drew in a deep breath and let it out.

If his door's unlocked, I'll take it as a sign to go in.

She turned the knob and the door swung open. "Damn," she said aloud.

She stepped inside and closed the door behind her. *Where to begin?* No way could she rifle through all his files. Too much of a risk she'd disturb something that he'd notice. She took a wild guess of a chance, and tried his top center desk drawer.

Locked.

She tried the other desk drawers. All locked. Then she tried the file cabinets along the wall. Everything locked. He was a careful one. And with good reason, considering what she was doing at that very moment.

The only option she saw had her going through the clutter on the top of his desk. But that presented a dangerous risk. Cluttered-desk types almost always knew the precise location of every piece of paper. Her boss would likely notice a single Post-it note out of place.

She stared at what she could see without touching anything. Every folder bore a neatly labeled tag. Except for one thin folder sitting alone on the edge of his desk in a spot closest to the door. A Post-it note on the outside of the folder, addressed to his secretary, read, "Please add the language we discussed, log it in as received, and return to me."

His secretary must have returned it after he'd left for the holiday.

She used the eraser end of a pencil to flip opened the folder. There they were, the missing notes on the Volandes murder. On the first page, her boss' name appeared as the person in charge, but typed next to it was, "See last page." She used the eraser to quickly shuffle to the final page. Above her signature someone had typed, "I hereby certify that all data and evidence recorded or described herein was gathered personally by me and is true and correct."

That miserable bastard.

She grabbed the folder, stuffed it into her backpack, and stormed out of the office. No reason to make a copy. Let him and his secretary blame each other for what happened to it.

She hoped it was their only copy.

•●●●•

Aryan told Malik he wasn't one to hold a grudge, so once Malik had given him the money, there was no need to sweeten the offer by giving him the keys to his Range Rover. Malik said his wife wanted Aryan to take it and leave. She worried how the children would react to a stranger in their home.

Aryan said he understood Malik's wife's concern for her children, but he simply couldn't leave until they'd worked out the details of their partnership. Malik said he'd need time to think that through. Aryan said that was fine with him but, as he hadn't slept in over thirty-six hours, they'd have to discuss it after he took a nap.

Malik quickly agreed and offered him their palatial guest room.

Aryan thanked him, but said sleeping in the home of someone who'd just tried to kill him required special accommodations. He took great pains to explain in detail to Malik and his wife what would happen should someone try to surprise him while he slept on the floor of their children's bedroom, between their beds.

Three hours into Aryan's sleep, the older boy awoke, followed soon by his younger brother. Aryan managed to negotiate more hours of sleep by promising the boys their father would buy them a pony if they lay in bed quietly for a few more hours.

It was mid-morning when Aryan led the children from their bedroom toward the sound of their parents' voices. He walked with his sword over his right shoulder and his left arm around the younger child.

"Don't forget to say thank you to your daddy," Aryan said, once they reached the room with the voices.

Their mother jumped up from between Malik and Jamal on the far side of a dining room size mahogany table, and ran to hug her children. She looked as if she hadn't slept for a month.

"Are you all right?" Her eyes jumped from one child to the other.

"Yes," said the older boy.

"Daddy, when do we get the pony?" said the younger.

"Run along with your mother," said Aryan. "I'll speak to your father about the pony."

She looked at Malik, he nodded, and she hurried them out of the room.

Aryan sat across the table from Malik and Jamal. He looked at Jamal. "I see you survived the airbag."

"Fuck—"

Malik quickly raised his hand to silence his brother-in-law.

Aryan smiled, and fixed his eyes on Malik. "And I see you've taken to heart our conversation about your colleagues."

"What's past is past," said Malik. "It's time to talk about our new relationship."

Aryan nodded. "It will prove very profitable for you."

"I would hope for us all." Malik looked at Jamal. "Do you understand?"

"He crippled me."

"You tried to kill him. That seems a small payback." Malik paused. "You know how much my wife and I value you, dear brother-in-law, but with the discourtesy you insist on showing our guest, I think it's best you not be here when he is present."

Jamal opened his mouth to speak, but said nothing.

"In fact, I think you should return to your home now."

With a brief glare at Aryan, Jamal left.

Malik turned his attention back to Aryan. "What are your plans?"

"To broaden your reach and increase your profits."

"Admirable goals, but there are others who will resist them."

"There are always those who cannot accept progress."

"But I'm speaking of very powerful, ruthless people. And there are many."

"Don't worry, I'll deal with them. I just need you to tell me the details of your organization."

"How will you deal with them?" Malik pointed at the sword resting on Aryan's shoulder. "With that?"

"This?" said Aryan lifting it off his shoulder. "No, that alone would never work. I plan on using a much sharper, more lethal weapon."

"And what is that?" asked Malik.

"This." He smiled and touched the sword to the top of his head. "The same one I've used with you."

●●●●●●

"What are you doing?"

"Nothing."

"You sound like a five-year-old caught with his hand in the cookie jar."

"It's not a cookie jar, it's a pan of your *galaktoboureko*, my love," said Tassos. "And there will be plenty left for tomorrow."

"Only if I lock the refrigerator."

"What can I say? I'm a sucker for custard in filo pastry, and yours is the best."

"Flattery isn't going to make that any smaller." Maggie pointed at his belly.

"All the more for you to love."

"More for me to worry about, you mean."

"My health is fine."

"When's the last time you saw a doctor?"

"I don't like doctors, they're—"

"For sick people," said Maggie shaking her head. "Get a new line. That one's older than the last time you exercised."

"Hey, lay off."

"Not on your life."

"I'm out of here, then."

"Fine. The walk will do you good. Just be back in time for church."

Tassos grabbed his sport jacket and headed out the door. There wasn't anything else to say. She was right. But he didn't want to admit it. He'd been attributing his pains to overeating. Maybe that's why he kept eating, to excuse the pain. He ought to see a doctor. Maybe after Easter. He didn't dare tell Maggie. She'd have him handcuffed and dragged off to a hospital.

He looked at his watch. Not even eleven yet. Maybe he'd walk to that new taverna with the outdoor terrace and lovely wrought-iron café chairs. Just for a coffee. Yes, that would work nicely. The taverna sat just around the corner from that bakery he liked. But he'd better not stop there. After all, he did just have that *galaktoboureko*.

A few paces before he reached the bakery, an old woman in black trundled out of the bakery loaded down with blue plastic grocery bags in each hand. He slowed to let her pass ahead of him. She reached the corner at the same time as a shiny motorcycle roared over the curb and shot across the sidewalk, missing the old woman by less than a step. She staggered backwards, dropping two of the bags as Tassos jumped forward to steady her.

"Are you all right, *keria*?" he asked, using the respectful title for a woman.

"O, Blessed Mother," she crossed herself. "He came so close."

Tassos bent down and picked up the dropped bags. "I know." He handed her the bags. "As long as you're okay."

"Look at him. He never even apologized."

The helmetless driver had stopped his motorcycle next to a metal post anchored to the sidewalk in front of the taverna's blue-awninged terrace. He stood about a half a head taller and forty years younger than Tassos. The driver paid them no attention, finished chaining up his cycle, walked into the taverna, and sat at a table on the terrace.

"Yes, I noticed, *keria*. Why don't you go home and forget about this? It's better to let it go. *Kalo Paska.*"

"You're right. It is a time of forgiveness. Bless you."

Tassos waited until the woman had crossed the street before he moved toward the taverna. He stopped by the motorcycle and stood perfectly still, staring at it.

After about a minute of his vigil, he heard the driver yell, "Hey, fat man, what are you looking at?"

Tassos didn't look up. "Nice bike."

"Yeah, now move on."

"Bet you paid a lot for it. Even more for the flames and demons paint job."

"I said move along."

Tassos raised his hands in a peaceful way. "No problem."

He turned and took two steps into the taverna.

"Don't come in here," said the driver. "I don't like your looks."

Tassos smiled. "Funny you should say that. I'm in the mood

to change looks." He picked up one of the iron chairs, stepped outside, and began beating on the motorcycle.

The driver jumped up from his table screaming and charged straight for Tassos. He reached him as Tassos completed disassembling the bike's rear lights and carrier assembly.

The driver swung for Tassos' head, but before he could land a punch, Tassos had swung the chair around legs first, pinning two legs above the driver's shoulders and two under his armpits. With a forward thrust of the chair and his left leg planted behind the driver's left, Tassos sent him stumbling down just inside the taverna entrance. The horizontal reinforcing metal cross-bars of the chair legs pinned the driver across his throat and chest. Tassos dropped down onto the chair, straddling it backwards, his feet firmly planted on the man's elbows, watching the man flail wildly about, trying to free himself.

"I'm going to kill you, fat man," the driver yelled.

Tassos leaned forward over the back of the chair and looked down at the driver's face. "Right now, I'd say your chances of pulling that off are pretty slim."

"You don't know who you're fucking with."

"Well, you sure as hell aren't a tough guy."

"Tough enough to mess you up bad."

"Since you've gone from threatening to kill me to threatening to mess me up bad, I guess you're beginning to appreciate your situation."

The driver started kicking, then tried rolling from side to side.

Tassos didn't budge. "Remember what you called me? Well, fat man ain't moving."

A waiter stood in the doorway, unsure what to do.

"Do you know this guy?" Tassos yelled over to him.

He gestured no.

"So, he doesn't work here?"

Again, he gestured no.

"Do me a favor. Bring me a Greek coffee, medium sweet."

Tassos looked down at the driver. "Would you like one?"

"Asshole."

"You really don't have any manners." Tassos crossed his forearms over the back of the chair and leaned his chin down on top of them. "Tell you what. I'm going to give you a fair chance."

"I'll kill you."

"Oh, we're back to that." Tassos stood up, driving his full weight onto the man's pinned elbows, and plopped back down hard onto the chair.

The man screamed.

"As I was saying, I'm going to give you a fair chance."

Pause.

"Good. You're learning manners. Here's the deal. I'm going to tell the waiter to call the cops and you can file a complaint against me. How's that sound?"

"I don't need any cops to deal with you."

"I know, but I feel bad after all I did to your bike. At least let me call them so you can file a claim with your insurance company. I mean, without a police report about a mad, fat man beating up on your bike, who's going to believe you?"

"You're crazy."

"You're probably right."

The waiter arrived with the coffee.

"Hand it to me. I'll hold it," said Tasso. "And by the way, please call the police."

"*No,*" shouted the driver. "No cops." He wrestled against the chair.

"Careful, I have hot coffee in my hands, right above your face."

Tassos looked at the waiter and silently mouthed, "Call the police."

Tassos took a sip of coffee. "Somehow it doesn't surprise me that you don't want me calling the cops."

"Fuck you."

Tassos leaned forward and stared at the driver's eyes. "I guessed right about you, didn't I?"

"What are you talking about?"

"You guys just can't help yourselves. You make some money dealing in drugs, prostitution, refugee smuggling, whatever, and the first thing you do is go for the gold chains, the glitzy watch, the high-roller routine in clubs. All the sort of shit that hangs a sign around your neck telling every cop to keep an eye on you." Tassos jerked his head toward the motorcycle. "Do you know what cops call that little rocket of yours?"

No answer.

"I guess if you knew, then you wouldn't be riding it. A *perp-mobile*. I can't remember the last time I saw a guy who makes an honest living riding one of those."

"I ain't done anything wrong."

"Of course not. All the pills and other shit in your busted open cargo carrier are for your aging mother in Kipseli."

The driver suddenly went still. "Who are you?"

"Just consider me a defender of old ladies with grocery bags."

"You're a cop?"

"Do you want to make a deal?"

"Sure, let me go and you can keep the stuff."

Tassos shook his head. "No, not that kind of deal. Just tell me who you work for."

"No chance. Never."

"Suit yourself." Tassos cocked his head toward the street. "Hey, do you hear that?" He looked down at the driver. "It's the sound of a siren announcing your Easter's about to get royally fucked." He waved for the waiter. "May I please see a menu? I've worked up a bit of an appetite."

● ● ● ● ●

The two young cops in a marked blue-and-white Toyota seemed unsure of what to make of the scene in the café. A heavy, old guy on a chair had a young, lanky punk pinned to the ground, and as soon as the punk saw the cops, he'd started screaming, "police brutality" at the top of his lungs.

"He's complaining about me, not you," said Tassos, holding out the ID he'd pulled from his jacket pocket when the cruiser drew up to the curb.

One cop took the ID, looked at it, and showed it to his partner. They both stood up a little straighter.

"What's the situation, Chief Investigator?" said the one holding the ID.

"Our friend here is a dirty, little drug dealer." Tassos stood, shifting his full weight onto the man's elbows, before stepping onto the ground.

The man screamed.

Tassos pointed a finger at him. "Stay there." He turned to the cops. "The suspect also drives illegally on the sidewalk, and I'd bet his bike's registration's expired."

The cop holding Tassos' ID took another look at it. "You're serious?"

"Yep, the drugs are in that open carrier on the back of his bike."

"He broke into it," yelled the suspect.

"Shh," said Tassos, putting a finger to his lips. "You'll get your chance to tell your story, but for now, just shut up and remember one thing: Never come back to this neighborhood, and if you happen to live here, *move.*"

The two cops walked over to the bike, and three minutes later had the suspect handcuffed and hustled into the back of the cruiser. They collected the evidence, took a statement from Tassos, and tried to get a statement from the waiter, an immigrant, but he insisted he'd seen and heard nothing. The cops called for a van to impound the motorcycle and Tassos agreed to stay there until it arrived.

It was after one by the time the two cops left, and Tassos' stomach growled with hunger. He estimated it would be at least another hour, possibly two, before the van picked up the bike, and so he'd better pace himself. He decided to start with something simple, like *gavros*, and along with those little deep-fried anchovies he ordered a small bottle of *tsipouro*. That brought him to thinking he'd better go healthier, so he added a Greek salad. Which, he concluded, justified his adding a fried cheese *saganaki* to go with it.

As he waited for the food, he thought about tomorrow's Easter meal, and how to go about getting Andreas the information he wanted on the Volandes murder. It seemed almost sacrilegious to bother someone about such grisly matters over Easter.

The proverbial light bulb went off in his head. *Unless the someone doesn't celebrate Easter.*

He pulled his phone from his pocket, looked up a number, and pressed connect.

"Hello?"

"Ibrahim, how are you? It's Tassos."

Pause. "Why are you calling me?"

"That's not a very warm way to greet a long lost friend."

"You're not a friend."

"My, oh my, what a short memory you have."

"No, I have a very long one, and getting a reduced sentence instead of freedom for my son, I do not consider the work of a friend."

"Your wife did."

"Mothers are more emotional."

"Yeah, I guess she made your life pretty miserable but, after all, it was you who decided to bring her baby into your drug-smuggling business. Has she ever forgiven you for screwing up his life?"

"Fuck you."

"Imagine how much worse it would have been for him if I hadn't stepped in. Not only would he have served five years instead of one, he'd also have done his time in a maximum-security prison, playing house with a bunch of real hard cases."

"As I said, I owe you nothing."

"How's your daughter? The one married to that Greek politician."

Silence.

"You know, the one with the three kids your wife idolizes. It was her husband, your son-in-law, who asked me to help out with your son. Or do you forget that too?"

"You can't do anything to them."

"Nor would I want to. They're decent folk who were just trying to do the right thing by helping out a family member who'd been betrayed by his selfish father. You had the chance to take the rap for him but refused to come to Greece and face trial."

"I'm hanging up."

"If you do, my next call is to someone who'll start the process for listing you and your wife as *persona non grata* in Greece. Enjoy explaining to your wife why she can't visit her grandchildren in Greece anymore. That should be fun to watch."

"No way you can bar us."

"Compared to what I did for your son, that will be child's play. How tough do you think it's going to be to get the Greek government to keep a notorious Turkish drug smuggler from entering the country? And if you think your son-in-law will jump in to help you out, pray on."

"Fuck you."

"Ibrahim, you're the one who decided to play hardball with me before even hearing why I'm calling. I always thought you were smarter than that, especially when you're the only one with something to lose."

While Tassos listened to the heavy breathing on the other end of the line, he waved to the waiter standing nearby with plates of food to put them on his table.

"What do you want from me?"

"What can you tell me about who was involved in the murder of that Greek shipowner on Lesvos?"

"I have no idea."

"You really don't expect me to accept that, wish you a nice life, and kiss you good-bye? Work with me, man. Give me your best guess."

"My best guess is the same as yours. Everyone knows the shipowner was trying to wreck the refugee-trafficking business, so it likely was someone in that business."

"Likely doesn't cut it. I need names."

"If you're asking me to name everyone in Turkey involved in refugee smuggling, go to hell. Even if you're just asking me to name the Greeks involved, same answer. Go to hell."

"That's fair. I can live with that. But I only want to know which of them are possibly—and I emphasize possibly—tied into the shipowner's murder."

More heavy breathing. "The night after the shipowner's murder, a guy involved in refugee smuggling north of Izmir turned up murdered in his car."

"So?" said Tassos. "Nothing unusual about that."

Ibrahim sighed. "It's the way he died."

"Meaning?"

"His head was sliced off with the single stroke of a sword. While he sat in his car."

"Jesus."

"I would put it differently, but you get the point."

"Any idea who did it?"

"Not a one, but you see the connection to the Lesvos murder, right, super cop?"

"Who'd the dead guy work for?"

"A local operator named Malik."

"Who's Malik's boss?"

"That's all I can give you. Malik heads up refugee-smuggling operations out of that part of Turkey into Lesvos."

"What about a last name and address for Malik?"

"Tiryaki, but no idea of an address. He lives in a big compound not too far from the sea, south of Ayvalik."

Tassos glanced at his food while he wrote the information on a small notepad. "What does he have to say about the murder of his man?"

"No idea. I don't know the man personally."

"No threats, no inquiries, no more bodies turning up?"

"Not a sound. And word is, he hasn't left his compound. If he knows anything, he's keeping it to himself."

Or dead. "That's it? Don't you have anything else for me?"

"Yeah. Go to hell." The connection ended.

Tassos put down his phone, picked up a fork, and tasted a bit of the *saganaki.*

Well, it's a start.

Chapter Seven

At Lila's urging, Andreas spent the afternoon in the National Gardens across the street from their apartment, playing with their son, Tassaki. Lila had told him that staying out of her way was the best thing he could do to help her ready their home for Sunday's festivities. Preparing Easter dinner on her own had become an annual tradition for Lila, but that meant no distractions by the other members of the household, namely the men in her family. The baby nurse would take care of their three-month-old daughter, Sofia. Besides, she wasn't old enough yet to create the sort of messes her brother and father were so good at.

Andreas watched his son run across the grass trying to keep up with older boys kicking a soccer ball. The older boys didn't seem to mind their five-year-old shadow, even encouraged him to put a boot to the ball every once in a while.

Andreas knew he was a lucky man. Despite Greece being in the throes of economic meltdown, and its Mediterranean neighbors battling wars and terrorists, his wife and children lived a home life removed from virtually all of that. He knew theirs was a life not to be taken for granted. Things could change rapidly in this world. That was not a thought he'd shared with his wife. New mothers had enough to worry about. So did fathers, old and new.

He couldn't imagine how he'd feel if his family had to flee

for their lives as trafficked refugees. How would he react to predators seeking to exploit or harm his children, his wife? Or to governments ignoring pleas for simple acts of human decency, such as food, shelter, or medical care for a sick child?

Not well. Not well at all.

Andreas' mobile rang.

"Tassos, what's up?"

"Can you talk?"

"Sure. I'm in the Gardens with Tassaki."

"I might have something for you on the Volandes murder."

Andreas listened as Tassos related his conversation with Ibrahim.

Once he'd finished, Andreas said, "It would be a hell of a coincidence if there's more than one killer taking a sword to folks tied into the Lesvos refugee situation. What's the chance that the decapitated guy simply pissed off some crazies who go in for beheadings?"

"You tell me," said Tassos. "He worked as low-level muscle in a refugee-trafficking ring. Why would anyone want to make an example of him? Besides, as far as I know, no one's taken responsibility for it. My guess is, if someone's sending a message with him, it's a private one intended for the beheaded guy's boss."

"Which brings us back to Lesvos refugee smugglers based in Turkey."

"And a dead end for me," said Tassos. "My contact won't give me anything else."

"I'll see if I can get anything from connections I once had in the Turkish Police."

"Once had?"

"They haven't been too cooperative lately. Everyone in Turkey is looking over his shoulder for someone who might be trying to label him disloyal to President Erdogan."

"Can you blame them? It's freaky what's going on over there, now that he has virtually unlimited power."

Tassos yawned. "I guess I should head back to Maggie's for a nap. This keep-out-of-the-house routine is hard work."

"Tell me about it." Andreas watched the older boys exchange high fives with Tassaki over a score.

"Let me know if you need anything else from me before I see you tomorrow," said Tassos.

"Will do, and thanks."

Andreas hung up his phone. He ought to head straight home and get to work on an official request for assistance from the Turkish Police. As he'd said to Tassos, he doubted his colleagues on the eastern side of the Aegean would cooperate unofficially. With the rampant paranoia of the Turkish leadership, person-to-person, informal cross-border cooperation of the sort most police relied upon had become downright dangerous for the Turks.

Thank God it's not like that here.

Tassaki came racing across the grass toward his father, smiling from ear to ear. "Daddy, this is my best day ever."

Andreas' face lit up and he swooped his son up in his arms.

"And it's only going to get better." Andreas kissed Tassaki on the cheek. "Next stop, ice cream."

Official police business could wait.

"Hi, Mommy, we're home." Tassaki ran ahead of his father through the rooms toward the kitchen.

"Shh," said Marietta. "Your sister's sleeping." She pulled off his jacket and pointed to a brown stain on the front. "I see someone had chocolate ice cream."

"That's the least of his laundry challenges," said Andreas. "He was a regular football star today, and has the grass stains to prove it. Don't you, champ?" Andreas lowered his hand to exchange a high five with his son.

"That's terrific," said Lila, poking her head out from the kitchen.

"It was so fun, Mom."

"You mean *such* fun." Lila bent down and gave her son a kiss. "Marietta, would you please give Tassaki a bath while I finish up in here?"

"Yes, Mrs. Lila."

"Thanks."

Andreas followed Lila into the kitchen. "He had an absolute blast. There were some older kids playing football and they let him play with them."

"That's unusual."

"I know. I hope he's not disappointed the next time. Kids can be difficult." He reached for a hard-boiled egg dyed red, sitting in a basket on the black granite countertop.

"So can their fathers." Lila smacked his hand away from the egg. "I spent Thursday dyeing them. You'll have to wait like everyone else. Don't you have something you can do besides 'help' me in the kitchen?" She put finger quotes around help.

"As a matter of fact, I do. We may have a lead on that Volandes murder."

"He was such a nice man. My father knew him well."

"Tassos told me that last night someone used a sword to decapitate a bad guy on the Turkish coast across from Lesvos."

"Oh, my God," said Lila. "That part of Turkey's becoming a hotbed for terrorists."

"Why do you say that?"

"It's all over the TV. Last night a Greek couple and their baby on holiday were gunned down there in a café. No apparent motive, but the Turks are trying to say it's not terrorism." Lila pointed to the television mounted in a corner of the kitchen. "There it is again." She picked up the remote and brought up the sound.

"Turkish authorities now claim to have found the van used by the killers, and also believe they've identified one of the men involved in the café murders. The bloody corpse of a known organized crime member was found in a stolen car not far from the café. Turkish police believe the Greek family was not the target of a terrorist attack, but rather, innocent victims of an organized crime dispute. Police are looking for a man shown on closed-circuit television as leaving the café on foot immediately after the shooting. Stay tuned for further developments."

Andreas kept staring at the screen while an advertisement started.

Lila clicked mute on the remote. "I take it you found that interesting."

"I've got to get a copy of the CCTV recording." He smacked his hand on the countertop. "I'll bet you anything Volandes' killer is the one who walked away from that café."

"Why?"

"Too many coincidences. Not sure why the shooters at the café wanted him dead, but they did. And badly enough to risk taking out tourists in the process."

Lila looked down at her hands. "Including a baby."

Andreas paused. "Our children are safe."

She looked up at his eyes. "How can you say that? The world's gone crazy. Everywhere you look, irrational people with myopic agendas are gaining power and hacking away at whatever aspects of civilized behavior they deem inappropriate for their purposes." Lila shut her eyes and shook her head.

She opened her eyes. "What do you honestly think will become of our children?"

Andreas swallowed. "No one's future is ever guaranteed, but I think we serve the children and ourselves best by doing all that we can to prepare them for living the sort of life we hope they'll have, and showing genuine respect, love, support, and optimism toward each other. All of that we can control. As for the bad stuff," Andreas shrugged his shoulders, "it's always going to happen to somebody. We can only pray it won't be us, help those who aren't as lucky…and be prepared to cut the balls off of any bad guys who dare to get too close."

Lila smiled. "You had to end your little pep talk on a tough guy note, didn't you?"

Andreas feigned a glare. "It's my style."

She shook her head and pointed at the television. "Okay, macho man, how do you plan on getting the recording?"

He moved away from the television and slid his arms around his wife's waist. "I'll worry about that later. For now, I'm all yours."

"Is that a threat or a promise?"

"You decide."

Lila draped her arms around her husband's neck. "I guess cooking can wait."

● ● ● ● ●

Andreas lay next to Lila, waiting for his heart rate to subside.

"My, weren't you the perfect picture of afternoon passion, my darling husband?"

"Something about the thought of you holding those eggs—"

"*Stop*, don't ruin the moment with your warped sense of humor."

Andreas rolled over and looped an arm across Lila's chest. "Your wish is my command."

"Remind me to take you up on that the next time your mother wants me to go clothes shopping with her."

"You love my mother."

"Of course I do, but I don't even go clothes shopping with *my* mother."

Andreas propped himself up on one elbow. "Imagine how you're going to feel when Sofia is old enough to say she doesn't to want to go clothes shopping with you."

"That will *never* happen."

Andreas smiled.

"Okay, wise guy, I get it. You think you're going to get to use our three-month-old daughter as an ongoing lesson plan for me. Think again."

He rocked his head from side to side. "Well, I guess you

could say it offers a symmetry of sorts…like how, whenever a certain five-year-old does something his mommy doesn't like, she says, 'He's just like his daddy.'"

Lila cocked her head at him. "Bastard," and poked him in the stomach.

"Such language. What kind of example is that for our daughter?" He shut his eyes, waiting for Lila to swat him with a pillow.

Nothing happened.

He opened his eyes and saw Lila staring at the ceiling. "What's up?"

"You made a good point."

"What was that?"

"Asking me what kind of example I'm setting for our daughter."

"I was only kidding. You're a terrific, loving mother."

She fixed her eyes on his. "But I once was a terrific, highly sought-after professional fund raiser. Now, I'm dying eggs, watching afternoon TV, and organizing play dates."

Andreas sat up, but didn't say a word.

"I feel like a Stepford Wife."

"You can't be serious."

"Oh, but I am. I'm not serving as the sort of role model I want to be for Sofia. *Or* for Tassaki."

Andreas bit at his lower lip. "Is it something I've done?"

She sat up and patted his cheek. "No, my husband, this is not about you. It's all about me."

Andreas raised his hands in surrender. "Okay, so what do you have in mind?"

Lila shrugged. "I don't know yet, but I've got to get back into the adult world. Not today, not tomorrow, but sooner rather than later."

Andreas' phone rang on the bedside table.

"I can't believe you didn't turn that off."

"I thought it was on vibrate." Andreas swung his legs out of bed and reached for his mobile.

"That was you, my love, not your phone."

"Glad your sense of humor's back."

She scrunched up her nose and headed toward the bathroom. "It's what gets me through the days."

The phone rang again.

He didn't recognize the number. "Hello, Kaldis here."

"Hi, it's me, calling about the information you wanted on that hit and run."

It took Andreas a moment to recognize the voice of the Lesvos police commander. He spoke like someone concerned about his conversation being overheard.

"Do you have it?"

"I've seen it."

"When can I get it?" said Andreas.

"There are complications that make that difficult."

"What sort of complications?"

"Let's just say it confirms your suspicions but compromises a second innocent."

Your daughter. "I understand."

"How many are involved?" said Andreas.

"I don't know yet, but you know what they say about a fish."

"Yeah." *It rots from the head.*

"Gotta run."

The phone went dead.

Andreas sat on the edge of the bed staring at the bathroom door. He wanted to continue the conversation with Lila, but sensed it best to let her decide when to raise it again. With the subject on her mind, he knew that one way or another she'd come up with a solution. Then she'd run it past him. That was the way she did things, and he was fine with that. She wasn't the sort that let things fester unaddressed.

His thoughts shifted back to his phone call with the commander. The Volandes murder had been far too intricately orchestrated to be spontaneous. Even though the Turkish police likely haven't yet tied what happened last night back to the

Volandes killing, by now they should be all over that Malik guy for anything he knew about his employee's beheading. They must be, what with the Turkish media reporting that their police had made the connection between the flunky's death last night and the slaughter earlier that evening of the Greek family in the café.

Unless that Malik character's protected.

Whether or not he is, Andreas doubted the Turkish police would pass along any information to the Greek police that might harm Turkish tourism. Then again, since a Greek mother, father, and baby were murdered in Turkey, they'd expect intense Greek police interest, even if they weren't likely to share anything meaningful until after they knew how it played out.

The more he thought about it, the more Andreas realized his only shot at identifying the likely killer anytime soon was through the CCTV recording.

But how to get it out of Turkey?

⚫ ⚫ ⚫ ⚫ ⚫

The police commander slid the cell phone back into his desk drawer. He rarely used it, and no one knew the number. Still, there was a risk. There was always a risk with something this big. If his daughter weren't involved, he would never have called Kaldis. But she was involved, albeit innocently, in something dark and nasty, and if the shit hit the fan, they both might need Kaldis as an ally.

He sighed. With Aleka being set up so masterfully, he wondered what they had in store for him. Strategists of the sort behind Volandes' assassination didn't go after the child of a powerful man unless they'd planned something for the father as well. Then again, getting her to sign the notes could have been her asshole boss acting on his own, thinking he'd found a way to cover his tracks should the overall plan blow up.

She'd shared the contents of the folder she'd taken from her boss' desk. The signed notes inside left no question that Ali was the killer. If anything went awry with that unjust accusation, then Aleka's signature would have her taking the heat.

Bastards.

Definitely, her boss was involved, but that opportunistic bottom-feeder wouldn't be at the top of the food chain on this one. There had to be someone else. The prosecutor? Hard to say. For sure he was an ambitious egomaniac, the type who, once having formed an opinion, refused to change it. But that didn't make him corrupt. Only easily manipulated. A trait the commander had used more than once to his advantage.

Aleka had rejected returning the report, saying it would make her party to ruining an innocent man's life. He couldn't disagree, yet the alternative raised serious threats to her own future, depending on her boss' reaction to the missing notes.

Assuming the forensic supervisor had another copy, but not one bearing Aleka's original signature, he'd likely ask her to sign the copy rather than forge her signature, sign the notes himself, or leave them unsigned. If he asked her to sign, she could insist on reading them, and object to signing them as written. Her boss could hardly blame her for that.

But if he suspected she'd taken the original, or word got back to him that Aleka had been bitching about what he'd done to her, he might panic and tell someone up the chain that they had a problem.

The commander hoped his daughter would keep her anger in check, and her mouth shut.

He shook his head. Too many maybes. And too many of them put his daughter at risk.

Perhaps she should leave the island for a while.

Good luck getting her to do that.

Chapter Eight

Evening church services in Athens on Holy Saturday generally started at ten, but midnight was the high point of the service. By midnight, Saint Dionysios on Skoufa Street in Kolonaki would be packed. That was Lila's parents' church, and in the years since Andreas' marriage, the entire family would gather there for services, including Andreas' mother and his sister's family. Only little Sofia missed the ceremony. She stayed at home with the nurse. Most Athenians who could afford it, tried to get out of Athens for Easter, many returning to their ancestral villages or summer homes, but for Andreas and Lila, staying in Athens meant keeping all sides of their family together in one place, and in doing so, they had established their own tradition.

At precisely midnight, church bells rang out across Greece and even total strangers exchanged the traditional *Christos Anesti* and *Alithos Anesti* greetings that Christ had risen, kissed each other, and lit each other's candles with fire flown into Greece each Easter from the Holy Flame of Christ's tomb in Jerusalem.

Most skipped out of church at that point rather than sit through the additional hours of services. They'd make their way home or to their favorite restaurants. For Andreas and his family, it meant another family tradition, one that had them all strolling to a restaurant in the National Gardens close by Andreas and Lila's home.

There, they'd challenge each other and friends with the customary smacking of dyed-red eggs, promising good luck to the winner, devour the traditional *mayiritsa* soup to break the fast, consume all sorts of salads, and drink lots of wine.

Lila sent Tassaki home with Marietta around one-thirty, and called it quits herself a half-hour later, saying she had too much left to do to prepare for the day's Easter dinner, the big feast of the week. Andreas rose to leave, but Lila told him to stay, so he did, until three.

After seeing his mother and sister's family into taxis, he walked home. He hadn't checked his phone in hours. He pulled it out. Only Easter wishes. No bad news.

A true Easter miracle.

• • ● • •

Dana McLaughlin's Easter holiday escape to 24/7 Mykonos was turning out far differently than she'd imagined. Her new friend Philipos insisted she join his family for Saturday evening church services, and after, for dinner at his son's restaurant, a cozy, garden-like bistro tucked away close by their church.

Philipos and his family had welcomed a foreign stranger into their midst, and a seemingly troubled one at that. This sort of village hospitality and generosity of spirit still surprised her, even though she'd seen the same shown by islanders to refugees on Lesvos, all without any expectation of compensation or public accolades for their efforts.

People simply did what they instinctively knew to be the right thing: going out to sea to search for lives to save; waiting on the beach to help bring to shore the panicked, traumatized, and wounded clinging to criminally overloaded boats; struggling to give solace to those who lost a loved one on the crossing; and feeding the hungry, clothing the needy, and caring for the sick who remained penned up until the world decided what to do with them.

She rolled over in bed and looked up at the ceiling. *The unselfish doing God's work in ungodly times,* she thought.

Sure, there were opportunists, tragedy drew them like flies Scum robbing bodies washed up on shore, sex traffickers preying on the dreams and fears of unaccompanied children, criminals using the cover of crisis to plunder a community, and profiteers garnering outrageous sums for food, water, or things as simple as a cell phone battery charge. But the good far outnumbered the bad, and to the extent evil thrived, it was not the islanders Dana faulted, but those governments and their agents who publicly pledged to help, yet, once away from the cameras and microphones, dedicated themselves to keeping refugees far away from their nations' borders.

That's why Mihalis died. His death was a message to anyone who dared tamper with the status quo, including Dana. Of course, her death wouldn't warrant more than a passing mention in the news, and within a week, no one would care beyond her parents.

Dana shut her eyes. She'd promised Philipos to be at his home for Easter dinner. She didn't want to go, given her own moody ways, but that was precisely why she had to go. She needed to get out of this funk.

"Funk it all," she yelled. "Funk every mother-funking one of you," banging her fists on the mattress.

She opened her eyes and waited for her breathing to slow.

Izmir raced through her mind. Everything had to tie back into Izmir. She just knew it. But how could she prove anything? Who could she turn to for help? There was no one to trust. That cop Kaldis had promised to help, but he didn't seem to care about Ali spending Easter in jail.

Whatever Kaldis' motives, she couldn't depend on him. She was back to where she couldn't depend on anyone anymore but herself.

But to do what? Find answers on her own? And answers to what? And once she had them, what would she do with them?

She squeezed the pillow beneath her head, trying to see a solution. Then it came to her.

She'd take what she found to the press. Not just any press—too many journalists were in bed with the politicians, pushing their patrons' agendas. She'd take it to the international media. That was the only way. Embarrass governments into action through the press.

She shook her head and laughed, *I must be mad.*

She sat up and swung her legs onto the floor. *I don't even know where to begin.*

She looked at the time on her phone.

I guess with Easter dinner.

Andreas felt uneasy about roasting a lamb on their apartment's terrace, even though he'd used the rear terrace facing away from the National Gardens and Acropolis. It violated a strict apartment building rule against any sort of cooking on any terrace. But on this day, the building's management benignly neglected enforcing that rule as a practical accommodation to the Greek national tradition of roasting lambs on Easter Sunday—provided they used electricity, not fire. Besides, virtually all the other residents in the building were away for the holiday, and Lila had invited those who weren't, to join them. Still, Andreas expected a knock on his front door at any moment, along with a lecture on how things just weren't done that way "in this neighborhood."

He stood on the terrace, drinking wine with Tassos, every so often tending to the slowly turning lamb by slicing off a piece to share with his buddy—just to make sure it was cooking properly.

Andreas' wife, mother, sister, mother- and father-in-law, and Maggie stayed inside with the grandchildren and a dozen other guests, enjoying a more formal sort of eating and drinking.

"I don't know about you," said Andreas, "but if I eat too much lamb it upsets my stomach."

"That's why you drink the wine," said Tassos. "So you forget all about what it does to your stomach."

"The key is moderation," said Andreas.

"That's a key for a lock I do not possess."

Andreas stared at Tassos' stomach. "I can see."

Tassos flashed him an open palm, the Greek equivalent of the middle finger. "So where's Petros? I thought he and Sappho would be here."

Andreas gestured no. "Our former team member is now a restaurateur. They opened a place together on Santorini, and Easter is a very busy time for them."

"He didn't know how easy he had it as a cop."

"Yeah, easy." Andreas sliced another bit off the lamb and held it out for Tassos.

"Anything new on the Volandes case?" said Tassos, taking the piece of lamb with his fingers.

Andreas gestured no. "On Tuesday I'll see if I can figure out a way to get the Turkish police to turn over a CCTV recording that might help us."

"Good luck with that," said Tassos. "I've a sense that whoever organized Volandes' assassination has a lot of political cover over there."

"For sure. Here, too." Andreas told him of his cryptic conversation with the Mytilini police commander. "This is getting way too Machiavellian."

"He was Italian," said Tassos.

"Would you prefer if I'd said Thucydides?"

Maggie slid open the terrace door, and stuck her head through the doorway. "How much longer until it's ready?"

"This is art, my dear. You can't rush it," said Tassos.

"It'll be soon," said Andreas. "Let's close the door before the smoke and smell off the lamb get inside the apartment."

Maggie stepped outside and slid the door closed behind her.

"I need an ETA, guys, so we can get the rest of the food ready to go."

"Twenty minutes," said Andreas.

"By then we'll have figured out the world's greatest mystery," said Tassos.

"And what would that be?" she said. "How to have any lamb left for the hungry horde inside once you two are finished 'testing' it?"

"Close," said Andreas. "How to get the Turks to turn over a CCTV recording of a crime scene."

"What scene?"

"We'll get into all that on Tuesday. For now, let's just concentrate on our cooking."

"Hey, you're the one wearing the apron, not me."

Tassos laughed and pointed his drink at Andreas. "Sexist."

Andreas shook his head. "I meant I don't feel like talking about the Volandes case anymore today."

"There's a CCTV of his murder?" said Maggie.

"We wish." Andreas studied the lamb. "We think it's our killer who got caught on a CCTV recording of the café scene where that Greek family got wiped out on the Turkish coast the night after Volandes' murder."

"The recording's all you want?"

Andreas turned his head to stare at Maggie. "Why do I sense you're about to make me feel like an idiot?"

"I'm sure it won't be anything quite that simple to achieve," said Tassos.

"Get me the details on what you're looking for," said Maggie, "and I'll see what I can do about getting it for you."

Andreas felt certain his jaw had dropped. "How the hell do you expect to accomplish that?"

"The way I always do. I'll ask my friend who works for one of the higher-ups in the Turkish police to get it for me, the same as she asks me to use my connections here to get Greek TV footage for her. If it's been playing over there or available, she'll get it for me." She tilted her head to the side. "Unless, of course, there's a formal embargo on it, because, let's say, some Greek police official made a formal request of the Turkish police."

"Ouch," said Tassos.

Maggie shrugged. "I'll just ask for it. No official reason, just curiosity. Low-key trumps official every time." She slid open the door. "Now, get back to work, cookie. Time's a wasting." She stuck her tongue out at them before stepping back inside and shutting the door.

"We deserved that," said Andreas.

"Nope," said Tassos, reaching for a dripping piece of lamb. "Just you."

● ● ● ● ●

Dana had eaten more than she thought possible, but there was little choice. It seemed as if Philipos' entire family kept piling food on her plate, prodding, "Try this, it's the best you'll ever taste." And they were right, though at times only because she doubted she'd ever again eat such a thing as a goat's eyeball.

As she struggled to resist her fifth proffered dessert, she wondered whether the tiny bikini she'd brought to Mykonos but not yet worn would ever fit her again. Perhaps, if she didn't eat again until July.

Still, she was having a blast.

Philipos waved for her to join him and his two sons in the living room. She said she preferred to stay with their wives to help with the dishes, but the women insisted she sit with the men. Philipos pointed her to a chair facing a pair of French doors opening out onto a terrace. The house stood on a treeless hilltop a half-mile northeast of the old town, looking down upon the old port. Its waning crescent-shaped sapphire-blue harbor curved away from a tangle of cloud-white centuries-old buildings set beneath a row of a sixteenth-century windmills capped in straw, running along a ridge south of the town.

"Wow, what a view," she said.

Philipos nodded. "Yes, it's hard to sit here without contemplating the fate of the universe."

Dana smiled. "You sound like an incurable romantic." *Just like Mr. Volandes.*

"For sure," said his older son.

"How can you ever find meaning to life if you don't take time to dream?" said Philipos.

"It is hard to dream when you're struggling just to survive to the end of the day," she said.

"I assume you're talking about the experiences of those in your care on Lesvos."

"As well as those fleeing Afghanistan, Syria, Iraq, Somalia, sub-Saharan Africa."

Philipos shook a finger at her. "But they wouldn't have fled those lands if they did not dream. Those without dreams are the ones who stay behind."

This time Dana laughed. "So, you're a philosopher, too."

"Right again," said the younger son.

"I am a dreamer," Philipos said, "but also a realist. And, as both, I dread the direction our world has taken, catapulted by a crisis more capable of rapidly transforming our world than any natural disaster or war. And by transforming, I mean not just the ethnic or religious makeup of Western societies, but their moral underpinnings."

She wondered where Philipos planned on going with this. For sure, his bottom-line crisis had to be the refugee crisis, but she hoped it wouldn't be as part of an anti-Muslim rant. He didn't strike her as the sort, but she'd been surprised far too many times on that subject to assume anything.

"For decades I've watched as our world permitted disease and civil wars to cull away masses of Third World souls, ignoring pleas for humanitarian intervention of the minimal sort necessary to save those only wishing to live with their families in peace. Instead, the West found an out-of-sight/out-of-mind approach far more suited to its citizens' sensibilities and politicians' careers."

He paused to take a sip of wine. "Even now, long after it's become obvious that shutting your eyes to reality does not change the scene in front of you, the West still refuses to confront the refugee crisis in a way that might actually make the world a better place."

"I'm wide open to any suggestions on how to change things," said Dana.

Philipos pointed at his chest. "From me? I'm just a simple museum watchman. But those capable of making things happen ought to open their eyes and do something before it's too late." He shook his head. "Though at times I think it's already too late." He took another sip of wine. "We've spawned haters of the West among generations, even among descendants of those who fled misery for hope, only to find ghettos and bigotry. Yes, part of that surely was self-imposed by some of them only wanting to live with their own kind, or unwilling to fit into new cultures. But rather than finding rational solutions, we allow haters on both sides to set the agenda. Now there are far too many people simmering, longing to strike back."

"You're forgetting about the millions still in transit," said his younger son.

Philipos shook his head. "Not at all. Though, for them, what hope is there, beyond the obvious? Like treating them as human beings, not penned or herded animals. As long as the West prefers funding detention camps and hoping that the trapped magically disappear, in lieu of finding ways to assuage the horrors refugees face in their homelands...." His voice trailed off and he shook his head.

"Or just give up and stop coming," said his older son.

Philipos shrugged. "But they won't stop coming, will they?" He looked to Dana. "Because they're all dreamers."

She smiled. "Just like us."

Chapter Nine

"Why do you choose to remain in my home? The police are looking for you everywhere. They have a picture of you now. It is only a matter of time until they find you."

Aryan reached for a bowl of fruit on the small wooden table between Malik and himself. "Your dear brother-in-law must be terribly anxious. After all, any photograph they have of me only shows me as a potential victim escaping a dreadful massacre. Should they find and question me, he's undoubtedly worried I might say I caught a glimpse of the shooter. And if they show me a photograph of Jamal…" He selected an orange and began to peel it. "By the way, has your government re-imposed the death penalty for the sort of thing Jamal did?"

"Don't be so confident. They may already know who you are…even what you did on Lesvos."

Aryan tore the orange in half and put one half on the highly polished tabletop. "I doubt that. I have no record, no agency possesses my photograph, and anyone who might recognize me knows better than to identify me. As for Lesvos, only you and Jamal know of my ties to that affair. I doubt you'd turn me in and implicate yourself as my employer." He shrugged. "If I had the slightest suspicion you might, neither you, nor anyone in your family, would still be alive."

Malik slid a napkin under the half-orange on the tabletop. "You know I would never do such a thing. But if the police find you, what will you tell them? How will you explain being at the café, staying in my home?"

"By telling the truth. I was in that café waiting to be met by your brother-in-law." He tore off a segment of the orange held in his hand and stuck it in his mouth.

"I don't understand," said Malik.

"It's simple," said Aryan. "I am your children's new language tutor. I was at the café waiting for transport to my new accommodations in your home."

"The police will never believe it."

"Of course they will. I am fluent in Turkish, Greek, French, German, Russian, and English. My luggage is in transit, and I get along famously with your children. What is there not to believe?" He tore off another orange segment. "I just happened to be in the wrong place at the wrong time, but unlike that poor unfortunate family, I survived and got away from the scene as quickly as possible after the attack. We all know from television that terrorists sometimes launch a second attack as soon as first responders arrive. I'm a teacher, I abhor violence, and so I ran away." He ate the bit of orange. "As for my face being known to the Turkish authorities, I no longer care. I am living a legitimate life here, with nothing to hide." Aryan smiled. "And they have no history to associate with it."

Malik sat staring at Aryan's face. "You really don't intend to leave, do you?"

"Why should I? I like it here." He popped the rest of the orange from his hand into his mouth, and reached over for the half on the tabletop, but instead of eating it, he carefully wrapped it in the napkin. "This half I'll share with your children." He stood up. "It's time to start their lessons," he said and walked out of the room.

Malik might think him insane, but Aryan knew better. At least he didn't think of himself as insane by any measure that mattered to him. He meant what he said about remaining in Malik's home. It stood as the safest place for him. The old adage about holding your friends close but your enemies closer applied tenfold to this situation.

If he didn't live literally on top of Malik's family, the bastard would dispatch a thousand men to kill him, blow up an entire hotel to destroy him. But here, in his home, he dared not even try to poison him, for fear his own children might fall victim… to a poisoned orange, perhaps.

Of course, he could leave Turkey, and Malik would no longer have a reason to pursue him, but Aryan saw a great deal of money to be made in Turkey, a golden opportunity.

Ultimately, his plans turned on convincing Malik's boss that he had nothing to fear from Aryan. As much as Malik might like to present himself to everyone as the big boss, he was neither smart nor efficient enough to be running more than a local organization. Nor would Malik have dared hire Aryan on his own, assuming Malik had even known of Aryan's existence. No, that required the participation of Malik's higher-up, whoever that might be. And that higher-up could not justifiably accuse Aryan of betraying his employer, for, after all, Malik tried to kill him rather than pay him what he'd agreed. That was the sort of ill-thought-out decision someone like Malik would make on his own, then try to cover up from his boss. Aryan might even be praised as charitable for only muscling in on Malik's business, rather than killing him in rightful revenge.

Somehow, Aryan had to connect with the boss at the top of the organization, and convince him that he possessed no grandiose visions of being anything more than a loyal lieutenant. After all, how could Aryan hope to amass the connections necessary to control such a vast enterprise in a foreign land? It would be insane for him to think that he could.

Aryan smiled. *Yes, surely insane.*

Aryan simply needed the opportunity of meeting with Malik's boss to make all his plans come to pass. At the moment, though, he faced a far more pressing concern. Staying alive. Obviously, Malik would kill him at his first opportunity. He was likely plotting it now. Aryan needed an ally. But who? The brother-in-law? Never. He was far too weak, too afraid, too untrustworthy.

He heard the children singing with their mother in the play-room down the hall. He smiled. He'd found the perfect ally. Now, to recruit her.

● ● ● ● ●

Andreas' Monday holiday had passed peacefully at home, capped by a leisurely afternoon family stroll through the National Gardens, one of the many serendipitous advantages of staying in Athens for Easter, and avoiding the rush back into town for the resumption of business as usual on Tuesday.

"Got it," said Maggie, bursting through the doorway of his office.

"Got what?"

"That footage you wanted from Turkey. I downloaded a copy for you." She stuck a USB stick into a slot on the back of Andreas' computer screen.

"Amazing."

"And way underpaid."

Andreas clicked on the USB icon, and a black-and-white image slowly moved across the screen.

"It came from a camera mounted on the corner of a bank across from the café. The recording runs from about two min-utes before the shooting starts, up until the cops get there."

Maggie walked behind Andreas' desk and watched from over his shoulder. She pointed at the screen. "That's the couple and their baby. It gets pretty gruesome." She crossed herself.

They watched it three times in silence.

"Bastards," said Maggie.

"I think we have our man," said Andreas.

"The one who walked away after the shooting?"

Andreas nodded. "He anticipated what happened. From

the number of times he looked at his watch, he was expecting someone. The logical place for him to sit in the café would have been where the family sat, but he chose a place that offered cover. And when the van eased up in front of the café, he slid his chair toward those large pots and dived behind them right before the first shots came. Then he walked away, didn't run. A real professional."

"So, we finally got a break."

"Thanks to you." Andreas froze the screen on a close-up of a light-haired, light-eyed, chiseled featured male as tall as Andreas but built as broadly as Yianni.

"Good-looking man. Looks fit too," said Maggie. "How nice of him to have walked straight at the camera when he left the café."

Andreas nodded. "As if he had nothing to hide. The picture of innocence. So, let's find out who Mister Calm-Cool-and-Collected really is. Send this to Europol and any other agency you think might have a shot at identifying him. Who knows, we've got a clear enough image that even our outdated facial recognition software might turn up something."

"One can hope."

• ● ● ● •

Dana's return to Lesvos on Monday began with an early morning fast boat to Athens' port of Rafina, a hurried taxi ride to the airport, and a bumpy flight to Chios to attend Mihalis Volandes' funeral on the island of his birth. From there she managed to hitchhike a boat ride back to Lesvos with one of the many from Lesvos who'd come to pay their respects.

She'd spent most of her travel time tossing ideas around in her head for drawing those behind Mihalis' murder out into the open. She felt strongly that her idea would attract the sort of attention Mihalis' killers wouldn't want, but wasn't nearly as certain how they'd react, beyond making her their bull's-eye.

By the time she reached her apartment near Mytilini's old harbor, she'd reached a decision to sleep on her admittedly not fully thought through plan. She hoped to wake up clear-headed, with a less risky strategy.

Instead, she awoke more determined than ever to launch Operation Squeaky Wheel. First stop, Mytilini Police Head-quarters.

The Mytilini police station sat approximately a half-kilometer due west of the Mytilini marina, close by a five-way intersection near the outskirts of the city. A strange complex of nine low buildings running up a hillside between two largely residential streets, the complex took up nearly a full city block. Yet, their uniform beige exterior walls, identical multi-paned windows trimmed in white and formed of black iron muntins, matching doors, and terra-cotta tile roofs, tied everything together nicely. For a police station.

"I'm here to see the commander," Dana announced in English.

"Do you have an appointment?" said the young cop sitting at the front desk.

"No."

"What's it about?"

"An employee of mine you're holding in custody."

"Your employee's name?"

"Ali Sera."

The cop shook his head. "Sorry, he's not allowed visitors."

"On whose orders?"

The cop stared at her. "For your purposes, take them as mine."

Dana stared back. "For your purposes, take that as a bad career move. Now get me your boss or tell me how to spell your name."

"Am I supposed to take that as some sort of threat?"

"Threat? Who's threatening? Take it any way you wish. I just want to make sure I spell your name correctly at my press conference tomorrow when I list you among the Turkish refugee smugglers and Greek government officials involved in covering up the truth about the murder of Mihalis Volandes. I'm sure they'll want to take a hard look into the background of the cop on whose orders visitors are denied to the man set up to take the fall for the real murderer." She set her jaw and waited.

It didn't take long. The cop glared at her for a moment, then stood, turned, and disappeared around a corner.

Three minutes later he returned, pointing in the direction from which he'd come. "Last door on the right."

At the end of the hall, Dana knocked on the door.

"Come in."

The commander stood behind his desk. She assumed the photographs on his desk were of family, but they sat turned away from her. She didn't see any of the sort of photographs that customarily adorned the office walls of government officials, posing its occupant with political leaders and celebrities. Perhaps they also were on his desk.

"Well, Ms. McLaughlin, how nice to see you again," he said in English.

She nodded. "Commander."

He pointed to the chair in front of his desk. "Please, sit."

She sat and crossed her legs.

He sat. "So, what is it you're here to see me about?"

"I want to see Ali Sera."

"About what?"

"NGO business."

"I thought it was about some sort of rip-roaring press conference you described to my officer."

"It involves both."

"I find it hard to believe you'll be dragging your NGO's name into the middle of that sort of 'press conference.'" He used finger quotes for emphasis.

"As opposed to the Greek 'justice system' dragging its name through the mud on the way to lynching our employee for a murder he didn't commit?" She, too, used finger quotes. "Frankly, Commander, I think it's time to drag a hell of a lot of other names into this."

"Is that wise?"

"There's only one way to find out."

"That could be dangerous."

She blinked. "I beg your pardon?"

"Don't look at me that way. You know precisely what I'm saying. You're as aware of the scum out there involved in this refugee-trafficking trade as am I. They killed Volandes and won't hesitate to do the same to anyone else they think threatens them."

"Are you telling me you know Ali didn't do it?"

"Are you taping this?"

"No. Are you?"

He gestured no. "The thing is…" he paused. "Your man's far safer in here than on the outside."

"What are you saying?"

The commander leaned toward her across his desk. "Assuming Ali didn't do it, you must admit he's been set up through a very well thought-out plan. The perfect ending for such a plan would be if the primary suspect turns up dead, in a manner establishing him as Volandes' killer. That gives everyone involved a simple solution to a messy situation. Case closed, end of story." He slapped his hands together.

"Are you serious?"

"I wish I weren't, but it's happened before."

"How close are you to finding the real killer?"

He shrugged. "The investigation is being run out of Athens."

"That's not an answer."

"It's the only one I have."

"Sounds like more political cover-up."

He gestured no. "The guy in charge isn't like that."

"Says who?"

"Everybody."

"Oh, good old *everybody*. That fellow seems to turn up whenever there's a call for a show of hands from those who believe in saving the lives of their fellow man, but conveniently disappears whenever asked to do something like feed, clothe, or allow a refugee to move into *everybody's* country."

"This isn't a political debate. I'm talking about a cop trying to do his job to help your friend."

"No, what you're telling me is to wait around doing nothing until something else happens. What's that going to be, a murder prosecution or funeral for Ali?"

"I think you ought to give our man in Athens time."

"For what? For you or him to get lucky and find the guy who swung the sword? Big deal if you have your killer, you're still no closer to those behind this 'very well-thought-out plan.'" More finger quotes. "Those bastards will still be out there, hiring others to murder the next caring soul who threatens their business."

"Which could be you."

"I'm willing to take that risk to stop them."

Knock knock.

"Who's there?" said the commander

"It's me," said an attractive young woman who wore no police uniform. "I need to speak with you. It's…oh, sorry, I didn't know you had someone in your office."

"That's all right, we'll be done soon, won't we, Ms. McLaughlin?"

"In a few minutes."

"Okay, but it's important, Dad. It has to do with that report because—"

"Excuse me, Ms. McLaughlin. I've been rude. Permit me to introduce you to my daughter. Aleka, this is Dana McLaughlin, she's the head of SafePassage, the NGO employing the young man accused of killing Mihalis Volandes."

"Pleased to meet you," said Dana.

"You, too," said Aleka. "I'll wait outside until you're finished." She closed the door.

Dana stared at the closed door. "She looks familiar."

"Not surprised, it's a small island."

Dana swung around to face the commander. "Not all that small. So, where were we?"

"You were telling me how you were willing to die to get to the bottom of this."

"Not quite, but you get my point."

"I trust you'll reconsider pressing for Ali's release."

Dana nodded. "I promise you I'll think about it. But I do want to see him."

"Okay. Just do me a favor."

"What is it?"

"Don't announce in your press conference that I gave you permission to see him."

"Fine," said Dana. "If it comes up, I'll blame it on the cop at the front desk."

"Please don't do that either; my sister would never forgive me."

"He's your nephew?"

The commander shrugged. "It's Greece."

"I get it, family matters."

"Which, if we're done here, reminds me that I'd better see what my daughter wants."

Dana got up to leave.

"Do yourself a favor, Ms. McLaughlin. If you trust me, please let me know before you say anything that might make you a target, and perhaps, together, we can figure out a way to move you out of the line of fire."

"That's very decent of you."

"I'd tell the same thing to my daughter if she were considering taking the sorts of risks you are." He looked at the door. "Just let me know. Okay?"

"I'll keep it in mind. Thanks. Bye."

Dana opened the door and left. Aleka rushed past her, through the open door, headed straight for the chair by her father's desk.

• • ● • •

"What was she doing here?"

"Close the door."

Aleka did, and sat in the chair. "So, why was she here?"

"Proving to me that you're not the only strong-willed woman on this island."

"What's that supposed to mean?"

The commander smiled. "Precisely what it sounded like." He sighed. "So what happened at work today?"

"My boss and his secretary spent the entire morning tearing the office apart, looking for his notes."

"What did they say to you?"

"Nothing until after they'd finished looking. He asked if I'd seen the notes and I said no. He asked if I'd been in the office over the weekend and I said no."

"That was it?"

"Until he asked me to sign a duplicate copy of the notes."

"What did you tell him?"

"That I'd like to read them."

"And?"

"He went ballistic. Screamed at me, called me disloyal, said that I risked putting his entire office at risk over my petulant attitude."

"He actually said that?"

"Called me petulant twice, and finished by yelling that if I didn't sign them at once, he'd fire me on the spot."

"So, you're here looking for a job?"

"Nope."

"I don't understand."

"I signed the notes."

"*You what?* Are you crazy?" He slammed his palms on his desk. "We went through all this before. You were going to refuse. I can't believe that after all the risks you took, you commit career suicide just because an asshole's ranting at you.

This doesn't sound like you at all."

"Well, I didn't think about it quite that way. I figured from how worked up he was, if I didn't sign, he'd likely panic, and who knew what he might do, or who else might get hurt."

"So, instead you decided to guarantee you'll get hurt."

"Not really."

He slapped the desktop again. "You signed the damn notes."

"Not really."

"Have you lost your mind? You just told me you signed the notes."

She smiled. "Yes, I did, but what I scribbled as my signature were the words, 'I disagree.'"

The commander stared at his daughter. "And he never bothered to read your signature?"

"How often do you check a signature you saw signed in front of you?"

He smiled. "As of this moment, always."

The cell stood barely wide enough for the man to stand beside a pair of metal bunk beds anchored lengthwise to the wall. A metal toilet and tiny sink mounted against the opposite wall took up much of the rest of the open space. Dana stood outside the flat vertical bars lining the front of the cell. The other three sides of the cell were made of dirty beige concrete, and none had a window. Light came in through translucent panels spaced along the vertical edge of the building's sawtooth-style roof and two barred windows at the end of a long hallway.

"How are you holding up, my friend?" she asked.

"They're feeding me, I have no cellmate, and I'm not being tortured, so life is good." Ali Sera smiled.

"How can you keep smiling?"

He shrugged. "I've lived through worse. Others on this island are living in far worse conditions than I. God knows I am innocent, and with God's help I shall be spared."

"But look at this place." She waved her hands all around her.

"My attorney said that by law I should be transferred to a different place. A place for those charged with crimes like mine."

"When will that be?"

"He said if the police don't do it by tomorrow, he will ask the court to order it."

Dana bit at her lip. "Do you want to go?"

He shrugged. "Do I have a choice?"

"My question is, do you want to leave?"

"I see no reason to move. I am comfortable here. I'm alone, and it's quiet."

The commander's words about Ali's death solving a lot of problems for a lot of people rang in her ears. A prison filled with serious criminals and cooperative authorities would be a perfect place for executing such arrangements. Literally.

"Do me a favor. Tell your lawyer *not* to ask the court to order your move."

"Why?"

She reached through the bars and patted his arm. "I want to keep you close by. We all do."

Ali sat staring out through the bars after Dana had left. He knew she meant well, she always had. She'd thrown her heart and soul into Volandes' plan, thinking that together they could forever change the dynamics of addressing refugees by infusing the process with dignity and common sense.

Volandes' plan stood based on the simple principle that no matter what the EU might wish, refugee migration would never end. They'd continue coming, risking death if necessary. Neither a callous disregard of their plight, nor free and open borders were viable solutions. A true solution required a workable platform allowing for a speedy determination of who may enter and who may not, operating in a civilized, humane, and organized environment.

The plan envisioned ferryboat-size ships, equipped with medical, social, and immigration services working side by side, processing refugees picked up on shores now ruled by traffickers. Their claims would be addressed on board with dignity and respect, and those granted entry, delivered to welcome centers and fully processed for the next step in their journey. Those denied entry would be set ashore in safe harbors outside the EU. All for a cost far less than what is now expended on an existing jumble of governmental policies and programs in shambles.

Ali kept staring. Even if Mihalis had lived, Ali wasn't sure his plan would have come to pass, much less actually have changed anything in a meaningful way. But to be fair, Ali had a different perspective than Dana or Mihalis, what with so much of his life spent looking up from the bottom of the refugee barrel.

Chapter Ten

Andreas sat with his eyes fixed on the computer screen, searching for a program that linked faces to names. If Facebook could do it, there must be others. There had to be. All he needed was the right database. Interpol had come up empty. Same with MI-6, CIA, Mossad. He'd not yet heard back from Greece's own intelligence services but wasn't holding his breath.

How the hell could there be no record of this guy anywhere?

He doubted he'd get any luckier on his own, but at least trying helped assuage his frustration.

Yianni poked his head in the doorway. "I heard from the Mytilini police commander. No luck on turning up whatever the killer used to spatter Ali with Volandes' blood. And no better word on the sword."

"Any other good news?"

"Only that I'm heading home if you don't need me."

"I'm pissed."

"At me?"

"The world." Andreas pointed at his screen. "How could there be no record in some database somewhere of this guy? He's a professional assassin."

Yianni nodded. "What are we dealing with? That Jackal guy from Venezuela?"

"He had KGB protection. People knew him."

"Maybe this guy's protected too?"

Andreas nodded toward the screen. "Yeah, but that was way before all this technology and mobile phone cameras existed. It's hard to imagine that no one knows him or ever took a picture of him that hasn't made it into some data file somewhere."

Yianni dropped onto the couch in front of the windows. "Maybe he goes in for plastic surgery."

Andreas shrugged. "Maybe. But he certainly doesn't show any concern over hiding his face. He walked straight at that camera, fully knowing what he was doing. It's as if he's daring us to identify him."

"Perhaps we're going at this the wrong way."

"What's that supposed to mean?" Andreas let go of his computer mouse and picked up a pencil.

"If none of the big boy agencies can identify our guy from his photo, either he's protected or not in their databases. If the former, we'll never hear about it. If the latter, he knows how to defeat the software and stay off the radar."

"How could he defeat the software? If he ever had a passport, driver's license, school ID, you name it, his photo would be in the system."

Yianni gestured no. "Not necessarily. Agencies know how to scrub their agents from those files. Like I said, it's how they protect their own."

"You're saying he's government?"

"No, I'm saying technology exists to keep him from turning up in searches. And since that exists, who's to say that, with the right sort of connections…" Yianni rubbed his thumb and forefinger together, "or cash, this guy couldn't make himself unofficially officially anonymous."

"That's a hell of a conspiracy theory, even for a Greek."

"I'll take that as a compliment."

"So, Detective Kouros, how do you propose we identify this guy if we can't find anything out about him officially?"

"To catch a thief…."

"It takes a thief?"

"Yep. If he's as efficient and deadly professional an assassin as we think, whether or not we've ever heard of him, he's probably known to his peers."

"Assuming you're right, how's that help us?" said Andreas. "I don't happen to know any international assassins willing to chit-chat with police about their colleagues."

"Yes, you do. At least one who might be willing."

"Who?"

"Oh, that's right, you never met him." Yianni paused. "But I did."

"You're beginning to be as much of a dramatic pain in the ass as Tassos. Get to your punch line already."

"I even know where he lives."

"Yianni, I swear—"

"Delphi."

Andreas paused. "Kharon?"

"Yep. If anyone might know him, it'd be Kharon."

"But why in the world do you think he'd talk to us?"

"He has a different life now. He's in the olive oil business. He's gone legit."

"And you think you're going to squeeze him into cooperating by threatening his new life?"

Yianni put up both hands. "Whoa. I'm not suicidal."

"But he's one hundred percent homicidal." Andreas shook his head. "Perhaps you forgot everything we did to stay off that maniac's radar. We didn't want him even suspecting we were on to him. Now you want us to drop in on his new life, tell him we know all about his past life—assuming it actually is past—ask that he please identify a fellow dirtbag killer, and hope he won't take that as some sort of threat. Are you crazy?"

"Probably. Otherwise, I wouldn't be a cop." Yianni stretched. "Do you have any other ideas on how to get a lead on our unidentifiable bad guy?"

"Not yet, but I'm working on it," said a clench-jawed Andreas.

"Great, you work on it your way, and I'll work on it mine."

Andreas pointed his pencil directly between Yianni's eyes. "Don't be a hero. He's not someone to mess with."

"No need to remind me of that. Trust me, I know I'd likely be dead if he'd not told me to walk out of that taverna in Thessaloniki."

"Not likely. Absolutely. And he didn't let you live because he liked you; he did it because not killing you served his plans."

"I still think it's worth the risk. We've hit a dead end and Kharon's our best, if not only, shot at identifying our killer."

Andreas shook his head. "I still don't like your idea."

"It beats a sharp stick in the eye."

"Maybe, but not by much."

● ● ● ● ●

On his way to the kitchen, Aryan caught Malik's wife sitting alone by the fire in the family room staring at the flames.

"A bit chilly tonight."

The woman jumped.

"Sorry, I didn't mean to startle you."

Her eyes watched him as if he were a wild dog threatening to attack.

"We really haven't had the chance to properly meet, what with all the excitement surrounding our initial meeting." He stepped forward extending his hand toward her.

She pulled back in her chair, clutching her hands tightly across her stomach, and staring at his outstretched hand.

He stopped a pace in front of her. "I understand why you are afraid of me. It's only natural. And, of course, you should be." He let his hand fall to his side. "But we can still be civil to one other." He dropped into a crouch, bringing his eyes level with hers. "After all, who better than I to appreciate how you dread the violence surrounding your life...the distractions you create in your mind to justify all of this," he waved a hand about the room, "and your constant fear at losing your never-ending battle to protect your children from learning the truth about their father."

She looked away, and he knew he had her.

He lowered his voice but kept his distance. "You carry a great burden as the lone protector of your children's innocence, fearing every day that they'll learn about the suffering exploited by your husband, the pain inflicted by him, the children who die at his hands to support your family's lifestyle…" Aryan's voice trailed off. "How often do you wish for a better life for your children, the life you once dreamed of for yourself?"

He stood. "We're not that different from one another. I made choices long ago, and now I regret how I must live my life. But, like you, I had little choice, coming from the desperate background that I did. You and I must live with our choices. I just hope that your children don't have to live with yours. Or, better yet, that you find a way to bring your life and your children's closer to your dreams."

He extended his hand. "I'm…Ari."

She stared at his hand, inches from her face, then at his eyes. "Deema. My name is Deema." She did not take his hand.

Yianni's drive northwest of Athens to the modern village of Delphi took just over two hours. A further twenty-minute descent along the limestone slopes of Mount Parnassus brought him to the heart the Amfissa-Chrisso-Itea Valley. Tens of thousands of hundred-year-old olive trees spread out in rows across broad expanses of this flat fertile triangle, stretching from the Gulf of Corinth's harbor town of Itea, northwest to the town of Amfissa, and northeast to the picture-perfect village of Chrisso. Here grew the finest olives in the region.

Here, too, Kharon made his home and ran his olive business in quiet, agrarian anonymity. A life far different from what one

might expect of a man still feared as one of Europe's most subtle, efficient, and highly paid assassins.

How all this had come to pass, Yianni did not know, but the
ingredients of Kharon's life were well known: orphaned on the
day he was born, raised on life lessons taught in government
orphanages for the unwanted children of the damned and
the poor, branded by the media a savage killer at thirteen for
defending younger boys from rape, and trained as a military
killing machine at eighteen. Now, anonymity and a life at
peace with the land were all Kharon desired.

Or so Yianni hoped.

Yianni had left Athens a half hour or so after dawn. By
ten a.m., he found what he was looking for. He parked his
unmarked police cruiser at the edge of a patch of dirt and gravel
directly across from the front door to an olive press facility of
weather-beaten stucco and old stone. Growers in the valley
came here to convert their olives into oil but, as harvest season
had just passed, the lot sat deserted except for a dusty, vintage
BMW motorcycle parked next to the front door.

This was Kharon's place of business, and Yianni gambled on
it being a less threatening spot to confront him than his home.
Yianni sat in the cruiser facing the windows along the first floor
of the building. He made no effort to get out or do anything
but sit. Fifteen minutes into his wait, the front door to the
building swung open and a man he'd met only once stood in
the doorway, gesturing for him to come inside.

Yianni swallowed hard, opened the car door, and stepped
out. He felt the gravel crunch beneath his feet as his mind went
blank, and he wondered why in the world he'd thought this a
good idea.

"Welcome, Officer. Long time no see."

He remembers me. Yianni cleared his throat. *Suck it up,
Kouros.*

He extended his right hand as he approached Kharon. "It's
detective, and I never had the chance to thank you for that pass
you gave me in Thessaloniki."

The tall, well-built man hesitated slightly before shaking Yianni's hand. He had a few years of age and a full head of dark hair over Yianni. "Now that we've cleared the decks of any pretenses over whom we know each other to be, perhaps you could tell me what you're doing here."

Kharon closed the front door and pointed Yianni toward two chairs next to a battered wooden table close by the windows. "I can make us some coffee if you'd like."

"Thank you, but no need to trouble yourself." Yianni turned his back to Kharon and walked toward the table.

"I like your style. Suggesting that you trust me by showing me your back."

"Why shouldn't I trust you?" said Yianni, turning to face him as he sat on one of the chairs.

Kharon sat on the other. His eyes suggested a smile, but not his face. "Oh, I don't know, but there must be some reason. I couldn't help but notice how you kept an eye on me in the reflection in the window."

Yianni smiled. "Force of habit."

"Military?"

"DYK."

Kharon nodded. "Greece's special ops brotherhood equivalent to America's Navy SEALs. I assume you already know my background."

Yianni nodded. "Impressive."

"So, why are you here?"

"I think what's likely most important to you is why I'm not here. I'm not here for anything that has to do with you. You are completely off our radar. Your past is your past. We don't care about it."

"That's hard for me to believe in light of one incontrovertible fact."

"Which is?"

"You're here because of my past."

"I think when you hear why I'm here you'll understand what I just said is true. This has nothing to do with you."

Kharon shrugged.

"We need your help with a name. Nothing more. If you can give it to me, great. If you can't, we're no worse off than we were before. I'm here unofficially. No one else knows. Whether you can help or not, I'll be out of here and you'll never hear from me again." He pulled a business card out of his pocket and laid it on the table. "Unless you want to reach me."

"What, no threats of tax or employee benefit audits? Of letting the world know who I am?" Kharon's voice had taken on a slight edge.

"Like I said. Period, end of story. I'm here because we need the name of a very bad guy. Just how bad I don't have to say, because if you know him, I'm sure you won't need any convincing from me."

"Are you wearing a wire?"

"No. And I'm not taking notes. All I'm hoping for is an ID."

Kharon stared at Yianni's eyes. "Show me what you have."

Yianni slowly pulled a folded photo out of his inside jacket pocket, opened it, and laid it on the table between them.

Kharon stared at the photo. "You took this off a CCTV?"

"Yes."

Kharon stared at it a bit longer. Without looking up he said, "How many children did he kill?"

Yianni felt goosebumps run up the back of his neck. "He sacrificed a baby."

Kharon turned his head toward a window looking out upon the olive trees. "Is he tied into that Greek family murdered in Turkey?"

Yianni nodded. "We think so."

"The Turkish police must be moving heaven and earth to find their assassin."

"We hope so."

Kharon jerked his head back from the window and fixed a dead cold glare on Yianni's eyes. "And what about the Greek police. Are you doing the same?"

Yianni felt his stomach tighten. "I don't follow. I meant it when I said this isn't about you."

"You understand me perfectly. This is not about a dead Greek family in Turkey, and it's not you I'm concerned about. It's all the other cops, on both sides of the Aegean, stumbling about looking for assassins. Who knows who they might unearth in the process?"

"I can assure you—"

Kharon held up his hand to stop him. "He goes by the name Aryan, but he's Swiss. Deadly with firearms and hand-to-hand, though he prefers to work with edged weapons. He considers them his trademark. If you ask me, his real trademark is his arrogance. It's also his primary weakness."

"Any idea where he lives?"

"No. But he's in his late-thirties, usually works as a mercenary in conflicts where atrocities are tolerated, even encouraged. He thrives on that, driven by some sort of bloodlust. He and I never saw eye-to-eye on his methods. There's no love lost between us." Kharon leaned back in his chair. "If you're here because of some new assassination he pulled off, let's say, for example, using a sword on an old man living on a Greek island off the Turkish coast, then I'd say he's branching out into new territory."

Yianni blinked. "Why would he be doing that?"

"Perhaps he's looking to retire. Trying to find himself an easier gig than facing death every day." His eyes seemed to twinkle for an instant. "Like pressing olives."

Yianni wasn't sure what to say to that, so he just nodded.

Kharon continued. "This guy is so twisted it's hard to imagine him walking away from the rush he gets taking lives. He might just be looking for a somewhat more controlled environment to operate in than a war zone. Too many chances to die in war."

"What sort of controlled environment?"

Kharon looked up at the ceiling. "Oh, I don't know, possibly something simpler." His gaze returned to Yianni. "Like refugee trafficking. After all, those victims don't shoot back."

"Do you have a real name for him?"

"Last name Kennel, as in dog. First name Alban or Adrian or something similar. I don't recall."

Yianni stood, and extended his hand. "Thank you. I owe you."

Kharon rose and shook it. "Twice."

* * *

He has guts, thought Kharon as he watched through the windows at Yianni driving away. *He knew where to find me. If he'd wanted to arrest me or bust my balls he could have done it without coming at me face-to-face.* He looked down at Yianni's card on the table. *This cop's not the problem. It's the ones that Swiss madman will attract that worry me.*

His eyes moved onto the photo of Aryan that Yianni had left on the table. *I've spent a lifetime surrounded by crazies. But this one's a megalomaniac obsessed with killing as the solution to any problem. He sees atrocities as a sign of his absolute power. And now he's moved into my neighborhood.*

That's not good. Not good at all.

* * *

"It's Yianni," yelled Maggie through the open door.

Andreas picked up the phone. "How did it go?"

"I'm still breathing." Yianni told him the details of his meeting with Kharon.

"Do you think he'll warn Aryan that we're on to him?"

"I don't think so. He had no reason to tell me what he did. And he clearly didn't like this Kennel guy at all."

"What you say makes sense, but who knows what sort of thinking motivates these kinds of guys?"

"That's why I got out of there as soon as I could. Calm, cool, logical-sounding killer types all have way too many parts missing."

"And a lot of what remains is seriously defective."

"But from the way he reacted to that photo, I'd say he considers Kennel a different species. One he wants us to catch."

"That's reassuring," said Andreas. "We've got one of the world's top assassins considering the guy we're after sick and twisted."

Yianni grunted agreement.

"As for Kharon's motive, I'd say he's given us that. Whenever cops are searching for a professional assassin in Greece, Kharon retired or not, is a potential target. This isn't about any altruistic desire on his part to better society. It's all tied into Kharon's primal instinct for self-preservation. He wants us to find Kennel in order to take the heat off himself."

"Either way, we've got an ID."

"I'll get Maggie working on Mister Kennel. If Kharon's right about Kennel working his way into the refugee trade, I think we're going to see a lot more bodies turning up, of both good guys and bad."

"Why do you think that?"

"I don't know. I just feel it. Perhaps I'll have a better idea after I see what Maggie comes up with."

"And if not?"

"We'll just have to wait and see what Kennel does next."

"If he returns to Greece, we can arrest him at the border," said Yianni.

"For what? Having his photo taken at a crime scene in Turkey? We have no reason to hold him, and every reason not to alert him that we're onto him. If we're lucky enough to catch him entering Greece, let's just hope it's someplace where we have people who can follow him."

"Good luck on that in these days of budget cuts."

"I'm more concerned with sword cuts."

Chapter Eleven

Malik's home sat inland, above an agrarian landscape that drew no crowds for its beauty. For scenery, you wandered down by the sea. Here, you came to work the land, to earn a living off it, to survive. Aryan chose to avoid it all. The outdoors made him too convenient a target for a sniper.

He remained inside the house biding his time, waiting for the opportunity he knew would come to make his move on the right people, and drawing Deema into conversations she'd never dare have with him in public.

Their first conversation lasted close to an hour, in hushed tones, as the children played videogames in their playroom. She told him how her parents immigrated to this area from the north when she was three and her brother, Jamal, nine. Her parents never spoke of why they'd moved, or of any of the family they'd left behind. She asked them once, and their reply was sharp and immediate: they had no life before the one they now lived, and she should always look forward, never back.

Aryan said each of his parents had been the only child of couples who'd fled Germany to Switzerland at the end of World War II and, as with Deema's family, neither his parents nor grandparents talked about their pasts. Aryan had no siblings, and not until his parents died in an automobile accident when he was seventeen did he have even an inkling of his family's past. That's when he learned he was heir to a vast fortune of artwork and gems, but of a sort he could not sell, except to special buyers who cared not for their provenance and paid only pennies on the dollar of their value.

He told Deema that she should be happy not knowing what her parents had kept from her, for once he realized his roots ran deep into a brutal Nazi past, his anger at the lies on which he'd been raised drove him nearly mad. He fled his fortune in search of wars to fight, wars where he could hopefully die fighting bravely for a just cause.

But he survived and only grew angrier each time he dodged death. He took greater chances, acted more brutally to draw retaliation, and gave up caring on which side he fought, as long as it promised the risk of dying in battle.

He paused at that point in his story to catch Deema's eyes. "That's when I realized I'd become more brutal than the worst of what I'd imagined of my own family's shameful past, and yet I felt strangely at peace. I'd found an answer offering me redemption: Our world runs on no single moral code of right and wrong. Only survival matters. You do what you must to protect your family, yourself."

He could tell his words were reaching her. He'd worked hard at telling his story, watching her eyes and measuring her breathing as he did, and in the process, almost believing it all himself.

Dana picked what she thought a dramatic venue for her press conference, then began wondering whether she'd be arrested. Arrests of international aid workers in Western countries had once attracted media attention, but with all the terrorist attacks these days, and her nation's wildly tweeting President, it took a hell of a story to break in on the news cycle, and a simple arrest wouldn't likely cut it.

But who knew? Perhaps one of Greece's *National Inquirer* clones would run a "Refugee Aid Worker Pleads for Her

Murdering Man" sort of story, though that wasn't the angle she was hoping for. No, she needed serious attention. Which was why she picked the front entrance to the Mytilini police station.

She'd teased the press conference with the various news services by announcing a "major international development in the Mihalis Volandes murder case," and kept interest building into the early afternoon by responding to all requests pressing her for a hint of what she'd be saying with the comment, "For the safety of my staff and myself, we can only reveal details in the presence of the police."

By the time Dana arrived, the cameras were waiting. So was the commander.

"What the hell is going on?" was his greeting.

"Hi, Commander. As I told you yesterday, we're having a press conference about the Volandes case."

"Not at my front door."

"I don't plan on saying anything bad about you or your police."

"That's nice to hear, but you're still not holding it here."

"Well, we can't move it now that everyone's here."

"You'll have to."

"Then you'll have to arrest me in front of all these cameras." She waved her hand in front of a phalanx of television cameras, some of which had begun filming. "I have the distinct impression that an image going out across the world of Lesvos police arresting the head of a widely respected NGO refugee organization just as she's about to reveal new developments in the brutal murder of its largest benefactor will overshadow any nice things I might have to say about you or your department in the undoubtedly far more widely anticipated and attended press conference I shall hold the moment I'm released." She put on a happy face for the cameras and patted him on the shoulder. "You might want to smile."

He simply stared at her. "Just don't block the entrance." He turned and walked inside.

She turned to face the cameras, and immediately a gaggle of reporters waved her toward an improvised lectern ringed with microphones. She still felt the adrenaline from her little victory over the police commander. But now what? This could be the biggest dud of a press conference of all time. Worse still, it could backfire and turn Ali into a whipping boy for refugee-haters. She took a deep breath to calm her nerves, and told herself to sound professional.

You better not fuck this up, McLaughlin.

"Ladies and gentlemen, my name is Dana McLaughlin, and I am executive director of operations on Lesvos for SafePassage. As I'm certain you know, all of us mourn the loss of a uniquely caring soul who sought no honors or profit for himself, but only to better the lives of hundreds of thousands of innocents seeking refuge in Europe from the terror and violence haunting their homelands. Children, wives and mothers, husbands and fathers simply looking for a place to live out their lives in peace.

"But that was not to be. Instead, those who find profit in terror and violence came to Mihalis Volandes' home, to his front door, and struck him down to send a brutal, bloody message to any others who might dare to threaten their multi-billion-euro refugee-trafficking business. It is the shame of our time, our world, the European Union, and this nation that we allow them to escape without so much as a whisper of blame.

"And I say shame because we know who is behind it, we know who profits, and yet we do not seem to care. But I care." Dana pointed to her colleagues. "We care."

She pointed at the cameras. "And I hope you care."

She paused. "I know you've all heard that Ali Sera, an employee of our organization, has been arrested for the murder. But we know he did not do it. Even the police know he's innocent. But for some, it's convenient to label him—a brave and loyal supporter of Mr. Volandes—as a scapegoat.

"Let there be no doubt in anyone's mind that Mihalis Volandes died on the direct orders of those who control refugee trafficking to Greece's shores. Nothing happens without their approval, and the lines of authority are clear and responsive."

A reporter yelled, "Give us names."

Dana smiled. "I'm afraid our friends on the Greek police would not take kindly to my disclosing their names at this point in their investigation."

"What investigation?" asked the same reporter.

"The one currently being conducted by the Greek Police's Special Crimes Unit."

"Are you sure of that?" said another reporter.

"Ask its chief, Andreas Kaldis."

"What makes you so sure it's some broad-based conspiracy, and not simply the act of your friend in police custody?"

"Ali is a friend, but he's also innocent, and when the hard evidence is made public, you'll see that it's true."

"Then why's he still in jail?" asked a female reporter.

"For his own protection. Mihalis Volandes' killer will not hesitate to do the same to anyone who could identify him."

A second of total silence broke into a cacophony of competing questions. "Are you saying Ali can identify the killer?" cried the loudest voice.

Dana raised her hand. "I really can't get into that."

The same question kept coming.

"I'm sorry, but I can't say any more on that."

"Well, what more can you say?" asked the same woman.

"That's fair. Permit me to point more precisely to where you'll find who's behind this evil stalking Greece and Europe, and with the investigative resources at your disposal, I'm certain at least one of you will be able to identify the person I'm not at liberty to name."

She paused and pointed southeast. "Izmir. That's where you'll find the man who ordered the assassination of Mihalis Volandes."

● ● ● ● ●

From the moment Dana pointed her finger at Izmir, the phone in Andreas' office hadn't stopped ringing. Apparently, nothing she'd said beyond that had anywhere near the impact of slandering Greece's biggest competitor for the Aegean tourist's euro, ruble, dollar, yuan, whatever.

Included among the calls was a tirade delivered to Maggie from Andreas' new boss for "not keeping him in the loop," and a request from the Prime Minister's office for an "immediate briefing." Andreas told Maggie to give them all the same answer. "The chief inspector has not yet seen the press conference and will have nothing to say until he has."

Networks immediately e-mailed Maggie links to Dana's performance.

A grim-faced Andreas sat watching in silence alongside Maggie and Yianni.

"What a dumb bitch," growled Maggie.

"Sure glad you said that and not me," said Yianni.

"What sort of a lunatic makes this stuff up? She's claiming there's a James Bond-style mastermind villain hanging out in Izmir, and that the chief knows who he is. Is she trying to get you killed?"

Andreas ran the fingers of his right hand across his forehead. "She might be a bitch, but she's certainly not dumb, and not likely a lunatic either." He leaned forward. "She just focused the entire nation on the plight of her friend by embellishing only slightly on the obvious. Yes, we are conducting an investigation, yes, I am in charge, and yes, we are convinced Ali didn't do it, and that someone is setting him up. It also didn't take much guesswork on her part to point a finger at Izmir as the heart of refugee smuggling out of Turkey into the Northern Aegean islands, and a very well-organized and politically protected heart, at that."

"How would she know it's protected?" said Yianni.

Andreas shrugged and picked up a pencil. "She deals with refugees more than any of us. It's not much of a secret. Or a leap of logic, for those who don't already know. Andreas twirled the pencil between his fingers. "The only thing I can't figure out, is why she decided to throw a dart at Izmir as home to whoever's at the top of the refugee-trafficking food chain. Does she really know who it is?"

"Maybe we should ask her," said Maggie.

"I doubt she'll have an answer, but by asking, at least it shows we care." Andreas looked at Yianni. "You haven't called her yet, have you?"

"I was going to give her a call today, but things got a bit hectic."

"No problem. Give her a call now, and see what she has for us. But don't give her any information beyond what she already knows, and be sure to keep your temper in check when she starts to go at you."

"Over what?"

"Who knows, but it will be something."

"Maybe you should make the call."

"Nope."

"Why not?"

"Because I won't be able to control my temper," said Andreas, snapping the pencil between his fingers.

As soon as the press conference ended, the commander motioned for Dana to follow him inside the building.

"Am I being arrested?"

"That would be too easy on you. I just want to get some details for my records, like the name and address of your next of kin."

"That's a bit dramatic, wouldn't you say?"

"Not after your performance out there. You do realize, of course, you just put a target the size of this island between your shoulder blades."

"Like I told you before, it's a risk I'm prepared to take."

"And pinned another on your buddy, Ali. Is he prepared to take the risk?"

"It had to be done."

"To do what? Piss off the only cop in Greece who might have been able to help you nail the bastards you're so convinced took out Volandes?"

"You think you're that cop?"

"Me? Not a chance. This situation is way outside my jurisdiction."

"If you're talking about Kaldis, he had it coming. It's been five days since he promised to help Ali, but he hasn't done a thing for him."

"You're as headstrong as my daughter."

"What's that supposed to mean? I don't owe Kaldis a thing, and whether this lights a fire under his ass or gets him fired, either way, Ali's better off."

The commander shook his head. "You ought to spend a lot less time talking and a hell of a lot more on learning what you're talking about."

"What? You're going to defend Kaldis now?" She shook her head. "Right. Of course. Cops always stick up for each other."

"That may be true, but it's clear you know nothing about Andreas Kaldis."

"What's to know? He's like every other cop, except he has a big-time job that he keeps by doing political favors and errands for his masters in Athens."

He stared at her. "I think the clinical term for the sort of incredibly off-the-wall scenarios you create in your mind to justify your behavior is *delusional.*"

"You have no basis for insulting me."

"I didn't call you an arrogant, ill-informed little shit, I called you *delusional,* and if you want confirmation of that," he pointed out the front door, "go back out there and repeat in front of the cameras what you just told me about Kaldis and see what happens. You'll be laughed off the island. In fact, out of Greece, because you'll just have proved to everyone who hears your rant that you have absolutely no idea what you're talking about."

Dana's right eye began to twitch. "Why, because he has a big title?"

"I'm amazed at how little you know about the political landscape of the country you're working in, not to mention the people you decide to piss off. Every bad guy in Greece knows Andreas Kaldis can't be bribed. He's married into one of Greece's most prominent and wealthy families. He's already served as Minister of Public Order and could do so again if he wanted, but prefers catching bad guys. As for political connections, he saved the Prime Minister's life. He's untouchable. And if he doesn't lift another finger on this case, it won't mean a damned thing one way or other to him, his career, or his life."

The commander sighed. "And you, in the delusional passion of your headstrong I'll-save-the-world fantasy, just tried to fuck him. Good luck."

She looked down. "You're wrong about me."

He turned and walked back toward his office, leaving Dana standing alone.

She watched him walk away, turned, and stared out toward the departing media trucks.

Now what?

Aryan found Deema draped in a black shawl reading alone in the second-floor sunroom. She sat framed in floor-to-ceiling windows, matted against an azure sky. He'd noticed she seemed to favor out-of-the-way places, shunning the home's grander, more ostentatiously furnished and gilded rooms.

He didn't know how long he'd been standing in the doorway before Deema caught him staring at her.

"What are you doing?"

"Watching you." He smiled.

She didn't smile. "You've got to stop this."

"Stop what?"

"Talking with me."

"You don't like talking to me?"

"Malik will be suspicious."

"Of what?" Aryan furrowed his brow as if confused.

"Of our talking."

"We're living in the same house. Why shouldn't we speak?"

Deema shook her head. "You do not understand. My husband is a very jealous man."

Aryan nodded. "Does he beat you?"

She looked down. Silent.

"Why do you stay with him?"

"I cannot leave him. He would kill me."

"What about your brother? Won't he protect you?"

She let loose with a quick nervous laugh. "Jamal? He'd help Malik do it. He's who drove me to marry Malik. Said it would be good for our entire family. Jamal does whatever Malik tells him."

Aryan stepped forward, stopping just in front of her. "Please, stand."

She looked behind him and out the window.

"Don't worry, there's no one here to see us."

"I, I can't...."

"Can't what?" He reached for her hand and gently pulled her to her feet. He put his hands on her shoulders, and pulled off the shawl. She wore a simple, white peasant-style blouse beneath it.

"Turn around, please."

She didn't look at him, but turned.

He placed his hands on her hips just below the bottom of the blouse. He felt her body tense, but she didn't move. He put his hands under her blouse, rested his palms against her skin, and slid them up along her back to her neck, pulling the blouse up along with his hands until it rested on top of her shoulders.

She still didn't move.

He ran the fingers of one hand between her shoulder blades. "He did all of this to you?"

She didn't move.

"You didn't answer me. He cut your skin like this?"

She nodded.

He ran the fingers of both hands softly along the sides of her body, watching goosebumps rise along her back as he did.

"How?"

"With his belt."

"Why?"

"Because I allowed you to see me naked."

"When did you do that?"

"That first night, in the garage."

"You did not allow me to see you. I cut away your clothes with a sword."

"To my husband, if you saw me naked, it was my fault."

Aryan touched her blouse to let it fall back into place. "Please, turn around."

She did, eyes fixed on the floor.

"If he ever hits you again, or even threatens to harm you, tell me."

Her eyes stayed locked on the floor. "I cannot do that, for if I did, the moment you leave us, he would kill me."

He cupped her chin in the palm of one hand and lifted her head until her eyes met his. "Who ever said I'm leaving?" He kissed her on the forehead.

A car roared up toward the front of the house, spitting gravel all the way.

"It's Malik! He knows about us." She ran to grab her shawl.

"There's nothing to know. Don't worry."

"But when he drives like that, he's very angry."

"Good to know. Stay here. I'll deal with him." He kissed her once more on the forehead and headed toward the stairs.

Malik came through the front door just as Aryan reached the bottom of the stairs. Malik waved for Aryan to follow him into his study. "I must speak to you immediately."

Aryan fingered the butt of the nine-millimeter in his small-of-the-back holster. "What's up?"

Malik closed the door behind them. "Your little escapade on Lesvos is now international news."

"Why?"

Malik turned on the television across from his desk. "Listen."

A young blond woman, affecting a serious glare at no one in particular, related what the screen below her flashed as BREAK-ING NEWS. "This morning the Greek government allowed an American representative of an NGO to slander the people of Turkey. At a press conference held outside Mytilini police headquarters, the representative made outrageous charges, linking Turkish citizens to last week's murder of a Greek ship-owner on Lesvos.

"The American said that the individual currently in custody could identify the actual killer, and that both she and the Greek police know who's behind the murder. The Greek police had no comment, and the American refused to disclose any names, though she did say that the one who ordered the assassination could be found 'in Izmir.'"

Aryan pointed at the screen. "That's what has you worked up? It's an obvious bluff intended to get us to make a mistake, or make the Greek police look as if they're actually doing something. If they knew who we were, they'd already be here."

"Maybe," said Malik, "but we're not in Izmir."

"See, I told you, it's all a bluff."

"Too bad my boss doesn't think the same way you do. Maybe then my life—make that our lives—wouldn't be at risk. But, then again, he has a different perspective than you or I, what with him living *in Izmir*."

"Then I think we should talk with him."

"That's precisely what he said. First thing tomorrow morning at his office in Izmir."

Aryan would have liked to be meeting Malik's boss under different circumstances, but then again, opportunities were for seizing.

● ● ● ● ●

It took until after nine p.m. before someone answered the number Yianni had been calling since mid-afternoon.

"Hello, Ms. McLauglin?"

"Speaking."

"My name is Detective Yianni Kouros and I work with Chief Inspector Andreas Kaldis."

"I must have received a half-dozen messages from you saying you wanted to speak with me. Frankly, I was hoping to talk to your boss."

"Hopefully, I'll be a suitable substitute."

"And *hopefully* you speak English."

Keep cool, Yianni. "I'll try my best. We understand you have information on a possible connection between the murder of Mihalis Volandes and a Turkish citizen living in Izmir."

"Is that your way of asking how I came to believe that the head of refugee trafficking into the northern Aegean Islands is based in Izmir?"

"If you wish to interpret it that way, fine. But I'm really just asking for the name of the person you referred to in your press conference earlier today, and any other details that might help us track down Mr. Volandes' killer."

"Oh, so you agree that the man in custody is not the killer?"

"I agree we must follow the evidence wherever it leads us, and if you're aware of anything that might help us find his killer, *whoever that may be*, please share it with us."

"Please excuse me, Detective, but so far I've heard nothing from you or your boss that leads me to believe you're doing anything to find the actual killer."

"Believe me, we are."

"Convince me."

"I'm not sure I know how to do that. You have every right to believe as you please, but we'd just appreciate it if you didn't hold any more press conferences without first running by us what you have in mind to say."

"Are you trying to censor me?"

Easy, Yianni. "No, just trying to make sure you don't inadvertently help the bad guys."

Yianni heard clapping on the other side of the phone.

"Wonderful line, Detective. Who wrote it for you?"

Maggie was right to call her a bitch. "I'm sorry if you see it that way, but from my perspective, all you achieved in your press conference was to warn those who thought they'd covered their tracks that we're on to them."

"Oh, the classic, 'you're interfering in the investigation' routine."

Yianni bit his lip. "It's a classic for a reason, Ms. McLaughlin."

"Fine, give me one reason why I should believe you've done anything to find the real killer."

"I can do better than that. I can tell you that we agree with what you said in the press conference."

"I don't...understand."

"We know who killed Volandes, but if you keep broadcasting that to the world, he'll vanish before we ever have a chance to catch him."

"What's the killer's name?"

"Sorry, I can't tell you."

She laughed. "Aha, more bureaucrat bullshit. How can I believe you if you won't tell me the name?"

Yianni laughed. "Sorry, I don't mean to laugh back at you, but it's hard not to when this conversation started with my asking you for a name and you saying you couldn't provide it. Now the shoe's on the other foot and you're indignant."

"But this is different."

"Only in the sense I never cursed at you."

He heard her swallow. "I'm not going to let you get away with this."

"I suggest you stop thinking of us as your enemy. I also suggest you consider that if you continue to talk to the media as you did today, the only ones likely to 'get away' with anything are those who murdered your friend."

Silence. Then Yianni broke it.

"Why don't you give us the name of the person in Izmir? We need to work together on this."

"Can I trust you with something?"

"What sort of trust?"

"Not to tell it to the press?"

"Yes."

"I don't have a name. I just know that someone sits atop Turkey's refugee-trafficking pyramid, and Izmir is the obvious place for him to be, because we all know it's the logistical center for smuggling refugees into the islands."

"May I ask you a question?" said Yianni.

"Yes."

"Are you recording this conversation?"

"No."

"Same trust stipulation?" said Yianni.

"Yes."

"We agree with you."

"So now what?"

"Let us do our job."

"What about me?"

"Keep your head down. People like this…they strike back hard."

"Are you trying to scare me?" she said.

"Absolutely."

Chapter Twelve

Three hundred kilometers due east of Athens, wrapped around a large blue bay at Turkey's western edge and set off against a mountain backdrop, sat Izmir, Turkey's third largest city behind Istanbul and Ankara. With a busy commercial center of wide boulevards, neighborhoods of modern high-rises mixed in among traditional architecture, and a metropolitan population equivalent in size to Athens, Izmir took pride in itself as a liberal and cultural center, a city of festivals and fairs, and the region's economic powerhouse.

Not so often acknowledged was the nostalgic longing of many residents for the more manageable times of decades past, before waves of immigration and virtually unfettered construction irreparably changed the face and culture of the city, burying some ancient sites in the process.

Izmir was one of the Mediterranean's oldest settlements, with four thousand years of recorded history as an urban center. But in classical times it was known by another name: Smryna. A name burned into Greek, Armenian, and Turkish memories by horrific events that took place there at the end of the Greco-Turkish War of 1919 through1922, and led to an almost unparalleled exchange of populations between Greece and Turkey. In this mutual expulsion, two million people found themselves banished from their homelands and forcibly turned into refugees, solely on the basis of their religions.

It took Aryan and Malik roughly two hours to drive the nearly one hundred fifty kilometers to Izmir, and another forty-five minutes cooling their heels in the reception area of a glass and glitz penthouse office atop one of Izmir's most dramatic and tallest towers. A receptionist with remarkable décolletage finally showed them into a conference room of equally impressive accouterments, each undoubtedly intended to draw similar, fawning attention to their possessor.

She pointed to a chrome-edged oval conference table topped in sleek gray leather and set upon two massive chrome pedestals. Surrounding the table stood twelve neatly arranged swivel chairs of matching chrome and leather, and beneath it all lay an Ardabil Persian rug of undoubtedly great value.

"Please wait there," she said.

Malik sat with his back to the windows, looking down at the tabletop, his hands folded in his lap.

Aryan sat next to him. He spent a moment glancing at the carefully displayed paintings and *objets d'art*, but fixed his eyes on a second door across the room from the one they'd entered by, and adjusted his chair to face it.

To Aryan, the most striking thing about Big Boss' office was the towering view staring west down the bay toward the Aegean, through a wall of floor-to-ceiling windows running the length of the room. In that and all else—the artwork, the furnishings, even the receptionist—he saw an identical purpose: to impress and distract. That's why he kept his focus on the second door.

Their forty-five-minute wait in reception, and a likely additional fifteen or so in here, struck him as a variation on a vintage mind game some practiced, thinking it put supplicants ill at ease. Keep them waiting amid the trappings of your power, work up their insecurities with a show of your prominence, and they'll be on their knees by the time you walk into the room.

Aryan saw it all quite differently. To him, the wait showed indecision on the part of Big Boss. Had they been shown in immediately, that most likely meant Big Boss had a fixed plan in mind for his visitors. The longer he kept them waiting, the calmer Aryan became.

From the way Malik kept wiping his brow with the rumpled handkerchief clutched in his fist, he hadn't reached the same conclusion.

Ten more minutes passed before the second door swung open and a man of Malik's height and build, but of much wider girth, strode through it wearing a dark blue tailored suit, white-on-white shirt, and gold and red Hermès tie. Two men of roughly Aryan's age and height, though more broadly built, followed him into the room, both dressed in dark suits and ties of far lesser quality than their boss'.

Malik jumped to attention. Aryan casually pushed back his chair and rose to his full height. The two men headed straight for him and without a word frisked him from head to toe. He didn't resist.

One man pulled a pen out of Aryan's pocket, and handed it to Big Boss. "Only this on him."

Big Boss studied the pen, unscrewed the cap and studied it some more. "A Montblanc fountain pen. Impressive choice." He sat across the table from Aryan and slid the pen to him.

Aryan stopped it with his fingertips. "Thank you."

"You, too, are impressive," said Big Boss. "At least by reputation."

"Thank you again," said Aryan.

The Big Boss squinted as he leaned in toward Aryan. "Then how come you fucked up so miserably at such a simple task as the killing of one old man?"

Aryan shrugged. "He's dead, the police have their killer, and your message is being broadcast throughout the region and the West, telling any who might think of screwing with your business what will happen to them if they do. The only 'fucked up' thing is how you're reacting."

Big Boss glared. "The world is pointing a finger at Izmir. Which means it's pointing its finger at me." He pounded his fist on the table and sat back.

Aryan smiled. "The world is not pointing a finger at you. One young woman is ranting at the gods in an effort to get you to make a mistake. All she's done is state the obvious and hope you'll do something stupid that exposes you."

Big Boss bristled at "stupid" but did not interrupt.

"Anyone with half a brain realizes that whoever's behind running refugees into Greece from this part of Turkey is based in Izmir. Where else would an operation that big be based? In a hut in the mountains, like my friend Malik's here?" He patted Malik on the back. "Izmir is the obvious guess, and that's all it is. A guess. The woman gave no name because she has no name to give. Nor will she ever, unless you do something that forces those with real power to expose you."

Big Boss stared. "You're a bold one, eh?"

"I think you mean thorough. Something your organization obviously is not. As I see it, you've come to rely on political protection instead of thinking. You react to a challenge with emotion, plan without reason, execute as amateurs, and when something unexpected occurs, panic, and fall back upon the same cycle of shabby thinking as got you into trouble in the first place."

Big Boss clenched his jaw. "I could have you killed for such talk."

"You could try, but I doubt there's anyone in this room capable of doing that."

Big Boss looked at the two men standing off to his left. "Are you sure he has no weapon?"

They nodded.

Aryan picked up the pen and twirled it between his fingers. Big Boss' eyes fixed on the pen.

"Remember what I told you about your organization not being thorough." He flipped the pen in the air with his right hand and caught it with his left.

One of the men reached inside his jacket.

"Uh-uh," said Aryan, pointing the pen at Big Boss with his thumb pressed tightly against the cap. "Not a good idea."

"*Stop*," yelled the boss, raising a hand to his men.

The man withdrew his hand from his jacket. Aryan put the pen back on the table.

"So, where were we?" said Aryan. "Oh, yes, I was giving you my observations on the status of your organization. And please understand I appreciate your reluctance to listen to an outsider, but I do have experience in the areas in which you need great help. For example, your two men are fine specimens, and I've no doubt with proper training they'd be invaluable security for you, but they sorely lack that sort of training."

Big Boss raised his chin. "They could tear you apart with their bare hands."

"Yes, but they're afraid of a simple fountain pen."

Big Boss blinked. "You mean it's not a weapon?"

"Does it matter what it is as long as I made you believe what I wanted you to think?"

Aryan stood and walked along the side of the table away from Malik in the direction of the two men. He'd left the pen on the table, and kept his hands held up in an I'm-not-a-threat gesture as he walked past the men.

"How do you think your men should react to this situation? I'm unarmed with my back to them, admiring all the wonderful antique implements hanging on your wall and attempting to offer you my professional opinion on how to make your business more profitable and less subject to international criticism. So, what is your decision? To address this in a rational, businesslike manner or to take out your anger on me because you need someone to blame for what you wrongly think of as a 'fuck up?'"

Aryan stopped with his back to the room and stared at the display on the wall.

"Why can I not have both?" said the boss. "I'll have them beat you, and listen to you after, once you've learned to show me the proper respect." He nodded at the men and they charged Aryan.

With the speed and grace of a dancer, Aryan stepped forward, placing a foot high on the wall before spinning counterclockwise in mid-air and landing with an antique sword arcing around behind his body in his right hand. The blade caught the first bodyguard squarely in the side of his neck.

The second reached for his gun but froze when the head of the first man bounced at his feet. Aryan stood with the sword poised to arc back clockwise at the second man's neck.

"I shall be merciful and give you the choice. Remove your hand from your jacket or I shall remove your head."

The man slowly lowered his hand. Aryan pressed the point of the sword tightly up against the man's throat as he removed the gun from the man's shoulder holster. "Now, sit next to your boss with your hands on the table."

Big Boss' eyes darted toward the second door as the bodyguard sat on the side of him farthest from Aryan.

"Whether you're thinking of running or praying for someone to come through that door, either will end badly for you. I now have this and I'm very good with it." Aryan lifted the pistol, then stuck it in his belt.

Aryan shook his head at Big Boss. "You're such a disappointment. I truly hoped you'd be more sensible than Malik. Be someone I could work with, serve with honor and loyalty. But you're just like all the others. Foolish, arrogant, and, utterly predictable."

Aryan stooped and picked up the dead man's head by the hair. "And, worst of all, you have no sense of loyalty to your people. You told this poor man," he held up the head, "to beat up a merciless professional killer because your delicate ego took offense. If you were so bothered by me, why didn't you just tell him to kill me and be done with it?"

Aryan walked slowly toward Big Boss. "Of course, I know the answer. You weren't sure yet whether or not you might need me. But you had to teach me a lesson. The same arrogance is what blinded you to my admiring your impressive collection of *kilij* sabers when you ordered this poor man to attack me." He brandished the head again.

"My compliments on your keeping your collection in such pristine fighting condition." He dropped the head onto the table in front of Big Boss. "Be careful, or your arrogance will be the death of you yet," he said softly.

Big Boss sat staring at Malik, his fists tightly clenched on the tabletop.

"I know you now believe you'll have to kill me," said Aryan. "I accept that. Which is why I'd like you to explain to me why I should not kill you first."

Malik's eyes went wide. "You cannot do that. He is my cousin."

"I see. So, if he dies, does that put you in line to take over the family business?"

"You are crazy," said Malik.

"What do you think?" Aryan said to Big Boss.

"You will never get out of here alive."

"Here you go again with the arrogance. If I kill you, who will be interested in coming after me? They'll be too busy trying to take over your empire. What do you say, Malik, would you like to be the new big boss?"

Malik paused for an instant.

Big Boss glared at his cousin. "I'll see you in hell."

"Sure will." Aryan swung the sword around in a powerful arc and a second head bounced onto the table. Malik threw up; the man sitting next to Big Boss stared up at Aryan but didn't move.

Aryan nodded in the direction of the second man and looked at Malik. "What about him, can we trust him?"

"He's not a relative. He's not even Turkish. He's new."

"Well, in that case," Aryan raised his sword above the second man's head. The man crossed himself and shut his eyes.

Aryan brought the sword down point-first into the table. "So, New Man, are you prepared to join us?"

The man swallowed, crossed himself again, and nodded. "Yes."

Aryan smiled. "Even if you don't mean it, that's the smart answer. I'll train you to be loyal. And if you aren't trainable, I'll kill you." He patted the second man on the back.

"Malik, we've got to get out of here, but before we do, we need to come to an agreement on something. As a result of all this," Aryan waved his hand around the room, "things will undoubtedly get very nasty very quickly, and I'm willing to reconsider my decision to stay and partner with you. If you wish, I'll simply disappear and leave you to sort this out on your own." He raised a finger before Malik could speak. "Or, if you prefer, I'll stay as your equal partner in all things, and do what I can to protect you while you try to convince your cousin's family that you weren't behind this.

"Whatever you decide, I suggest you take care or someday soon you'll likely find your own head gracing a table somewhere at the hands of your family." Aryan crossed his arms in a waiting pose. "So, what is your preference? Should I stay or should I go?"

Malik furiously rubbed at his forehead with his handkerchief, trying to avoid looking at the heads in front of him. He stood and headed for the door. "Stay," he said. "Please stay."

Aryan picked up his pen from the table. "Agreed."

Malik drove, his eyes on the rearview as often as on the road before them. Aryan sat in the backseat, directly behind Big Boss' former bodyguard. He gave his name as Tomislav and his origin as Serbian. Aryan spent the trip telling tales of his service at the end of the Yugoslav Wars and barraging Tomislav with questions.

As they turned off the highway onto the road leading up to Malik's home, Aryan leaned forward and patted Tomislav on the shoulder. "Interview complete. You'll do just fine."

Tomislav nodded and forced a smile.

"By the way," said Aryan. "Would you please hand me the automatic I left in the glove compartment when I went up to meet your former boss."

Tomislav hesitated, but opened the glove compartment, picked up the gun by its barrel and handed it to Aryan.

"Well done," said Aryan, reaching for the gun with his left hand. "And I believe this one is yours." He reached around Tomislav's right side and handed him the gun he'd been holding in his hand all the way from Izmir.

Tomislav quickly put it away in his shoulder holster.

The car slid to a stop at the front door to the house. Malik jumped out and ran for the door, headed straight for a bathroom. Aryan strolled into the house behind Tomislav and asked the maid to bring them coffee and something to eat.

Malik came out of the guest bathroom off the entrance foyer, his shirt damp from water he'd tossed on his face. Splashes of blood from his cousin's beheading still stained the front of his shirt, and splotches of dried blood missed by his washing stuck to his hair.

"*Deema*," he yelled.

"Yes?" came a tentative voice from upstairs.

"Don't say yes, come here this instant."

"Malik, we should talk about our arrangement," said Aryan.

"Not now. I must first speak to my wife."

Deema hurried down the stairs. "Yes, Malik, what is…my God, what's happened to you?"

"Don't ask questions, just bring me a new shirt."

"You have blood in your hair." She reached up to touch his hair and he batted her hand away.

"Just do as I *say*."

"But—"

He raised his hand to strike her, but before he could, Aryan grabbed his arm.

Malik spun around to meet him. "How dare you interfere

with how I deal with my wife?"

Aryan held on to Malik's arm for another few seconds before letting go. Deema turned to leave the room.

"No, don't go," said Aryan. "Stay here. You should hear this."

Aryan looked at Malik. "As I said to you, we should talk about our arrangement."

"Later, I—"

Aryan put his finger to his lips, and Malik fell silent. "The agreement we reached in your late cousin's office has me as your 'equal partner in all things.' Do you recall that?"

"Yes, of course."

"Good. Then do not harm the wife that I share with you."

Malik's eyes widened and his jaw dropped. "What are you talking about? She is *my* wife."

Without taking his eyes off of Malik, Aryan said, "Tomislav, when Malik and I reached that agreement in your former employer's office, did he say anything excluding his wife from the arrangement?"

"No," said a firm voice.

"So, you see, Malik, if you refuse my equal rights to your wife, I shall have no choice but to treat it as a breach of our agreement and, well, you know what that will mean."

Malik's head lowered slightly. "But she's my wife."

Aryan put his hand on Malik's shoulder, "No, my friend and partner, *our* wife."

Malik started to tremble.

"Tomislav, please show my partner up to his bedroom. I think he needs to rest."

Aryan pointed Tomislav up the stairs. "Second door to the left."

Deema started to follow them.

"No, stay here," Aryan said.

She stopped and looked down at the floor.

Aryan walked over and stood beside her as the two men

ascended the stairs. He put his arm around her shoulders and pulled her close to him.

He moved his hand to between her shoulder blades and gently ran his fingertips up and down her spine, dropping down every so often to trace the outline of her rear. "See, I told you I would protect you."

The maid came bursting in from the kitchen with a tray of coffee and food.

"We won't be needing that. Please take it upstairs to Mr. Malik. Mrs. Deema and I will be in the living room. We do not wish to be disturbed."

The maid nodded and hurried up the stairs.

"Come," said Ayran, steering her toward the living room.

She did not resist.

Once inside, he closed the doors behind them.

She did not resist.

Chapter Thirteen

"Sounds like you had a productive conversation last night with McLaughlin," said Andreas.

Yianni smacked his hands on the arms of his chair opposite Andreas' desk. "It took about all the patience I had, but I think she's come around to believing she can trust us."

"That's a big step."

"But I'm not sure how long that'll keep if we don't get this guy Aryan."

"You mean Kennel."

"I prefer calling him Aryan. Kennel reminds me of dogs, and I like dogs."

Andreas shrugged. "Call him whatever you want. Maggie couldn't come up with anything recent on him under either name. School records show he was raised in Switzerland, but he fell off the grid at seventeen and has no living next of kin."

"Terrific."

Maggie burst into the office. "Chief, I just got a call from my friend in Turkey."

"Did they catch the killer?"

She gestured no. "I'd told her I wanted the video for research into potential similarities among gruesome killings in this part of the world. She called to tell me they'd just had a double murder to put at the top of my gruesome list."

Andreas leaned forward. "What sort of murder?"

"A double beheading."

"Terrorists?" said Yianni.

"The police don't seem to think so. And because the country's tourist industry is apoplectic at the thought of something like this being picked up internationally as another terrorist attack, the police are releasing a lot more details about the incident than they normally would. They're even telling the Turkish media to discourage any suggestion of terrorism. One victim was a hugely important man, an ex-government minister and the son of a former general of the Turkish Army. The murders took place in his office, and the second victim worked for him."

"When did it happen?" asked Yianni.

"According to the receptionist, a couple of hours ago. Two men showed up for an appointment with her boss. He made them wait in reception for almost an hour, they were inside for about a half-hour, and left with a third man who'd also worked for her boss."

"Who found the bodies?" said Yianni.

"She did, about a half an hour later. The boss' wife called to say she'd been trying to reach her husband but he hadn't answered his phone. She asked the receptionist to tell him to call her. When she went to see what was going on, *voila*, she found two heads in the middle of a conference table with a bloody sword driven into the tabletop beside them. I don't know if she called the police or they just heard her screams."

"Where did this happen?"

"A penthouse office in one of the chicest buildings in Izmir."

Andreas shut his eyes, then opened them. "Did the receptionist identify the visitors?"

"She's new and didn't recognize them. Both spoke Turkish, but only one looked Turkish, the one who said her boss was expecting them."

"Did she give a more detailed description of the men?"

"My friend didn't say, but I assume the police got whatever

they could from her. Perhaps we should suggest to the police that they show the receptionist Aryan's picture from the CCTV?"

Andreas picked up a pencil. "And how do we explain how we got that photo, what made us interested in it in the first place, and why we think those two events are linked, without implicitly suggesting some very bad things about one of Turkey's most prominent, recently deceased citizens?"

"You think he's the big guy McLaughlin had in mind?" said Yianni.

"If Aryan's involved in this, I've no doubt these murders are somehow connected to refugee trafficking. As to precisely how the two dead guys are tied in, and why Aryan killed them, I've not a clue."

"I've an idea, Chief," said Maggie. "Why don't you reach out to the Turkish police in sympathy? Tell them we recently had a similar horrific sword murder of a prominent citizen just across the sea from Izmir on Lesvos. Suggest that they might be able to help you solve your case if they have a description of possible suspects in their double beheading murder."

"I like that idea," said Yianni. "That way we don't have to let on that we know anything more than what hit the news today. It also allows the Turks to claim they're cooperating with us, with virtually no work required on their part."

Andreas nodded. "I like it, too, unless they already know who's involved, or have a damn good idea and don't want them exposed."

"You mean until they're in a position to arrest them, or never because they're protected?" said Yianni.

Andreas shrugged. "Another question to which I don't have an answer. But, I'll make the telephone call and see if I can get our colleagues in Izmir to cooperate."

"Nothing ventured, nothing gained," agreed Maggie.

Andreas picked up his phone. "As Lila once pointed out to me, that quote happens to come from the same American who once stood out in the middle of a field in a rainstorm flying a kite trying to attract electricity."

"Sounds like a sure-fire way to get yourself killed," said Yianni.

Andreas dialed a number and listened to it ring. "I think that was Lila's point."

It took three conversations with three different Turkish cops before Andreas found a police inspector willing to speak with him about the double beheadings. Modern Turkish police served as the Turkish president's balance to the military's propensity for *coups*. That made senior police officials antsy when faced with potentially politically tinged decisions, such as exchanging information with the Greeks. Retribution was swift in Turkey.

Unlike the two other Turkish police Andreas had spoken with, this inspector seemed relatively unconcerned about possible political miscues. But, then again, he had a strong vested interest in identifying the suspects. The Izmir slaughter was his case, and that meant bosses screaming for results ASAP. For him, the upside of a break in his investigation in exchange for cooperating with Andreas far outweighed maintaining political purity.

Andreas told the inspector what he knew about the Lesvos murder, including his doubts about the guilt of the person in custody, but he left out the part about the photo at the Turkish café. No need to put a suspect in the inspector's sights. Especially a foreigner like Aryan. The inspector might be tempted not to take aim at anyone beyond Aryan, for if a non-Turk took the fall, the inspector would be a hero without stepping on any Turkish toes, no matter how many might be dancing around him. This approach offered him not only the easiest solution, but the surest route to promotion.

The inspector said he hoped to pick something up off the building's security cameras, but hadn't as yet. If he did, he'd send them on straightaway to Andreas. Beyond that thin offer of assistance, he offered no more details than Maggie had obtained from her friend. Andreas felt certain the inspector hadn't told him everything, but that was to be expected. After all, Andreas had done the same to him. Andreas thanked him profusely before hanging up.

Andreas looked to Yianni. "Well, at least we're talking."

"Nothing, huh?"

Andreas nodded.

"Sounds like cops protecting their turf," said Maggie.

Andreas stretched. "Probably so. But they haven't finished looking at the building's security cameras. That should yield something. The question is whether they'll actually share it."

"By when?"

Andreas shrugged. "Soon. I hope."

Aryan spent an hour alone with Deema in the living room. When he left, she did not join him. He climbed the stairs, turned, and stopped at Malik's bedroom door. He knocked and Tomislav opened it. Malik sat across the room on the edge of the bed, staring at the floor.

"Oh, I thought you'd be resting," said Aryan walking toward Malik. "All that's happened this morning must have been quite stressful for you. After all, it's not every day you see a cousin beheaded."

Aryan stopped two steps in front of Malik. "He was not an honorable man. He did not wish to share. He thought only of himself. He let his ego fog his judgment. We are all better off with you as our new leader."

Malik did not lift his gaze from the floor. Nor did he speak.

"I sense you're still in shock. You will get over it, for I know you're a practical man. Now, we must talk about the future. Your cousin's men will want to come at you for revenge. If not his men, at least his family, or perhaps business rivals wanting to claim his enterprise for their own. You must act at once to stabilize the situation."

Silence.

"Or you will die."

Malik looked at him. "I wondered when you'd get around to that."

Aryan sat on the bed next to him. "Me? I have no reason to kill you. This organization can never be mine. I am not of your family's blood. I'm not even Turkish. No, as I said before, if you die because of what happened today, it will be at the hands of others." He paused. "*Unless* you show them strength, and convince them that your cousin left you no choice but to defend yourself by taking his life."

Malik swallowed. "How can I convince them of that?"

"Easily, because they probably already know your cousin intended to harm us. Isn't that correct, Tomislav?" Aryan glanced at Tomislav.

Tomislav nodded yes.

"His death at your hands showed strength. All you need to do now is show your willingness to continue down that path if they make it necessary, while offering them a plan for a more profitable, better-run operation. Show them your willingness to use both the stick and the carrot, and they will follow you."

"How can you sound so certain?"

"Human nature. Those who might dare to go against you will have seen the risk of what happens to them if they try."

"You speak of arrogance. It is yours that will get us all killed."

"Perhaps," said Aryan. "But if you do not act at once, your indecision will guarantee you die first. I'm certain you can think of any number of persons planning at this very moment to kill you."

Silence.

"What are you suggesting I do?" said Malik at last.

"Call those who will come at you. Tell them you wish to meet under a flag of truce in an effort to spare further bloodshed.

Tell them your cousin left you no choice but to defend your life from him, and that if, after you've met, they still believe you acted unjustifiably, they can do with you as they please."

"They will never agree to meet except to try and kill me."

Aryan shrugged. "Perhaps not at first, but once some try to kill you, and their lives end instead, the others will come around."

"You're mad."

"Of course, but it is my madness that will keep you alive." He put his arm around Malik's shoulder. "After all, you are my partner."

Malik cringed at the word partner.

Aryan patted Malik's shoulder. "You make the calls. I'll take care of the rest."

● ● ● ● ●

Deema had dressed quickly after Aryan left, but did not leave the living room. She sat wondering what now would become of her life. She'd long ago learned to put up with abuse at the hands of men, and come to accept it as the curse of her gender. She'd also realized it would not have mattered had she been born ugly, because men did what they did to women for reasons unrelated to beauty or the lack thereof. They abused because they could, and often for purposes understood far better by their victims than by the men themselves.

Deema knew that her husband beat her to excuse himself for his own insecurities. She'd learned to anticipate those moments, and to be prepared for what followed. But that was before the foreigner.

Aryan had changed the rules. The night he entered their lives Malik beat her mercilessly, venting upon her his anger at himself for his lack of courage in confronting Aryan. When Aryan later forbid Malik from striking her, Deema knew Aryan hadn't come to her defense out of any concern for her safety, but to humiliate her husband, compounding his shaming by lecturing him in front of her.

Aryan had raped her for the same purpose. Not for the pleasure of her body, but to complete Malik's humiliation with an act he would forever blame on his wife as much, if not more, as on her rapist.

Deema saw her life as over. Soon, one of her abusers would kill her; either Malik worked into a holy rage over festering thoughts of adultery, or Aryan simply because he decided it was time. Fears of what would become of her children after she was gone were all that pushed her to live. She longed to escape with them, but could think of no place on Earth to flee where her husband could not find them.

Even the most despondent of her husband's trafficked refugees had a better chance of finding freedom than did she from her tormentors.

Death will be the only escape.

Dana's second visit to Ali did not meet with the same official opposition as her first. This time the officer showed her into an interview room and even asked if she wanted coffee while she waited for Ali to be brought to her.

"Hi, Dana," said a smiling Ali as an officer led him shackled into the room and sat him in a chair across the table from Dana.

"Just yell if you need me," said the officer to Dana. "I'll be right outside."

"You seem happy," she said.

"Ever since you spoke to the commander and I told my jailer that I'd asked not to be transferred to another jail, I've been treated as if I gave them a five-star rating on TripAdvisor."

Dana laughed. "They're probably not used to satisfied customers."

He shrugged. "As long as they're happy, I'm happy. Any word from the police on finding the real killer?"

She hesitated. "I don't know. They're willing to say off the record that you're not the killer, but they won't go public with it. They claim you're safer inside."

"Safer from whom?"

"The real killer." She glanced at the door and lowered her voice. "But that's just what they say, and until you're told you're free, I wouldn't assume anything other than you're the one they plan on pinning this on."

He nodded. "I'll just keep smiling and not say anything when they try to get me to talk again."

Dana sat up straight. "Someone's trying to get you to talk about the case?"

He nodded again. "A woman about your age, maybe a little younger, came by this morning asking me questions. But I wouldn't answer any of them."

"Who's she with?"

"She said she's a forensic examiner."

"She's works for the people who put you in here."

"She told me that, too, but said she wanted to help me."

"I bet. Good thing you didn't talk to her. What's her name?"

"Aleka something or other."

The police commander's daughter. "I know her."

"She seemed nice enough."

"Yeah, I'm sure she's as sweet, innocent, and understanding as a friendly insurance investigator trying to get you to tell him what he needs in order to deny your claim. It's in their genes. Don't talk to her. Please."

"I hear you, but she said she'd stop by again tomorrow to see if I've changed my mind."

Dana made a mental note to tell the woman to stop pestering Ali. They chatted for another ten minutes about NGO business unrelated to his case, and Dana passed along the good wishes of Ali's coworkers, explaining how everyone wanted to visit him but the police wouldn't allow it. She said she didn't want to make a fuss over that because it might jeopardize the relatively free access she now had to him.

He said he understood, but as he was led away still in shackles, she watched his sunny smile fade away.

• • ● • •

Malik spent the early afternoon on the telephone cajoling, convincing, and conniving with people he knew wanted him dead. As far as they were concerned, he was complicit in the murder of their leader, who to some was also a cousin, brother, or father. Malik faced a hard sell, but Aryan wanted the meeting and that meant he had to arrange one, even if on dangerous terms.

They agreed to meet that day before dark on flat, open farmland halfway between Izmir and Malik's home. It offered both sides a safeguard from ambush, as anyone approaching could be seen from kilometers away, but its utterly deserted environs offered no limitation on what one side could do to the other once there.

The odds definitely favored the other side's twelve men—plus one driver and one bodyguard each—versus Malik, Aryan, and Tomislav.

Thirty-six potential guns, cried Malik, but Aryan shrugged it off as a meaningless concern. "Not one of them wants to die needlessly any more than we do."

"But they could kill us on the road before we get there. These men have great power, they could use a military attack helicopter," said a nearly hysterical Malik.

"If you wish to fantasize, think drone. No, my friend, if they have such power, we are dead men anyway. They will be curious to hear what we have to say, and those who just want to see us dead will want to see our faces as we die." He smiled at Malik. "Perhaps even want to behead us themselves."

Malik turned away. "You're mad."

"Come, let's get ready."

"What's your hurry?" said Malik. "We don't have to leave for hours."

"Yes, but we must dress appropriately for our funerals."

Dana planned on heading straight back to the office from her visit with Ali. She had work to do on a grant application she intended on submitting to a foundation established by one of the most charitable shipowning families in Greece. It seemed logical to ask Greek shipowners to continue Mihalis Volandes' good work. She might even suggest a joint venture of sorts with the Greek Church. No reason not to aim high. But as she walked to her car she remembered she had a more urgent matter to attend to.

When she entered the office of the forensic supervisor, she headed straight for the reception desk.

"Hi, my name's Dana McLaughlin, and I'm here to see Aleka."

"Is she expecting you?" said the dour-faced woman sitting at the desk.

"No."

"What is your business with her?"

"She knows me."

"Just a moment." The woman dialed an extension, repeated what Dana had told her, and hung up. "She'll be right with you."

Twenty seconds later, a tall, young woman with a quizzical look on her face appeared at the reception desk. She stared at Dana for second. "Oh, it's you," said Aleka, the look now gone. "I didn't place a face with your name. What can I do for you?"

"Is there a place we can talk?" said Dana.

"You can talk here, it won't bother me," said the woman behind the desk.

"That's very nice of you to offer," said Dana, "but my mother raised me not to be an imposition, so, I'd rather be somewhere that won't make me feel that I am."

Aleka nodded. "Follow me." She led Dana down a hallway of institutional green walls and beige linoleum floor tiles to a door marked EXAMINATION ROOM. "No one's in here now."

As she stepped into the room Dana felt a chill run down her spine. She realized she stood where many of the people she tried to help ended up when she failed. "Is this where they bring the drowning victims?"

Aleka nodded, grim-faced. "Among others."

Dana stared around the room.

Aleka broke the silence. "I appreciate your not talking in front of that woman. She's my boss' secretary and his eyes and ears around this place."

Dana focused on Aleka's eyes. "Should I take that as an admission you realize you're way out of line in trying to speak to my coworker, Ali?"

"No, that's not the reason at all," said Aleka in a cold voice. "If you'd mentioned any of that in front of her, you'd have made things worse for him."

"Don't run your 'I'm only here to help you' hustle by me, sister."

Aleka clenched her teeth. "I see what my father meant."

"I beg your pardon?"

"Beg all you want. You're one strong-willed bitch. Bitch being my word, not his."

"Fuck you," said Dana.

"Good, now we can have a conversation on a level we both understand," said Aleka. "I know your guy isn't guilty, but a lot of people around here don't seem to care. I went to see him to find out if he had even an inkling of who the actual killer might be. Volandes' killer stood in the garden that night only steps away from Ali, facing him head on. I don't think anyone's ever told Ali that before. I wanted him to concentrate on what he could remember or even just sense about that moment. But I never got around to asking him, because he wouldn't talk to me about that night."

"How do you know all this?" asked Dana.

"From the police in Athens."

"Then why is Ali still in jail?"

"My boss doesn't agree, and the prosecutor will run with the case if it works for him politically."

"That seems to be the party line."

Aleka shrugged. "Believe it or not, that's up to you. I just wanted to help. If you don't need it, fine. I've a lot of other things to do."

Dana paused. "No, I think it's okay. In fact, to be honest, I think your interest might have made Ali feel better. I'm his friend, he expects my support, but you represent the government to him, and that gives him more confidence. He's a naturally cheerful guy, but I sense jail is wearing down his spirits."

"As if our lines of work don't do the same to us."

Dana smiled. "Touché."

Aleka crossed her arms and leaned back against an examination table. "Perhaps you could answer a question for me."

"I'll try."

"I've lived here all my life. Never even been out of Greece except twice with my father to visit my mother's family. You're from America, and I'm sure you've seen a lot of places." Aleka bit at her lower lip. "I can't help but wonder if anyone out there really cares anymore about what's happening here? As far as I can tell, many who once claimed genuine concern have moved on to mourn new crises, forgetting all about the refugees and us in the process. I've even heard that some NGOs created here and bearing the name Lesvos, have not only moved on, but removed Lesvos from their names."

Dana shrugged. "I'm afraid that represents a sad reality of the state of our world. Crisis brings media attention. Media attention brings openhearted people who translate into money. Along with money come profiteers who don't give a serious shit about the people in crisis. They're only interested in their own image and fundraising. Slick PR and sound bites draw in the donations, and for them, that's all that matters."

Aleka nodded. "We islanders know who they are. The EU gives money directly to NGOs, and the aggressive ones are damn good at getting more than their fair share."

"That's because the EU doesn't trust your government."

"With good reason, but instead of putting time and attention into establishing a mechanism that actually achieves what the EU claims to want, it just passes out the money and says, 'See, we care.'"

"We're of like mind on that score," said Dana. "Good intentions don't always succeed."

Aleka stared at Dana. "I have something else to ask you."

Dana cocked her head and nodded.

"Do you really know who's behind refugee smuggling in Turkey?"

"Why do you want to know?"

"Pure curiosity. I can't help but wonder what drives someone to do what you did. Most would say you're nuts to have held that press conference, because whether or not you actually do know the name, simply threatening to release it to the press must have sent your life insurance rates sailing off the chart."

Dana nodded. "You know, I never thought of it that way before. But I get your point. Your father made sort of the same one to me."

"He makes good points to me, too. Many times, on many subjects. Even if I don't admit it to him." Aleka smiled. "But you didn't listen to him, did you?"

Dana grinned. "We bitches rarely do."

Chapter Fourteen

"Here it is," said Maggie, bursting into Andreas' office.

"Here's what?" said Andreas.

"This." She placed a photo on his desk. "It's from the Turkish police, taken off a camera in the lobby of the dead man's office building."

Andreas stared at an image of three men walking together. Aryan's face stared straight back at him. Andreas patted the face with his forefinger. "That's our guy." He looked at the other faces. "But what's with this? One of the faces is blurry."

"That's the way it came in."

"Looks like someone doesn't want the third face identified."

"What do you want to do?"

"Tell Yianni to come in here, and please get me that Turkish police inspector on the phone."

Andreas' eyes went back to staring at the photo.

Yianni walked into Andreas' office just as Maggie yelled, "He's on."

Andreas motioned for Yianni to sit in the chair by his desk, and handed him the photo as Andreas picked up the phone. "Hi, Inspector. My colleague just walked into the room so, if you don't mind, I'll put you on speakerphone."

At that, Maggie came inside the office and closed the door.

"First of all, thank you for sending me that photo."

"Always glad to help our Greek colleagues."

Yianni made a gesture that Andreas ignored.

"But there seems to be a technical glitch in the photo. One of the faces is blurry. Do you have a better copy?"

"Oh, you needn't worry about that man. He's not relevant to your investigation."

"I see," said Andreas. "But could you at least tell me who he is?"

"No. As I said, he is not relevant."

"What about the other two men in the photo?" said Andreas.

"One is a former employee of the victim. He is a Serbian national, all we have for a name at this point is Tomislav."

"And the other man?" Andreas waggled his eyebrows at Yianni.

"Uh, we're hoping you might be able to help us with that one. We can't seem to identify him."

"So sorry to hear that. We know who he is, and would like to help you out, but frankly, I don't think he's relevant to your investigation."

Yianni smiled.

"I think he is," said the inspector in a clipped voice.

"Aha," said Andreas. "A professional difference of opinion. And I respect that. I have a similar reaction to the blurry man." He waited a beat. "Why don't you reconsider your position on the relevance of blurry man, and I'll do the same with mine on your killer."

"Are you saying the man you won't identify is the killer?"

"For sure."

"I demand that you tell me."

"Duly noted. But first, I need to know about blurry man."

"This is the last time you'll ever get help from me."

"Sorry to hear that. I thought you wanted the name of your killer."

"We can get it without the help of the Greek police."

Andreas rolled his eyes. "Good luck, but don't let pride stand in your way if you need our help. I'll be more than happy to show you mine, if you show me yours."

The inspector exhaled into the phone. "I doubt I can trust you."

"I guess you'll just have to if you want to know who you're looking for."

"That's blackmail."

"No, it's professional cooperation between neighbors." Andreas made the same gesture Yianni had used.

"Good-bye," said the inspector.

"Thank you, bye." Andreas hung up.

"I wonder who the blurry guy is," said Yianni.

"My bet is he'll tell us," said Maggie. "He's desperate for Aryan's name."

Andreas leaned back in his chair and clasped his hands together behind his head. "Somehow, I sense negotiations are not yet completed."

* * * * * *

Malik wanted to reach the meeting site early, but Aryan opted for being right on time. He figured whatever surprises the other side undoubtedly had in store for them would be hidden in their vehicles, be they rocket-propelled grenade launchers or something more prosaic than RPGs. Arriving early would gain no advantage, and only show anxiety. Aryan saw this as a business meeting and intended to treat it as such, with slight preparatory modifications in recognition of the circumstances.

Malik drove, with Tomislav next to him in the front seat, but he didn't say a word as he sped along the four-lane highway through nothing but wide open farmland and the occasional town that made even the farmland look interesting. Ragged hills rose up in the distance to the east, and somewhere off to the west sat the sea. When they turned east toward Bergama, the scenery remained uninterestingly the same.

That suited Aryan just fine. He sat in the back, grilling Tomislav for his views on the men likely to be at the site. He

wasn't interested in the twelve leaders; he'd received information on them from Malik. He wanted to know about the
muscle that would be with them. Tomislav only knew some of
the men, but of those he did, few were seasoned professionals.
Most were relatives paid to look tough and deal with problems
in packs.

About twenty kilometers east of Bergama, they turned south
off the highway onto a flat, treeless dirt road aimed straight at
the distant mountains. Two kilometers later they turned east
onto a rutted dirt road, toward a large open section of brown
fallow farmland a kilometer ahead, bounded on the north and
south by struggling olive groves. The other side had chosen
wisely. Cluster bombs could go off here without attracting
attention.

Dust hung in the air above the road as Malik's Range Rover
closed in on the site. Aryan saw two SUVs ahead of them also
heading east, and seven vehicles parked nose-to-butt in semi-
circular fashion in front of the olive grove to the south.

Aryan twisted to look out the rear window. Out of the
approaching evening redness in the western sky, three black
SUVs hurried along behind them. *Good*, he thought. Everyone
wants to be on time.

"When we get to the field, park inside the semi-circle with
your nose pointed at the vehicle in the middle of the line."

"I don't like this," said Malik.

"I didn't expect you to," said Aryan. "Just remember, do
exactly as I told you, precisely when I told you to do it, and
everything will work out fine. Otherwise you'll die, if not by
them, by me."

As they pulled off the road into the field, headed toward
the line of vehicles, a group of men chatting next to one of the
vehicles broke up and spread out along the line, each man's eyes
fixed on the Range Rover. None showed visible weapons, but
each wore a long coat, likely concealing more than enough fire-
power to take out the Range Rover and everyone in it. Another

row of men stood partially concealed behind the hoods of the vehicles. They, too, showed no visible weapons, but likely had automatic weapons, if not RPG launchers, at their feet.

Once the Range Rover stopped, Aryan told Malik and Tomislav to prepare. He watched as the twelfth vehicle arrived and took up its place in the semi-circle.

"Okay, Malik, you're on."

"I'm scared."

"You should be. Now, just do as I told you."

"I can't."

Aryan leaned forward.

Malik braced as if expecting a sword across his throat.

"Yes, you can." Aryan patted him on the shoulder. "It's your time to shine."

Malik looked as if he might hyperventilate.

Aryan nodded to Tomislav, who leaned across the front seat and opened Malik's door.

The moment the door opened, some of the men standing in the front row swung open their coats and gripped AK-47s.

The scent of manure drifted through the Range Rover. Tomislav pushed Malik out the door.

Malik struggled to keep his footing on the uneven ground and raise his hands above his head at the same time. "I come in peace. I have no weapons."

"Walk toward me," said a young, swarthy man in a red beret.

"Not until everyone is out of their vehicles," Malik answered.

The man in the red beret raised his voice. "I said walk toward me."

Malik started, then stopped. Aryan had told him that if he didn't stay where he was he was a dead man. "I can't."

Red Beret lifted his rifle and sprayed a quick burst at Malik's feet. Malik cringed, but did not move. "Is this how your bosses honor their commitments to meet in peace?"

"Shut up and do as I say," said Red Beret.

"I cannot."

A door opened in the vehicle behind Red Beret and a portly, middle-aged man in a tailored business suit stepped out. "That will be enough of that," he said to Red Beret. "Malik, I see you have gained some admirable courage."

"It comes with the confidence of my convictions that I did nothing wrong, and that you will agree once we have the chance to talk."

"Liar," yelled Red Beret.

"Silence," said portly man. He turned to Malik. "I apologize for his temper, but he is the only son of your recently departed cousin who would come to listen. The other two refused."

Malik nodded. "Yes, it is understandable how they feel. I just hope that they are willing to listen to the truth."

"The truth! The truth is you murdered my father." Red Beret again raised his rifle, but before he could train it on Malik, a man in army fatigues standing next to him tripped him to the ground and disarmed him.

Portly Man shook his head. "I was afraid that might happen, so I took certain precautions to see that he be kept under control. I hope you'll take that as a sign of our good faith."

Malik nodded. "Thank you."

Eleven other doors opened and soon twelve men stood together across from Malik.

The passenger doors to the Range Rover opened and Aryan and Tomislav stepped out, each in car coats, with hands raised above their heads. They took up positions ten meters to either side of Malik, facing the vehicles.

"You betrayed my father," Red Beret yelled at Tomislav from the ground.

"No," said Malik. "That's not what happened. Your father called a meeting in peace, but then tried to assassinate us. It was only after the attempt failed—"

"Liar, you're—"

"I told you to be silent," said Portly Man. He nodded at the man who'd disarmed Red Beret. "Put him in the backseat, and if he won't shut up, gag him." He drew in and let out a deep breath.

"What is it you wish to tell us, Malik, that brings us out to this god-forsaken place? I trust you understand that although I disapprove of our young colleague's lack of restraint, I share his desire to take revenge on you for the death of his father. All three of you will die here today if you cannot convince us why you should live. And you better do so quickly, for we're all of one mind on that."

The other eleven men nodded.

All stood silent. Not a bird, not a dog, not a cricket to be heard.

Malik's knees appeared to buckle.

"Bravo, bravo," said Aryan. "I love a man who tells the truth up front. It makes discussion all the more pertinent and to the point."

"And you, I assume, are the assassin Malik recruited for that bit of work on Lesvos."

"Actually, we're partners. Right, Malik?"

Malik bit at his lip. "Yes."

"Equal partners in all things," said Aryan.

Portly man smiled. "Then you shall be equal partners in death."

"You are so insightful," said Aryan. "You took the words right out of my mouth. Well, mine are slightly different. I'd phrase it as, 'If things don't work out here today, we'll *all* be equal partners in death.'"

Portly Man smirked. "One word from me and the three of you will instantly die where you're standing." The men in front of the vehicles swung their automatic weapons up from beneath their coats and took aim at the three facing them. The men on the other side of the vehicles did the same.

"Nicely choreographed move," said Aryan. "But before you get any more carried away with the theatrics, permit me to suggest one thing."

"What's that?"

"Have your men frisk us. But please tell them to be careful. We wouldn't want any accidents before we've at least had the chance to talk."

Portly Man hesitated for a moment, then nodded for three men to do as Aryan had suggested.

Beneath their coats, Aryan, Malik, and Tomislav wore vests composed of C-4 and thousands of ball bearings, and each held a small triggering device in the palm of their right hand.

"As you may already know, they're called suicide vests," said Aryan to the group, "and what we're each holding is a dead-man trigger. Meaning, if you should follow up on your threat, we're all going off together."

Some men started to move away.

"Uh-uh, don't move or else I might just let go." Aryan opened his hand to show the trigger. "And for those of you thinking I wouldn't dare commit suicide, think again. You just told me we're dead men. So my current motto is, the more the merrier."

Portly Man reached for a handkerchief and patted at his forehead. "Okay, what is it you want to tell us?"

"First of all, have your men on the other side of the vehicles join us."

A few hesitated to leave the security of engine blocks between them and the suicide vests, but ultimately did as Aryan asked when ordered by Portly Man.

"Now that we understand we're all in this together, I assume no one objects to us lowering our arms." He and the other two dropped their arms to their sides. "If you don't mind, we'll keep the vests on, even though they're quite heavy."

He paused. "That was a joke."

Portly Man was perspiring freely now.

"Okay, let's start off with something that's unconvertible about what happened this morning. We arrived at the meeting unarmed. If you won't take Tomislav's word on that,

or somehow think your ex-boss wouldn't have frisked us—
especially considering what he had in mind for us—what can I
say except, look how everything turned out?

"I'm sure you know by now that your boss came into the
meeting intent on killing Malik and me for that 'bit of work on
Lesvos', as you put it," he said, staring at Portly Man.

"I should say for the record that I did that bit of work on
Lesvos for *him*. We all know your boss gave the go-ahead for
that job, yes?" Aryan waited until the men in the other group
nodded. "No matter, he called the meeting because he was
angry at a news story coming out of Lesvos where some NGO
woman close to the man I eliminated on *his orders*, claimed
that the head of refugee-smuggling operations lived in Izmir.

"I told him she was guessing and had no name to tell. He
wouldn't listen to reason. He'd made up his mind that someone
had screwed up, and his delicate ego couldn't tolerate the possibility he might be wrong. He felt so offended by my insisting
he had nothing to worry about, that he wouldn't even give us
the time to explain the idea Malik and I had for him."

"What idea?" said Portly Man.

"A method for transforming your refugee trafficking from
a business that has the world labeling you as perpetrators of
crimes against humanity into one that brings honor to you. All
without sacrificing profitability in any meaningful way."

Aryan paused. "But I digress. You want to know what happened in that office. Simply this. Your big boss made the same
mistake so many have made. He thought he could treat me as
he did anyone else who offended him, order someone to get rid
of me. Surprise. I'm not like everyone else, and when he told
two men to kill me, I used a weapon mounted on his own conference room wall to defend myself. I did precisely what any of
you would have done. No more, no less."

"Okay," said a slim man in a khaki suit who looked as if
he'd be more comfortable in a military uniform. "Assuming
we believe your self-defense story, what's your grand plan for
making us all heroes and rich at the same time?"

"Ah, a man who gets right down to business. I like that."

Aryan began pacing as if in a theater-in-the-round. "All of you are involved in a business directly responsible for the death of masses of innocent people every day, many of them children. You supply them with boats, life jackets, and GPS equipment that fail and cost lives. You make martyrs of those who oppose you, even inspire talk of resurrecting the death sentence to punish your actions.

"All that grief you bring down upon yourselves, despite being in bed with some of the most influential political powers in governments all along your refugee routes. Why? Because your business plan is so abhorrent to their constituencies that even your protectors dare not risk being linked to you in any way. They are the first to find a sacrificial lamb among you when they think it necessary to prove that they are not allied with you. Who among you will be the next sacrifice?"

"Okay, we get that," said Portly Man. "Tell us something we don't know."

Aryan sighed. "It's all so very simple that I'm afraid you'll be reluctant to give me the credit I deserve for my brilliant idea. So, before I tell you, does anyone have any idea of what I'm about to suggest?"

Silence.

He stared up and down the line. "Oh, come on, you're all in the same business and can't even venture a guess on a better way to do things?"

More silence.

"Okay, here it is, but don't any of you claim you already thought of it." He cleared his throat. "Go legit."

"What?" said Portly Man.

"Okay, not completely legitimate, but at least with a keen eye to what plays out best in public relations."

"What are you talking about?"

Aryan paced back and forth more quickly, looking at the ground and wildly waving the hand holding the trigger. Some men flinched. "What I mean is this. Stop sending the refugees out in death trap boats, stop selling them life jackets that sink, start handing them boxed lunches when you put them in a boat, even give them Dramamine if they want. You get the idea?"

"Are you crazy?" said the slim man.

"Like a fox," said a well-dressed young man with dark hair. "The lunch costs us half a euro, the Dramamine less, and I'm sure we can work out something with the Greeks to get the better boats back to re-use. Same thing with the life vests. Europe uses the way we treat our inventory as its basis for convincing the world to shut us down. It's not the fee-gouging or even stories about those who disappear along the way into sex and labor work that get serious attention anymore. The media's numb to all that. What galvanizes people are pictures of dead children on beaches, overcrowded boats sinking in the water, and masses of floating bodies."

Aryan nodded for the young man to continue.

"If we could pull off what he suggests, just make those few changes in the areas of greatest press attention, it could do wonders for our image. It might even gain us allies among some of those NGOs trying to get refugees out of Turkey and into Europe. I bet with the right image we could work out a deal to use our boats to get refugees from our launch points in Turkey transferred mid-sea to their boats for the rest of the trip, and still make our full fee off the refugees. We could ride on their claims that Europe is anti-refugee, and portray ourselves as good guys simply trying to help the suffering ones reach their promised land."

"You make some very good points," said Aryan. "To which I'd like to add that the media is full of reports decrying how horribly Greece and the rest of the EU treat your clients once out of your control. They herd them into overcrowded concentration camp-like facilities, riddled with poor food and water, vermin, unusable toilets, a dearth of medical care, and angry men fighting among each other while doing far worse to the women they harass. Think of how little you would have to do to accommodate your clients on a two-hour boat ride—or less, if you work out that mid-sea transfer deal with NGOs—to make yourself look better than the Europeans for the cameras? I submit to you that the bar is very low for putting you on the side of the angels in this."

"We could force the independent smugglers to keep to our standards," said the young man.

"I like the political cover it gives us for a lot of the more profitable stuff that happens away from the cameras," said another.

"For very little cost, we could dramatically change our very negative public image," said the young man, looking directly at Portly Man.

"What do you think?" Aryan asked.

Portly Man looked at his colleagues.

They nodded.

He looked at Aryan. "I think you've come up with a reasonable proposal that deserves further consideration. I'm sorry our recently departed colleague did not see the wisdom in your ideas. At least to the extent of running it past us."

"To be honest, he didn't give me the chance of presenting it to him."

"Even sadder. Perhaps he thought you were seeking to challenge his leadership."

Aryan shook his head. "Not a chance. We're content being loyal lieutenants to whoever's in charge." He looked to Malik. "Right?"

Malik nodded.

"We only sought to suggest a way of bettering the business, nothing more. We came in peace, he wanted war, we gave him death."

Aryan's eyes ran down the line of twelve men, catching each man's gaze as he did. "I trust you agree living in peace is a wiser alternative."

Again the men looked at each other and back at Portly Man.

Portly Man nodded at Aryan. "Agreed." He extended his right hand.

Aryan stepped forward, extending his left. "Sorry, the right one's busy at the moment." He waved the trigger in the air.

A few men laughed. Most didn't.

The Range Rover stayed until the twelve other vehicles had left, all headed west. Aryan told Malik to head east. Malik said that way added an hour to the journey home. Aryan said one disgruntled of the twelve could be waiting up the road with an RPG. That would add a lot more than an hour to the trip.

"But they gave their word. Even shook hands on it," said Malik.

Aryan stared at the back of Malik's head. "I used my left hand. Some might see that as an out."

Malik drove east.

* ● ● ● *

Maggie was just about to leave for home when her phone rang. "Chief Inspector Kaldis' office."

She listened. "Yes, Inspector, I'll put you right through." She placed him on hold and yelled though the open doorway. "Looks like I win the bet. It's your Turkish police inspector buddy."

Andreas picked up the phone. "Yes, Inspector, what can I do for you?"

"I've reconsidered your proposal. I'm under tremendous pressure from my superiors to keep the identity of the third man confidential. He is unrelated to the investigation, but someone with great influence."

"I understand all that," said Andreas. "We face the same considerations here, but I still need to know his identity."

"Yes, I understand, and I am going to trust you with information that could ruin my career if it gets out."

"Understood, my lips are sealed." He glanced at Maggie standing in the doorway.

"Thank you. I will give you my information first as a sign of trust."

Andreas picked up a pencil and began tapping it on the desktop. "I appreciate that."

"By way of background, the man I'm about to identify had been taken hostage by your killer and brought against his will to the victim's office as the killer's means of gaining access to the victim. He is a respected businessman and we've cleared him of any involvement in any of this."

Andreas tapped the eraser end of the pencil on the desktop. "I'm sure. So what's his name?"

"Ivir Zivir."

Andreas wrote down the name. "Thank you."

"And what is the name of our killer?" asked the inspector.

Andreas replied, spelling out the name.

"Strange name."

"Sure is."

"Thank you. Bye."

The inspector hung up before Andreas had the chance to say good-bye. "The poor man's in a real hurry."

"Why did you tell him what you did?" said Maggie.

"What's the matter, don't you trust me to know what I'm doing?"

"You know what I mean."

"Here, do me a favor and see what you can come up with on this Ivir Zivir character."

"Now?"

Andreas stared at her. "Feel free to put in for overtime."

Maggie headed for her desk. "And what will you be doing?"

Andreas smiled. "Waiting for the inspector to call back."

• ● ● ● •

Thirty minutes later the inspector called back.

"Kaldis here."

"You're a dishonorable man."

"Ah, so you checked out the name."

"I trusted you."

"Just tell me when you're done performing for whoever's in your office."

"There's no one here but me."

"Strange, you didn't strike me as the sort who'd lie to himself. To others, yes, but yourself?"

"How dare you insult me!" the inspector shouted.

"As much fun as I'm having with this, let's cut the bullshit. That name you gave me was phony. You know it and I know it. It was like an American giving John Doe as his name. You could have at least tried to be creative."

Silence.

"Like I was. I really liked my guy's name."

"Mott Leigh Crew?" said the inspector.

"It rocks." Andreas laughed. "So, are we done playing games?"

The inspector sighed. "Malik Tiryaki."

Sounds like the same name Tassos got from his source in Turkey. "Tell me about him."

"He's a cousin of the dead man."

"Were they in the same business?"

"Yes."

"What the hell's going on over there in your backyard?"

"I wish I knew. Looks like there could be a war brewing among refugee smugglers all up and down the coast."

"That must put a lot of heat on you."

"You have no idea," said the inspector. "Everyone has a protector, and they're all letting me know it. All I want to know is who's swinging the sword."

"I can give you that name, but I'm sure you understand I can't do that until I verify what you just gave me is legit."

"Understood. But when can I expect to hear from you?"

"Tomorrow." He glanced at Maggie in the doorway. "Everyone's gone for the day."

Maggie gave a fist pump.

"First thing tomorrow, then. No exceptions."

"Absolutely. I'll speak to you tomorrow," said Andreas.

"Thanks, and sorry about our little misunderstanding. You have no idea what it's like over here these days."

Or here.

Chapter Fifteen

He slid his hand along her left hip, his body pressed tight up against her from behind, his own hips rocking in rhythm to a moaning he heard in his mind. They lay on their right sides in the deep shadows of the room, sheets kicked off onto the floor, curtains to the bedroom windows open to a cloudless, crescent moon middle of the night.

It was the third time tonight he'd taken her. The first, soon after he'd returned with Malik from their meeting in the field. He'd made a point of offering her first to Malik, who refused, only to find himself listening to the sounds of another man mating with his wife coming from their bedroom. Later, Aryan made the three of them eat dinner together. That's when he announced he'd be sleeping in the master bedroom that evening with Deema. Malik said nothing, just finished his meal and went off to a guest bedroom. Their second time had come an hour later.

Aryan slid his left hand from her hip up to grip her breast. He pulled her back toward him and pressed harder. She groaned and he twisted her over so that he lay mounted on her from behind, ramming hard against her and bringing himself to the verge of—

BOOM.

The explosion took out the wall between the bedroom windows, shattering every pane in the process. Aryan grabbed for his gun and raced out the door, leaving Deema screaming in her bed.

He reached the bottom of the stairs as the second RPG hit the bedroom. He saw Tomislav taking cover in an interior room and yelled, "Get two rifles, they'll be inside any second."

Aryan made his way to the side of the house opposite the blown-out bedroom wall and took up a position close by a door leading to the outside. The lock disappeared in a spray of automatic weapons fire, and the door sprung open followed by two men carrying AK-47s.

Aryan put a bullet in each man's head.

He bent to pick up one man's rifle when he heard the spurt of a rifle behind him. He dived for the floor and did not move until the firing ended. He looked back to see Tomislav pointing toward the open door at a now dead third man that Aryan had not seen.

Carefully, Aryan and Tomislav made their way outside. Not a sound. Aryan pointed right, toward the edge of the house, and they crept toward the corner. There, they waited and listened. Still no sound.

Aryan nodded, and they hugged the side of the house, headed toward the front. Somewhere out there sat someone with a grenade launcher. Aryan had been lucky that the first RPG hit the thick masonry wall instead of crashing through the bedroom window. Otherwise he'd have been dead. He had no desire to test his luck a second time tonight. Enough moonlight shone down to catch any movement against the horizon, but that applied to both sides. If the shooter was out there, let him come to them. Once the sun came up, he'd be the sitting duck target, not them.

Twenty minutes later, Aryan heard an engine starting about a half-kilometer away. A bit later headlights came on and disappeared down the road. Apparently, the shooter had reached the same conclusion as Aryan.

He whispered to Tomislav. "Stay here, just in case there's

still someone out there. I'm going back inside to put on some clothes. I'm freezing my ass off running around out here naked."

He found Malik standing inside the back door, staring at the three bodies. Then he caught him staring at Aryan's crotch.

"What's on your mind, partner?"

"My wife. What's happened to my wife?"

Aryan shrugged. "Don't know."

"And my children?"

Aryan shrugged again. "Do you recognize any of these dead guys?"

Malik nodded. "Two are sons of my dead cousin, another is their friend."

"Brothers of Red Beret?"

"Red Beret?" asked Malik.

"The guy who shot at your feet in that field."

Malik nodded. "Yes, they're his brothers."

"Well, I guess that means we know who was out there launching RPGs at your bedroom. Now, if you'll excuse me, I'm going to put on some clothes."

"It's your fault for all of this."

"Mine? Think again, partner. If I hadn't been upstairs in your bed, you'd likely be dead right now. They were here to kill you, not me."

Aryan watched Malik clench his fists.

"That is, unless you happened to tell someone that I'd be sleeping with Deema tonight."

He patted Malik on the shoulder. "I suggest you figure out what you're going to tell the police about all this. Of course, you might think you can get rid of these bodies the same as you had your brother-in-law dispose of the three from the night we first met. I caution you, though, that denying them a proper burial might create even bigger problems for you with their families. I leave that to your judgment." With a second pat to Malik's shoulder, he headed upstairs.

At the top of the stairs he hesitated at a sound coming from

down the hallway. He slid his feet along the carpet, a gun raised
in his hand, toward the sound. He stopped when he recognized
it as Deema whispering a story to her children. She must have
run to them before the second RPG hit her bedroom.

Malik would be happy about that.

● ● ● ● ●

Deema sat on her older son's bed, an arm clenched tightly
around each child, rocking as she told them one story after
another, whether they wanted to hear them or not. *They are not
safe here. No one is safe here. We will all die here.*

● ● ● ● ●

When Andreas got to his office, he found three voice-mail messages from the Turkish inspector, each asking that Andreas call
him back immediately. The first message had come in at five in
the morning and the most recent thirty minutes ago, at seven,
the last one in a decidedly irritated tone.

Andreas turned on the coffeemaker and looked at his watch.
Thirty minutes more until Maggie got in. The inspector hadn't
struck him as the anxious sort. Still, he'd just have to wait until
Maggie confirmed with Tassos that the Malik character named
by the inspector was the same Malik identified by Tassos'
source. He'd tried reaching Tassos on his own but had no luck.
And in light of the elaborate games the inspector had played
on the first go-round over names, Andreas wasn't about to give
that information away without confirmation.

The coffee had just started to brew when his phone rang. He
knew who it likely was, but answered anyway. "Kaldis here."

"Didn't you get my messages?"

"Yes, Inspector, I got them two minutes ago when I walked
into my office. Let me tell you straight out, as I said last night,
the moment I check out the name you gave me, I'll give you

what I promised you. And that should happen this morning."

"What I want to know is what you did with the name I gave you?"

"I don't understand," said Andreas.

"I want to know who you gave Malik's name to."

Andreas hesitated. "I'm not sure why I should tell you that, but the only person I told was my secretary."

"And whom did she tell?"

"I assume no one. She had no reason to."

"I need to know if she told anyone."

"Okay," said an irritated Andreas, "it's time you tell me what this is all about."

"I'll assume you're not involved in what I'm about to tell you, though I'm afraid that if my paranoid superiors ever learn that I gave you Malik's name, they will not give you—or me—the same benefit of the doubt."

"Just get to the point," said Andreas sharply.

"Approximately eight hours after I gave you Malik's name, three armed men attacked his home, attempting to kill him and his wife as they slept in their bed."

"Holy Mother of God. And you think I had something to do with that?"

"As I said, if I did, I wouldn't be telling you this, but you have to agree the coincidence is striking. How would you react if the shoe were on the other foot?"

Andreas ran the fingers of one hand through his hair. *I'd think someone tied into the Turkish police had tipped off the bad guys that Malik was attracting police attention.* "What happened to Malik?"

"The assassination failed. His security guy managed to kill the intruders."

"How'd he do that?"

"An RPG missed its mark, and woke everyone up, allowing security to catch the three breaking into the house."

"Did the security guy, by chance, happen to be our guy?"

"If by 'our guy' you mean the man you have yet to identify to me, no. But it was the other man in the photograph,
Tomislav, a former Serbian military man."

"He works for Malik?" said Andreas. "I thought he'd been a
bodyguard for the dead cousin?"

"He had been, but according to Malik, both he and Tomislav
were taken hostage by the third man in that photograph, and
when he let them go, Malik asked Tomislav on the spot to
work for him as security. At least until the police caught his
cousin's killer. Malik said he needed security because he feared
his cousin's sons might do something irrational. He said they
were hotheads who might not realize he was an innocent victim
of the same attacker of their father."

"Do you believe his story?"

"Well, the part about the sons proved true. Two of them
ended up among the three dead intruders."

"Oh, boy."

"You've got that right. You can't imagine all the hell that's
broken loose over here. I'd appreciate it if you'd give me the
name of the third man in the photo. It will take a lot of heat
off me."

Andreas shut his eyes. He knew he should wait to confirm
this wasn't another ruse to get the name.

Sometimes you've got to trust your instincts.

"Alban Kennel."

Portly Man sat reading his newspaper and sipping his coffee
in the same hookah café as he did every morning, two doors
down from his large marine supply shop on one of Izmir's main
shopping streets. He took no notice of the other customers
until one abruptly sat down at his table.

"Do you mind company?"

The man stared. "What are you doing here?"

"We had a deal, remember? A deal that we'd live in peace."

"Yes, we have such a deal."

Aryan sighed "Not everyone seems to agree, and that makes me very uneasy."

Portly Man put down his paper. "What are you talking about?"

"Last night, uninvited visitors paid a visit to Malik's home. Three of them are no longer with us. The fourth I trust you will arrange to soon join them."

"You're making no sense to me."

"Assuming your newspaper doesn't cover it, I'm sure with your contacts in the police, you'll be able to figure it out quickly enough. And quickly is when I expect you to resolve this dissension in your ranks." He patted Portly Man's hand. "Make that *our* ranks."

"What is it you want me to do?"

Aryan smiled beneath a serpent-like stare. "I could easily do it myself, but I thought it best to ask you to use your influence with the others to take this opportunity to demonstrate your commitment to our agreement, and to provide proof that no one else had anything to do with last night's betrayal of trust."

Portly Man reached for his coffee but stopped when he realized his hand was shaking. "I will speak to them."

"Fine," said Aryan, standing. "I expect it resolved today. Enjoy the rest of your morning."

Portly Man watched Aryan leave before reaching for his coffee and, holding it with two hands, said a quick prayer.

Next, he called his cousin on the police force.

Maggie, Yianni, and Andreas sat in Andreas' office staring at television coverage of the Greek Coast Guard caught up in yet another capsized refugee boat-rescue.

"Our boys deserve a lot of credit," said Maggie.

"But all they'll likely get is blame for whatever goes wrong," said Yianni.

"And if they don't, we will," said Andreas.

"It's the way of the world, boys," said Maggie. "The public needs someone to blame, otherwise there's no one left to fault but themselves."

"My guess is they'll pick us if we can't prove Aryan killed Volandes," said Andreas.

"But your investigation will save an innocent man wrongly accused of the murder," said Maggie.

"Some would call that soft on crime," said Yianni.

"How long do you think before your friend McLaughlin feels compelled to tee off again with the press at refugee smugglers?" asked Andreas.

"Don't know," shrugged Yianni. "I guess it depends on what happens next."

"Sure wish I had an answer to that," said Andreas. "We've got a world-class assassin hired to make an example on Lesvos of a prominent adversary of refugee smuggling, running up and down the Turkish coast taking out at least a half-dozen refugee smugglers of various levels of prominence."

Yianni smiled. "Maybe he saw the light and went over to our side."

Andreas flashed him an open palm. "Plus, we've got a prosecutor and forensic supervisor back on Lesvos trying to pin Volandes' murder on someone we know is innocent, who just happens to be employed by an NGO with an executive director hell-bent on committing suicide by threatening to publicly name the real killer. A name she does not know, I should add."

"To be fair," said Yianni, "it looks like she guessed right about Izmir being the big guy's headquarters."

"That could turn out to be a pyrrhic victory. A lot of people in Turkey might get nervous about what else she could know, and see her as too big a risk to ignore."

"I think she's going to cool it for now," said Yianni.

"Let's hope so, especially since we have no idea where Aryan is."

"What about that Malik guy?" asked Maggie.

Andreas picked up a pencil. "We know from Tassos' informant that Malik runs refugee smuggling out of Turkey into Lesvos, and according to the Turkish inspector, he's a cousin of the businessman beheaded in his office in Izmir. Plus, the guy found beheaded in a stolen car in Malik's territory the night after Volandes' murder worked with Malik's brother-in-law in refugee smuggling."

"A very cozy family arrangement," said Maggie.

Yianni nodded. "Until someone badly pissed off Aryan."

Andreas began tapping the pencil onto his desk. "Yianni, you've just given me an idea."

"Would you like to share it?" said Maggie.

"*Pissed off.* That's the key to nailing Aryan. We've got to find someone pissed off badly enough at Aryan to testify that he's our killer."

"And how do you suggest we go about finding someone willing to risk a literal beheading to help us put Aryan away?" asked Yianni.

"Let's start with the Greek family killed in the Turkish café. We know they weren't the targets, Aryan was. That's likely what set him off, and the guy found later that night beheaded in the stolen car, who must have been tied into the botched hit, worked with Malik's brother-in-law."

"Which meant Aryan knew Malik was involved."

Andreas nodded. "And possibly others."

"Like the late Izmir businessman," said Yianni.

"Which brings me back to wondering why that Malik guy's still breathing," said Maggie.

Yianni shrugged. "Perhaps because he fingered the Izmir bad guy to Aryan as the big boss behind everything?"

"Could be," said Andreas, "but that still has Malik involved in the hit, and Aryan doesn't strike me as the sort who gives a pass to someone who tried to kill him."

"Maybe he's using him for something else?" said Maggie.

"Aryan used Malik to get him in to see that guy in Izmir, and Malik later told the police he only did it because Aryan had him as a hostage."

"A bullshit story," said Yianni.

Andreas pointed the pencil at Yianni. "But what if he really is some sort of hostage? That would explain why he's still breathing. Because he's more valuable to Aryan alive than dead."

"For how long is that going to last?" said Maggie.

"Precisely." Andreas slammed the pencil on the desk. "And I bet you Malik knows that, too. All we have to do is find a way to get to Malik, and let him know that if he's willing to testify against Aryan, we'll protect him."

"He's going to want immunity for his part in the killing."

"If we get to the point of negotiations, I'd say we're way ahead of where we are now. Let's cross that bridge if we ever get to it. For now, though, we need to find some way to get to Malik. And we can't use the Turkish police. Who knows what they'll do."

"How about through one of his family?" said Maggie.

"If you happen to know a family member willing to turn on him, I'm all ears," said Andreas.

She waved her hand at Andreas in a less than ladylike gesture.

"So, how then do we get to Malik?" said Yianni.

"That's the sixty-four-thousand-euro question, and the only way I can think of finding the answer is from someone on the ground in Turkey who moves in those circles." Andreas leaned in toward Maggie and smiled. "Or perhaps through someone who knows such a person with access to Malik's world."

"If you're talking about Tassos, don't look at me. I'm more pissed at him than Aryan is at the Turks."

"A lover's quarrel?" said Yianni.

"No. Two people have to speak to each other in order to quarrel. And the son of a bitch hasn't called me or answered my calls since he left here after Easter."

Andreas started to say something, but stopped.

"Sounds like he's all wrapped up in a case," said Yianni.

"Nice try, Detective. That's the same sort of bullshit I'm getting from his office when I call Syros asking to speak with him." She twisted her shoulders back and forth and mimicked a coy young thing saying, "'I'm sorry, he's on assignment and unavailable.'"

Yianni laughed. "Do you really think something's wrong?"

"If there isn't, there damn sure will be by tomorrow, because if I don't hear from him by the end of the day, I'm on the first boat out of Piraeus to Syros Saturday morning."

Andreas pushed his pencil away. "I'm sure everything's fine and there's no need to worry."

Maggie closed her eyes and sighed. "I hope so. God, I hope so."

Aryan did not return to Malik's house until well after dark, first calling Tomislav to tell him he would be knocking on the back door.

"Where have you been?" said a somewhat hysterical Malik when Aryan strode into the living room.

"Making the world safe for you, my partner." He nodded at Deema. She looked away.

"The police have been here three times. Twice this morning and once this afternoon. The last time they searched the house."

"Did they find anything?"

"No."

"Good, then what are you worried about?" Aryan stretched and yawned.

"They might come back and find you."

"So what? They have no reason to arrest me."

"You killed my cousin."

"No, we killed your cousin. And if I am arrested, you're arrested. Our defense is self-defense. Pure and simple."

"But I told them I was not involved in the meeting where you murdered him."

"You were nervous, so you lied, because you were afraid of his proven vengeful children. But no matter, your only way out is to claim self-defense, and Tomislav here—a former employee of the decedent and the only objective observer in the room at the time—will back us up on that."

Tomislav nodded.

"But what if they find out about your past? There may be others who want to arrest you."

He smiled. "I have no past."

Malik shook his head, and pointed toward an ivory inlaid coffee table. "That package on the table came for you."

Aryan picked up a book-size envelope. "It's light." He turned it over in his hands several times, sniffing at it as he did, before carefully opening it at one end. He smiled as soon as he saw inside. "Ah, how I love efficiency."

He dumped the contents on the table: a blood-soaked red beret with bullet hole through the top.

Deema walked out of the room.

Malik stared at the beret. "He was the last of my cousin's bloodline."

"A lesson to be taken," said Aryan. "I'm hungry, what do we have to eat?"

Malik called for the maid, his face pale.

"Don't be so disheartened, it's a new life for us. Everything will work out just fine." He eyed a bowl of dried apricots on a sideboard across the room.

"The police will be back," said Malik.

"Why do you keep saying that? They have nothing to go on as long as we keep saying self-defense." He walked toward the sideboard.

"No, it's not that. They think I know someone I do not

know. They asked me, they asked my wife, they asked the maid, they asked Tomislav, they asked me again."

Aryan reached for a dried apricot. "Who are they looking for?"

"Someone named Alban Kennel."

Aryan blinked and withdrew his hand. He'd lost his appetite.

Deema hurried up the stairs toward her children's room. She knew the meaning of the bloody beret: another life taken by the two men who one day soon would take hers.

Then who would look after her children? Who would keep them from turning into their father, or the foreigner?

She stood outside her children's bedroom staring at the door.

It is better they die now than face such a fate.

She shut her eyes, and did what so many seeking refuge did in such moments of total despair. She prayed.

Chapter Sixteen

At five years old, Tassaki had begun the process of schooling that would take him on a fixed route though the traditional institutions attended by Greece's rich and prominent. Rarely did the routine vary, except for those who went off to boarding schools in foreign lands, because the camaraderie of childhood translated into lifelong connections and support.

The big adjustment in his life, though, came in the form of a three-month-old sister. His friends had siblings, so did his cousins, but having one of your own living with you on your once-exclusive turf was different. His mother and father went out of their way to tell him how lucky they all were to have another person to love and love them, but he wasn't so sure. She didn't talk, slept a lot, and cried sometimes, but no one seemed to mind. A lot of visitors came to the apartment to see her. They'd bring her gifts, tickle her toes, and make sounds and faces he thought silly. They'd also say nice things to him, and some even brought him gifts, but he knew they'd really come to see her.

Babies needed a lot of attention. They weren't grown up like he was. His father had told him he had a duty as her brother to protect his sister. He knew a duty was something important, but how would he know that his sister needed help when she couldn't talk? It wasn't like with those babies he saw on television, the ones who'd fallen into the sea and couldn't swim. He could tell they needed help.

He was lucky. He knew how to swim.

• • ● • •

"Why are you looking so serious, son?" said Andreas tousling Tassaki's hair.

"I want to teach Sofia to swim."

Andreas smiled. "We'll do it this summer."

"She needs to know, Dad, before she gets on a boat."

"She'll be fine. She'll have her own life jacket, just like yours."

"Life jackets didn't save the children on television."

Andreas' smile disappeared, and he knelt down to his son's eye level. "What children?"

"The ones in the boats that sank."

"Where did you see that?" Lila and he had been careful not to watch that sort of news in front of their son, out of concern for the very worry he now saw on his son's face.

"I told you, on TV."

Andreas drew in and let out a breath. No reason to cross-examine his son. It could have happened anywhere. A careless night watching a show together in bed thinking him asleep when a breaking news update came on, a television running when no one thought him around, or something he saw at a friend's house on a play date. It didn't matter now, the image had fixed in his mind.

"Your sister is safe."

"I don't want her to drown."

Andreas hugged him. "Don't worry. I won't let that happen."

"Promise?"

Andreas swallowed. "Promise."

Tassaki hugged his father. "I'm doing my duty, Daddy, just like you told me. Protecting our family."

Andreas smiled and kissed him on the forehead. "Time for your bath. Run along. I'll be in to read you a story later."

Tassaki took off like a shot.

How quickly they grow up. He felt proud to hear his son embrace duty to family so passionately. It reminded him of something he'd meant to do earlier. He walked into the living room, picked up the phone, and dialed. He sat on the couch, looking out at the brightly lit Acropolis while waiting for someone to answer.

"Syros Police, Sergeant Tsappas."

"Sergeant, this is Chief Inspector Andreas Kaldis, and I'm looking to speak to Chief Homicide Investigator Stamatos."

"He's away on—"

"Assignment. Yes, Sergeant, I know the official line, but let me put it to you differently. I repeat, this is Chief Inspector Andreas Kaldis, Head of Special Crimes and the former Minister of Public Order. So, whose bad side would you prefer to be on, Tassos' or mine? And before you answer, please consider that, one way or the other, I'm going to find out what's going on with my friend."

A whisper came through the phone. "He's okay, Chief, honest. He just doesn't want anyone to know."

"To know what?"

"Promise you won't tell him I told you."

"Sergeant Tsappas—"

"He had a heart incident and has been in the hospital for the past couple of days."

Andreas' own heart skipped a beat. "A heart attack?"

"No, they said it wasn't a heart attack, but he's going to need surgery."

"My God," said Andreas. "What hospital is he in?"

"I—I'm not so sure it's a good idea to tell you."

"Just give me the goddamned hospital's number!" Andreas shouted.

"Uh, Chief, if you call him in the state you're in now, you might do him a lot more harm than good. He needs to take it easy."

An Aegean April   201

Andreas shut his eyes. "You're right, Sergeant. Absolutely right. I'm sorry I yelled. It's just that he's like family to me."

"I know, he speaks the same way about you."

Andreas held back a tear. "I promise to stay calm. Honest."

The sergeant gave Andreas the number and five minutes later, after a few more rounds of you-better-let-me-talk-to-him with the hospital operator and various supervisors, the phone rang in Tassos' room.

"Hello."

"Hi, buddy," said Andreas.

"I assumed that sooner or later you'd find me. Sure took you long enough."

"I'm not as efficient a detective as you."

"Damn straight." Tassos coughed.

"How are you feeling?"

"About as you'd expect. Tubes everywhere, lights on all the time, nurses running in and out checking the machines and prodding me. They act as if I'm someone important."

"If you'd like, I could set them straight about you."

"Spoken like a true friend."

"So, what's on the agenda?"

Tassos paused. "Does Maggie know?"

"Not from me."

"Promise you won't tell her."

"It's not up to me; that's your call." Andreas hesitated, not sure if he should say what he was thinking. "But I have to ask, why don't you want her to know?"

He could hear Tassos breathing deeply.

"She's too caring. If she knows there's something wrong she'd come running."

"And that's bad?"

"She'll feel the need to care for me. I don't want her to feel responsible for an invalid. It will cripple her life too."

Andreas felt a rush of anxiety. "You're making it sound very serious."

"They found two nearly blocked arteries and an aortic valve that has to be replaced."

"That's it?"

"Isn't that enough?"

"Jeez, Tassos, that sort of surgery is done every day. My father-in-law had the same things done at a dozen years older than you, and was up and about in no time."

"Honest?"

"Listen, my friend, you've got to face up to this and realize you've got a lot of friends out there willing to pitch in to help you—in ways like bringing you up to speed on what's really going on in this world beyond chasing bad guys. Your medical knowledge seems stuck back in the days of bloodletting and leeches. All you have to do is ask."

"Who do you suggest I talk to?"

"If I gave you any name other than Maggie's in response to that question, I'd be in the bed next to you once she found out."

"She'll tell me, 'I told you so.'"

"And if she's right, maybe next time you'll listen."

"She'll put me on a diet."

"Did I just hear you correctly?"

"Okay, the doctor's already told me I can either lose weight or lose years."

"Nicely put."

Tassos paused. "I guess I should call her."

"All I can tell you is that if you don't, you're going to see her anyway, because she told me she'll be on the first boat tomorrow to Syros."

Tassos laughed. "If she does that, she'll kill me for sure… assuming the surgery doesn't get the job done first, because they're airlifting me to Athens tomorrow morning. They wanted to stabilize me here before moving me there."

"You better call her. And let me know where you'll be. Otherwise, I'll be in just as deep shit with the love of my life as you'll be in with yours if you don't tell her everything ASAP."

Tassos chuckled. "I got you covered. Thanks for calling. And for that gentle kick in the ass. I better get off and call Maggie before it's too late. Bye."

"Bye." Andreas drew in and let out a deep breath as he hung up the phone.

"Nicely done."

Andreas spun his head around to see Lila standing by the doorway.

"You heard?"

"With you screaming at the top of your lungs, how could I resist finding out what had you so worked up. I assume that was Tassos. Is he okay?"

"I hope so. It sounds like he's going in for a cardiac catheterization on two arteries and a valve replacement."

"Like my father."

"That's what I told him. I think his head's in a better place now."

Lila walked over and sat down next to him. "Promise me, Andreas, that you'd never keep any bad health news from me."

"Why would I ever do that?"

"Because certain macho men types have problems along that line."

Andreas patted her thigh "Don't worry. I don't have that hang-up. I know that someday that sort of bad news will come—if we're lucky. Otherwise it's just one big bye-bye-world moment."

She waved her hand. "No need to overdo it with the reassurances. I just wanted you to understand that I took the 'in sickness and in health vow' very seriously."

"But what about the 'obey' part?"

"I must have been day-dreaming and missed it."

Andreas smiled. "There's something I should tell you."

Lila crossed herself. "Don't you dare make a joke about your health. It's not funny."

"No, it's nothing like that. Tassaki knows about refugee children drowning. I don't know how he knows, but he does."

"Is he frightened?"

"No, just worried for Sofia. He wants us to teach her to swim."

Lila squeezed Andreas' hand. "I guess it's a good sign when a five-year-old learns about the dark side of life and thinks only of how best to protect his sister."

Andreas smiled. "Good point. I hadn't thought of it quite that way."

"*Daddy,*" came echoing down the hall.

"Like father like son," said Lila. "He's developing a very robust scream."

"It's storytelling time." Andreas stood up. He reached out his hand for Lila's. "Let's do it together."

Lila stood. "I'd like that.

Andreas kissed her on the cheek. "It's all about family."

She patted him on the butt. "And, if we're lucky, friends like you."

Aryan went to bed alone that night. He had no desire to be with anyone. Nor did he sleep.

How could they know his true name? Where had he fucked up? He'd spent half the night running through every conceivable source. He had no fingerprints or DNA on record. At least none that he knew of, and he'd changed his appearance. It could be someone who knew him after the plastic surgery. He compiled a list in his mind of every possible betrayer. He would have to deal with each one. He couldn't afford for this to happen again. But that would have to wait. The urgent problem was here.

He paused. No, not here. On Lesvos. It must be tied into that woman who spoke to the press. Everything flowed from that press conference. She'd drawn worldwide attention to his work on Lesvos, and someone, some enemy somewhere, could have recognized the swordplay and revealed his name. But who would dare? Again, he could trust no one.

He tossed in bed. He had to be careful. His knee-jerk reaction to grab the Lesvos woman and force her to tell who might know his true identity wouldn't work. He'd done interrogations that way many times before in many different situations, but then he'd worked anonymously in the fog of war, with no one caring what he did. Things were different now. Too many here would like to see him disposed of by the police. That would conveniently end his threat to their interests.

Killing an American always came with risks, but killing an American aid worker from an organization that had just seen another of its members murdered on the same island would inevitably generate relentless pressure on the police to find her killer. He needed to find a more subtle approach, one that ended her life before she publicly revealed his name to the world, yet satisfied the police without drawing him into the mix.

Yes, he needed to plan much more carefully.

Lila and Andreas spent a few hours on Saturday and Sunday visiting with Tassos and Maggie at the hospital. Yianni stopped by each day and, together, they watched Maggie dote on Tassos while he faked that he minded the attention. Maggie said she wouldn't be back at work, "until this is all straightened out," but that she'd arranged for a friend to cover for her.

Andreas told her not to worry.

"I have to worry," she said. "I'm a Greek woman."

Other than that, the weekend had passed as peacefully as the calm before a storm.

Andreas was headed out the door to lunch with Yianni when his office phone rang.

"It's the Mytilini police commander," said Maggie's friend. "Shall I tell him you're at lunch?"

He gestured no and pointed at Yianni. "I'll spend the whole time listening to him speculating on what the commander has to tell me. Put it through."

He walked back to his office, followed by Yianni, and reached across his desk to put the call on speakerphone. "Hi, you caught me just as Yianni and I were headed out. What's up?"

"We've got a strange development in the Volandes case. Make that *bizarre* development."

Andreas dropped into one of the chairs in front of his desk. "Is it good bizarre or bad?"

"Depends on who you talk to. The prosecutor has agreed to release Ali."

"That sounds good," said Yianni.

"For Ali," said the commander.

"Why's he letting him out?" said Andreas.

"According to the prosecutor's forensic supervisor, who also happens to be my daughter's boss, the evidence doesn't support a case against Ali."

"So he's come around to agreeing that Ali isn't the killer?" said Yianni.

"Not exactly," said the commander. "He's saying the evidence won't make it a slam-dunk conviction, which to this prosecutor makes it a no-go prosecution."

"I thought you said the forensic supervisor does whatever it takes to get that prosecutor convictions," said Andreas.

"And on this investigation he went out of its way to set Ali up to take the fall," added Yianni.

"Yes to both points," said the commander. "Which is precisely what makes this development so bizarre. First thing this morning, the forensic supervisor had a letter delivered to the prosecutor's office stating that his department's report was riddled with errors and faulty observations, making it impossible to rely upon it in any prosecution. In other words, bye-bye physical evidence."

"Wow, that's quite a screw-up to own up to," said Yianni.

"Don't start admiring him. The only blame he admitted to was entrusting my daughter to know what she was doing, claiming the professional disaster was all her fault. Well, not quite all her fault because he did go out of his way in his letter to write—and I quote—'Her techniques typify the same absence of attention to readily observable details as features so prominently in her father's many botched investigations,' end quote."

"How nice of him to give you credit," said Andreas.

"Yes, I can't wait to find his car illegally parked."

"That's quite a serious charge. How's your daughter taking it?" said Yianni.

"She's laughing."

"What?" said Andreas.

The commander told him how his daughter had given in to her boss' demand that she blindly sign his report, but did so using the words, "I disagree" as her signature.

Andreas laughed. "That's quick thinking. How long do you think it will be until someone picks up on that?"

"If someone does, it won't affect Ali's release because the forensic supervisor has admitted the facts are wrong, regardless of who recorded them. As for my daughter, she's out of there anyway, as soon as she finds a new job, and if either her boss or the prosecutor tries pushing this any further against her, whether they know the truth or not about the report, at the appropriate moment I'll shove that report up their asses. Sideways."

"Sounds like a plan," said Yianni.

"But why do you think the supervisor decided to do this, since we know his reason is bullshit?" asked Andreas.

Yianni said, "Maybe he was worried about the observations in the report coming out at trial as phony, and he didn't want to risk the public humiliation?"

"My vote," said the commander, "is any explanation that involves putting profit in his pocket or covering up one of his many past transgressions."

"I see you hold him in high regard," said Andreas.

"You have no idea. And I'm not talking about calling a suicide an accidental death so that some tortured soul can be buried in consecrated ground. I'm talking about finding the most outrageous practitioners of unsafe, illegal procedures as 'not at fault' for horrendous outcomes. As I see it, he relishes every disaster requiring his involvement as a potential profit opportunity."

"Like mass drownings at sea?" asked Yianni.

"You get my point."

"With what came out at that press conference, Ali's going to have a target on his back," said Andreas.

"I know."

"So, when do you let him out?"

"I can't do that until I officially hear from the prosecutor. My guess is that won't happen until tomorrow."

"If you haven't heard from the prosecutor, how do you know what you just told us?" asked Andreas.

"From my daughter. Her boss had the memo typed up this morning before his secretary got in, and the one who did the typing was my niece. She smuggled my daughter a copy."

"Quite a loyal office he runs."

"That's a reason to hire your own relatives. Unless you have any more questions, gentlemen, I've told you all I know."

"Thanks. Catch you later. Bye." Andreas didn't move from his chair, just stared at the speaker until he heard the commander hang up. "Something's not right here. I feel it in my bones."

"Me too," said Yianni.

"Too quick a reversal on the prosecution without any justifiable new reason."

"At least none we know of."

"There's some other story playing out here, Yianni, and I don't see a happy ending in it for Ali."

"So, what do we do?"

"Call the McLaughlin woman and see what she knows about this."

"But what about protecting Ali?"

"Yes," said Andreas. "Alert immigration on Lesvos to be on the lookout for Aryan trying to get back on the island."

"You mean Alban Kennel?"

"I have no idea what name he'll be using. Send them his photo. That's likely all we'll have to go on."

"Do you think he'd try to come to Lesvos through an official point of entry?"

"It's all we can hope for."

"But why would he come back?"

"That's something I hope we never get an answer to."

"Why?"

"Because I'm afraid it will involve more dead bodies."

Dana looked at the number ringing on her mobile. An Athens number. She recognized it as that of the detective she'd spoken to before. She knew what he must be calling about. Aleka had called her an hour before with the news about Ali. Aleka said she'd told her father. He must have told the Athens cops. Now they were calling her. At least they were thinking of her.

Dana's big question to Aleka had been why the sudden change of mind? Aleka gave no answer, just told her to meet her in an hour at a taverna down by the old harbor. A bit dramatic, Dana thought, but then again, her entire life had turned into a BBC murder mystery, albeit set on an Aegean island.

Dana arrived in the old harbor at the end of Ermou Street precisely on time, but she'd forgotten in which of the half-dozen tavernas lined up across the road from their open-air, summertime seaside venues she was supposed to meet Aleka. So, she went from taverna to taverna until she found her sitting at a table in the rear of the one with the least number of windows open to the street.

"I take it from where you chose to sit that you don't want to be seen with me," said Dana smiling as she sat down.

"Not sure which of us benefits more from that, but I figured it wouldn't hurt to be cautious."

"Cautious of what?"

"Of whatever the hell is going on in my office," said Aleka. "Look, I'm a cop's kid, I grew up surrounded by paranoid thinkers, I get all of that. But something's not right about this lock-him-up, now let-him-go scenario. Since day one my boss has been wound up to get your friend Ali tried for the murder of Mihalis Volandes. Now he's suddenly all fired up for letting him go. I don't get the sudden change of heart."

"Guilty conscience?" shrugged Dana.

"Not a chance. I know Ali's your friend and you want him out, but something's wrong about this."

"You think someone wants him out to get at him?"

"If by 'get at him' you mean kill him…." Aleka shrugged.

"I've heard this scenario before. From your father and the Athens cop."

Aleka forced a smile. "Is that your way of saying there's nothing more for us to do about his fate?"

Dana raised her hands in a gesture of surrender. "Whoa, I'm not criticizing you, just letting you know that you're not the only one who feels that way."

Aleka let out a breath. "Sorry. I'm just tired of too many on this island seeing bad endings as inevitable."

"Well, I'm certainly not one of them."

Aleka waved for the waiter, and Dana ordered a coffee.

Aleka let out a deep breath. "I realize I'm edgy at times. It gets me to wondering how long it will take for me—make that everyone on my island—to recover our footing. The media talks about how refugees are affected by experiences so far beyond the scope of any rational coping mechanism. What about us? We've seen too much, experienced too much."

Aleka shook her head. "I've watched folks on Lesvos who'd once praised their neighbors' efforts at helping refugees—and basked in our island's nomination for the Nobel Peace Prize because of those efforts—turn angry at those same neighbors, even boycott their businesses, arguing they shared in the blame many now cast upon the refugees for the island's struggling economy."

Aleka took a sip of her coffee. "We've changed. My generation, for sure...dead babies on the beach, armies of desperate people trekking across our island begging for help, good people helping, others taking advantage, most refugees considerate, others criminal, the media making a show, the government setting up internment camps, international celebrities showing up for photo ops." She threw up her hands. "Why am I telling you all this? You know it as well as I do."

Dana leaned across the table and patted Aleka's arm. "It's not just your island that's affected. We who come to help are conflicted too, sometimes by people whose motives most see as saintly. For example, we get volunteers who come here on their school breaks wanting to help the refugees. How can you fault them? Yet, what they too often do is force us to assign full-time workers to train them, and just when they're able to function on their own as a true on-the-ground benefit to our efforts, they're off and back to school."

"That must be very frustrating for your people."

"I wouldn't be surprised if that's one of the reasons Ali didn't mind being in jail. It's Easter break, and a big-time draw for refugee tourism."

"Ouch, that's a rather harsh phrase for describing people trying to help," said Aleka.

"Not nearly as harsh as the feelings I hold for media types who flock to refugee centers looking for a 'new take' on the same story." Dana flashed finger quotes. "They seek out the refugee with the most horrific, heartbreaking story, thinking that their brilliant reporting will help the desperate refugee gain assistance. So, they get the poor soul to rip off the scab once more, get the story, and then disappear, never to be heard from again."

Aleka nodded. "All of which brings us around to why I asked for you to meet me here."

Dana sat up. "That sounds intriguing."

"I think you should call another press conference."

"What?"

Aleka nodded. "You heard me. This time to announce a vast conspiracy aimed at concealing the true circumstances of the murder of Mihalis Volandes."

Dana stared at her. "Well, so much for my thinking you're a parrot for law enforcement's official line. They've all been telling me to lay low and keep my mouth shut."

"I know, but with what happened this morning I don't see that as the way to go."

"You mean the decision to release Ali?"

Aleka nodded. "Like I said, it makes no sense to me. Not only does it run counter to everything my boss has been doing to get Ali convicted, it galvanizes the press into wondering who might be the real killer. In unexpectedly releasing Ali, they've gone ahead and stirred up the hornets' nest they'd been working so very hard at keeping under control."

"Who are *they*?"

"I wish I knew. But letting this play out the way my boss and whoever else is trying to re-position things, strikes me as definitely the wrong way to go."

"Convince me."

"My boss now says the physical evidence is useless, not that Ali didn't do it, only that they can't prove it. That still dangles Ali out there as a suspect, and if somehow he's made to look guilty, perhaps even die in the process, it would resolve a lot of problems for a lot of people."

"I've heard that scenario before, too."

"That doesn't mean it's not true."

Dana nodded. "But where does a press conference come in?"

"The last one you held set a lot of things in motion. Sitting back and doing nothing allows whatever the bad guys have planned—and there's definitely something in mind—to move forward according to their schedule. But if you seize the initiative it might force them to change plans."

"You mean kill Ali sooner?" said Dana.

"If it's a question of trying to kill him sooner or later, don't you think it better to get the killer to attempt to do it on our terms?"

"Who's 'our'? You and me?"

Aleka smiled. "Hardly. I never was into Nancy Drew. Call the conference, then we'll tell the police all about our plan."

"Why don't we tell them before I call the press conference?"

"Because I know my father. He'll lock us both up."

Dana nodded with a faint smile. "I believe you."

"So you're in?"

"Let me think about it. But I like it. After all, what do I have to lose?"

Chapter Seventeen

"Any news?" said Yianni, poking his head into Andreas' office first thing Tuesday morning.

"About what?"

"Turkey. It's been all quiet on the eastern front since Friday."

"I doubt it's going to stay that way."

Yianni stepped inside the office. "Why do you say that?"

Andreas shrugged. "Not sure. It just bothers me that a hot-to-trot prosecutor decides out of the blue to release his only suspect. I'm waiting for the other shoe to drop. Have you spoken to McLaughlin?"

"No. She's back to not answering my calls."

"Any word from Immigration?"

Yianni gestured no.

"Great."

"Maybe our phones aren't working?"

As if on cue, Andreas' phone rang. He reached for it before Maggie's stand-in had the chance to answer for him. "Kaldis here."

A woman's voice said, "Chief Inspector, I have the Minister of Public Order on the line for you. One moment please."

He looked at Yianni. "Great, our boss. Now what?"

"Kaldis?"

"Yes, Minister?"

"What the hell's going on over on Lesvos?"

Andreas cleared his throat. "From what I understand, the prosecutor no longer believes the evidence supports a case against his suspect and so he's releasing him from custody."

"I'm not talking about that, I'm talking about this damn press conference that's all over the news."

Andreas blanched and pointed Yianni at the television mounted on the wall. Yianni grabbed the remote and turned it on. A still picture of Dana McLaughlin filled the screen above a banner headline running across the bottom of the screen: PRESS CONFERENCE NAMING KILLER OF MIHALIS VOLANDES SCHEDULED FOR LATER TODAY.

"Son of a bitch," said Andreas.

"I assume that's not directed at me," said the minister.

Not this time.

"Do you have an answer I can pass on to the Prime Minister for why a private citizen seems to have more information on who killed one of our leading citizens than do our police?"

"She doesn't know any more than we do, just has a hell of a lot worse judgment. As to why she's claiming to know, I can't say, but we're on the next plane to Lesvos to find out."

Yianni walked to the doorway, leaned out, and told Maggie's friend, "The Chief and I need tickets on the next flight to Lesvos."

He looked back at Andreas and added, "Leave them open return."

Dana heard the Mytilini police commander yelling for her well before he barged into her office.

"Ms. McLaughlin, have you gone insane?"

"How nice to see you, Commander. Is Ali with you?"

He slammed his hand on her desktop. "This is not a game, young lady."

Dana straightened a photograph of her family knocked over

by the commander's smack to the desk. "No need to remind me that we're talking about real lives here. Remember, it's my organization's benefactor and friend who was murdered, and my employee who's wrongfully accused, arrested, and likely *still* sitting in your jail."

He leaned across her desk. "If you're keeping a body count, you've left out a few."

Dana cocked her head. "I don't understand."

"I just got off the phone with Chief Inspector Kaldis. It appears the killer you're so hell-bent on identifying has been a very busy boy."

She fidgeted with the hair beside her ear. "What are you saying?"

"Bottom line?" He scowled. "You just publicly threatened to announce the name of a world-class, maniacal killer across the planet for God-knows-what reason."

"To protect Ali," she said. "We were always going to tell you. Our plan is to draw him out so you could catch him."

"We? Who are we?"

Dana paused. "I meant me."

He dropped into a chair across the desk from her. "I don't know what sort of crazy thinking has ahold of you, but from here on out, I'm just following orders. It's someone else's problem to figure you out."

"What's that supposed to mean?"

"Kaldis told me not to let you out of my sight until he gets here."

She tugged at her hair and bit her lip. "He's coming. Good."

The commander stared at her. "From the way he sounded, I'm not sure 'good' is the word I'd use."

• • ● • •

As the more recent visitor of the pair to Mytilini, Yianni drove from the airport while Andreas took in the scenery. They headed toward Dana's office on the northern edge of Mytilini, close by the road leading to her NGO's primary remaining work locations on Lesvos: Kara Tepe and Moria Relocation Centers. Her office sat along a road running next to the sea, but in a far-from-elegant setting. A heavily littered, narrow strip of beach across from the office served as home to several rusting container ship pods, and abandoned or rundown industrial buildings peppered the neighborhood.

They parked off the road on the side away from the sea, close up against a concrete wall next door to a small, three-story, dirty-yellow apartment building. A discreet sign on the second floor door of that building read SAFEPASSAGE. Obviously, this NGO chose to plow its money into good works over image.

Andreas wondered how Aryan would react to Dana's latest mad act. Flight or fight are the natural choices for a threatened animal, but that presumed a rational animal. Even the fiercest tiger had enough sense to flee if it could. Aryan could be gone from this part of the world by now, never to be found. So why would he want to stay? But *if* he stayed, he needed to protect his lair, and that did not bode well for those he perceived as threats.

Andreas knocked on the door, and a voice from inside yelled, "It's open."

Not a wise way to keep the unwanted at bay.

Inside, the vestibule walls stood covered in posters, flyers, photographs, and messages, giving the place a homey feel, but one in keeping with the unkempt neighborhood.

They followed the sound of voices into what looked to have been a living room in the place's days as an apartment. A deep brown area rug in a tight-tufted industrial weave sat in the middle of the room, atop the same sort of book-size, beige faux-marble tiles as covered the other rooms' floors. Overall, it reflected a match-as-cheaply-as-possible approach to decorating.

Andreas nodded to the commander sitting across a small rectangular table from a woman matching the image of Dana McLaughlin on television. Both stood, but Andreas motioned for them to sit. He'd never met her before, and come to think of it, neither had Yianni. She looked younger, slenderer, and more fit in person than on TV. In fact, she looked very much like a freckle-faced, red-headed marathoner.

Yianni walked over and introduced himself to Dana, but Andreas simply sat next to the commander and stared across the table at her. He wasn't playing mind games, just immersed in searching for some sign or sense of what made this obviously bright young woman so distrusting of him that she'd rather blindly leap into an abyss than talk to him first.

Obviously, she saw him as part of an uncaring, non-evolved establishment that ignored the most basic needs of the refugees she'd dedicated her life to saving. But he sensed something more, a deeper underlying anger and mistrust of police, perhaps of all authority. He knew it a waste of time to attempt challenging her perceptions directly. Her image of him and what he represented stood as fixed as those her critics held of her, her views of life, and those she served. It was humankind at war with itself, few caring to look beyond his or her own agendas. For both sides, all was black or white, good or bad, faith or heresy.

After saying hello to Yianni, she simply stared straight back at Andreas.

"Ms. McLaughin," Andreas said in English. "I'm sure your motives were well-intended, but—"

"Stop patronizing me, Chief Inspector," snapped Dana.

Andreas' expression did not change. "I'm sure your motives were well-intended, but I'm afraid they've upset the proverbial applecart."

"In order to upset an applecart, you need to have one in the first place, and as far as I can tell you have absolutely no strategy for capturing Mihalis' true killer."

"Frankly, it would have been better for all concerned had you taken the time to ask me that question before unilaterally deciding to torpedo our plans."

"You're mixing your metaphors."

"And you're risking lives."

"He's already made that point," said Dana, nodding at the commander sitting between Yianni and Andreas.

"And I bet you don't believe him either," said Andreas.

"Why would the killer want to come after me? If I know his name, he has to assume the police know it too, so what does he gain by killing me?"

Andreas stared at her. "That sounds perfectly logical to a rational mind. The trouble is, this killer's logic board is irretrievably warped. To him, killing you could easily serve as an example to others never to mention his name, or as proof to himself of his power over all things. You're not playing with fire here. Fire at least has some predictability. You're playing with the mind of a madman."

She shrugged. "So what's your great plan I destroyed?"

"A simple, elemental one. With so many people dying every day, adrenaline had taken over for thought. We wanted things to calm down, give the killer a chance to evaluate his options, not just react, and for those in direct battle with him to do the same. We needed to convince those closest to him that helping us capture him stood as their only viable way of protecting themselves from him."

"Diplomacy?" she said. "What makes you think your killer won't just disappear while you're playing the long game?"

"He might, and that would certainly be in your best interests, but somehow I don't think your sending in beaters with television cameras to flush him out like a tiger is the way to do it, because this uniquely dangerous tiger is particularly adept at devouring its pursuers."

"I'm tired of your analogies."

"Well, then how about these facts? The Turkish police can't

find him even though they know who he is, what he looks like, and whom he's likely with. Three guys who crossed him have been decapitated, three others shot to death, and who knows how many more he's killed who haven't turned up yet. The man is a killing machine. Does it make you more comfortable now knowing you're not dealing with my tigers?"

She shut her eyes, opened them again. "Look at it from our point of view. What other choice did I have? If we do nothing, he simply kills Ali. You know that's why Ali's free. You also must realize it's the killer who somehow got him released."

"I'm not disagreeing with that, but now you've put your own head on the literal chopping block, and given us two targets to worry about."

"But if the killer's as insane as you say, he'll try to stop me from holding the press conference."

"How does that possibly help you?"

"It gives you the chance to catch him."

Andreas threw up his hands. "And how, pray tell, do you suggest we do that?"

"I don't know. That's your job, not mine."

Andreas gritted his teeth. "I'm all out of magic potions and incantations. You started this and unless you announce right now that it was just a publicity stunt aimed at getting the police to work harder on solving the case, and you get on the very the next plane out of Greece, I don't see how we can protect you from the many potential ways and opportunities this killer has for taking you out."

"What's that supposed to mean?"

"Where do you plan on holding the press conference?"

"At the murder scene."

The commander barked a laugh. "Great. The one place on the island our killer likely knows better than we do."

"What do you intend on doing after the press conference?" said Andreas.

She shrugged. "I haven't thought about that. Just keep doing the usual things."

Andreas nodded. "Like spending time at refugee camps, driving long distances over lonely deserted stretches of island roads, sleeping where you always sleep, seeing the same friends—"

"Okay, I get your point, Chief Inspector. My routine makes me a target."

"Frankly," said the commander. "It's your mouth that makes you a target. Your routine just makes you an *easy* target."

"No reason to be rude," she said.

Andreas jumped in. "You don't seem to appreciate the situation. I'm not sure if it's out of false bravado, masked fear, or something else, but we're telling you that someone very skilled at killing people likely wants you dead, and you have absolutely no idea who he is."

She bit at her lip. "Maybe if I don't go through with the press conference he'll take it as a sign I don't know and forget about me."

Andreas glanced at Yianni.

"Well, at least you're coming around to appreciating the situation," said Yianni.

"Do you think that would convince him to leave me alone?" She looked at her hands.

Andreas gestured no. "I think it's too late. This sort of killer isn't likely to change his mindset once he's fixed on his prey."

"So, what do I do?"

"What do you want to do? It's your life on the line," said Andreas.

"I have no name to announce at the press conference. It's all a bluff on my part to smoke out the killer." She ran her hands through her hair. "If what you say is correct, then it's the worst of all worlds for me. Even if I don't name him at the press conference, he may still kill me."

"Just to be sure that you can't name him," said the commander.

She rubbed at her eyes. "It might be better if I could name

him, because then I'd have done all I could to harm him, and no longer be a threat to your tiger, only an object of revenge."

Andreas nodded. "Possibly."

She put her head in her hands.

Andreas paused before speaking. "I think we'd all agree you've really fucked up. But let's see what we can do to minimize the risk, yours and Ali's, as I agree he's also a target." Andreas turned to the commander. "Can you get Ali here so we can figure out a strategy?"

"I don't know where he is. The prosecutor ordered his release while I was here baby-sitting Ms. McLaughlin and he left before anyone let me know."

Andreas drew in and let out a breath. He looked at Yianni. "Remember when I was talking before about that other shoe?"

Yianni nodded.

"Let's hope it hasn't dropped."

Ali had smiled throughout the discharge process, though his jailer labored solemn-faced while explaining to him that he was free to go once he signed papers he didn't really understand. Ali didn't care, he just wanted to leave, though he sensed he must have shown surprise when the jailer handed him all the things taken from him when he'd been arrested. That hadn't been his experience with other police in other lands. They would arrest refugees just to see what they could take from them. Back then, he did the same as he did now: never questioned, always smiled.

He behaved the same way today, not even asking why he'd been released. That did not seem a wise question to ask, for in his experience, police saw those who asked questions as trouble-makers. They preferred their subjects to smile, especially if your skin was as dark as Ali's.

He left the jail expecting to hear someone yelling, "Stop, come back!" He wanted to get as far away from the jail as fast as he could, but didn't dare run. A man of color running through a city street invited problems. So he strolled briskly in the direction of a bus stop that would take him back to where he had friends.

That thought reminded him to call Dana. He pulled his phone from his pocket. Dead. The jailer had returned it, but not charged it.

Ali recognized a taverna close by the bus stop. The food was cheap, and the décor slightly better than the cell he'd just left. He went inside and ordered a cheese toast and Coca-Cola. It would be his celebratory meal. He sat at a table as far back in the rear as he could find. No one could see him from the outside. He wanted to be alone and possibly get his mind off the stress of being in jail, not knowing what the law had in store for him. He still wasn't sure, but at least he was free for now and that was good.

He wondered if he'd ever be able to truly relax. For him, that required a sense of home, a truly safe place. His life now ran in perpetual transit; no family here, no family wherever he might end up, no family back in his homeland. He remained an unwelcome visitor in someone else's homeland, always conspicuous and far too likely viewed as a potential rapist, robber, disease carrier, or terrorist; never simply as another man.

Ali nibbled at his toast. He sat alone in the taverna, except for a tall white man who came in a few minutes after he did. The man sat two tables away, sipping a coffee and facing him. Ali sensed the man watching him, much like a cop might watch. Maybe he was a cop, and Ali's release was only conditional? Maybe he wasn't a cop, and was only curious? But the man seemed more interested than curious.

Ali wondered if the man might try to speak to him. He hoped not. He had no desire to play the role of accommodating refugee. He wanted to be free of that sort of subtle harassment. At least for now. There'd be time to fall back into that role later, after he went back to the NGO's office.

He'd thought about quitting his work with Dana, trying to head north to Germany, perhaps through a boat to Italy, like all those he dealt with on a daily basis dreamed of doing, searching desperately for a way north into Europe. North was the way to freedom—the same as for the American slaves he'd read about in school. Yes, he'd been educated, and would have been in college if his life hadn't exploded.

Literally exploded, killing his mother, father, and two younger sisters. At the moment of the bomb, he wanted to die with them, but something deep inside him convinced him to live on.

The same voice now told him to continue on in his work with Dana.

Right after he finished his Coke and toast.

Malik wasn't sure what to do next. The rash of murdered practitioners in the refugee-smuggling trade had severely spooked Malik's long-time political protectors, and though Aryan dismissed Malik's concerns by telling him to simply offer them a temporary larger share of the profits, the political heat burned too intensely. The male lineage of a politically prominent family had been wiped off the face of the earth in a matter of days. No one was willing to risk going forward with business as usual without a clear resolution of the conflict.

Malik dared not act without Aryan's input, but Aryan was nowhere to be found. He'd left first thing that morning on what he'd described as "personal business." He'd left no way to be reached, and Malik knew not what to do. So he did nothing.

Chapter Eighteen

His plane from Athens arrived early enough for him to be in position across from the jail before Ali came out. He'd called the jail from the airport to ask about visiting hours, hoping to catch the McLaughlin woman visiting with Ali before her press conference. The perfect assassination would have required the two of them together.

Pure luck landed him an officious officer who insisted on knowing the name of the inmate before answering his question, only to announce that a visit would be a waste of time, because he was being released this morning.

He'd followed Ali to a taverna and purposely sat close enough to him to gauge his state of mind. He could tell Ali sensed being watched from the stress showing on his face, even though he tended to default into a smile. He'd just spent days in jail accused of a murder he knew he didn't commit, lived as a refugee In a land growing angrier every day at the presence of his kind, and his skin stood out as dark amid a sea of white. All legitimate reasons for stress. But did he realize he'd soon die in a second assassination?

I think not.

• • ● • •

Ali left the taverna and headed straight for the bus stop. The man had left a moment before him, but Ali saw him standing at a nearby kiosk buying a newspaper. The man seemed to pay him no mind, but Ali kept glancing back over his shoulder at him. He hadn't moved from the kiosk, and a minute or so after Ali reached the bus stop, the man turned and walked the other way.

Ali breathed a sigh of relief. Five minutes later he was on a blue-and-white bus headed north toward his NGO's office, passing through neighborhoods he'd only hours before wondered whether he'd ever see again.

His mind wandered back to the moment he'd first landed on Lesvos, stepping off that wavering, overloaded, Chinese-made rubber boat into the surf, and that feeling of relief at having arrived alive, no longer in fear of war or drowning. Others might describe the emotion as joy or happiness, but he carried too many sad memories to call it that. Those who met the new arrivals on that scraggy, hilly beach offered directions to where each should go—Ali to Moria Relocation Center—but also told them to expect few services there, a decidedly different scenario from what the smugglers promised would be waiting for them in Greece.

But those were lies told by smugglers, not Greeks, and did not erode the promise of a new life flowering in the heart of each arriving refugee at having safely reached Greek shores. Disappointment would come later, once it sunk in that their arduous journey through EU bureaucracy had only just begun.

Little did he realize at the time that the long trek along hilly dirt roads and two-lane highways toward Moria symbolized so much more yet to come. Taxis, cars, and buses passed them by without offering to pick up even the very young, very old, or disabled. Only later did he learn that Greek law forbade all drivers but those with express police permission from giving refugees a ride, making even that simplest act of human kindness bureaucratically complex.

But what truly changed him lay only ten kilometers north-west of Mytilini: Moria. It changed many of its occupants. Just the mention of the name Moria triggered a vision in Ali's mind of the soaring chain link and razor wire containment fence surrounding much of the interior camp. That fence stood out to him not as a sign of where he had been confined, but of what the world thought him to be.

His next thought always ran to cardboard.

You'd find it everywhere. Underfoot, overhead. Detainees relied on it as a floor, a crib, a mattress shielding them from the bare ground, and held it above their heads as protection from the sun while standing in lines waiting...for something...for everything.

European governments called Moria a hotspot or detention center, but those who'd spent time there, as a worker, detainee, or visitor, knew the truth. This former military compound built to accommodate a maximum of four hundred, had become a concentration camp for three thousand.

And then there were the odors. Ali swallowed and stared out the bus window at the passing buildings.

But some good, too, had come to him through Moria. He'd found it in the children of the camp. Some with families, some without, many listless, defeated, afraid, unsmiling, and all looking for hope. They'd given him a means for honoring his own family's memory, a renewed purpose for smiling, and a reason for staying behind when his own chance at moving on arrived.

He sighed as his thoughts had led him back to Dana. She's who gave him the opportunity to work with the children. He prayed she hadn't lost hope now that Volandes was gone. So many NGOs had given up and left the island after Turkey's agreement with the EU dramatically curtailed the migrant flow. They felt there was nothing left for them to do, even though thousands still remained detained on Lesvos. Their departure left voids in services local volunteers tried to fill, as they'd done before the NGOs arrived. But now that was more difficult.

A sense of violence pervaded the camp, fueled by frustration, anger, disappointment, and fear. On top of that, Moria operated as a closed camp, meaning no visitors, only approved NGOs allowed, and an inevitable close-minded perspective on how things should be done…leading to riots.

A simple difference of color, religion, or culture summoned up such intense fears and biases in so many who thought of themselves as part of the civilized world, as to offer Ali little hope for his or the world's future. After all, what sort of fiendish subliminal intolerances caused otherwise decent souls shown a photograph of a dead child to measure the intensity of their reactions in direct proportion to the child's skin tone?

Despite all that, he persevered, because not to do so meant ceding his life to hopelessness. That was something he would never do. Nor, he believed, would Dana.

He got off the bus and walked the two blocks to the office. He noticed several strange cars parked outside. His reception committee, he presumed.

Time to practice his smile.

"Where have you been?" shouted Dana as Ali walked into the room. "I've been worried sick." She jumped up, ran around the table, and hugged him.

Ali let his hands dangle by his sides and smiled at the three men at the table through Dana's bear hug.

"Ali," she said, "these men are police, so be careful what you say."

Andreas shut his eyes and shook his head. "Not a very constructive way to start a conversation designed to keep you both alive." He opened his eyes.

"They think the only reason you're out of jail is because someone intends on killing you," said Dana.

"What the hell is wrong with you, McLaughlin?" said the

police commander. "Are you trying to scare the poor man to death?"

"It's the truth, isn't it?" she said,

"Yes," said the commander, "but how you tell it matters."

She crossed her arms. "I believe in telling it straight."

"Like you did to the media in announcing how you'd give them the name of Volandes' killer?" said Yianni. "A name you do not know."

She glared at Yianni.

"Well, have we all sufficiently vented?" Andreas rose to his feet. He extended his hand to Ali, "Hi, my name is Andreas Kaldis."

Ali shook it.

"I'm in charge of the Greek police force's special crimes unit, and I'm here with my assistant, Detective Yianni Kouros, and the Mytilini police commander, whom you already know, because we believe you're innocent of Mihalis Volandes' murder, and that your and Ms. McLaughlin's lives may be in danger from his real killer. We want to talk with you about how best to protect you and capture the killer."

Andreas turned to Dana. "Do you disagree with any of that?"

She clenched her lips but jerked her head straight up.

Andreas turned back to Ali. "Did you recognize that gesture as meaning no?"

Ali smiled as he jerked his head down, signifying yes in the Greek style.

Andreas smiled back, telling Ali what he'd told Dana about events in Turkey, and how Dana's threat of naming the killer to the media might draw him back to Lesvos.

Ali began blinking and his smile faded.

"What's wrong?" said Andreas.

"There was a man in the taverna where I got something to eat in town before coming here. I thought he was watching me. He stood outside the taverna when I left, and didn't leave until I reached the bus stop."

"Do you think he was following you?"

"I don't know."

"What did he look like?"

Ali shrugged. "Taller than me, white."

"How old?"'

"I have a hard time telling ages, as most people I know look much older than they are. I think under forty."

Andreas nodded at Yianni, and Yianni handed Ali a photograph.

"Is this the man?" asked Andreas.

Ali studied it intently. "I don't know, could be, but I can't be sure."

"Let me see it," said Dana.

"Only if you promise not to tell the media we have a photo of the possible killer," said Andreas.

"Why should I agree to that?"

"So that I show it to you."

She clenched her fists. "Okay."

Andreas held it up in front of her. She reached for it, but Andreas did not let her touch it. She dropped her hands and stared at the photo. "I've never seen him."

"It was taken at the scene of a triple murder north of Izmir," said Andreas.

Dana's eyes widened. "So I was right about Izmir."

"My gripe with you has nothing to do with whether you're right or wrong, but with the way you do things. You might think you're helping to catch your friend's killer, but you're actually screwing things up. I wish you'd somehow understand that we're all on the same side in this."

Ali cleared his throat. "Sirs, what is it you want of me?"

"Ali, you don't—"

Ali raised his hand. "Dana, I trust these men. If I am wrong, how am I any worse off? I have nothing to hide because I did not kill Mr. Volandes, and there is nothing more I can tell them about that night." He swallowed. "But if they are right, and I do not help them, both you and I will likely be dead. I see no choice but to cooperate."

Dana shrugged. "It's your life. Do as you choose."

Ali did not smile. "It is not just my life, it is yours too. I watched my entire family die." He paused. "It has taken me much time, but I have accepted that I had been helpless to save them. Now *you* are like family to me, the only family I have left, and I'm offered this chance to save you." He paused again. "Do you understand why I must do what I can to help?"

Dana shut her eyes and nodded.

Andreas drew in and let out a breath. Now all they had left to do was to come up with a plan.

Chapter Nineteen

Tassos instinctively looked at his watch when his cell phone rang. He could easily have checked for the time on his phone, but that glance at his wrist hung on as one of many old-fashioned habits he just couldn't break.

He did, though, check the caller ID. Maggie had told him to leave his phone on while she did some shopping, just in case she needed to reach him. She'd been with him from the instant he arrived at Athens Onassis Cardiac Surgery Center, and from that moment on she'd forbidden him to take calls, saying he needed his rest.

Caller ID read BLOCKED, so he ignored the call.

His catheterization surgery had gone well, and he'd likely be released tomorrow. The valve replacement surgery they'd schedule later. How much later he did not know. But getting out of here would be good, if only for a little while.

The phone rang again. The same BLOCKED ID message appeared on the screen.

"Wondering who the hell that is riles me up more than whatever it's about," he mumbled as he answered the phone with a brusque, "Hello."

"It's Ibrahim."

It took Tassos an instant to recognize the caller as his Turkish source who'd reluctantly given him the information he'd passed on to Andreas about the refugee smuggler named Malik.

"Well, aren't you a pleasant surprise? Never thought I'd hear from you again so soon."

"Spare me. I'm calling to do us both a favor," said Ibrahim in a decidedly impatient voice. "A lot of people are dying over here, and from what you squeezed out of me in our last conversation, I'm pretty sure everyone's interested in the same madman."

"Who would that be?"

"Don't play games with me. The one who killed your ship-owner on Lesvos."

"What's on your mind?" said Tassos, shifting in his hospital bed.

"The man's crazy. He's killed more than a half-dozen here and moved in on Malik's smuggling operation. No one believes he's going to stop there."

"Why don't you guys just follow your government's lead and do what you do best, eliminate the opposition?"

Ibrahim's voice rose. "Screw you. You think your politicians are any better?" He paused, and in a calmer voice said, "This is not about politics, but since you asked, those who feel threatened by the madman are too afraid to take the risk of eliminating him. They're convinced if they try and fail, he'll wipe out their families…as he did to one already."

Tassos' tone turned serious. "What do you think I can do for you from over here?"

"If you want him for that murder on Lesvos, now's your chance to catch him, because that's where he is right now."

Tassos propped himself upright in the bed. "How do you know he's on Lesvos?"

"Early this morning he hired a smuggler to drop him there. The smuggler's being paid handsomely to return at midnight tonight to pick him up."

"What makes you think the story's true?"

"The smuggler bragged about the deal to some of his buddies when he got back from dropping him off. The passenger's name meant nothing to any of them, but from the description the smuggler gave of him, one of them recognized the passenger as the guy who'd moved in on Malik."

"How'd he know that?"

"He's Malik's brother-in-law, and before you ask, he hates your guy and wants him out of the way."

Tassos leaned back in bed. "So, he's who asked you to call me."

"He's a friend and knows of my connections with the Greek police. How could I refuse this opportunity to help you?"

Tassos ignored the sarcasm. "If your madman is part of Malik's operation, why didn't he use one of Malik's smugglers' boats to take him to Lesvos?"

"My guess is he chose to pay a stranger because he didn't want Malik knowing he'd left for Lesvos. He probably worried about Malik doing the very thing his brother-in-law asked me to do, tip off the Greek police."

Works for me, thought Tassos. "So, where's tonight's pickup up spot?"

"Mantamados, on the northeast coast of Lesvos, about thirty kilometers north of Mytilini, and a dozen kilometers southeast of the refugee-friendly landing beach of Skala Sikamineas."

"That's a pretty big area. Do you have anything more precise?"

"The smuggler's supposed to hang off the coast and wait for a call around midnight for specific pickup location details."

"Can you get me those pickup coordinates?"

"Hard to say," said Ibrahim. "No telling how a Turkish smuggler might react to being asked to cooperate with the Greek police. Besides, it could all be a ruse to distract your police from his real plan for getting off the island, just in case someone like you happens to get wind of his plans from someone like me. I hear this guy's a big time paranoid."

"Sounds like there's more than one involved in this."

"Fuck you."

"Just get Malik's brother-in-law to get the pickup coordinates from his smuggler friend, and to text them to me at this number as soon as he has them—that is if he wants me to do what I can to rid your smuggler cronies of their madman problem. Understand?"

"Yes." Ibrahim hung up without saying another word.

Good. Tassos smiled. He felt back in the action and alive again. Now to call Andreas.

Before Maggie gets back.

Jamal had delivered his information on Aryan's secret trip to Lesvos to his brother-in-law personally. He saw it as his chance to resurrect himself into Malik's good graces, and demonstrate just how valuable he was to Malik's business.

"Are you certain?" said a visibly excited Malik. "I mean *absolutely* certain that Aryan is back on Lesvos *and* that the Greek police want to arrest him there?"

Jamal assumed an air of unaccustomed confidence in the presence of his brother-in-law. "No question. The smuggler identified him, and I verified through a friend with high-level contacts in the Greek police that the Greeks are anxious to arrest him for the murder of Volandes. The Greek police want us to provide them with the coordinates for Aryan's pickup as soon as he gets them to the smuggler."

Jamal lowered his head, but kept an eye on Malik. "If you wish to be rid of this foreign devil, now is your chance. Just give me the word and I'll arrange to pass along the pickup coordinates to the Greek police."

Malik bit at his lower lip and paced the living room. "You're certain?"

Jamal nodded.

"But the Greek police still must prove he killed Volandes, or else they'll have to release him." Malik pressed the heel of his hand to his chin and patted at his cheek with his fingers. "And he'll surely return here to murder us all."

"Brother-in-law, I'm certain that with all of your resources you can find witnesses to testify that he was the assassin, though you may not need to do so. He must have returned to Lesvos to deal with that troublesome NGO woman. If he's successful, they'll have him for her murder. But no matter, for once he's in a Greek jail there are ways to assure he never leaves alive."

Malik drew his hand away from his face. "Yes, you're right. All of that can be arranged." He walked over to his brother-in-law and placed his hands on Jamal's shoulders. "You have done well. Now do whatever you must to see that the Greek police capture him tonight. I will take steps to assure that this arrogant defiler never leaves their custody alive."

Tassos spent the first few minutes reassuring Andreas that all was going fine on his end, and the phone calls were not a strain on his health, though he did ask that Andreas not mention them to Maggie.

By the time he finished telling Andreas of his conversation with his Turkish contact, Andreas had no doubt Aryan planned on killing Dana or Ali before midnight. Possibly both. He looked at them as he hung up the phone. How to tell them without sending them off the deep end came as his first challenge. Keeping them alive, let alone capturing Aryan, was a whole different story.

Andreas told the group, "I have news." He turned to the commander. "How many men can you spare to work security at the press conference?"

"In this economy? You must be kidding."

"What are the chances of getting other commanders on the island to spare a few cops?"

"They have less to work with than I do. What's on your mind?"

Andreas' eyes jumped between Dana and Ali. "The possibility we talked about is now a reality. Mihalis Volandes' killer is back on the Island."

"What?"

"He arrived on a smuggler's boat this morning, and plans to leave the same way before midnight."

"Why?" asked Dana.

"Why do you think?" said the commander.

"Your press conference," said Ali.

"Why would he want to come to my press conference?"

No one said a word.

Dana shut her eyes. "Yes, I don't believe I just said such a stupid thing." She opened her eyes. "He doesn't plan on there being a press conference."

"I can get you both off the island right away," said Andreas.

"To where?" asked Dana.

"Athens. From there, go wherever you want."

"What about Ali?" she asked.

"I can get him to Athens. Where he goes from there is out of my hands."

"Because he's a refugee?" said Dana.

Andreas shrugged.

"Couldn't the killer follow us to Athens?" asked Ali.

"Yes," said Andreas. He looked at Dana. "But my guess is he won't bother to come after you if he believes you don't actually know his identity and have given up on trying to learn it."

"But that's just a guess," she said.

Andreas nodded.

"What if we stay?" she asked.

Andreas looked her straight in the eyes. "I believe he'll try to kill at least one of you before midnight."

"Another guess?"

"I'd say that one's closer to a sure thing."

Dana stared at the ceiling. "What are the chances of your catching him if we stay on Lesvos?"

"Depends."

"That's not very reassuring."

"Depends on how willing you are to listen to me, and how many local police we can get to help out." Andreas looked at the commander.

"I'll call in some favors and get a few of my cops to work double shifts. How's six sound?"

"Better than none."

"What do you want me to do?" Dana said.

Andreas smiled. "Whatever I tell you."

She forced a smile. "Some particulars, please."

"First, we have to move the site of the press conference."

"But everything's set to go at Volandes' house. If we change locations, we'll likely lose press coverage."

"And if you don't, you'll likely gain funerals," said Yianni.

"A bit dramatic, but he's right," said the commander. "You picked a location in the heart of the city, one that gives the killer way too many options for how, when, and where to take you out. We can't possibly cover them all."

"But doesn't he kill with a sword?" said Ali.

"That's his favorite weapon," said Andreas. "But he's just as deadly with firearms."

"Or a bomb," added Yianni.

"Something I'd prefer not to think of," said the commander, "but again, the site you've chosen lends itself to all those possibilities."

"Where do you suggest we move it to?" Dana asked Andreas.

"Someplace outside of town where it's not so easy to ambush you. A location not familiar to the killer, but yet not so far out of his comfort zone as to discourage him from going after you."

"How the hell do you expect to find a place like that?" said the commander.

"I don't," smiled Andreas. "As the local cop, that's your job."

The commander waved an open palm in Andreas' general direction. "How am I supposed to know what's out of his 'comfort zone?'"

"I can help you with that," said Andreas. "He came ashore this morning in Mantamados, and expects to be picked up in the same general area after midnight."

Dana spread her arms wide. "But if we switch the press conference to Mantamados, won't that make him suspicious?"

"Or, he might see it as fate," said Andreas. "We'll just have to come up with a convincing reason for the shift, and hope it passes a paranoid psychopath's sniff test. The bottom line is, you have to move the conference site. For certain the killer already has a plan in place based on the location you picked. We've got to shake up his planning if we expect to catch him without endangering you *unnecessarily.*"

Andreas let the word hang in the room for a moment, then looked directly at Dana and Ali. "Before going any further with this, I must ask again whether you're each willing to take the risk. This is no longer a hypothetical threat. The danger is real and now. We'll do our best to keep you safe, but you will be targets, no doubt about it."

"Excuse me, Chief Inspector," said Ali, "but from what you've told us, we've been targets since this morning."

Dana's eyes shot toward a window across the room facing the street and an open sea beyond. Yianni got up and pulled the curtains closed.

She smiled at him. "I guess my anxieties are showing. Obviously I'm not psychologically cut out for being a human target."

"That's nothing to be ashamed of," said Andreas. "Shall I make the arrangements to get you to Athens?"

Dana gestured no. "You misunderstood. What I meant was, if you don't catch this killer I'll likely spend the rest of my life looking over my shoulder, wondering if he's out there searching for me." She looked at Ali. "But as you said before, this is not just about one of us. You're as much a target as I. What do you want to do?"

"I'm used to people trying to do me great harm. Some have

succeeded. Those who failed only did so either because I fled them or I did what they asked. This man is but one of many of his sort from my past, and of likely many more to come." Ali hesitated. "But he's the first one I've had the chance to strike back at."

Andreas told the commander, "Sounds like they're set to go. So I guess it's up to you to come up with a new location for the press conference."

The commander rocked his head from side to side. "There's a place that could work, and it comes with a terrific backstory that might even justify the last minute change of venue. At least to the press, because I'm not sure there's any change that won't spook our killer."

"If the place is as good as you say," said Andreas, "there might just be a way to push the killer's buttons hard enough to overcome any second thoughts he might have."

Yianni leaned forward. "What sort of magic button-pusher do you have in mind?"

"A press release."

"What makes you think he's going to read a press release?" said the commander.

"Because Dana's going to issue one announcing a change of location for the press conference."

"That still doesn't answer my question. What makes you think he'll read it?"

"Because he's thorough in his planning. The night of Volandes' murder, do you think Aryan just happened to be hanging around Volandes' garden, hoping his victim would appear? Or that, when Ali received a call telling him Volandes had something important for Dana, there was any chance of Dana showing up instead of Ali? Aryan knew Volandes was on Chios for the day and would return late, likely tired and wanting to head straight home, and that Dana was away on Mykonos." Andreas tapped his finger on the table. "Believe me, he'll read it."

Andreas looked at Dana. "It's time to write it."
Dana reached for her keyboard. "In the beginning...."

For Immediate Release

CHANGE OF LOCATION for Dana McLaughlin Press Conference

Dana McLaughlin, Executive Director of Safe-Passage, is honored to announce that at the urging of the beloved Bishop of Mytilini, the press conference scheduled for 16:00 today will be held instead at Taxiarchis—the Holy Monastery of Archangel Michael in Mantamados.

The Bishop will conduct a brief memorial service in the presence of the monastery's most holy icon of the Archangel, a sacred treasure created with the blood of tenth-century Christian martyrs slaughtered during Easter Week within the monastery's walls by pirates in service to the Ottomans. The Bishop wishes to bestow this distinct honor upon one named after the Blessed Archangel, his friend Mihalis Volandes, another resolute Christian slaughtered during Easter Week within the sanctity of his own walls, the same as those whose blood now blesses the holy icon.

At the conclusion of the service, Ms. McLaughlin will hold a press conference to address recent developments in the Mihalis Volandes investigation and announce the names of both the audacious killer and his migrant trader employer.

Chapter Twenty

Aryan had returned to Lesvos early that morning, prepared to implement a simple plan designed for finishing off the refugee and the NGO woman by the end of the day in a manner that left no doubt Ali had killed both Volandes and McLaughlin. The forensic supervisor had done as Aryan had instructed him, accomplishing the critical first step: convincing the prosecutor to release Ali.

Aryan planned on Ali dying of the same cause as the McLaughlin woman, with a simple suicide note in his pocket: "I loved her. But she only loved him. I thought if he were gone she'd love me. But she doesn't care. I don't want to live. But first she must die."

All Aryan needed to make it work was a venue that played well with his storyline. He couldn't believe his good fortune when that morning McLaughlin announced she'd scheduled a press conference on the very spot where Ali had allegedly killed Volandes—Ali's competitor for McLaughlin's affections in Aryan's tale. She'd picked the perfect place for a conclusion uniting Ali and McLaughlin in death at Ali's hand.

The press would eat it up. Some would play it as a dramatic end to a love triangle among McLaughlin, Volandes, and a refugee, while others as proof of how ungrateful refugees could so easily turn on their saintly benefactors. Either way, the heat would be off Aryan, and two potential problems eliminated:

the refugee as the only person who could conceivably identify him as Volandes' killer, and the McLaughlin woman, the only one pushing to tie Aryan and the Turks to the murder.

McLaughlin's new press release changing the venue was not good news. It meant he'd wasted a half-day preparing a now useless setting for the perfect assassination. It had been such a good plan, too. Brilliant, in fact, if he had to say so himself.

But brilliant as it was, he doubted he could modify his plan in time for the rescheduled press conference. In order for it to work he'd need to scout the new location for what he needed, and yet still find a way to kidnap Ali before killing McLaughlin. Too little time, and too risky.

He knew he should leave the island and forget all about those two. After all, what was the real downside of walking away? There was no evidence tying him to the Volandes murder, only his paranoia that had him thinking the refugee could possibly identify him. And, scream and shout all she liked, the McLaughlin woman had to be bluffing with her claim to know his name, let alone anything about his affairs.

Of course, once back in Turkey he'd have to get to the bottom of how the Turkish police learned his real name, and eliminate those responsible for betraying him, but to think the McLaughlin woman had anything to do with that exceeded even his customary level of paranoia.

Then again, even paranoids had enemies. He took another look at the press release. Moving the press conference to Mantamados bothered him. He distrusted coincidences. But, then again, it was plausible that the Bishop wished to honor his friend with a service at a place befitting his death in a church dedicated to the saint after which Volandes had been named. Aryan hadn't realized that his method of killing Volandes fit perfectly with the legend surrounding that monastery. He smiled. One coincidence might be said to have cancelled out the other on that choice of location.

But even assuming the change of location was legitimate, the McLaughlin woman must be bluffing about what she knew.

He chuckled to himself as he imitated a reporter asking, "And who, pray tell, Ms. McLaughlin, *are* your audacious killer and his migrant trader employer?"

Yes, the time had come to stop giving in to his paranoia, and to check out the boat schedule for the next ferry back to Turkey. No reason to wait until midnight. That only gave his migrant trader partner more time to develop rambunctious ideas.

He grinned. The McLaughlin woman couldn't even get their relationship right. Malik Tiryaki wasn't his migrant trader *employer*, but his *partner*.

In an instant all glee drained from Aryan's face.

Migrant Trader…M and T…Malik Teriyaki.
Audacious Killer…A and K…Alban Kennel.

The bitch not only knew his name but also Malik's. And she'd taunted him by using their initials in the press release.

Time to revise plans.

•●●●•

Malik sat at his dining room table. The bottle of raki in front of him had served its purpose. At forty-five percent alcohol, the distilled grape and aniseed national drink of secular Turkey had given him the courage and insight he sought. He poured more of the clear liquor into his glass, added a bit of water and watched the combination turn into a milky white cloud. He stared at his glass and thought of how rapidly his own life had changed, except the clouds engulfing him were an ugly bloody-black.

But the sun would soon shine again. Even brighter than before. *Once Aryan is arrested by the Greeks he's as good as dead. We have friends in Greek prisons to see to that.*

Malik took a sip of raki.

When my colleagues realize how efficiently I've arranged to eliminate our collective problem, even to the extent of first allowing him time to liquidate that difficult NGO woman, they'll all be

*clamoring for me to lead them. Malik smirked. I guess I should
thank Aryan for all he's done to make me look so good.*

He took another sip. His look turned sullen.

*But how can they respect me as their leader when I cannot con-
trol my own wife?* He gulped down another swallow.

He glared out the doorway toward the living room. *That's
where they first did it. Where the adulteress humiliated me. I'll
rain hell down on that whore as soon as he's gone.* Malik swigged
down the rest of his drink. *But why must I wait? He's as good as
dead now.*

Malik pushed himself back from the table and staggered
toward the door.

"Wife, where are you? It is your husband calling for you.
Come to me now, *you whore!*"

Andreas wasn't sure their subtle psychological ploy with the
initials in the press release would work. Nor was he sure he
wanted it to work. If it did, a killer as unhinged as this one
might do something drastic, just to prove he couldn't be toyed
with.

That was the phrase Dana had used: "I think the best way to
get at him is to toy with his mind."

Letting Aryan know Dana actually knew his name seemed
the obvious way to go, but if she simply announced it in a press
release, he'd no longer have a reason beyond revenge to risk
going after her. It would also make the press conference anti-
climactic. No, they needed a more subtle way of letting Aryan
know Dana intended to expose him.

Yianni had suggested using Aryan's initials.

"Somehow calling him 'A K' doesn't seem much more subtle
than using his name," said Andreas.

"They're also your initials, Chief," added Dana.

"That certainly will attract the attention of the press," smiled
the commander.

"We have to do it in a way that appeals to his intellect," said Dana. "Something that gets him to realize I am telling only him that I know who he is."

"Sounds a bit complicated, and if we make it too subtle he might miss it completely," said Yianni.

"What if we use words starting with his initials to describe him?" said Dana.

"Like, 'Today, I'll name the *asshole killer*?'" said Yianni.

"That's the idea," said Dana, "but still too subtle. We need something more definitively tied to him. Something he won't miss."

"Maybe we should use capital letters for 'asshole' and 'killer' or underline his initials in those words?" said the commander.

Dana gestured no. "That's way too obvious. It tells the whole world we're trying to say something with the initials."

"It also screams *trap*." Andreas leaned back in his chair. "I like the idea of using the initials of the men you'll be identifying at the press conference in the words you use to describe them in the press release. If our killer's as smart as we think, he'll pick up on the two sets of initials as being far too precise to be a coincidence."

"I think it's still too subtle," said the commander. "And our killer may not be that smart."

"If you're right, the worst that happens is nothing beyond a very uneventful press conference." Andreas looked at Dana. "Because aside from their initials, I'm not going to risk your life by giving you their names to shout to the press."

Dana smiled. "I'll take that as a gesture of kindness rather than distrust."

"Good," said Andreas. "So, let's come up with some perfect words for describing AK and MT."

While the others had worked on the press release, the commander called his friend, the Bishop, to request the use of the monastery and his participation in the service. The Bishop required no convincing because he'd considered Mihalis a true friend. Nor did he fear the danger when told of the risk for, as he explained, such battles with the devil's minions bespoke the very the history of the monastery.

The commander patiently listened as the Bishop recounted a story the commander had heard before. In the tenth century, Lesvos and many other Aegean islands found themselves plagued by Saracen pirates, who'd plunder, kill, or enslave all those they found. The high, thick walls of the monastery at Mantamados protected its monks from such battles. But early one spring night, as the monks prepared the monastery for Easter, they'd failed to anticipate a pirate raid that early in the year, and posted no lookout to keep watch.

While the monks were at prayer, pirates crept into the monastery and slaughtered every soul but a novice monk, Gabriel, who'd managed to escape to the roof. As the pirates retreated with their plunder, they spied Gabriel on the roof and returned to kill him. They used ladders to climb to him, but as they set foot on the roof, it turned into a raging sea, above which loomed a mighty ferocious fighter in his metal shoes wielding a sword spouting tongues of fire, and he plunged into the mass of pirates, sending them fleeing for their lives and abandoning their plunder.

When Gabriel came down from the roof, he saw his colleagues all dead, and realized he'd been the only one saved by Archangel Michael. From the blood of the slaughtered, and the soil of the place where they perished, he fashioned the bas-relief icon of Archangel Michael that survived to this day in the monastery as one of few such embossed icons in all of Orthodoxy.

The Bishop continued on, and by the time he'd finished and hung up, the others were well into completing the press release.

"So, how did it go?" said Andreas.

"The Bishop's all in with the plan."

"Great," said Andreas.

The commander drew in and let out a breath. "He reminded me of something I'd forgotten about the monastery. It has me thinking fate might be playing a big hand in steering us there to honor Volandes." He repeated the story leading up to Gabriel's creation of the icon.

"I've heard that story before," said Dana, "but I don't see how any of that ties fate into our situation."

"It's what happened afterwards," said the commander. "A shepherd boy saw the pirate ships close by the shore and ran to the monastery to warn the monks, but he was too late. He raced off to tell the villagers of the slaughter, and after confirming what the boy had seen, the villagers charged off in pursuit of the pirates. When they reached a high point overlooking the shore, the bodies of pirates lay scattered everywhere."

The commander paused to swallow. "Each one killed by an identical single blow from the sword of Archangel Michael."

He paused again. "Slicing each pirate cleanly in half, from his forehead down through his crotch."

Chapter Twenty-one

The man knew what to expect. The change in location would disrupt planning, but not change the ultimate result. The assassination might not meet professional standards but no bomb would be used. Bombs killed indiscriminately, and brought with them frenzied media attention. No, this would be done as a personal, directed attack. One that the media would find only brief value in covering.

After all, he thought, *that's the essential purpose of what's underway on Lesvos, to stay anonymous, unnoticed, and uninteresting to all but those who hire you to do their killing.*

In order to get a fix on the assassin's revised plan, he had to visit the monastery at once. He knew the police would be expecting the assassin to do just that, but he had no choice. The risk had to be taken. The question was, how to make his pilgrimage inconspicuous?

I must keep my presence a surprise.

● ● **●** ● ●

As Andreas saw it, the response to Dana's press release so exceeded expectations as to fall into the category of unbridled nightmare. The media went wild promoting details of a promised live announcement later that afternoon of both Mihalis Volandes' killer and the man who'd hired him. When the people of Lesvos heard that the Bishop had scheduled a special service at Taxiarchis in the presence of the holy icon of Archangel Michael to honor one bearing his name, many who worshipped the icon's legendary healing powers took it as a divine sign for anyone in serious need of hope, healing, or salvation to attend.

By mid-afternoon, pious and curious from all over Lesvos had joined together in a growing processional. Some trekked toward the monastery by foot or on horseback, the same as many would during the soon-to-be-held Festival of Taxiarchis, but others drove, each now part of a spontaneous pilgrimage, hoping for some promised revelation.

The commander hung up his phone after taking a call from a colleague reporting on the masses headed toward the monastery. He looked at Andreas. "So much for moving the conference out of town to keep the crowds down."

Andreas shook his head. "It's called shit happens. We'll find a way to deal with it."

"The crowds make it a lot easier for the killer to blend in among the faithful."

"Look at the upside," said Andreas. "It makes it unlikely he'll use a bomb. Setting one off in a large crowd would label him a terrorist and trigger a relentless worldwide search. Something he definitely doesn't want."

"Should I take that as hope, prayer, or fact?" said Dana.

"Any way you'd like," said Andreas, "but don't get too comfortable. As far as you're concerned, it doesn't change a thing. He'll just choose a more selective targeting method to try and take you out."

"So, now what do we do?" asked the commander.

"Distribute the killer's photo and description to every cop working the crowd, and make sure they pay particular attention to males. Especially any dressed as priests or monks."

"I'd also keep an eye out for bent-over *yiayias* wrapped in black shawls," said Yianni.

"Noted," said the commander, "though I doubt he'll go in for the grandmotherly look."

"He'll go for whatever gets him out alive," said Yianni.

"What about in?" said Dana.

"He's probably already where he wants to be," said Andreas.

"How are you going to find him?" asked Dana.

"Don't worry, we will," said Andreas.

"But how?" Her voice cracked. "Or are you waiting for him to find me?"

The commander leaned forward. "He's only one man, not a superman, not even Harry Potter with a cloak of invisibility."

"Nice try, Commander," said Dana, "but that's not reassuring. It's condescending bullshit."

Andreas slapped his hands on his thighs. "Okay, folks, time to head out to the monastery."

"How are we getting there?" asked Dana.

"With us," said Andreas.

"If Ali and I show up in a police car, won't that scare the killer away? I think we should get there on our own."

"I think she's right, Chief," said Yianni. "He'll expect police to be there for crowd control, but if she shows up with us in the same car it'll look like we're all in it together and smell like a setup."

Andreas bit at his lip. "Fine, if you want to drive yourself, go ahead. But not with Ali in the same car. That makes it too easy for him to take you both out at once."

"But I have no way to get there on my own," said Ali.

Dana turned to the commander. "What about your daughter? Can she give Ali a ride?"

"What does she have to do with this?"

"Nothing," said Dana, not looking him in the eye. "But she once offered to help in any way that she could, and this would be a big help."

"I don't want her involved."

Dana shrugged. "If it's as safe as you say, and the killer's not superman, what's the risk to her of simply giving Ali a ride to the monastery?"

Andreas winked at Yianni.

"Just ask her, please," said Dana.

Andreas stood up. "Whatever you decide, do it quickly, because we've got to get moving. There's a lot to do at the monastery, and not a lot of time in which to do it."

The commander picked up his phone and hit a speed dial number, staring at Dana as he did. "Why do I sense there's something you're not telling me?"

Dana shrugged.

Andreas stage whispered to Yianni. "Parental intuition."

Aleka knocked on her boss' door, wondering how to explain that her father wanted her to take off from work so that she could provide taxi service for her boss' former number one murder suspect. She couldn't lie about the reason; the entire island would soon know where she'd been and with whom. Nor could she let him know she knew about the letter he'd sent off to the prosecutor that morning, wrongly accusing her of incompetence. She expected him to be aggressive, so she drew a deep breath and let it out.

"Come in."

Aleka opened the door. "Sir—"

"What is it?" He sounded more abrupt than usual.

"I need to take the rest of the day off."

"Why not?" He waved his hands around in front of him. "You have me here to do all your work. Perhaps you'd like to come in around noon tomorrow, so you have ample time to recuperate from your imperative social demands?"

"It's not something personal."

"You mean you're doing lab business on the side?"

Keep your cool. "My father needs me to drive someone to Taxiarchis."

"So, our illustrious police commander is reduced to poaching on my manpower? Excuse me, *woman*power."

He's trying to rile me. "I guess you could ask him if you'd like. From what I understand, the suspect in the Volandes murder case released this morning is to attend a press conference at the monastery, but the suspect doesn't feel comfortable being asked to take a ride in the country in a police car."

"Ah, and of course, he'll be far more comfortable with you. Go please." He shooed her away with his fingers. "And close the door behind you."

She did as he asked, but left thoroughly confused. He'd gone from active belligerence to defeated resignation in a single sentence.

All she could think as she headed to her car was, *Why?*

He sat at his desk, biting his lip and staring at the door Aleka had just closed. How had he ever gotten this deeply involved with a madman? Then again, what choice did he have? The killer somehow knew of his past indiscretions in other cases, and though this was a far more celebrated victim than any of the others he'd helped creatively inter over the years, it would be his undoing if he refused. The killer had all the facts he needed to expose him in a scandal that would land him in prison.

The money he'd been paid for placing blame on the refugee was secondary. He agreed to do as the killer asked in order to protect his reputation and family. Well, his reputation. His wife had left him, taking the children with her, two years before. Besides, the killer would have murdered Volandes anyway. It wasn't as if he could have saved him.

But now things had taken a decidedly grim turn. The situation no longer loomed as simply a matter of his being exposed as corrupt, but of him making decisions that could end up with him dead. The killer had called yesterday morning and told him to change his report so that the refugee suspect was released at once. He'd told the killer that was impossible. That's when the killer said, "Do it or die," and hung up.

In a panic, he dictated a letter to the prosecutor, announcing how he'd no choice but to overrule Aleka's findings in the Volandes investigation due to her grossly incompetent work, and had it delivered to the prosecutor along with his recommendation that the accused refugee be released at once. Only later, in preparation for a possible call from the prosecutor for specific details, did he take another look at the report. That's when he saw she'd not signed her name, but written instead, "I disagree."

He'd screamed so loudly that his secretary had come running into his office. He pointed at the report, and said Aleka must have stolen the original version from his desk. That's when his secretary told him that Dana McLaughlin, the foreign activist and employer of the murder suspect, had met with Aleka in one of the examination rooms after refusing to speak in front of her.

Not knowing what to do, he'd kept his temper in check and not said a word to the bitch until she walked into his office with that request from her asshole father. The bastard had probably put her up to what she'd done to him.

Now all three of them would be together at a press conference. Who knew what they were up to? Nothing good for him, that was certain. He shut his eyes. *What should I do? What can I do?*

His eyes popped open and he grabbed for his mobile phone. He scanned through recent calls, found the number he wanted, and called it. He crossed himself, hoping for a voice to answer.

"Yes."

"I have some information on who will be attending that press conference this afternoon which may be of interest to you."

"I'm all ears," said Aryan.

• • ● ● •

Now Aryan had three to dispose of. Possibly four, depending on how he later felt about the forensic supervisor. Lucky for the supervisor, they'd never met. Aryan only knew of him from some who'd used his services, otherwise there'd be no question of his fate. But for now he lived, because today was all about creating an illusion, one that sold a story to the media that would allow Aryan to retreat into Turkey, free of further Greek police interference.

He'd come around to seeing the media circus created by switching the press conference to the monastery as a stroke of good fortune for his plan, for it drew the national press attention he needed to make it work. But in Ali and the police commander's daughter traveling together without police protection, he saw a twist that would make his murder-suicide story line irresistible to the international press. That development he saw akin to miraculous intervention.

Aryan sensed from his conversation with the forensic supervisor that this was a police trap, but he saw that as giving him the element of surprise, for they did not know that he knew. More important, if the press went with his story line, it spared the Greek police worldwide embarrassment and ended their investigation in a neatly tied-up bow. Yes, the police commander wouldn't like it—his daughter being dead, and all that—but the Greek police powers-that-be surely would want the case closed and story over.

An American NGO executive killed by her jealous refugee employee still stood as his central story line, but the introduction of the police commander's daughter offered a potentially irresistible subplot to both the mainstream conservative press and edgy scandal rags.

All he needed to do was tinker with the suicide note he'd created for Ali by adding Aleka to the list of suitors for McLaughlin's affections. Again, jealousy would serve as

Ali's motive for killing Aleka—the same as it had for killing Volandes—though her death would likely require a bit of sexual perversion, as Ali would undoubtedly be embittered by Dana having chosen passion for a woman over him.

It was all working out remarkably well. The forensic supervisor's secretary would attest to Dana and Aleka enjoying tryst time in Aleka's office examination room, elaborating, no doubt, on the sounds she heard emanating from their time together. He could count on the good supervisor to arrange for that, even to corroborate with other details and, of course, eliminate any evidence that might point back to Aryan. After all, how enthusiastically he cooperated would directly affect his lifespan.

He imagined headline writers across the planet going wild over a murder-suicide involving lesbian lovers on Lesvos, a wealthy old Greek shipowner, and a young male Arab refugee raging with jealous passion as the perpetrator. He smacked his hands together. *It might even make late night American television.*

All he had to do now was wait for the two of them to show up in the sun-bleached red Fiat Panda described by Aleka's boss. They'd both fit quite nicely into his revised plan.

Chapter Twenty-two

The commander told Andreas it should take a little more than an hour to cover the fifty kilometers between Mytilini and Mantamados. He suggested they take the route closest to the sea.

Once past the outskirts of Mytilini, the two-lane road bounced back and forth between seascapes in hues of brown, beige, and blue, and country hillsides of grays into greens; always seeming to land by a centuries-old olive grove or stone wall. The towns the road passed through lay largely by the sea, some quaint, some not, but all painted in the island's pastel palette. Even the occasional hotel, Quonset hut structure, or bit of graffiti along the way, couldn't dampen the sense of bygone times evoked by the drive.

They passed a group of horses grazing in a sunny hillside pasture. "I bet Tassaki would love all the horses here," said Yianni.

"For sure." Andreas reached for his mobile. "And soon Sofia will too."

"They grow up so fast. I can't believe Tassaki's already five."

"Tell me about it." Andreas hit a speed-dial button.

The phone rang twice before he heard, "Yes, my darling, I know you're calling to tell me you miss me terribly."

"Amazing. I'm married to a mind reader."

"And don't you forget it."

Andreas smiled. "Yianni and I were just talking about how much the kids would like Lesvos, so I decided to call and check in."

"All's fine here. How about with you?"

Andreas paused. "We have to make sure to instill in the kids the importance of keeping an open mind, and enough confidence that, no matter what might happen in life, they know they're loved."

Lila cleared her throat. "May I ask what brought on this epiphany?"

"I just had a headache of a conversation with a young woman who's sorely lacking in trust. So much so, that it's put her life at risk."

Lila's voice dropped. "Are you safe?"

"Yes, I'm fine. I didn't mean to alarm you."

"Well, you're doing a good job of it anyway."

"I'm just thinking of the kids and how lucky we are that they're as well-adjusted as they are."

"Uh, yes, I'd say they're as well-adjusted as any five-year-old and three-month-old could be expected to be."

Andreas chuckled. "I guess I'm sounding a bit foolish."

"No, you're sounding affectionate toward your family. Which is the perfect thing for a new mother to hear. Especially one who's recently told her husband she feels the need to get back to work in the adult world."

"I was wondering when you'd raise that again. Any ideas on what you might like to do?"

"I'm working on it."

"Whatever you decide, I'm behind you a hundred percent."

"I know."

"I love you."

"I love you, too," said Lila, with a kiss. "Now, get back to concentrating on your work. I'll tell Tassaki you called, and give them both hugs and kisses from you. Bye."

"Bye." Andreas turned off the phone.

"Chief. May I ask you a question?"

"Sure."

"Do you love me too?"

Andreas smiled. "Just shut up and drive."

They arrived at the upper edge of Mantamados right on time. The monastery lay on the other side of town. Looking down from above, the town appeared a gem of gray stone buildings, none taller than two levels and all tiled in terra-cotta hip roofs. As they descended, the gem showed a bit ragged in places, but still sparkled.

"The commander said to stay to the right at the market and follow the signs to the monastery," said Andreas.

"I have GPS, Chief. Besides, we've been following the commander's daughter's Fiat all the way from Mytilini."

"Just passing along what he told me. He said it's the second right past a barbed wire-protected installation, and that from the road we'll be able to see a real F5A fighter jet mounted at the entrance to the monastery. It's a gift from the Greek Air Force in honor of its protector, Saint Michael."

"That's a lot more detail than I get from my GPS friend."

"He also suggested we park in the lower parking lot next to the steps, and find our way inside from there."

Andreas looked out the side window. He hadn't told Ali or Dana of his plan, in part because he wasn't sure it would work. After all, he'd never been to the monastery and the little time they'd have to learn its layout gave Aryan a decided advantage. An assassin only needed to find one hiding place and develop one exit strategy, while Andreas had to find and counter all possibilities.

But Andreas had another reason for not sharing his plan. He'd told Dana not to arrive at the monastery until the very last moment, but wanted Ali there ASAP. As Andreas saw it,

Dana was Aryan's primary target, and he wouldn't jeopardize that target by taking out Ali first. Nor would it likely spook Aryan to see cops keeping an eye on Ali. After all, free or not, he remained their only suspect in a still open murder case.

All of which made Ali the perfect distraction, or to use a less politically correct word, bait. Andreas wanted Ali wandering around the monastery to give Andreas the opportunity of seeing what sort of attention he attracted.

Andreas hadn't actually told Ali he'd be bait, but from their conversation back at the NGO office, and Ali's street instincts, he must have figured that out. More significantly, Andreas knew if he told Dana of his plan for Ali, she would never go along with it, even though Andreas saw it as the best way of improving the chances at catching Aryan, and saving both their lives in the process.

Andreas had to admire Dana's loyalty to her friend, but then again, by Ali tacitly offering himself up as bait, he'd shown reciprocal loyalty to her. Andreas saw no reason to inject himself into dueling acts of loyalty among friends.

He smiled as he shook his head at his own logic. *God bless rationalization.*

"What's so funny, Chief?" Yianni glanced at Andreas from the driver seat.

"How our minds work to justify potential morally unjustifiable acts as serving a higher purpose."

"That's a bit heavy for this time of day. Maybe you'd like to talk about football?"

"As a matter of fact, I would," said Andreas, "but since the monastery is just up ahead, let's go over again what we're going to do when we get there."

Then he saw it. Classic Byzantine, two-story, gray stone perimeter walls, complete with a four-story matching bell tower, all topped in terra-cotta roof tiles and set off against a sylvan background of greens and browns. Beyond the monastery's archway entrance at its southwest corner, a gray square-cut stone courtyard encircled a rose-and-beige stone church of arched doorways and windows soaring up to meet a gabled terra-cotta roof. Trees stretched from within and without the monastery walls toward a cloudless, bright blue sky.

"That's a pretty sight," said Yianni. "I'd much rather be checking out the grounds than burrowing around inside the buildings like you have me doing."

"Just make sure you get the Bishop's assistant to show you every centimeter of the monastery. That means every hiding place, abandoned or not. A monastery that old, besieged, and attacked as much as it's been, must have a lot of them."

"And what will you be doing while I'm battling bats, bugs, and snakes?"

Andreas shrugged. "Damned if I know. I'm going to start out by keeping an eye on Ali. See what he attracts."

"Do you really think he'll draw out Aryan?"

"One can hope. I'm counting on Aryan's arrogance to bring him down. He wants to pull this off, even with cops here. A sane man would walk away. But if he's here, he's going to try to put on a big show, I'm sure of that. I just hope Ali's not the first act."

"Sounds like the curtain's about to go up on a performance by the Lesvian Thespian Centurions."

Andreas stared at the side of Yianni's face. "Please, spare me the comedy efforts and just keep following that red Panda."

Yianni grinned. "I can bear it if you can."

Andreas shut his eyes at the bad pun. *Yes, we're both anxious. How could any sane person not be? Another disadvantage to battling a madman.*

● ● ● ● ●

Deema crawled from her marriage bed along the floor, blood from her broken nose caked across her face, blood from other parts of her body more brutally and relentlessly assaulted by her husband streaked down her legs.

He'd attacked her far more savagely than ever before. She knew she'd be dead by now if he hadn't passed out from the raki. Her time had come. She'd prayed to God for deliverance but her prayers had not been answered.

Or perhaps they had been, for she still breathed. But only until Malik awakened. The anger would be back, and once sober he would kill her, for sure. She crawled toward the place she'd seen Aryan go when he thought she was asleep in the bed. There, she might find what she needed to end her misery.

Please, my Lord, grant me that prayer.

Aleka parked at the far northeast end of the monastery's upper parking lot, as far away from the television crews gathered around the main entrance as she could find. It must have been a slow newsday for so many to be on site for a press conference not scheduled to begin for two hours. Though they did have a wide array of pilgrims to choose among for interviews out of the crowd already milling around for the promised afternoon event.

She thought of waiting in the car with Ali until Dana got there, concerned that if just one of the reporters recognized Ali as the one-time suspect-in-chief in the Volandes case, they'd descend on him like a murder of crows. But her father had told them to walk around the monastery grounds as if they were tourists. He'd also told them to stay within sight of the police at all times. She didn't know how to accomplish both, what with the monastery as filled with twists and turns as it was, and only six cops patrolling the grounds, all anxiously searching for the face of a killer.

No way they could be expected to keep an undistracted eye on her, even if she was the boss' daughter. Then there were the two cops who'd followed her from Mytilini. The younger one had hurried off inside the monastery the moment they'd parked. The other one still sat in the unmarked police car. Perhaps he was to be their chaperone.

"Okay, Ali, time to get out and explore. Have you ever been here before?"

"No."

They got out of the car and walked toward the monastery.

"Well, you're in for an experience. I'm not going to bore you with a lot of history, but this place really is special. Though we call it a monastery, it's no longer used as one, but as a monument to the architecture of fortress-like Byzantine monasteries. There's a church inside the walls that's still very active and holds a lot of important relics besides its famous icon. A small church built in the seventeenth century was replaced by a larger one in the eighteenth century, followed in 1879 with the current one. Some consider it a cathedral, because of its size and architectural layout as a three-aisled basilica."

Aleka paused. "I think your eyes are glazing over. Am I losing you?"

Ali smiled. "Not at all. I just can't believe a few hours ago I was in jail for murder, and now here I am amid a place of miracles. That in and of itself is a miracle to me."

"There's a big festival here in a couple of weeks, on the third Sunday after Easter. Maybe you could come back for it. It takes up the whole weekend, beginning with a parade starring a bull draped in gold, precious objects, and flowers. The bull's led to the slaughter, then it's cooked all night and served the next day in a traditional stew called *kistek*."

"To be perfectly honest," said Ali, "at the moment, I'm not sure I want to be hearing about things being led to the slaughter. Especially around here."

Aleka nodded with an unsure grin. "Touché. Any place in particular you'd like to see?"

"No." Ali looked back over his shoulder at Andreas strolling a dozen paces behind them. "Let's just make sure not to lose him."

She nodded again. "Understood."

They walked along a gray stone path leading up to the monastery's main gate as flute music drifted toward them from up ahead. Close by the monastery wall, a ragged, gray-haired old man in a long dark coat sat cross-legged playing a nearly meter-long wooden flute. Aleka stopped to listen. The flute looked to be Native American, with a traditional-looking carved bird mounted near the mouthpiece.

Ali looked back at Andreas, who gestured with his head for them to move along.

"Let's go," said Ali.

"He's good." Aleka reached into her bag and pulled out a euro. She dropped the coin in a cup by the old man's feet, and he nodded at her without missing a note. They moved on to the monastery's entrance.

Andreas stopped and stared at the old man. He, too, left a euro and moved on.

Andreas stood by the side entrance to the church, pulled out his phone, and hit a speed-dial button.

"What's up, Chief?" answered Yianni.

"Nothing, but I'm getting quite a tour following these two around everywhere."

"Bet it can't match mine. We're in an underground maze. You were lucky to catch me by a basement window. Otherwise, I'd never get a signal."

"Have you checked out above-ground areas?" Andreas looked up at the stone bell tower.

"We're headed there next. The Bishop's aide is very cooperative, but he knows about as much about the intricacies of this part of the monastery as I do. He said no one ever comes here, so we're working off copies of old maps he found in the monastery's library."

"Terrific. Sounds like the plot to one of those American movies starring that actor who's married to a Greek."

"I think you're talking about Tom Hanks and *The Da Vinci Code*."

"That's it."

"Sorry to disappoint you, but no strange characters, bodies, or cryptic signs have turned up down here. At least not yet. Just a lot of empty old spaces and dead end tunnels. What about you?"

"The strangest character I've seen up here so far is a flute player, but he's not our guy."

"When's McLaughlin getting here?"

"In less than an hour."

"That's not much time. I better get moving," said Yianni.

"Check back with me in twenty minutes."

"Will do."

Andreas slid the phone back into his pocket, watching as Ali and Alcka stood mesmerized by the holy icon. Perhaps they were praying. In a place like this it wasn't hard to be overcome with the sense of a higher order of things, a spiritual power capable of overcoming the worst that our secular world had to offer.

For some, perhaps, that feeling came from the trappings of crystal chandeliers, fixtures of gold, silver, and precious gems, elaborate icons and banners, or perhaps the special offerings unique to the Archangel—rare military paraphernalia from reverent armed forces followers, or the metal shoes that tradition has Taxiarchis wearing when he appears as a vision—contributed by the prayerful in hope they'll be worn by the Archangel when answering their prayers.

Others may have found it in the majestic architectural bones of the church, with its elaborate fluted pillars soaring up from inlaid marble floors, to flower into arching ribs of burgundy and cream, spanning across the basilica's vaulted ceilings to frame a panoply of artistic masterpieces floating high above all else.

If Andreas had to guess what did it for Aleka and Ali, he'd pick the unmistakable power emanating from the icon itself. In a four-sided canopy of gilt and crimson sat the reason for all that surrounded it. Graced by a crown and wings of silver, the massive head of Taxiarchis stared at the world through austere yet benevolent, black eyes—set in a face far darker than Ali's.

Andreas saw a message in that. At least for some.

A half-dozen tourists wandered in and out of the church, taking photos and reading about the displayed treasures. A tall, sturdy man in a dark sweater, dark pants, and running shoes stood against a far wall with his arms crossed and staring at the couple. All at once he uncrossed his arms and headed straight for them, his eyes glued on Ali.

"What are you doing here, *mavro*? This is a Christian country, not a place for *Mousoulmanos*. We don't want your kind here stealing, raping, and murdering. Get out now, and take your Greek *putana* with you." He pushed Aleka to the side and swung his body around to hit Ali at precisely the moment that the heel of Andreas' right hand, in full upward thrust, met his jaw.

The man went down like a rock.

"Are you okay?" Andreas asked Aleka.

"Yes, it's sort of an honor to be called a whore by a *Chrysi Avyi* Nazi skinhead."

"And I've been called a lot worse than a black and a Muslim," said Ali.

"Sorry about this, but that's the trouble in a democracy: you've got all kinds to deal with."

"I like the way you dealt with this one," said Ali.

Andreas smiled. "Me too."

The man started to come around, and Andreas yanked him to his feet. "Come along, sir, I have some friends I want you to meet."

"Fucking Muslim-lover."

"Oh, you're really going to like them."

The man tried to pull away. Andreas grabbed his hand and twisted it into a wristlock.

"Ow, that hurts."

"Then just do as I say and don't struggle." Andreas looked at Aleka and Ali. "You two don't move from here until I get back. Understand?"

Each nodded yes, and Andreas led the man out the main entrance of the church into the courtyard, headed toward the monastery's main entrance. He waved over the first cop he saw.

"This man just assaulted your police commander's daughter. Get whatever ID information you can from him, and put him somewhere safe where he can't do any more harm. We'll get him back to town after this is over."

"Cocksucker," screamed the man.

Andreas smiled, and looked at the cop. "Safe is the primary concern, comfortable a distant second."

The cop nodded, cuffed the man with his hands behind his back, and led him away.

Andreas turned and headed back to the church. The tourists had left by the time he returned, and Ali and Aleka weren't by the icon. He looked right. He looked left. He looked behind him. He walked up and down the aisles, and looked behind the iconostasis separating the priests' area from the main sanctuary. No Ali or Aleka. He ran out the side door. Not there. He retraced their steps back out into the parking lot. Nothing.

He jogged back toward the monastery and stopped where they'd seen the old man with the flute. He'd left too.

Andreas bit at his lower lip. Had he just been played, or just been careless? How could he face the police commander? He thought of his own children and how he'd react to one who'd promised to keep them safe but failed.

He shut his eyes, shook his head, looked straight ahead, and ran off to find the skinhead who'd drawn him away from his promise to protect another man's child. He prayed as he ran, but doubted he'd find anything to rid him of the sick feeling now occupying the pit of his stomach.

• • ● • •

As the man saw it, the trick to being inconspicuous lay in knowing your audience, and being prepared for a quick change of appearance, be it by donning or discarding a coat, a wig, or face putty. Showing up at a monastery dressed like a monk was far too obvious, especially when police had likely alerted monastery personnel to point out any monk they did not recognize. That's why he'd settled on portraying a long-coated, itinerant flute-playing beggar.

Sometimes, the best way to distract attention is by attracting it.

Chapter Twenty-three

At the main entrance to the monastery, Andreas caught up with the cop who'd taken the skinhead away. He pointed Andreas toward a building off to the right, beyond the mounted fighter jet.

"Your guy's over there, on the far side of that building, locked in the back of a police van." The cop reached in his pocket. "Here are the keys."

Andreas took them and ran along the tree-lined stone path leading toward the jet, dodging people streaming into the monastery. He cut off the path at a tree break and headed across open ground straight for the building. He found the van and paused to catch his breath. Whether this guy worked for Aryan or simply was an asshole bigot, Andreas needed his cooperation.

He banged on the side of the van. "I'm coming in." He unlocked the windowless sliding door and slid it back. The man sat on the far side of the second row of seats, his hands still cuffed behind his back.

"Is it your turn to have fun with me?" A plum-red bruise had taken hold over his left eye.

"You stumbled, I see," said Andreas sliding in next to him on the seat.

"Fuck you. I'm going to get a lawyer as soon as I get my phone call."

Andreas nodded. "A very wise decision for someone in your situation."

The man snickered. "*My situation?* The most I did was insult a fucking *Mousoulmanos*. I'll get a medal for that."

"I'm sure your Chrysi Avyi colleagues will oblige you on that score, but if I were you I'd be more concerned for the bigger mess you're in than in mouthing Golden Dawn bullshit."

"What bigger mess?"

Andreas leaned forward. "Accessory to a double murder."

"You're out of your fucking mind."

Andreas brought his finger close to the man's face. "I promise you that when that couple you went after turns up dead here because you distracted me from protecting them, you're going down for their murders."

"They were alive when we left them, and I've been in police custody ever since. No way I could be involved in their murders."

"I said accessory. Your job involved creating a diversion. It's not going to be hard convincing a judge of that, what with your deep love of refugees. Especially since one of the victims is a local police commander's daughter."

The man's eyes began twitching. "I had nothing to do with any of that. I don't know what you're talking about."

"Come on, someone in that church expected you to do precisely what you did. Who's going to believe it a coincidence that you attacked the very couple I'm there to protect, and that while I'm turning you over to another cop, the couple disappears, only to later turn up murdered?" Andreas shook his head. "If I were you, I'd make sure my phone call is to the best damn criminal defense lawyer I can find."

"Fuck, fuck, fuck," yelled the man as he bounced back and forth in his seat.

"If you're done beating yourself up, do you care to take a shot at convincing me why you're not involved in a double murder?"

The man leaned back on the seat and closed his eyes. "A buddy of mine works maintenance at the monastery. He sometimes gets me work when they need help. He called me in to do cleanup today after the crowd leaves. But they paid me to come in early to keep an eye on things inside the main church. Watch out for potential vandals or thieves. I've done that sort of thing for them before when they expect a lot of visitors."

He swallowed. "I saw the two of them come in the church. I knew immediately who he was. That Muslim who'd killed the shipowner. Couldn't believe he dared step inside the church. Their kind doesn't belong here. They're—"

"You're not helping your case with that sort of talk, fella."

The man sighed. "So, I watched the two of them come in. I saw you at the doorway making a phone call and looking at them, but I didn't realize you were with them. I thought you were looking at them for the same reason I was. If I had to guess who was the cop I'd have picked the other guy."

"What other guy?" said Andreas.

"While you were talking on the phone a guy came in another door walking behind two fat, gray-haired German lady tourists. He walked as if he was with them, but from the way the women talked to each other and ignored him I don't think they knew him. He stood back in a corner on the far side of the church away from the Muslim and his girlfriend. He kept taking photographs of things most tourists aren't interested in. It made no sense to me, but a lot of things tourists do make no sense to me. Besides, I was angry with the girl who'd brought the Muslim into the church."

"Tell me about the tourist guy," said Andreas.

The man shut his eyes. "He wore one of those cheap straw fedoras all the tourist shops sell. His was black. A dark blue, long trench coat, and dark pants."

"What did he look like?"

"Hard to say, he stayed in the shadows and stood bent over, like some old men are. He had a partially grey beard and big nose. Not a Spartan nose, more like one of those Jewish noses."

A Chrysi Avyi bastard to the core. "Anything else?"

"Just the big camera hanging around his neck."

"What made you think he could be a cop?"

"Cops act interested in things normal people don't care about, trying to distract you from what's really on their mind. That's how this guy was treating everything but the Muslim and his girlfriend—and they were the most obvious things in the place. Even the fat German ladies stared at them."

Andreas leaned back. As much as he hated to admit it, this bigot's frame of reference may have picked up on something. Andreas had left Aleka and Ali alone in the church while he spoke with Yianni, and this skinhead had gone after Ali just as Andreas walked inside. Andreas never had the chance to check out the others in the church.

The Fates had worked against him. He thought to damn them, but decided better of it. He needed them back on his side. And soon.

Andreas' phone rang. It was Yianni. He looked at the man. "Thank you for your help."

"Fuck you."

Andreas shook his head. The depth and source of such unbridled hatred always amazed him. It spewed forth unbound by reason or even common sense. This man faced prison, yet he couldn't restrain himself from lashing out not just at the objects of his hatred, but at anyone keeping him from his targets.

Andreas stepped out of the van onto the ground, slid the door closed, locked it, and answered his phone.

Time to share the bad news.

What a stroke of luck. That skinhead chose to show how much he hated Muslims just when Aryan wondered how he might separate that cop from his wards. He couldn't have planned it better. He was certain he could convince the two to come with him if he had the chance, but their cop chaperone had complicated things.

Come to think of it, that skinhead turned out to be a lucky break for the cop, too. Aryan had begun to improvise a modification to his story line that accounted for a bloody ending to the policeman's life. He'd kill him when he caught the three of them alone and make it appear but yet one more violent act perpetrated by refugee and killer Ali—using the same *nodachi* sword he'd taken to Volandes and retrieved from its hiding place.

But, on balance, that idiot skinhead wandering into the middle of his script made it neater and all the simpler.

He'd merely strolled over to the two of them, looking every bit the foreign tourist he'd worked so hard to master, and said matter-of-factly, "Come with me and no one gets hurt. Refuse, and you both die here."

He had to admit that opening his coat to flash the sword scabbarded across his chest in a Kevlar and Velcro tear-open sheath, added the appropriate element of dramatic realism necessary to make them comply so effortlessly.

Now, on to the next act.

• • ● • •

Andreas hurried through an explanation to Yianni of what just happened. "I really screwed up. Those two kids might be dead because of me."

"Go easy on yourself, Chief. It sounds like Aryan spotted you and was waiting for the right moment to make his move. If that skinhead hadn't come after Ali and forced your hand, no telling what Aryan might have done to get them away from you."

"If you're trying to make me feel better by suggesting he might have tried taking me out, it's not working. I promised to protect them."

"I hate to sound like the adult in this relationship, but I think we better forget about whether or not you fucked up, and figure out how to find them if they're still alive. Not to mention protecting Dana, who's due here in about thirty minutes."

Andreas nodded at his phone. "I get it, no more moping." He drew in and let out a deep breath. "So, have you finished checking out the monastery?"

"The place is bigger than it looks, and filled with all sorts of potential hiding places. I'm into triage, going after the most obvious places, the ones with sight lines on approaches from the parking lot and into open areas inside the monastery walls."

"I was afraid you'd say that. It sounds like Aryan's way too many steps ahead of us. Probably has Ali and Aleka far from here by now." Andreas kicked the ground. "If he hasn't already killed them."

"Maybe he intends on using them as hostages, to trade in exchange for Dana calling off the press conference?"

"That's what I'd call big time wishful thinking. I can't see him letting them live. I think we're better off focusing on the *why* if we want to figure out the *where*."

"I don't follow," said Yianni.

"If Aryan could have taken them anywhere, the question is why does he want them in the first place?"

"To frame Ali for the Volandes murder."

"Yes, that's the most likely scenario for hoping they're still alive," said Andreas. "But why Aleka?"

"No idea, but I'm sure it's tied into some plan hatched in his warped dramatic mind."

"No doubt set to kick off once Dana gets here, and before her press conference."

"Maybe we should stop her?" said Yianni.

"We can try. But once she learns about the kidnapping, I doubt she'll run off. That would mean certain death for Ali and Aleka. We both know Aryan won't let them go now that they've seen him. If Dana's a no-show, he'll kill them and disappear. This is a guy who cuts off heads as a message."

"So when do we tell Dana about her friends?" said Yianni.

"We'll cross that bridge when she gets here. Which, as you said, now is less than thirty minutes away, and there's still a hell of a lot of this place to check out before then."

"The two of us can't do it."

"Grab every cop you can find and assign them an area to search."

"I thought they're supposed to be scanning the crowds for Aryan."

Andreas swallowed. "I think I've demonstrated that he's better at hiding than we are at finding. Let's get them searching the buildings and grounds. It's a better use of their time."

"What are you going to do?"

Andreas sighed. "Try to figure out Aryan's next move." He paused. "After speaking to Aleka's father."

In Andreas' call to the commander, he spent more time and carefully chosen words explaining what had happened to the man's daughter than he had in telling Yianni.

The commander did not interrupt, and when Andreas finished, he said nothing immediately.

Andreas waited in silence.

"Do you think she's still alive?"

Andreas swallowed. "Yes, I do."

"Do you think you'll find her while she still is?" The commander's voice came across as flat and professional.

"We're trying our best."

Pause.

"Then don't let me keep you on the phone. I'm coming out there to be with Aleka when you rescue her. Bye."

Andreas stared at the phone. The man had the class and

experience to realize it made no sense to lose his temper or vent at the only person who could help him find his child. He also likely realized that nothing he said to Andreas could make him feel any worse than he already did.

Chapter Twenty-four

Andreas stood by the western entrance to the church, in the stone courtyard running between the church and the monastery's main entrance. A surprisingly patient crowd stood lined up three to-four across outside the church's arched massive wood and glass doors.

Andreas had decided to keep the public waiting outside the church until Dana arrived and been seated inside, away from a potential sharpshooter's line of sight. Only clergy vouched for by the Bishop's aide were allowed inside before Dana's arrival.

Andreas looked at the crowd, wondering how much longer its patience would last. The line snaked across the courtyard, back out through the entrance to the monastery. It continued on along the terraced brick walkway, past a taverna on the right, and out toward the air force jet emblazoned with an image of Archangel Michael on its tail.

He shook his head. No way this crowd would fit inside the church. The courtyard would be packed. He'd stationed three of his six cops at different spots along the line, with instructions to scrutinize every face and pull out and interrogate anyone who piqued their police instincts. He gave similar instructions to the other three, two of whom he'd assigned to patrol other means of access into the church, and one he'd sent up into the bell tower on the monastery's west wall with binoculars and a sniper rifle. He delivered his instructions at ear-shattering volume, knowing full well he was directing his anger at himself.

Neither Yianni nor anyone else had found a thing in searching the grounds and buildings, and though Andreas doubted Aryan stood waiting in line to get inside, perhaps his screaming might fire someone up enough to think outside the box and come up with an idea on how to find the bastard or his hostages.

For sure, Aryan thought that way. Always be prepared to improvise. Andreas doubted he'd anticipated a crowd this large, and he certainly didn't know where the press conference would be held. He couldn't know, because Andreas hadn't decided on a location for it yet. Aryan probably assumed Dana would attend the service, and might even have guessed they'd bring her into the church through the entrance on its south wall, but that's about all he could count on.

Everything else depended on improvisation. On both sides. Andreas would take his best shot and hope Aryan's wasn't better.

Andreas looked up. A lot of places around here for a shooter. He better remind the cop in the bell tower to keep his eyes on the crowd. Once the service started, he'd pull two cops off crowd control and get them patrolling the balconies looking down into the courtyard.

He still had to make the big decision: where to hold the press conference? Keeping it inside the church would work for the television crews, who would love the setting, but the crush of the crowd made it almost impossible to protect Dana. The devout packed themselves into important church services like this one tighter than so many sardines in a tin, and once they saw the TV cameras, forget about trying to clear Greeks out of their church. It would be bedlam.

Crowds were a big threat. All Aryan needed to do was get close enough to Dana for a quick jab with the right poison, and he'd be long gone before she died.

As Andreas saw it, the only way to go was to hold the press conference outside. Though still risky, it at least gave them a better angle on crowd control.

Angle.

Andreas' mobile rang. "What's up?"

"Dana's here," said Yianni.

"Did you tell her about Ali and Aleka?"

"Yes."

"What did she say?"

"Just what we thought. She's all in."

"The woman has guts. Bring her in the side door and let's get this show underway. No one sits within an aisle of her. No physical contact with anyone."

"Got it."

Andreas hung up, and returned to his thought. *Angle.* He had to take away whatever advantage Aryan saw in the crowd, be it inside or out. He looked up at a lattice-covered balcony running along the north wall of the monastery. If he put her up there for the conference, she'd be away from the media and the crowd. And trees partially screened her from the courtyard. That would likely push Aryan into using a gun, giving them a better chance at spotting him making his move than if he came at Dana through a jostling crowd.

What Andreas didn't know was how forcing Aryan to change his plans for Dana would impact what the killer had in mind for Ali and Aleka. Could it cause the twisted bastard to kill them sooner? He drew in a deep breath. *Too many questions, and too few answers.* He exhaled.

Seems like a good time to go to church.

Aleka knew her father would be angry. He'd told her never to go willingly with a kidnapper, because kidnappings inevitably turned into murder investigations. If you tried to get away up front, you had far better odds on not becoming a murder statistic, and even if the kidnapper had a gun and shot you, you probably wouldn't die from it.

But this was different. She'd seen the results of this killer's work on Volandes, and had no doubt he'd have used that same sword on them in the church. At least now they had a chance of being rescued.

It all happened so quickly. He'd walked them straight out of church, off into the parking lot, and into the back of a van. That's all she remembered, other than a pinprick at the back of her neck, until waking up bound and gagged inside an abandoned goat herder's hut in the middle of nowhere. Ali still looked unconscious. The killer must have drugged them both.

But where is he now?

Aleka began to tremble. He must have gone back to the monastery for Dana. If he came back, that meant he would kill them. If he didn't return, they'd likely die because no one would find them.

Tears welled up in her eyes. *I should have listened to my father.*

●●●●●

The new disguise worked better than his last. A pious old farmer arriving on horseback added local authenticity to its rider. It even brought him a nod from the cop who watched him carefully tie up his horse in the shade.

The idea came to him when he saw a string of horses tied up just beyond the eastern wall of the monastery, near where he'd parked the van. He borrowed one of the horses to make his entrance. His exit depended on how he eliminated the McLaughlin woman. He planned on using the van to cover the three kilometers back to the goat herder's hut, eliminate the refugee and girl there, and disappear into the town of Mantamados while waiting for his midnight pickup back to Turkey. As for what he needed to complete his performance within the monastery walls, he'd long ago smuggled and hidden all that inside.

Aryan strolled into the monastery a few moments after the

service had begun. He had a hard time finding a place to stand in the packed courtyard that offered a view inside the church. The view he did have gave him no idea where Dana sat, but he doubted he'd be able to get to her even if he knew.

He wanted to work his way around the church, peering in the windows to find her, but thought better of it when he noticed a cop with binoculars up in the bell tower scanning the crowd, and two more walking along balconies doing the same.

So much for window peeking. He couldn't risk doing anything that might attract attention. This would be tough enough to pull off as it was.

He doubted he'd be able to get close enough to her to go with plan A. So much for his Romeo and Juliet scenario that had star-crossed lovers Dana and Ali dying of the same poison. He'd so liked the symmetry of that ending, though taking a blade to Dana would have been more in keeping with Shakespeare's original.

Still, the paramount purpose of his storyline was for Ali the refugee to end up as the undisputed killer, and Aryan off the radar. How Ali now died depended on what end Aryan came up with for Dana. As for the other, she'd die as planned — the victim of a jealous, raging lunatic who hacked her to death with perverted sexual furor, using the same sword as he'd used on his first victim. Of course, the suicide note must again be changed. But even Shakespeare had to rewrite.

This had become a challenge.

And he loved it.

• • ● • •

Andreas pushed his way through the crowd inside the church to where Dana sat alone, no one in front, behind, or beside her. Yianni was telling one angry worshipper after another that no one could sit in those empty seats. From what Andreas could tell, Yianni would likely need an evil eye *mati* the size of the holy icon itself to ward off all the evil thoughts cast at him by so many churchgoers denied a place to sit.

Andreas whispered his plans in Yianni's ear, adding that at the conclusion of the service they'd announce the location of the press conference. No need to give Aryan more time to prepare than absolutely necessary.

"Do you actually think he's in here?" whispered Yianni, his eyes darting around the church.

"I wouldn't bet against it. Let's wait until the place empties out before moving her. We'll use the side door and head around the back way up to the balcony along the monastery's north wall. That looks like our best shot at avoiding crowds."

"I wish you hadn't said, 'best shot.'"

Andreas smiled and nodded toward the Bishop stepping forward. "The service is about to start. We better sit down if we don't want to be conspicuous." Andreas sat behind Dana, and turned his head to scan the room.

Yianni sat next to her, leaned back toward Andreas, and whispered, "I think you mean *more* conspicuous."

Aryan needed to find a place within the monastery walls that offered him the flexibility to cover potential venues for the press conference. From what he'd seen, the police had taken great care to keep the McLaughlin woman isolated from crowds. He assumed they'd do the same thing for her press conference, but they also needed a location with sufficient space to accommodate the media and the curious.

They'd also want to eliminate as many sight lines at her as possible. That meant no view down on her from the bell tower, because even though a cop stood up there now, cautious cops wouldn't discount the risk of Aryan taking their man out to get at his target.

He saw two likely venues, both on the west side of the

monastery and looking out on the courtyard at the west entrance to the church.

The first stood just inside the monastery's main entrance: a prayer vestibule shielded by an overhanging wooden second floor, and featuring a full-length, glass-enclosed icon of the Archangel. The icon, and burning candles offered by the faithful, presented a dramatic backdrop for the media. Plus, the vestibule had an exit to the outside, and bad sight lines on it from the tower. It also had a serious downside; his target would be standing at the same level as the crowds.

The second possibility sat just beneath the bell tower on a balcony running along the north monastery wall. Partially shielded from the courtyard below by trees and latticework, cameras could still catch her, but no one could reach out and touch her.

Aryan deliberated on where to set up to get off the best shot, regardless of which of the two venues ended up the chosen one. He toyed with finding something underground that offered him an angle on both, through a grate or basement window, but that took away his flexibility should the cops surprise him and settle on a third location. No, he needed to be above ground.

He found a perfect place for taking his shot should the choice be the balcony, and an acceptable place less than ten seconds away if the ground level vestibule ended up the venue. He hoped it would be the balcony, because he'd be less exposed for that shot. Either way, he'd be dressed to give would-be witnesses a fleeting glimpse of a crouched over assassin of unrecognizable height, caped and masked in the fashion expected of Muslim terrorists. Another touch he'd added for the benefit of Ali.

Aryan would patiently wait for the media to flock into position once they'd learned the press conference site. Yes, there were risks in going through with this, but so far he'd guessed right or been treated kindly by the Fates, and he felt confident things would continue breaking his way.

Soon, the McLaughlin woman would be dead, Ali blamed for it all, and—once Aryan had made an example of whoever might have given his name to the Turkish police—he'd be set to take over Malik's operation in Turkey. The other smugglers would soon fall in line.

He could hardly wait.

• ● ● ● •

Deema found what she was looking for hidden in a floor vent. Now, all she had to do was find the courage to use it to end her misery. She pulled herself up onto her feet and staggered back in the direction from which she'd crawled. She stopped at the foot of the bed and stared at her sleeping husband.

"You are the father of my children," she whispered. "You are the provider for my family."

She stepped around the side of the bed to be closer to his snoring, and raised her voice. "But you are not our protector. You are our tormentor."

He stirred, and she moved closer to him.

"Don't worry, soon you'll no longer have me in your life. That is what you want, and so that is what you shall have."

She lifted the gun. "Wake up," she shouted. "Wake up, you cursed man, so that you may see how you've succeeded at driving me to end my life."

Malik's eyes opened.

Deema pulled the trigger.

Her husband's blood streamed onto the pillow.

Her eyes did not move from his face. "Now, I must sit with you, waiting for my other tormentor to return, so that I may do the same to him." She thought of the words Aryan had once said to her. *You do what you must to protect yourself, your family.*

She drew a deep breath and exhaled. "I may fail and die, or if not, I will surely go to prison. My life is over. But I have spared my children the fate of a merciless father who preys on the helpless, and takes pleasure in torturing the desperate."

Deema sat on the edge of the bed, shut her eyes, and dropped her head. "I cannot even bring myself to ask God to take pity on your soul."

● ● ● ● ●

Midway through the service, the commander walked in the side door of the church and sat next to Andreas. Grim-faced, he whispered, "Any news?"

Andreas bit at his lip and whispered back, "No."

He nodded. "What's your plan?"

Andreas told him.

"Sounds risky for Dana."

"She's all in on it."

"I misjudged her."

"Look," said Andreas, "if anyone's at fault—"

The commander held up his hand. "No need to go there." He paused "To help my daughter, Dana's making herself target practice for a professional assassin."

"And, being honest, I'm worried," said Andreas. "We've picked a spot that cuts down on his potential shooting angles, and Dana will be wearing a ballistic vest, but he'll most likely try a head shot, and if he gets one off...." Andreas shook his head.

"You've given me an idea. There's something in this monastery that just might help with that. Let me see what I can do." He stood and hurried out the door.

Yianni leaned back toward Andreas. "What was all that about?"

"Beats me," said Andreas. "He said there's something in this monastery that might help protect Dana from Aryan, and took off."

"Archangel Michael?"

"We should only be so lucky.

"I think you mean blessed."

"Amen." Andreas crossed himself three times.

"Add my amen to that," said Dana.

"I didn't know you were listening," said Andreas.

"To every word," she said in English. "My understanding of Greek is better than my speaking it."

"How do you feel?"

"Scared, anxious, excited."

"Sounds about right," said Andreas with a nod.

She stared down at the floor. "What are my honest chances of surviving the press conference?"

"Very good," said Andreas.

"Does that mean better than fifty-fifty?"

"For sure," said Yianni.

Dana cleared her throat and stared straight ahead. "I had a baby brother once. He adored me, trusted me. We lived in rural New Jersey. He was seven and I was eleven. One day we were playing in the front yard. I had him stand by the split rail fence running alongside the road, so I could roll the ball down to him to kick back up toward the house. That way, the ball wouldn't go out onto the road."

She looked down at her hands. "He never saw the driver who swerved through the fence up onto the grass and killed him. The driver never stopped. Just backed up and drove off."

She looked at Yianni. "But I saw the driver, and the car. I told the police everything, even the license number, and they assured my parents and me that they would catch him.

"The driver turned out to be the son of a very powerful man in our county. But it was a big story in the media, so the police had to find someone to blame. They arrested a Pakistani refugee, claiming he'd stolen the car and killed my brother. The prosecutor went along with that lie even though I insisted he wasn't the driver and the son was. The prosecutor characterized me as a traumatized child who obviously was confused.

"The Pakistani's legal aid lawyer worked out a plea bargain giving his client a reduced sentence of five years in exchange for an admission of guilt. Five years for something he hadn't done, so that the son of a powerful man could get away with murder."

She looked Andreas squarely in the face, "That's why I feel as I do about police and prosecutors, especially when political stakes are high." She swallowed. "It might also help to explain why I do what I do. Somewhere out there in my head must linger some twisted sense of guilt that I hadn't done enough to save my baby brother's life, or rescue that innocent refugee from being chewed up in the system."

Andreas placed his hand on her shoulder. "I don't know what to say."

She shook her head. "You don't have to say anything. This is my problem, not yours." He removed his hand. Dana shut her eyes.

"What are Aleka's and Ali's chances if I don't go through with it?"

Yianni looked at Andreas.

"Zero," said Andreas.

Dana opened her eyes. "That's what I thought."

She paused. "Even refugees in a leaking boat have better odds than that. I've spent much of my life wrapped in NGO good intentions trying to better the odds for refugees facing death for reasons not of their making. Never, though, have I actually been in one of those boats. Given my friends' situation, I guess it's finally time for me to jump into one."

She turned to Andreas, "Just promise me one thing."

"What?"

"You'll nail the bastard no matter what happens to me."

Andreas nodded firmly. "Promise."

Chapter Twenty-five

At the conclusion of the service, the Bishop's aide announced that a press conference would be held in the courtyard north of the west entrance to the church. Andreas and Yianni waited inside with Dana until the church emptied out. They then took the south door and, rather than heading west directly into the courtyard, turned east and made their way around the church to its north side.

A long line stood gathered there waiting to use the toilets by the northeast end of the monastery wall. Andreas pushed through the line, taking care to keep Dana between him and Yianni.

An old woman dressed in black screeched, "Wait your turn."

Andreas smiled. "Sorry, *yiayia*, but we're not in need." He pointed west. "We're headed over there."

"Can you believe that with all the people here there's only one working toilet?" she grumbled.

Andreas shook his head. "Cutbacks. They're everywhere these days."

A few paces on, Andreas led them up a set of stone steps onto a patio potted in greenery, and then up a few more steps onto the open first-floor porch of a two-floor structure running the length of the north monastery wall, housing what Andreas assumed had been the monks' cells when it functioned as a monastery. They'd made it about halfway to where the conference would take place when a blond female reporter saw them and climbed onto the patio and up on the porch.

Andreas held up his hands, "Please, stay back."

The reporter shouted a question at Dana.

"Ms. McLaughlin will answer all your questions, but please stay back so she can get to where she'll be able to do so."

The reporter tried pushing her way past Andreas to Dana, still shouting her question. By now other reporters had followed her onto the patio.

Andreas took the reporter by her upper arms, lifted her off the porch floor, and gently deposited her back on the patio. "As I said, everyone stay away. *Please.*"

The reporter yelled at Andreas, "That's police brutality."

Andreas smiled. "Not yet."

Yianni quickly ushered Dana behind Andreas and up a set of stairs to the second-floor balcony.

Andreas waited until the reporters had retreated from the patio back into the courtyard before heading up the stairs.

The commander stood waiting for him at the top. "I hope you don't mind my telling Dana where to stand."

She stood to the right of what appeared to be a large window in a polished wood frame raised off the floor on stones. It towered over her, and intersected the balcony railing at a forty-five-degree angle running away to her left.

"What is that?" said Andreas.

"My idea," said the commander.

"It's a window," said Yianni.

"And it was a bitch of a time hauling it up here. The sucker's heavy."

"But it's just a window?" said Yianni. "How's that going to protect her?"

"I'm feeling ill," said Dana.

Andreas' mind quickly retraced in his mind their steps from the church to here. No one had touched her. "What do you mean by ill?"

"I'm scared. I think I'm going to throw up."

"It's normal to feel that way," said Andreas.

"I need to use the bathroom."

"But we're ready to start the press conference."

"I really need a bathroom."

"Are you sure?"

"*Yes.*"

Andreas looked at the commander. "Is there a toilet nearby?"

He pointed east. "They're down there, at the end of this wall."

Andreas gestured no. "Only one's working and there's a long line of very unhappy people between us and the first available toilet."

"What do you mean they're not working?" said the commander. "I used one fifteen minutes ago and men and women were going in and out without any problem or complaint."

Andreas felt the hair rising on the back of his neck. He stared down the monastery wall into a window for the toilet area, and lunged for Dana. "He's in the toilets."

He heard the shot hit the window, heard Dana scream, and felt her fall just as he reached her. He heard a second shot as he covered her body with his own. He looked up and saw Yianni and the commander taking aim back toward the toilets from behind the unshattered window. He looked at Dana. No blood. She must have fainted. He heard the screams and shouts of people fleeing in panic from the courtyard below.

Andreas jumped up and pulled his gun. "Where is he?"

"I don't know. He stopped firing after the second round," said Yianni. "We didn't return fire. Too risky with all the people around the toilets."

"Be careful," said Andreas. "He could be waiting for us to come out from behind whatever the hell this glass is."

"It's what protects the full-size icon of the Archangel at the entrance to the monastery," said the commander. "It's bulletproof."

"Thank God for that," said Yianni.

"But we can't just hide here," said the commander." We've got to go after him and catch him alive. That's the only chance my daughter has."

Andreas looked up. He thought of his own children. "I'll go first. I lost your daughter. It's my risk to take to get her back. Just keep an eye on the toilet window and fire the shit out of it if you see any movement."

Andreas crossed himself and crouched at the edge of the window, ready to dart for the cover of a doorway ten steps toward the toilets, when he heard someone shout, "*ARYAN*," and a loud thud above him on the roof.

Andreas looked up. "What the hell was that?"

"Sounded like something landed on the roof," said Yianni.

The sound of footsteps running across the roof tiles in the direction of the toilets quickly followed.

"Maybe it's the cop you put in the bell tower," said the commander.

"Maybe," said Andreas, "but how would he know Aryan's name?"

People in the courtyard started chanting, "*Taxiarchis, Taxiarchis.*"

"Now what's happening?" said Yianni.

"Sounds like somebody's calling out to the Archangel Michael," said the commander.

"I'm out of here," said Andreas. "Yianni, stay with Dana until we know what's happening."

Andreas crept around the window to the stairs, hurried down and out into the courtyard, followed by the commander.

Up on the roof, at the east end of the north monastery wall, two men stood battling each another. One, masked in black Arab dress, held a sword. The other wore an ancient Greek battle garment and metal shoes in a style reminiscent of Archangel Michael in full avenging fury, but instead of a sword, he held only a flute, and fought masked.

"What's going on?" said the commander.

"No idea," said Andreas, "but for sure, one of the two of them up there's our bad guy, which means I'm rooting for the other one. Whoever the hell he might be."

• • ● • •

Aryan had become far too cocky for his own good. The madman's decision to go with a rifle significantly increased his chance of capture in the case of a strong, immediate police response. Poison remained the way to do it, even though the police undoubtedly expected it. But if Aryan insisted on using a rifle, why in the world wait until his target stood before the media to take the shot? Obviously, the fool had fallen in love with his own dramatic psycho fantasies. That made him easy to anticipate.

The man in the bell tower smiled. *At least to another psycho.*

The man had overpowered the cop in the tower within minutes of learning the location of the press conference. From the tower, he could monitor Aryan's potential escape routes. The simplest escape involved blending in with those gathered by the toilets, moving away from the commotion into the parking lot, and driving off in his van for the goat herder's shed and the two he'd kidnapped.

But there could be alternate routes, and when he saw the figure coming out of the toilet dressed in Middle Eastern terrorist garb, he knew it wouldn't be a simple inconspicuous dash to the van for Aryan. The psychopath *wanted* to be seen.

Down in the courtyard, cameras filmed the chaos as reporters scurried about talking into their microphones. This had to be Aryan's moment. The man took off his long coat, revealing an ancient Greek battle garment beneath, and pulled on a pair of metal shoes, both of which he'd purchased in a local tourist shop catering to the Taxiarchis faithful. Dressed in the image of Taxiarchis, he stood waiting for Aryan to make his move.

That would be his cue to enter Aryan's staged drama, but

masked, thus playing his part anonymously, leaving those who believed in the Archangel to decide for themselves what they'd witnessed. He saw his costume as the perfect distraction for the gathered crowd of Taxiarchis' faithful at this site of the Archangel's ancient miraculous performance. There was more glory to be found by the pious in believing they'd been blessed to witness a new miracle by their beloved Taxiarchis, than in looking to unmask an impersonator. Or so he hoped.

Up until now the man held a decided advantage over Aryan: Aryan didn't expect him to be here. That's why the man's flute-playing cover had worked so well, allowing him to sit in one place and watch unnoticed the comings and goings of Aryan and the other players in the cast. It's also why he'd been able to follow Aryan's van so easily. But now he would have to make his entrance and bring down the curtain on Aryan's performance.

Another hope.

The man stared out across the rooftops, the flute he'd brought with him from home tucked into his waistband. By the east side of the monastery's north wall, he saw a hand reach up onto the roof. From there Aryan could easily make it up the slightly peaked roof, down the other side, and over the monastery wall out to the parking lot, offering all below but a brief glimpse of him in his terrorist getup.

The Greek-garbed man yelled, "*ARYAN*," dropped down onto the roof, and headed straight for his target.

Showtime.

Aryan froze. Who'd called his name? And who was *that*, charging straight for him along the ridge of the roof? A cop? The assailant wore a costume and had no visible weapon.

He must be mad.

Having given the crowd below their brief glimpse, he had to get off the roof now if he wanted to escape the police. He ran crouching toward the monastery wall.

"Stop, coward Alban Kennel!" shouted the man.

Aryan stopped and spun around. "You're who betrayed me to the police!"

"You're too predictable, Alban." The man stopped three paces from Aryan. "When I heard the media announce this morning that your name would be revealed at a press conference, I knew you'd try to stop it. And, being the sick fuck that you are, you'd game yourself into going after everyone you could think of who might be able to identify you. I can't risk having a danger like you running around loose. You left me no choice but to… intervene."

Aryan pulled a *kilij* sword from the scabbard across his blouse. "You've saved me a trip to the mainland."

"Ah, so you recognize me." The man gestured to the crowd below. "Though perhaps our audience will believe their Taxiarchis savior has returned."

Voices from below yelled for Aryan to drop his weapon.

"I guess the police want you to get this over with," said the man.

"Happy to oblige."

Aryan leaped forward, sweeping his blade at the man's neck, but the man ducked, pulling the flute out of his waistband as he did, and driving it hard against Aryan's right elbow, eliciting a wince from Aryan and a stumble on the roof tiles.

"You've always been overconfident of your blade skills," said the man.

"We both know they're far better than yours." Aryan circled to his left and up onto the ridge.

"Knowledge is power."

The shouts for Aryan to drop his weapon grew louder.

"Sounds like you better hurry up, before they start shooting at you."

"They won't dare, because if I die, they'll never find the missing girl and Muslim."

"You mean the ones in that goat-herder's hut?"

Anger burned in Aryan's chest. He lunged forward with his blade.

The man parried and deflected a follow-up slash on the body of the flute. "Bet you didn't think a wooden flute could handle your steel."

Aryan slashed out in tight arcs but the man countered each move with his flute.

"That's because it's not what it appears." The man backed up. "It has a steel bore."

Aryan charged forward, swinging the sword relentlessly.

A chant of "*Taxiarchis, Taxiarchis*" rose up from the courtyard.

"I think I have more fans than you do." The masked man backed up toward the base of the bell tower.

Aryan pressed closer, his sword pointed level.

"I know what you're thinking," said the man. "Sooner or later the flute's going to give out, or I'm going to give out. I have a better plan for you. Surrender to the police and I'll let you live."

His face burning with rage, Aryan slashed at his opponent's neck, driving him farther back.

The instant the man's back touched the bell tower wall, Aryan stopped his slashing and lunged for the man's heart, but the man parried the maneuver, swung his body away from the bell tower, and skipped east along the roofline. "I'll take that as a no."

"That's right," said Aryan. "Run."

The man stopped with his back to Aryan, fidgeting with what looked like a carved bird mounted near the mouthpiece of his flute.

"I see your weapon holds up no better than your courage," said Aryan striding toward the man.

The man turned and tilted his head. "Once again your arrogance gets the better of you. You love a weaker opponent. Like a flute player armed with nothing but his flute."

"You chose your weapon, now die with it." Aryan charged.

The man pointed the flute at Aryan's throat. "Like I said, it's not what it appears." He pulled back on the bird.

The sound of a twelve-gauge, double-aught buckshot shell reverberated off the monastery walls. Smoke from the barrel of the flute hung in the air as Aryan stumbled backward, fell to the roof, and rolled off into the courtyard.

Every eye in the courtyard fixed on the body on the ground. When they looked back up to the roof, the warrior Greek had disappeared.

Shouts of "miracle" echoed across the courtyard from the wild-eyed crowd rejoicing in this latest miracle of Archangel Michael. Andreas struggled to press through to the nearest exit, but by the time he'd made it outside the monastery walls, the mortal form of Alban Kennel's slayer had vanished.

• • ● • •

The commander stood in the courtyard, staring down at the nearly decapitated body of his daughter's kidnapper.

Yianni stood off to the side near Dana, his eyes fixed on the father's face. He saw the first tear and turned away.

Andreas came running up to them. "The other one's gone." He looked at the body, then up at the commander. Tears now rolled freely down the older cop's cheeks. Andreas looked down.

"Any idea of the identity of the one that got away?" said the commander.

"No," said Andreas softly.

"How about where my daughter might be?"

Andreas looked up. "Since they're not in the monastery, they must be somewhere nearby. To have snatched them when he did and been back in time to set all this up, they couldn't be more than twenty minutes away."

"That covers a lot of ground on this island. And if he had an accomplice...."

"Let's get the search going," said Andreas. "He's dead. He can't harm them now."

"Unless he's already done it," said the commander.

"I don't want this to sound wrong, but we need to stay positive."

The commander raised an eyebrow as he turned to face Andreas.

A loud ping went off.

"What's that?" said Andreas.

"A text message," said Yianni reaching for his phone.

Andreas turned his attention back to the commander. "What's the fastest way to get word out to all the cops in the area?"

Yianni touched Andreas' shoulder before the commander could reply.

"Chief?"

"What is it?"

"Take a look at this." Yianni held up his phone.

"What are you showing me? It's a bunch of numbers, letters, and symbols."

"I know. That's the message I just received."

"Who sent it?"

"No caller ID."

"It's spam, then." Andreas turned away.

"This is my police phone. I don't get junk mail here."

Andreas took another look at it, then grabbed the phone from Yianni.

"Look at this and tell me what you think." Andreas handed the phone to the commander.

The commander wiped his eyes, and studied the phone. "I don't see anything different than you did. Gibberish."

"Do you have a map of the area?" said Andreas.

"I can get you one, but we won't need it to get the search going."

"It's not for the search," said Andreas. "I think this 'gibberish' may be map coordinates."

"Give me back my phone." Yianni snatched it from the commander. He tinkered with some keys and within a minute had a Google map homed in on a spot less than three kilometers from where they stood.

Before Andreas or Yianni said a word, the commander had taken off like a shot for his car, yelling into his phone for an ambulance to meet him at that spot on the map.

Andreas looked at Yianni. "If that's where the hostages are, who the hell sent you that message?"

Yianni shook his head. "I have no idea. Maybe the techies back in GADA can pick something up from the phone or get it from the carrier."

Andreas stared up at the roof. "Why am I getting this nagging suspicion that it's our Archangel who's behind it?"

"Which one? Today's or the original version?"

Andreas waved his hand at the people in the courtyard. "With the way fantasy has become reality in the world these days, I'm not sure we could convince many of them that there's a difference."

Andreas noticed Dana sitting on the edge of the stone patio, her head down and tears running down her cheeks. He gestured for Yianni to join her with him. They sat beside her.

"You were very brave," said Andreas.

"I was scared to death."

"We all were."

"And now Aleka and Ali will die." She buried her face in her hands.

"Let's take a ride." Andreas stood up.

Dana didn't move.

"We might have a lead on your friends," said Yianni.

"But don't get your hopes up," said Andreas.

She jumped up. "The way my life has been going, that's the only direction my hopes can go."

Andreas smiled. "Glad to help out."

As they left the monastery, the crowd's chanting continued

undiminished: "Thank you for blessing us with your protection, *Taxiarchis.*"

Don't thank him just yet, thought Andreas, as they left to join the search for Ali and Aleka.

Chapter Twenty-six

By the time Andreas, Yianni, and Dana reached the goat-herder's hut, the commander had found and freed Aleka and Ali and canceled the ambulance. Tears and hugs continued, as Dana immediately added hers to the mix.

Andreas and Yianni stood off to the side, watching.

"We've got some serious loose ends here," said Andreas.

"Starting with who was the other guy up on the roof?" said Yianni.

"Likely the same one who sent you the map coordinates."

"But how did he get my phone number?"

"And why did he come out of nowhere to blow Aryan away?" said Andreas.

"He wasn't there by accident," said Yianni. "He knew he'd be there. I even heard him yell, 'Aryan.'"

Andreas nodded. "I heard it too."

Yianni's mouth dropped open and he smacked his hands together. "'*Aryan.*' That's it."

"What is?"

"I stayed with Dana on the balcony, so I never saw the guy on the roof, but I heard him call Aryan 'Alban Kennel.' He knew his real name. I need to see a photograph of that guy."

"I'm sure the press has loads of pictures. They're probably all over the Internet by now."

Yianni pulled out his phone and began typing. "Keep your fingers crossed. I think I know our mystery man."

"So who is he?"

"Someone I gave my business card to. It had my mobile number on it." Yianni turned his phone toward Andreas. A close-up of the face of a man wearing a mask covering all but his eyes, mouth, and chin filled the screen. "The same man who gave me Aryan's real name."

"Kharon?"

Yianni nodded. "He disguised himself pretty well. There's no way I could swear in court that I recognized him, but it was Kharon."

"Why would he be here?"

"I know he didn't like Aryan, but beyond that I haven't a clue."

"He didn't lift a finger to stop Aryan from trying to kill Dana, but he sends you a text message that saves Ali and Aleka. What's he thinking?"

"Maybe he thought we could protect Dana without his help," said Yianni.

"More likely he didn't think we could handle Aryan on our own. I don't think he gave a damn about anything other than killing Aryan, and only after he'd done that on camera did he think it might be a good idea to stay in our good graces by saving the other two. Pure self-preservation."

Yianni shrugged. "Could be. But don't forget, he already has two big favors out there to call in on us."

Andreas watched the commander lead his daughter, Dana, and Ali toward his car. "I doubt we'll ever know what motivated Kharon to do what he did, but he did get rid of Aryan, and no matter what the truth might be, I think it's safe to assume those four folks over there would say we owe him three favors."

"At least."

Andreas patted Yianni on the shoulder. "Time to head back home."

Maggie charged into Tassos' hospital room holding her mobile phone in her hand. "I just heard from Andreas."

"How nice," deadpanned Tassos. "How's he doing?"

"From his message, I'd say a lot better than when you two spoke earlier."

Tassos blinked, trying hard to look as innocent as a baby. "Spoke? Earlier?"

Maggie shook her finger at him. "I leave you alone for five minutes and you're right back in the thick of things."

Tassos shrugged. "Not really. I just took a message and passed it along to Andreas."

"Don't you get it?" She waved her arms around the room. "You're supposed to take it easy and…and…" Maggie shook her head and flopped into a chair next to Tassos' bed, tears welling up in her eyes.

Tassos rolled over on his side and reached out with one hand to caress the side of her face. "I'm sorry, my love. It's just my nature. I didn't mean to upset you."

Maggie shook her head. "I know you didn't, but if by your nature you mean you'll keep doing whatever you please, even if it means I might lose you…" she shook her head again.

"But my friend needed me."

"We all do. That's why we don't want you dying on us."

Tassos sighed. "I sense I'm in a losing argument."

"Damn straight you are, and while we're on the subject of losing, once we get home tomorrow, don't you even think of cheating on that diet the doctor put you on."

"I'm sure none of this is why Andreas called you."

"No, he called me because your phone was off, and he didn't want you worrying about having missed a message about tonight's rendezvous at sea."

"Oh."

"Apparently, Volandes' killer won't be able to make it, due to an unexpected interaction with a shotgun blast to his head."

"Ouch, that must have hurt."

"I think that's a good vision for you to keep in mind if you don't start following orders."

"Whose orders?"

She patted his hand. "Just think of it as *my* shotgun, and things should work out fine."

• ● ● ● •

The next day, Andreas called his police colleague in Turkey to inform him he no longer needed to worry about looking for Aryan, a/k/a Alban Kennel. The Turkish inspector didn't sound surprised at learning Aryan was dead, so Andreas asked why he wasn't. The inspector said a lot of things had happened last night in Turkey to fit with that scenario. Andreas pressed him for details, and after reaching an off-the-record understanding, the inspector told him of the events of the night before.

"A smuggler waiting to pick up Aryan after midnight off the coast of Lesvos was monitoring Greek police and Coast Guard radio channels when he picked up chatter about a Greek ship-owner's murderer getting killed that afternoon in a monastery near the pickup location. The smuggler later spoke to Malik's brother-in-law back in Turkey, who'd paid the smuggler to give him Aryan's pickup details as soon as he had them. The smuggler told him that Aryan was a no-show, and he wasn't going to wait around any longer for him. The brother-in-law insisted he stay, and that's when the smuggler told him what he'd heard over the radio.

"The brother-in-law told him to wait for further instructions if he wanted to keep what he'd been paid. The smuggler never heard back from him, but hung around until close to dawn before returning to Turkey.

"Right after hanging up on the smuggler, the brother-in-law tried calling Malik—who I now understand was Aryan's partner, not hostage—to tell him what the smuggler had heard on the radio, but he never got an answer, so he drove over to

Malik's house. That's when he found him dead in his bed, shot to death by his wife."

"How do you know all this?" said Andreas.

"Malik's wife called me after her brother told her what had happened to Aryan. She made him tell her everything at gunpoint."

"Gunpoint?"

"Yes, she seemed almost as afraid of her brother as she was of her late husband."

"But why'd she call you?"

"We'd been out to the house several times, and she said I was the only cop she knew. She said that her husband had beaten and raped her in a drunken rage, and kept at it for hours until passing out. She was convinced he'd kill her the moment he woke up. That's when she found a handgun, one I suspect belonged to Aryan, and used it to kill her husband."

"Do you believe her?"

"I saw the bruises…and worse. And I went back up the chain confirming what she'd told me with her brother-in-law and the smuggler—in exchange for promising not to prosecute them for anything tied into last night."

"Sounds like self-defense."

The commander paused. "Here many see the beating of a wife as acceptable. I will make my recommendations, but it is out of my hands."

"How's she now?"

"Considering all she'd been through, I'd say she seemed strangely at peace. When I interviewed her, she wouldn't let go of her children and kept repeating, 'Thank you, God.'"

"I have an angle for you on her brother," said Andreas, "one that at least might help keep her at peace from him, by putting him away for a very long time. If you look hard, you'll likely find that he was involved in the murder of that Greek family ten days ago."

"I figured he might be, from his connection to the guy we

found beheaded in a stolen car that same night. We found some yet unidentified prints along with that dead guy's in a van tied to those killings. I'm not sure how the politics will play out. Too many want this put behind us, with Aryan taking the blame for everything."

Andreas sighed. "I find myself wondering more and more these days, how the decent are expected to survive among all the disgusting types out there running our world."

"You and me both."

They said good-bye.

Andreas stared out the window for a moment. "Maggie, get me the Mytilini police commander, please."

He paused. He'd forgotten. Maggie still wasn't there. They'd spoken that morning after she'd brought Tassos home from the hospital. Her exact words were, "I'm staying home to keep a close eye on the patient and make sure things continue to go well."

Andreas picked up his phone and dialed. He heard, "Mytilini Police."

Andreas identified himself and asked to speak to the commander. A minute passed.

"Hello."

"Hi, I'm just calling to see how your daughter's doing."

"A lot better, thanks. Especially after I told her of my early morning meeting with the prosecutor."

"How did that go?"

"I followed your suggestion, and told him he had a very simple choice. Either cooperate in the investigation and prosecution of his friend the forensic supervisor for his crimes and corrupt practices, or himself be the target of an investigation spearheaded by GADA's Special Crimes Unit."

"Glad to have been of service. I assume it worked."

"He's already obtained an order barring the supervisor and his secretary from access to their office, its files, and computers. He's also assigned an assistant to work full time combing through the bastard's files searching for areas of potential prosecution."

"Sounds promising."

"Knowing the prosecutor as I do, I'd say the forensic supervisor has quite a few years in prison to look forward to."

"I'm curious, with budgets being what they are these days, where did he find the funds to assign an assistant full time to one case?"

"He didn't. I volunteered Aleka."

Andreas laughed. "No wonder she's feeling better. Payback's great."

"Sure is." He paused. "The one I'm worried about is Dana."

"Why's that?"

"She strikes me as depressed."

Andreas' voice dropped. "Hard to imagine how she wouldn't be, considering all she's been through and the nature of her work. Refugees keep coming, smugglers keep preying on them as if they're less than human. Babies, siblings, and parents keep drowning, or survive only to live concentration-camp existences, while our allegedly civilized world does not much more than spout empty promises and platitudes."

"That pretty well sums up the views of my Coast Guard buddies who go out every day looking and hoping to rescue more poor souls from the sea."

"Sounds like Dana could use a break from the insanity of our times."

"Couldn't we all?" said the commander. "She told Aleka she has friends on Mykonos she met over Easter who she thinks could help her clear her head. She plans on visiting them in a week or so."

"Amen to that. How's Ali?"

"Still smiling, but not sure if he'll stay here much longer. Lesvos hasn't exactly welcomed him with open arms."

"He's a resilient, good kid. I hope things work out for him, wherever he ends up."

"Me, too."

"Well, like I said, I was just calling to check in. Stay safe, and be well."

"Same to you, my friend."

They hung up.

Andreas rubbed the side of his face. Two phone calls, two less-than-encouraging views of the state of the world.

He stood, grabbed his coat, and headed out the door. "Bye, Maggie. I'm taking the rest of the day off to hug my wife and kids."

Maggie didn't answer, but he knew she'd approve.

To see more Poisoned Pen Press titles:

Visit our website:
poisonedpenpress.com
Request a digital catalog:
info@poisonedpenpress.com